PEGGY

PEGGY

A NOVEL

REBECCA GODFREY

with LESLIE JAMISON

RANDOM HOUSE • NEW YORK

Copyright © 2024 by the Estate of Rebecca Godfrey

All rights reserved.

Published in the United States by Random House,
an imprint and division of Penguin Random House LLC, New York.

Random House and the House colophon are
registered trademarks of Penguin Random House LLC.

Hardback ISBN 9780385538282
International edition ISBN 9780593736937
Ebook ISBN 9780385538275

Printed in the United States of America on acid-free paper

randomhousebooks.com

2 4 6 8 9 7 5 3 1

FIRST EDITION

Title-page typography by Lynn Buckley

Contents

I. OLD MASTERS   *1*

Prologue   *3*

CHAPTER 1: The Silver Prince   *8*

CHAPTER 2: Twirl   *25*

CHAPTER 3: Libertines   *41*

CHAPTER 4: Sulfur   *67*

CHAPTER 5: Aviators   *72*

CHAPTER 6: The Sunwise Turn   *90*

CHAPTER 7: Hooligans   *108*

CHAPTER 8: Eternal Wound   *118*

II. SURREALISM   *123*

CHAPTER 9: The Silver Princess   *125*

CHAPTER 10: The Interloper   *163*

CHAPTER 11: The White Envelope   *172*

CHAPTER 12: An Imperious Urge   *193*

CHAPTER 13: The Dangerous Month   *216*

CHAPTER 14: Bird Bones   *255*

III. MODERNISM   *297*

CHAPTER 15: Borrowed Bedroom   *299*

CHAPTER 16: Bird in Space   *322*

Epilogue   *349*

ACKNOWLEDGMENTS   *363*

I.

OLD MASTERS

———

"I adore floating."

—PEGGY GUGGENHEIM

Prologue

I AM THE DAUGHTER OF TWO DYNASTIES; I AM BELIEVED to have more money than anyone in this city, second only to our neighbor, Rockefeller. Both my grandfathers were born in stables, like Jesus, and both came to America in steerage, running from Bavaria and Switzerland. These are not fables. These are not myths of the American Dream. The facts: both were fourteen, dark-haired boys, mute at first, then stumbling with the consonants of English; Joseph and Meyer, these were my grandfathers, and both men were peddlers, peasants, despised. In the Midwest, they knew neither cowboy nor coal miner. They sold shoehorns, spectacles, shoelaces, glue, cigars. If they got word two hens were sick in a village, they walked twenty miles to this village and sold off their own two hens. Soon Meyer invented a kind of stove polish; soon he was selling uniforms to the US Army. Then it was mines, amassing one, a hundred, all the silver mines in Alaska and Chile, all the copper mines in Mexico. Joseph learned math, stocks, and began his own bank. President Grant wished him to run the Department of Treasury. (He said no; he was too shy.) By the time I was born, in 1898, Manhattan was hurtling toward a kind of European regality, and my grandfathers were no longer peasants but kings, driven toward the gilded palaces all along Fifth Avenue.

I have twelve uncles. Washington, Samuel, Eugene, Jefferson, DeWitt, Isaac, Daniel, Murry, Solomon, Robert, William, Simon. It is these brothers who will be placed in charge of the fortunes. Anyone could know this would cause trouble, but no one does. My mother's family, the Seligmans, are a discreet, distinguished family. Whispers suggest my father married her for her *cachet*. Her ancestors were from a less bawdy part of Germany. The Guggenheim fortune came not from banks or offices but from the dank dirt of mines, underground, filth. Eldest Daniel is said to be the wisest, Senator Simon the most powerful, but it is my father Benjamin who compels the city. He's *dashing,* the papers say, he's nicknamed the Silver Prince. In the portrait of Guggenheim & Sons, the men are all unsmiling, mustached, with high wide collars and heavy waistcoats. They've erased every trace of peasant. Only my father grins. He's at the end of the long burnished mahogany table; he's sitting on the arm of a chair, leaning back. All the other men stare straight ahead, a kind of confrontation, a unified posture of assurance, but my father looks off as if to another room. His brothers hold an open book, a fountain pen; his father touches the model of a mine. Even then, I see now, my father was plotting his glorious escape.

The tragedy of our family, at least the tragedy before the one I am about to unfold here, is simply that my parents had only three daughters. In a portrait taken in Switzerland, the three of us are dressed in white. We wear wide boater hats, white cotton dresses, ruffled ankle socks. I'm ten; I hold a bouquet of flowers on my lap; my dress has pleats and a soft line of lace. Hazel is five, with ringlets and dimples, a bow in her hair. Benita is fourteen. She stands over us, her long neck, her tapering fingers, her chin lifted only slightly. Her sleeves are puffed at the shoulder, ruffled at the wrists. We appear lush and crisp. We're clouds; we're temporary; we're pure sweetness; the tipped flower of a wedding cake. We're the white of things that hover and tempt. Groomed for silliness and ease. And so I am the daughter of a dynasty, but I became nothing more than a dilettante. My sister known as a murderess. Are you surprised? Perhaps you should be. Perhaps this is only what they've said about us. Only the beginning of what we became.

———

I WAS BORN ON Park Avenue. 1898. We lived in a strange and lavish mansion. My father filled the home with his whims and treasures: a bald eagle he'd shot; a Corot, a Watteau, caged slippers from Morocco. There was a glass dome that let in the stars, an immense stairwell, a separate floor for his daughters, an elevator that terrified us all. The walls were gloomy and heavy with gray-green oil paintings of grandfathers, immense gilt mirrors, and the dark weight of tapestries depicting such scenes as Alexander the Great's triumph in Rome. It seemed strange to us, almost illicit, that my father let us live this way. We were supposed to be quiet and hidden and discreet, partly out of imitation of the Havemeyers and Huntingtons and Rockefellers, but partly because we weren't supposed to be here at all. It was understood that if we made too much noise or show, the world would come out as they did when my grandfather was shuffling about in Ohio. *Jew, Sheeny, Christ-killer!* Men stoned him; threw him into the dirt. My mother wore a single diamond. My sisters and I hid under white sailor hats and gloves. We were ushered by governesses between 60th and 80th streets, between the small world bordered by Park and Fifth. Even our clocks ticked quietly; the elevator made no sound; the servants' feet were silent. The worst you could say about a girl was she's "showy." Our clothes came from Paris, silent as they were slipped onto our quiet bodies. These dresses must be of the best fabrics but never be too bright, must never look too new. We spoke in code, in abbreviations. Our home was known as "15," and to others in our crowd, we were known simply as "the Googs." When we, the quiet girls with our Christian names, became ill, we were sent away to hotels in New Jersey. A mere cough, it seemed to us, might sicken the calm of these clean, pleasing rooms. The wealthier you were, the more inconspicuous you must be.

Three years after my father supposedly disappeared, my sister tries to do the same. In the papers, a headline will appear: GUGGENHEIM HEIRESS LOST. In White Plains, Hazel and my mother rested together at the Willets Mansion. At ten in the morning, after receiving a scolding from my mother, Hazel simply disappeared. Hours went by; the sun began to fall. My mother waited a few hours before calling the police, and then an entire force of deputies was brought in; every room of the mansion was inspected. Guests and grooms at a nearby hotel joined in the search; the green fields bloomed with men in white linen waistcoats. It was assumed that she'd been kidnapped. It was assumed, wrongly, that my sister was the daughter of a great fortune. Guards were placed at the railroad station. My mother insisted the men widen their circles; she believed my sister must have run beyond the searched route. At the railroad station, all trolley cars were stopped; on the roads, every auto held in place. *Have you seen a little girl?*

One sheriff left the group and went alone toward the old ruins near the mansion. Crumbling stone; ivy and wisteria tangling at his feet; he headed toward the faint skeleton of a wide wall. He saw a glimpse of something white through the trees. He ran after the whiteness, which turned out to be a fleeing girl. He expressed surprise at my sister's silence, but why would she, even when lost, not stay silent? When we had been taught the worst thing was to be noticed.

CHAPTER I

The Silver Prince

1912

STRIPED AND SHOT, THE TIGER LAY FLAT, AND I STRETCHED
my hungry body across him. He was part treasure, part prey.
Though we had so much, I often ignored the chaises and satin
chairs, instead gathering my book and lying upon this tattered dead animal. Move, my mother would say, if she happened to be in the room. Peggy, move away from the beast!
This request would send my sister, Benita, into fits of giggles.
Move away from the beast, Benita would later imitate. The
tongue had fallen out, at one point, replaced by a hapless plas-
ter replica. As I read, I would dangle my fingers into the
mouth, touching the jagged rise of ebony. Often the head
would loll abruptly; the mouth red and raw and somehow
alive below the still, crystal eyes.

Oh, Peggy, my mother said, move away from the tiger
and *get off the floor*. I would brush the tiger fur with my hand,
and stare up at the ceiling, entranced. For a moment, everything in the elegant room felt savage, uneasy.

———

WE WERE LIVING AT the Waldorf-Astoria. We moved there from our former house on 15 East 72nd, right across from the entrance to Central Park. My father was in Paris for business; this is what we were told and what we would dutifully repeat. After weeks of waiting for his expected return, my mother moved us to the hotel. Not to worry. Daniel, my father's brother, lived there as well. The entire floor below ours was for his family; I imagine the Astors were mortified. *The Googs are taking over the hotel.* Like money and love, these sudden changes in residence were never spoken of in my family. I'm fourteen, but believe I'm possessed of a knowledge that eludes the rest of them. I know my father will not return.

THE MORNING HE LEFT, I begged Victor, his valet, to let me brush my father's mustache. We sang together, a sweet, secret song he'd invented for me. French and English. *Oui, oui, Peggy. A whistle, a dun-la-dun,* and I would twirl. Into his pocket, I sneaked the tiger's tongue.

With him, my father took his secrets, and his shame, packed in one of his seventeen trunks. Silver to the end, he held us each in his arms while all around us the cherry trees of Fifth Avenue erupted into bloom. Clouds above us broke apart. We ran after him. Corseted, silk skirts to our ankles, we were hobbled. Our sailor hats fell off in the breeze, floating lightly over the wheels of his carriage.

Hazel's sobs were heard all up and down Park Avenue. Adeline Havemeyer and Alma Harrington looked down from their windows. My father's carriage continued toward the dark strands of river in a part of the city we'd never been. A business trip, my uncle Daniel informed my mother. "He seems to have got in his head to start his own company, the— I believe, it's to be called the International Steam Company." He looked appalled, for my grandfather had always told the brothers the story of Aesop, they should stick together like a bundle of sticks. "Florette, has he ever spoken to you of his business matters?"

"Do you think he has? Really, Daniel."

"Has he ever mentioned—" He stopped, catching sight of me on the rug. "Peggy," he said softly. "I did not realize you were there."

"She is having an unhealthy love affair with that beast," my mother said. "I can't imagine how their children will look."

"I am sure they'll be clever," he said.

"Dangerous," I countered, flailing backward with arched back and bared teeth.

The St. Regis was sumptuous and dull. The windows were covered with bars and dirty glass. The park was only a sliver of light through the window. I missed my father's whims and treasures, however morbid and lavish.

My mother turned sentry. The fact that her own marriage, a merging of fiefdoms, was clearly in decline seemed to only raise her interest in marrying off her brother's daughters. Weeks on weeks went by without my father's return, yet she grew perversely more attuned to the possibility of romance. A dinner was held for Mr. Harry Loeb; a lunch for Mr. Roger Straus. She sent battalions to Barrytown for strawberries; ermine arrived from a valley in Russia. She wore bustles and blouses buttoned to her neck. *N.G.,* she would say of a name on the guest list. *Not good.* Strike of the pen. The poorer erased.

Why would my father not wish to stay in Paris when this was the woman in his home? I began to despise her.

In Paris, my father must have been elated never to attend another ball, another stuffy Fifth Avenue party. The more my mother neglected us, the more I grew certain that my father would stay in another city with other women who were slim and joyful. I imagined them with such beauty, I almost fell in love with these creatures myself. Peacock feathers in ringlets; the white dive of breasts.

He's freed himself from all of us, I told Benita. His silly daughters, his greedy brothers, his snobbish wife. Don't you see it? He's freed himself from the Havemeyers and the Harringtons and the Loebs and the Strauses and the perfectly lovely Rockefellers.

She always answered me; we spoke sometimes like a song. Our words entwined; giddy. It was a kind of language through a forbidden melody. But when I said this, she walked toward the piano. She played Wagner perfectly from memory. I decided not to mention it again, since she looked so wounded, banging the C sharp, staring into the sheet music for a song she wasn't playing.

He wrote us letters. Benita and I read them to each other as we lay across our mother's bed. We ransacked the notes from my mother's jewelry box, where she kept them under ribbons and emeralds. In April, he wrote me. He'd been gone for nine months. *I am glad to receive your kind letter and hope that you will frequently find time to write me. I have found—*

Here I stopped reading. Found what? Benita asked. A nice gift for Hazel, I lied.

Oh Haze, she said, sighing.

Why didn't I tell Benita then? I suppose the rest of the sentence set off such a fierce joy that I felt if shared, I might receive a reprimand. *It's just a promise; he's always making those.* I folded the letter seventeen times, until it was thin as a match. I slid it into my leather ankle boot while Benita stood, asking me to act like a boy and help her practice her curtsy.

IN PARIS, MY FATHER was building elevators that would climb to the top of the Eiffel Tower. This fact alone filled me with love. My father! Setting off to the clouds while all his old-fashioned brothers still sent men down into the infernal mines. It seemed to me that my father was unafraid of modern machines; he refused to return to the places his father sent him—the barren rock of northern Mexico, the choking furnaces of all-night smelters in an empty Colorado. My father believed in the unproven, in volition, in a closer view of the clouds.

One morning, soon after I received the hopeful letter from my father, I was stopped on Fifth by Mr. Rockefeller. He waved his cane and summoned me closer. I had not seen him since we'd moved from 15. He was older now; with white flecks in his eyes; a scent of lily and pines. I was always looking close at these men, trying to see what it was we were all trying so achingly to be. His voice was clipped and magnetic. The clever Miss Guggenheim, he said. He placed emphasis on the *heim*. Scratchy, German, a sound as if he were clearing his throat.

I started a curtsy, then without completing it, exclaimed. "My father is in Paris," I announced. "He's building elevators for the Eiffel Tower!" I knew I sounded ludicrous and impolite, but I enjoyed the announcement.

"Is that right?" he said. He seemed to consider whether the idea was worth his considering. "Elevators?"

"The Eiffel Tower is the highest building in Paris," I informed him.

He nodded. "Yes, the higher to fall."

His amusement didn't bother me. I imagined my father, straddling the immense scaffolding, suspended. Below him the arches of Notre-Dame, the Louvre.

I began to speak again, but the governess Cora squeezed my hand. The high sun brushed her face; she lifted her parasol off the ground. "Peggy," she said. "Do you not know? Has Hazel not told you?"

She was not allowed to embrace me, but it seemed she wanted to lift me as her hands weaved near my chest. That was when she told me, my father had booked a return ticket for Hazel's birthday. In three weeks, she said, your father will be home.

———

AS WELL AS BEING inconspicuous, it was important for the princes to be *cultivated*.

The brothers were sent to Europe to attend operas and

learn about literature, languages, and art. Their sisters were finished in Switzerland. This was partly an attempt to imitate a British idea of the civilized, but there was a genuine desire to appreciate something beyond the often-savage accumulation of coal, ore, metals, and other men's property. When we were little girls, my father insisted we spend our summers in Europe as well, to learn what he called "good taste." My mother spent most of her time at the couturiers, while we went to museums with a lady called Miss Hartman. My father told her it was her duty to teach us about culture. She took us to the Louvre, the Carnavalet, and to the châteaux of the Loire. She taught us French history, and read us Dickens and Eliot. On the last of these trips I would make with my father, we went to a Salon, as he'd heard the show there had caused some outrage. "Let's you and I go see what the furor is about," he said. We walked through the park as he sang his silly song. "Peg-ee, oui—oui."

"Arrêtez-vous!" I screamed, as he swung me high. Pigeons swarmed near his feet. The streets were dirty here, but neither of us would ever mind.

We stood before a painting of a simple French country house. White with green shutters, behind two bare but pretty trees.

"What has Miss Hartman taught you?" he said. "What can you tell me about this painting?"

I was then, as I am now, quite proud to state my opinions, but felt suddenly terrified, so rarely was I asked by anyone to reveal my thoughts.

"This is Braque, I believe," I said. I was twelve, but I enjoyed the lessons of the Louvre. "He's an Impressionist, born in 1882."

"Yes, yes. What can you tell me about this painting?" He pointed at the flowers in the corner, rendered as pink blurs. "What kind of a mess is this?"

"These paintings look unfinished, but they're deliberately haphazard," I said. I wasn't even sure what this meant, but I'd gathered this much about Impressionism. "This technique is called broken color. The painter is not preparing or mixing his paint on the palette; he's adding strokes on canvas until the color appears. He's not interested in re-creating something staged, so this moment, this house, it's meant to seem like something beautiful he stumbled upon, perhaps by accident."

"Looks unfinished but is deliberately haphazard. I like the observation, my clever Peggy. But all you need to know," he said, pointing at the painting, "is that this is life. And this," he said, dropping a coin to the ground, "is death." He kicked his leg forward, as if uplifting some piece of filth. "Show me some more of these messes," he said, and we wandered around looking at paintings for the rest of the afternoon.

PERHAPS IT WAS BECAUSE of the lessons of Miss Hartman, but there were moments in my own life that I preferred to stand away from and see as if they were paintings. They seemed more understandable with the distance, more beautiful with some element of composition.

So when I heard of my father's return, which I found dif-

ficult to reconcile with the message in his letter, I thought of
him as if in a painting. He is in Paris, of course, and rather
predictably, in a café. Not the grimy ones with burgundy
banquettes I will later frequent, with chicken grease on the
wineglasses, the clatter of angry poets. His is more formal; he
sits in the amber light under a dustless chandelier. He is with
Daniel's son Henry, who has recently finished his studies at
Harvard and is now apprenticing at the International Steam
Company. They're discussing the perils of smelting, the riots
in Angola, the latticework of burned hands versus the plea-
sures of steam and elevators. The numbers of floors will light
up one day, my father says, a red light will shine, a bell will
announce another height. Ninth floor, he sings out, la-ling.

Or maybe he's with Miss Léontine Aubart, a French girl
he calls Ninette. She dips an oyster into his cognac, plucks it
with her perfect lips. My father is carefree with Ninette; he
pulls her to his lap and asks her to sing the song she sang last
night on stage when she wore a dress that seemed to be made
entirely of feathers. As she sings, some sense of responsibility
clutches at him. Perhaps it's his daughter's letters. Not mine,
but Hazel's. *Dear Father, Will you be home for my ninth birthday
party?*

It is for her, my sister, that he walks the ten blocks to the
offices of the White Star. He inquires if there is a liner that
will arrive in New York City in time for his daughter's birthday party on April 30. He buys a ticket himself. He buys
a ticket for Mademoiselle Aubart under the name of Mrs.
B. Guggenheim. He buys tickets for his valet, Victor, and her
maid Emma. Each of these tickets is extraordinarily expen-
sive, even for my father who heedlessly refuses to for one mo-

ment be frugal. He is pleased to see John Jacob Astor is also on board, but wonders about the gossip that might occur due to his traveling with Ninette.

For a moment, he considers canceling the trip, then recalls all the gossip surrounding Astor, who's done what is rarely done among these princes—divorced Ava Willing, his wife, and now will be traveling with his pregnant teenage bride. Tickets purchased, he returns to the café of my painting. Ninette is already demanding twenty-four chemises and a Vuitton valise. He turns the conversation to speed. This brand-new boat, this *Titanic,* will be a grand ride; this liner, they promised me, will set a transatlantic record.

Ninette scoffs. It will take weeks to get to New York, she knows.

Not true, he says. Haven't I told you, he says, lifting her ungloved hand to his lips, settling back into the lights now dusky and burgundy, the world is getting faster. They'll board in Cherbourg, he tells her, and be in New York in seven days.

Such a frenzy for his return. Lavish, heady flowers on the mantelpiece collapsed under their own weight. My mother's back bore pinpricks from so many fittings. She burnished every mirror herself; tore away any petals with a touch of wilt.

AT BENITA'S ELOCUTION LESSONS, I sat cross-legged on the floor reading *The Lustful Turk.* Benita trilled. There were ways a girl should say her *ah*'s at the end of every sentence, ways she should hush the hardness of her *t*'s and *n*'s. It was another code, meant to alert the sons of our crowd that she was ready; she was worthy. But she was practicing for my father too. Would he love her enough this time? Would he decide to stay?

Hearing her sorrow when she lingered too long on a vowel caused a certain kick in the closed part of my heart. How could I tell her what I knew? All this exercise so futile when father was not going to return. Should I find the letter, show her his promise to me?

The instructor, a Dutch woman with a black mole between her eyes, pushed roughly on Benita's throat, her palm so brusque and forceful that my sister's teeth clenched. And yet she remained poised on the stand, her gentle smile untroubled. I might have pushed back at the instructor; I was certain then I would never trill. I craved only school, which my mother forbade. I read Thackeray, Trollope, whatever books Isaac, my downstairs cousin, brought home from school. I couldn't think of anything more dull than being a debutante, but Benita was ecstatic for her ball.

It seemed in those days before my father's expected return, we calcified into the roles we would never fully depart from. Hazel was scattered and careless; she left her jeweled doll in the carriage; she misspelled her middle name. There was a sweetness about her, though. She sobbed if she saw a limping animal; she smuggled pastries into the rooms of a sick maid. Benita was the beauty, graceful and good. Even before her elocution and dance lessons, she'd achieved the great goal— erase the *gug,* the *heim,* the *lig,* the *mann.* Now her voice trilled; her spine was straight; her nose tiny and tip-tilted.

My nose was elegant as a potato; my hair rugged. I was

not ugly; I never felt ugly, and so I never felt envy for my more beautiful sister. I was indifferent to my face, to my body. I rarely looked in mirrors.

On the day my father was supposed to walk into the St. Regis, I tossed on a dress and ran away before my maid could pull the sash properly.

MY FATHER'S BOAT MOVED with its decadent surge through the Atlantic, leaving Cherbourg on a warm April day. Crystal chandeliers reflected into the surface of the swimming pool; camellias twined around ropes of frail bamboo; every aisle was a garden path of velvet and marble. It was a kind of wealth that served to only adorn and dazzle; anyone fragile would fall from the force of it all. Evenings, my father separated from Ninette, and with his valet returned to Deck B to smoke cigars with the Englishmen. Near midnight, as the liner sped toward America, an iceberg ripped open the bottom of the boat with such force the bow and stern tilted toward the ocean floor.

Handed a life preserver, my father placed it on, then helped the women and children into the boats. This life preserver, this ludicrous buoyancy, bothered him. He was not a man used to discomfort. Perhaps he was dizzy from the parting kiss of Miss Aubart. He'd helped her to the last boat; told Emma, her maid, it's just an iceberg, for God's sake. We'll see you soon. Once all the boats were full of women, children, and a few men from steerage, the Englishmen smoked cigars and played cards. My father decided to return to his room and remove his life preserver. He asked Victor to release him from the silly device. Ever faithful, Victor took off his own. Both men changed into their dining jackets and wandered through the dark decks. Maybe he was heading toward the sounds of an orchestra playing ragtime; even a cymbal or a drumbeat could tempt my father from safety.

The rift: split open now, a gash of ice.

Who could paint the scene? When the whole world starts to tilt; when those who are underneath are rescued, and those great kings of New York are swallowed up in a black violence. Who paints these things—the taking of fathers, the sky cruel as a coffin? Bodies, hundreds in the icy waters.

THE PIANIST AND THE silk horse leave. The diamond tiara is taken from Hazel's tresses. Streamers and garlands lifted off the walls. Little nine-year-old girls are lied to by their governesses. A procession of grave men enter with envelopes. The uncles arrive, and we're all waiting, together, at Daniel's. Even my grandfather Joseph, with his flowing white beard and terrifying gaze, is with us, a canary oddly perched on his shoulder. I keep my eyes perched on the canary, as though the mere absurdity of this orange, squawking bird will keep me alive. Names of other missing men are announced, as if it matters that my father was in proper company. Edgar Meyer, John Thayer, Isidor Straus. *Isidor Straus! I heard his wife refused to leave him, and now she's missing too.*

"Modern ingenuity," Daniel is saying. "We can construct a swimming pool on an ocean liner, but can't find room aboard for enough lifeboats. What, please tell me, do we need with a swimming pool and gymnasium?"

When the newspapers report the missing, they include Mrs. Benjamin Guggenheim. Her friends arrive en masse, *Oh Florette, you are here, oh you are alive!* My mother herself only wants to see the lists. The lists of those who have been saved. Seven hundred were pulled aboard the *Carpathia,* now on its way to New York from Newfoundland. My mother insists my father is alive and for the first time disobeys Daniel. "I'll go to the office myself, if you do not choose to accompany me," she says, "I'm certain he's on the boat from Newfoundland."

Murry interrupts. "Why were there no soldiers on this liner? Men with pistols?"

"Seven hundred have been rescued, Daniel. Don't you think those would include the more prominent, the men from the higher decks?"

"Perhaps, Florette," Murry, Daniel, Simon, Meyer, Robert, and William say. "Florette, we are all hoping he will be found."

Once she's left us, off to the White Star offices with her brother-in-law DeWitt, I enter alone into my uncle Daniel's office. I've not been invited; I walk into the room. There is the chair from the photograph, the chair in which my father careened. I sit down in this chair. "I know," I tell them, "I know he's not on the rescue boat."

Daniel nods; his eyes are sharp but blurry at once, the first time I've been close enough to him to notice his splintering eyes are both blue and green. He holds my hand, uses my full name: "Marguerite."

There's the terrible sadness of so many men; it's almost violent; the heaving breaths, the strangled sobs. My uncle, the senator in Colorado, was able to wire the captain of this boat, the *Carpathia.*

"Your father," he says, "is most certainly not on that ship. They have found many bodies but he, but his—hasn't yet been found."

"I know, I—" *Read them the letter,* I tell myself.

But Simon now sits beside me, takes my other hand. Tells me how the brothers have arranged to have the steamers scouring the seas. An expert aviator named F. C. Ditmar in California is offering to send aeroplanes equipped with calcium phosphate signals. They'll scout for a hundred miles from the site of the downed boat, searching just for him, searching for his body.

WHEN MY MOTHER COMES home, it is only a brief moment; so she can order us all into black. These stiff dresses, lace like charcoal and boots like ash. She disappears to a hotel in New Jersey with a nurse. The papers describe her as distraught.

Every night for a week, it seems, another steward or valet arrives in the lobby. They plead to see my mother; they say they were the last to see my father alive. Daniel finds me; he brings me with him to hear their stories. My mother is distraught, he explains to the earnest visitors.

"Oh," James Etches sighs. His hair is carefully combed, but he's missing cuff links. He tells us he was the assistant steward; and he has a message only for Mrs. Benjamin Guggenheim. "We were together almost to the end. I was saved. He went down with the ship. He was going from one lifeboat to another, shouting out, 'Women first.' I saw him later and asked him why he'd changed into his dining jacket. He said, 'We are prepared to go down like gentlemen.'"

"Possibly true," I tell Daniel.

"Very possible," he agrees.

Orange-haired and knock-kneed, John Johnson scratches his neck; insists he was an expert swimmer. "I have a message for the widow," he says. "I can only deliver it to her."

"Look here, she's prostrate with grief. Deliver it to her daughter," Daniel says.

"Well, Mr. Guggenheim said, 'This is a man's game, and I will play it to the end.'" The boy with the unlikely name of John Johnson tears up. "He said, 'Tell her, Johnson, that I played the game straight to the end and that no woman was left on board this ship because Ben Guggenheim was a coward. Tell her that my last thoughts will be of her and our girls.'"

"A hoaxer," I tell Daniel.

"A hoaxer," he agrees.

The papers have reported that my father has left $92 million to his family. A week after we send John Johnson away, a deck chair is found in West Africa. The next week Mr. Astor is found floating up, his body proud, his gold watch still telling the time in New York, and his pockets full of all this useless money.

I SLEPT NEXT TO Benita, in our black dresses. We walked to the synagogue and stood up together to say the Kaddish. My mother was gone; the governesses let us sleep in our dresses; they left us alone. When I heard Benita's breath, safe and soft,

I let myself unroll the letter. *Tell Mummie I will be asking if she wants me to rent a beautiful country place at Saint-Cloud near Paris for July.* I knew my father was there. I knew the house he had found near Paris was white with green shutters. Perhaps he hurtled down into the depths at first, but then he rose, and the water was warm, and with his pockets full of jewels and gold, he paid a pirate to take him somewhere better.

In this painting, my father waits for me to arrive. In this painting, I see the brightest swath of yellow you can imagine: sunflowers, sparrows, shadows of light on the two bare trees, and my father smiling, in a suit of sun-bleached linen, reclining on a faded, rough bench. All around him the light has been painted with rough strokes to keep the scene from becoming too sentimental, too nostalgic. There are a few lilies in the corner of the garden, only one or two unkempt.

CHAPTER 2

Twirl

1914

TWIRL, HE SAID, AND I FOLLOWED HIM. I AM NOT ONE TO follow, but something about Mr. Erlesto's earnest quality, as if this mattered, as if he were teaching Dante instead of another Park Avenue girl to twirl for her cotillion, appealed to my sense of the perverse.

Like this, he said, for five. *Retreat, lightly, now on the toes.*

Mr. Erlesto is stocky and good-natured. He likes to wink, to saunter, to sing songs he says are from Brazil. I will dance perfectly, I promised him. I don't need to spend these next years practicing. Those boys, I said, winking back at him. Horace Homer, Robert Stillman. You can bet they'll be lined up against the wall.

I am fifteen; I am being prepared. My mother believes I am too unruly and somber; she must begin my training now. Are you coming out? the ladies ask me at my mother's teas. Are you making your debut? Benita's was such a splash. The front page of the *Times*! Oh, wasn't she the most beautiful girl to ever walk into the Ritz.

Benita had been at the dressmaker with my mother while

I was at my lesson. In her room, I undressed. Her dress of tulle lay on the bed, stiff and immense, as if a creature from a morbid ballet. We were unaware that this was to be our last day of dancing lessons and dressmakers, that after this afternoon, we would never again be so adored and carefree.

Benita had all the latest magazines, opened carefully and arranged in rows across the floor. *Vogue, Harper's Bazaar.* She has marked certain pages to show me, using her silver combs as bookmarks. "This one is too showy," she says, inspecting the model with the endless train of lace. "Hazel Goodman wore one of these my year, and it was a catastrophe. So garish! No one would ask her to dance, except the little Bernheim boy. The one with the lip. Poor thing, he didn't know any better."

She kept flipping through the glossy pages. "You are so slim; you should wear one of the newer lengths. Like this one. Sister, you should show off your ankles."

"Oh, I will," I say.

Hazel, the interloper, knocks on the door. "Can I join you?"

"No," I say decisively.

"No," Benita says tenderly.

Hazel, that interloper, that killer. It was a kind of vengeance to ignore our younger sister, who had, we believed, lured our father to his last voyage.

Oh, Father! At the thought of him, I stand, naked, before my sister. We are often undressed, us two. As though in this hotel we are suffocating, with the tapestries and portraits and silver, the weight of it all, not merely wealth, but just the *of it all,* the crystal and china and rabbit furs. Benita is naked as well. With her knees pressed to her chest, she is working on her enunciation. This month, a Russian specialist has been brought in; he insists she work on the lilt. Where to place the lilt. So her every word rises, in the right place, the perfected pause that conveys pure delight. And though it seemed to me impossible, this lilt has made Benita even lovelier.

Now the best families of New York invite her to tea; their heir sons contemplate a marriage. Your nose, I tell her, reminds me of this poem. I stand upon the tulle, reciting Tennyson. *Lightly was her slender nose / Tip-tilted like the petal of a flower.*

Stop, Peggy, she says, laughing. You're crushing my dress. Her smile has the lure of joy, while mine is sly. This is our biggest difference, our smiles, after the nose. But I must no longer spend time dissecting why Benita can pass, and I can't, into the worlds of the Fricks and Rockefellers. Marriage seems grotesque to me; I must make other plans.

Hazel is knocking.

Tenderly, Benita says, Maybe in a while, Haze.

But I am already opening the door. Naked, I ascend the stairs.

Haze will later kill her children. She will say she dropped the two boys from her warm arms, but everyone on Park Avenue will say she threw them like paper bags off the penthouse roof. And of the many moments of my cruelty in my life, I will, for some reason, always remember this particular one, when I walked right by Hazel and ascended naked up the servants' stairs.

I've never been up here before, in the high, hidden corners of the thirteenth floor. Ashes and pigeon's feathers.

Downstairs the maids bustle past me with their downcast eyes. Here I am not certain what they will do. So I walk like I'm a pistol of a girl; tilted; ready to aim. *Are you thinking of asking my mother why I am wandering around naked upstairs. Dismiss that idea! Toss it from your mind.* I find my black dress easily, in the sewing room, hung from a taut, unswaying line. The seamstress upstairs has been instructed to take it in, for I've lost eight, then ten pounds. Daniel is the only one to be alarmed. *She must go see someone. Florette, she's withering.*

I'm just preparing, I sing to him, preparing for the ball. For a while after my father failed to come home, I was Daniel's sidekick. He took me in his carriage to his offices by the seaport; spoke to me of his adventures. How lovely was the silver in Soweto. All winter, while the snow fell over Wall Street, he showed me around. We toured the vaults; watched Isaac fluster about in a courtroom. Might I be the first girl groomed to take over the fortune? I was fifteen, as I said, and easily able to muster such fantasy. He showed me the number machines, watched closely as I attempted calculation. Have you seen those machines? Quicksilver, the sums fly forward on a screen. I had a gift with the keys; I memorized the location of numbers, then typed, listening to the hum.

As winter ended, Daniel stopped inviting me, and now this June, he seemed fearful and guilty whenever he looked at me. When he spoke now, it was as though I weren't in the room.

I heard the voices of the maids. They must have been in the room behind me, the room with deep green, heavily scuffed doors. At first I thought it was Moira, and so I moved my ear closer to the door. For seven weeks, I'd lived alone with Moira, while I had whooping cough and Benita was being prepared. My mother did not want me near my sister. She sent me off with Moira to a hotel on 82nd.

Moira was lanky, with her shining black hair held still in two braids. She was constantly twisting her braids; she had a drifting, lazy eye. I loved Moira; she taught me to wink; she was healthy and greedy. She ordered coq au vin for herself; she took me to William Gillette plays, explained the code of mobsters, the Irish threat. Nights, she drank whiskey from her tea while I read Tolstoy. It was a kind of heaven. When I coughed and lost breath, she stroked my hair. When I told her how I longed to see my sister, she arranged it with startling precision. We would walk by the window of the St. Regis at 3:15. Benita would be at the living room window, brought there by Agnes, and at 3:20 we would wave at each other, my hands reaching upward toward her illuminated face.

But on this Saturday, it is not Moira saying with sorrow, *Oh, c'est très triste . . . les jeune filles.* The black dress is in my hands, damp and unaltered: I slip it on. If Moira were here, she would translate for me. The maids are speaking too rapidly, with the urgency of a great and terrible piece of new gossip. Genevieve, my cousin Gladys's governess, I recognize her sweet, worried voice. I move closer to the doorframe. *Retreat, lightly, now on the toes.*

Maids are never in paintings. I cannot imagine the scene behind the door. How they smile, how they drape their hands. I hear only their words, followed by a gasp. *Père deux,* they say. This is what I think they are saying, something about two fathers, but later, I will realize, they are saying *perdu,* they are saying, lost, as they gasp, they are saying gone, all gone.

———

IN THE SYNAGOGUE, THERE is a boy I think I should kiss before I become a debutante. His name is Morris, but I say it quickly, only with the side of my mouth, so it sounds like Morse. He is easily charmed. Call me Morse, he says, I'm your code. His Hebrew is lousy. He has a crooked nose, he looks like he's been beaten. That is enough for me; I know he is not one of us. Soon after I misheard the maids, Morse and I walked to the lake. He was not the first boy I'd kissed, but I pretended he was. Even then, I knew I was special. No other girl had lips like flames. His hand on my breast; he fell backward. I lay down in the slope of grass. Where the green ended, the lake began, and upon the lake, couples in white linen rowed. It is 1914, and my father has been gone for two years, but we still have not found or buried his body. If only we were not Jewish, I could have believed in his reincarnation.

Every seagull and rose may have borne his soul. If only Ninette had not made such a public scene, writing letters to the newspapers and suing our family for the repayment of every valuable in her lost valise, I might have continued to believe he ran away with her to Paris. Everyone believed what they were told. But I would not believe he was at the bottom of the sea, cold and still and unmoving. Instead, I held to the belief that he was still descending, as if he were forever in the place where his body left the boat and went hurtling into the blue below. I saw this image of him so often, I think it became part of me. He must have been bruised, I had decided, he must have bashed his head on a heavy cruel crevice. For my father, he would not have floated like Astor. He would have risen and hailed a rescue boat. I'd done research.

I went down to the Grolier Club and asked to see every newspaper from April 1912. The Grolier Club was on 32nd Street; I announced myself as Daniel Guggenheim's niece. They opened the doors for me and offered me tea. Moira waited for me across the street at Steiner's. Moira was not so easy to fool. I had to tell her I was doing some research for the rabbi, and she obliged, too frightened of seeming suspicious of our religion. I read every detail of every survivor. I learned of Ninette's lawsuit. I learned of the saviors in Newfoundland. And still I continued to hold on to this image of my father's body. Every time a wave would come, it would cast his body forward. He was forever in a current, tumbling, unharmed.

BENITA WAS WAITING FOR me in the lobby. Saturdays at three, we were allowed to walk unattended to an ice cream shop on Central Park South. But that day, as we walked together, she said, we must talk; we must skip the cherries, the sweetness. We walked down Fifth Avenue holding hands; and it was only after a few minutes, that she confronted me.

"Did you know Mother just asked all the maids to leave?" Of course not, I said.

She told me they were lined up that afternoon, as if in a firing range, and one by one, Mother told them they must immediately leave the St. Regis.

"What happened when you went up to the servants' quarters this morning? And *why* did you do that?" she whispered. "Why did you go up there undressed? We are not allowed to be up there. Did someone see you? Did someone scream?"

I tried to calm her. I just took a dress from the laundry room; I listened at the door. I was unseen; I didn't linger.

"Something terribly strange is happening," she said accusingly. "I saw Isaac in the lobby, and he walked very proudly, right by me, without even saying 'Good afternoon.' And when I caught his eye, he looked at me as if I were a hideous beast. I don't know how to describe it to you, Peggy. It wasn't like when Father died. It was something more heartless. It was disgust, I suppose, disgust or pity."

The careful lift of her vowels was forgotten; the words rushed out of her, and they were shimmering with panic. My sister was always serene, implacable; I felt a certain dread to see her so undone.

"It will be fun without maids," I told her, trying to cheer her. "Except I'll miss Moira. We had such a grand time when I had the whooping cough. She told me—"

"We are here as guests, Peggy," she said sharply, interrupting me. "It's something you don't seem to realize. Papa spoiled you that way. With me, he let me know."

"Where? The St. Regis?"

"Here." She spread her hands toward the park, the lovely park, the long fields of green. "We can have the president invite us for dinner. All our millions. We're still just guests."

"I don't know what you're saying, Benita."

"You need to be less careless. You can't walk around like some nubile, besotted orphan. You shouldn't kiss that Morris boy in the park. You shouldn't tell the doormen at 1125 that your name is Raskolnikov. Any whiff that we're strange or odd, the *Googs,* we won't be *here.*"

"And would that be so bad?"

"It would be," Benita said, with tears in her eyes, "a tragedy."

When we arrived at our apartment, a man in a grimy overcoat was carting off my father's portrait.

———

"YOUR FATHER LEFT HIS business affairs in an awful muddle," Mr. Harris told us. After Benita and I tried to wrestle the portrait from the grimy man's hands, my mother pushed us into the library. There Mr. Harris, her lawyer, upon her instruction, told us about our father's secrets. "These girls worship their father," she said to Mr. Harris, when she saw he was reluctant to tell us, girls in sailor shirts and linen skirts, "They should know the truth of the matter, or else they'll continue with this senseless idealization of the man."

"Yes, well you see, it is quite complicated, but essentially, your father made some unfortunate business decisions that I have just discovered. I informed your mother of the financial muddle this afternoon." Mr. Harris was a very tall man; even sitting in a chair, he seemed to loom and tower. His smooth, dark face was shrewd, but he acted bewildered.

"Unbeknownst to your mother and to myself, several years before he went to Paris, he discontinued his partnership with his brothers. This meant he was no longer a shareholder of the Guggenheim Company. His brothers have made some intelligent, even brilliant choices, so this was perhaps a rash decision."

"And in Paris," my mother said.

"And in Paris, yes, he lived quite extravagantly. There were demands on his generosity from some rather . . . from his many friends. And he believed in companies, in inventions, that were ultimately not worthy of his faith. He lost a staggering amount of money."

"You don't need to be specific," my mother said. "These girls have no notion of such things. I myself find it hard to grasp."

"How can we just find this out now?" Benita said rather sensibly. "Father has been dead for more than two years. If he lost all our money, how have we been living as we have?"

"As we have learned, your uncles have rather nobly, and discreetly, been providing your family with the necessary funds."

"While keeping us in supreme ignorance," my mother said. She was enraged, her nose quivered. "I must put an end to this false situation immediately. We will sell what we have. We will move to a more modest apartment."

Beside me, Benita had begun to giggle. It was a giddy, rueful kind of laughter, and I wanted to laugh as well, but I was struck silent by my mother's courage. The day we'd learned of the liner's sinking, she'd collapsed, inept and fumbling. Now she seemed almost noble, and when I reached for her hand, I saw her bare fingers and imagined she'd already begun the task of selling her rings. On this, I was right, for in

the following days, she would lose any sentimental attach-
ment toward her many possessions. She would spend mornings wrapping and shining and folding, then dash out
furtively. She would manage to sell her paintings, her tapestries, her jewelry. It was as if she'd summoned the skills of her
ancestors and become as they had once been, a gifted if reluctant peddler.

WE LEFT THE ST. REGIS. We moved to a perfectly fine apartment on the corner of 58th, which meant, as if it mattered
anymore, that we could still have an address on Fifth. I missed
nothing of our former home, and soon it seemed like a dream,
or a scene in a film, those days when we lived in an apartment
that stretched across blocks of the city. Our new apartment
was rather bare, though Hazel insisted on taping up paintings
and drawings of horses she'd torn from various editions of
Black Beauty. Benita and I shared a room, but we had always
done this, unofficially, and so it hardly seemed a deprivation.
We pushed our beds together, so tightly there was no chance
of falling down into the space between us.

There were two large windows in our bedroom, and lying
there, in our narrow, unmade beds, we could see into the
windows of a violinist's apartment. He was perpetually placing his bow on the strings and weaving it back and forth with
a great dramatic thrust, and we came to love his part, the part
we heard of a symphony. To this day, I cannot remember my
mother's room or Hazel's. I cannot remember their location,
or their décor. But I can still remember the brass lamp with

the crimson shade that I'd rigged up to hang from the wall in just such a way that it would allow me to read into the night while not waking my sister from her dreaming.

For a few months, my mother did her best to be frugal. Her efforts were comedic and doomed. She washed tuna in the sink; she polished our shoes with white towels. She had no idea how to cook; she served us raw chicken and scorched carrots. We will not summer in Europe, she announced; we will join my family in Elberon. Elberon was in New Jersey, and the mansions were hideously Gothic, like the homes of some mad Victorian.

The coast was desolate. The few rosebushes were paltry and vicious with thorns. In nearby Allenhurst, there was a hotel that turned away Jews, and on the night it burned down, my cousins and I all ran outside at five in the morning to eagerly watch the flames. But none of this mattered, the terrible food, the end of Europe. I began to believe I could love my mother again; I admired the way she turned scrappy and careful; her pride, once roused, seemed insistent.

She refused to ask her brothers and father for help. There was the Seligman inheritance; her father was ninety-two. She would soon be able to pay back my uncles; she would avoid them until that day. Evenings, she spent with a wide green book, scratching out numbers, looking entirely content. It was hard to believe she'd ever busied herself with gossip and teas.

When I brought up school again, she relented. I suppose it was because she could no longer cast me off to governesses. And besides, she said, all the nice girls go to the Jacobi School now. Esther Allinger, Rose Sulzberger, Adeline Kuhn. She thought it was a finishing school, like the others, where I would learn languages and manners. If she'd known I would soon be taught Oscar Wilde and anarchism, I am certain she would never have allowed me to attend. But once my education began, I was careful to keep my lessons secret.

SHORTLY BEFORE I BEGAN to attend the Jacobi School, I was abducted. Outside the synagogue one afternoon, while walking with Morse. It was Uncle Daniel who approached me and ushered me into a waiting auto. He would not have needed to pull me with him; I would have walked willingly by his side. I leaned into his shoulder, and he smelled like my father: lavender and tobacco.

Daniel embraced me and, with his watch, measured my wrist, seeing if the band slid off. I know you've been suffering immensely, he said. You notice more than most of us, Peggy. I thought you might like to talk to someone. I went into a building, and he left me there. The building was near our old mansion. It was on 72nd, in a ground-floor apartment. I had never been in a ground-floor apartment before that day, and it felt almost illicit to be in a room so close to the noise of the street.

Of course, Dr. Beren was the best, and of course, he was very distinguished. Cropped silver hair and a fine mahogany cane. I had not yet heard of Freud, but I sensed, with what may be my only talent, that there would soon be a great interest in what my uncle called the talking cure.

I lay on the long leather chaise. I tried to keep my eyes closed, as he suggested, but I couldn't help but look. Upward to his certificates, a shelf with a collection of Guatemalan artifacts. How much sorrow has been in this room? I wondered. Has he heard of murders? Has he heard of rapes, or just girls fainting and wandering? Looking at him, he seemed untroubled, immune to melancholy. I saw my own knees, grazed where I'd just knelt that morning, and brushed off the grime. Then I gazed upward once more, absorbing the cool beige of the room, the perfect quiet stillness of the unmoving ceiling fan.

"I suppose," I said, "you would like me to talk about my father, but I'd rather not."

He didn't answer, and I formed the reply precisely in my mind, as one constructs an apology. I do see him floating at times; I imagine how he must have felt, that is how he haunts me. My sisters don't wonder how he felt with that tug, that undertow. But I imagine this moment most of my days. I now wonder if he chose this death to escape his debts. You didn't know he had debts? Well, ask his brothers. Eight million, he frittered away in Paris.

And you see, he *was* wearing a lifejacket, and he took it off and put on an evening jacket. Isn't that the most wonderful thing? I imagine he felt the tilt of the boat, yet he walked with his mistress toward the orchestra room. *Oh Benjamin,* she said. She is quite lovely, Cupid's bow lips, hair in pin curls, alabaster skin. I saw her photo in the *Herald*. One day I'll go to Paris and I'll find her and I'll say, Just tell me what my father's last words were, and why he put on that goddamn dining jacket!

"Doctor," I finally said aloud, "they like to say, in the papers, that he was a hero, and he gave his lifejacket to a woman or child. I don't believe that to be true. You see, I know my father, we were very close."

"Oh yes?" he says, interested now.

"Oh yes, I was his favorite daughter."

This is not true, Benita was, and who could blame him, for Benita is also my favorite, patient and content.

Then, abruptly, I confess.

"I look for matches," I told the doctor.

How silly it sounded, how trivial. I felt my voice rising, pleading. The clipped, affected, vaguely British accent that Park Avenue girls were using that season was not mine. I preferred guttural sounds. I may have been the first teenage girl on the Upper East Side to make such sounds. Machine-gun rat-a-tat, my voice was ridiculous and full of bravado, the voice you would later hear in movies starring Jimmy Cagney. I used it on the doctor, hoping to shake him up.

"I walk around picking up matches from the sidewalks."

"Why matches?" he said pleasantly.

How did one keep such a flat tone? Later in my life, I will run from anyone with a tone like this, detached, pleasant, immune to sorrow, and this means I will run from bankers, and doctors, and run toward those with violence or filth in their voice.

"Why matches," he asked, "as opposed to, say, stones?"

"I pick them up so they won't start fires."

This is not wholly true, for I picked up dead matches, fingering the charred ends, hoping for the residue of flame.

"You likely think I am seeking warmth, but I am not."

"No," he said. "I can see that."

"It just feels sinful to leave them there. And the thing is, they are everywhere."

Wandering home along the carriage path. I picked up seven, then twenty matches. I was always looking for the virgin, the one that hadn't yet been used, the one that still might ignite.

CHAPTER 3

Libertines

1915

My FIRST LOVE WAS A GIRL I MET WHEN I STARTED TO attend school. Her name was Fay Lewisohn. She was the one who told me the frightening story about the black birds. I didn't realize it at the time, but this simple story would change me forever. It seemed impossibly macabre, but Fay swore it was true.

Here it is:

At Ava Fairchild's debutante ball, white doves were placed in the alcove of the Stratford Hotel in Philadelphia. Perhaps the alcove was airless; perhaps the boys in charge of the birds were vengeful. These doves were, almost immediately, forgotten and untended, until it came time for Ava Fairchild to be presented. She wore a gown of pale tulle; it billowed below her breasts and when she bent to bow, her hands trembled nervously. *Where are the doves?* she must have wondered. Had her mother been so mesmerized by the dress that she forgot to give the signal?

Ava could not rise and ask herself. Rising after bowing is forbidden for a debutante. She waited, in her obligatory crouch, more awkward than demure. Her silk gloves slipped beneath her elbows. Eyes downcast, she heard first a thud, then gasps, and minutes went by in which she heard only the odd sound of hardness, of heaviness. All around her, the birds were falling, not flying, falling from the shaft above. Corpses now, feathers darkened by death, the birds descended onto the dinner table.

All her family had wanted was a fluttering. A symbol of purity. Instead, the dead doves lay around their daughter, leaden and still. Several fell into the immense chandelier, the weight of their bodies causing a spark, a crash of crystal, a quickening above, like lightning's flicker.

I wasn't surprised Fay was the one who told me this story. She was the first girl I wanted to befriend; I followed her around like a fierce shadow.

The Lewisohns lived in a white limestone mansion on Fifth Avenue built by the king of railroads, Mr. Edward Harriman. For a Jewish family to have been able to buy what once belonged to the WASP tycoon was of course symbolic and allowed the family to be admired by all. I will tell you more about the mansion and what I witnessed there later, for like the story of the black birds, observing the way the Lewisohns lived, particularly Fay's mother, Adele, would change me.

But, before that, I was most taken by the rooftop of their mansion. There, above the city, above the park, there were six caryatids, stone women standing, versions of the statues of the great goddesses of the Acropolis, and it seemed fitting to me that Fay would live in a home with Athena and Artemis on the roof above her. She herself had the air of a modern goddess; she was long-legged and serene, with remarkably beautiful eyes, a color that flickered, once violet, then blue. She wore her hair parted on the side and smoked Corona cigarettes from a simple, unadorned black holder. Our grandfathers battled over control of mines in Arizona, I'd later learn. Our grandfathers were not good men, she told me warily, when I naïvely mentioned that my grandfather discovered copper. *My* grandfather discovered copper, she said, sighing, your grandfather discovered charcoal. Either way, they're both bastards.

—

EARLY IN THE NIGHT, Benita returned to our bedroom, intoxicated from her hours with Count Litsky. She wore a fuchsia-red silk dress in the Empire style, black velvet ribbon tied in a bow above her breasts. It seemed perfectly fitting to me that my sister would marry a Russian nobleman. In fact, I was overjoyed and irritated her with my curiosity. Had he mentioned his castle? Had he caroused with a bear?

Peggy, you are misled by imagination, my sister often said when I asked such questions. The real world is not *War and Peace.* But wasn't it? Why couldn't it be? Here she was now, a princess from two dynasties enamored with a dashing man who wore ermine and ducked his head out of habit, after his father's assassination. A dimple in his chin, a dark crest of hair, eyes rather cruel and emerald.

That evening I considered telling her about the black birds, but she rushed past me, throwing a gift of some sort, wrapped in pink tissue and lilac branches, onto her bed. She drew a bath, and I could smell the water, overly scented, the heavy perfume, an odd smell of lilies and calamine.

I'd left my uniform on; I always found it difficult to undress. I loved the plainness. The simple white shirt, the long navy blue wool skirt. I felt, in that moment, that I belonged to some secret army, a troop of incendiary girls, all of us dressed alike. The alikeness had surprised me as I'd only felt a misfit, near orphaned, before Jacobi. For sixteen years, my mother carefully kept me confined and cosseted. I'd never had a friend. And so I expected to be teased at the school. Like Jane Eyre, I'd be mocked and disliked—the bookish, melancholy girl left alone.

Instead, the girls at Jacobi, even Fay, seemed to adore me for reasons I couldn't quite comprehend. The girls, even the daughters of my mother's friends, the Loebs and the Warburgs, were sullen and witty. They argued with each other over anarchism and labor. Each one of them might have been my mirror image, with their dark, unruly hair, their vivid, watchful eyes. When I took the uniform off, I always felt a tinge of loss. Without it, I was once again ordinary, unloved, at the mercy of my mother's rigid rules and relentless demands.

I smelled like Fay's smoke. I inhaled the dark musk on my very thin wrist. At the fitting for my debutante dress, my mother had declared that my breasts were too small, *nothing there really.* With a terrible sneer, the tailor nodded, then stuffed cotton down into my bodice, while my mother laced me tightly, as though I were a rearing horse and she must re-

strain me with reins. This cotton stuffed against my skin satisfied my mother: this cushioning, this fakery. I *was* too delicate,
too thin, but I didn't care. I thought of Fay's laugh, when she
told me about the bird corpses on porcelain plates. Sitting beside her, I'd felt jolted, as if a crucial electric wire had been
placed into the bones of my body. *You* should have dead birds
fall down from the roof at your ball, she said. It was a kind of
dare. *Are you as dangerous as I am? Are you ready to mount a disas-
ter that will become legendary?*

My ball was months away; my mother had rented the Tea
Room at the Ritz. I certainly had time to discover a stall selling dead crows. I was almost sixteen; I believed I might find
stalls of diseased and discarded animals if I could muster the
bravery to wander into unknown parts of the city.

What a farce a debutante ball is, Fay had said dramatically
when we sat on the steps, looking at the scarlet leaves fall. It's
really about offering us up as virgins for the tribe.

What a farce, I agreed loudly, as though I were on stage.
What a tedious display of frivolity!

Now Benita came back into our bedroom, her skin warm
and flushed, her hair soft from steam. She looked so serene
and untroubled that I decided not to mention the story of
Ava Fairchild, though it seemed worthwhile to investigate if
Fay's account was true. My sister and I were summoned for
supper by a frantic and abrupt bell. We looked at each other
with worry, perhaps because both of us had guilt in our heart.
Quickly, I pulled off my uniform, covering myself with a ridiculous flouncy dress, a billowing contraption of muslin,
with a top pinafore patterned like a green and white checker-

board. Quickly, Benita dabbed at her damp skin; she seemed to press her legs together as though concealing some secret softness.

We clasped hands. We knew from the sharpness of the bell's ring that we were about to be berated. I looked ahead at the large windows facing the park and was certain I saw two crows fly up from the coppery leaves. Frightened, I took it as a good omen, but I was foolish. *Misled by imagination.* Had I been more attuned to the atmosphere in our home, I might have known my mother had discovered a trespass. My sister and I were to be treated as errant soldiers, for my mother had learned that morning of a crossed boundary.

Benita was cheerful. She sat erect and still, her face as pleasing and innocent as possible. She'd placed the lilacs from her unopened gift loosely into her chignon, her skin still as dappled as if she'd emerged from a silvery brook. She called to mind the portrait of a girl reading by Fragonard. Suddenly, I vividly remembered a time in Paris when I was ten years old. My father brought me to a private home. There, he promised, I was to see the famous painting *Girl Reading,* which was owned by a man who might invest "capital" into the Eiffel Tower elevators. This man was a surgeon from Texas; his name was Theodore. My father wished me to explain why he found the painting so moving. Let my daughter explain this masterpiece, he'd said to Theodore, a ruddy man who seemed addled and boisterous, strutting about with a peculiar twang and that particular American arrogance.

This is *Young Girl Reading,* I said quietly, awed by the pure color of the painting, the bright strokes of yellow. It was painted by Jean-Honoré Fragonard in—I paused, forgetting.

Was my father trying to show me off as an intelligent, cultured girl? I wasn't certain why I'd been prompted to speak, but I sensed it was important for me to win over this man. Even then I hated the idea of hoarding, of "collecting," and though I was only twelve, I bit my lip so as not to chastise Theodore for hiding such a beautiful painting in his library on the Avenue Montaigne, next to bullhorns and a gilded surgical instrument.

"Jean-Honoré Fragonard shows his subject in profile in order to accentuate the act of reading," I said. "He uses light to illuminate her face and suggest the act of reading is akin to enlightenment. Fragonard is known for his vigorous brushstrokes and use of vivid color. The yellow and crimson in this portrait are an example of the use of both color and form to create solemnity rather than whimsy."

Theodore looked taken aback.

Peggy has studied with Madame Hartman at the Louvre, my father said, and for the first time, I wondered if he wanted me to learn about art for more calculated purposes, as a form of showmanship, no different than besting another man by gunning down a pheasant on a hunt.

It's a shame such a beautiful painting is not in a museum, I said, only because the men had moved away and were now discussing something incomprehensible: wax cylinders, sealed boxes, Edison's phonograph.

Alone, I stared at the yellow of the girl's dress. My exposition had been bland. I could not find the language for such beauty; I could not find the words for what I sensed—that all that mattered about the painting was the light from the window, the color of her dress, a color I was startled by, for in the reproductions the color was flat, familiar, but here the dress felt combustible and bold, as though the artist had meant the girl to be adorned in the shade of fire.

AFTER BENITA BEGAN TO eat, I tried to do the same. I pushed my food around, repulsed by the color of mustard and bone, a marbled protrusion. Peggy, my mother said sharply. Her voice could be astonishingly rude for a woman who was so enamored of manners. *Peggy, where did you go today?*

To school, I said softly, observing the flowers painted into the fluted porcelain of my untouched plate. For the past four months, since I'd been at Jacobi, I'd been fearing my mother might discover my subterfuge. I'd deceived her constantly, telling her I was studying Venetian pottery when really I was reading about riots in Angola. Only last week, when I'd gone with Helen Kastor to see her father's knife factory on Canal Street, I'd told my mother I'd been helping Ava Bernheim with Latin. I lied with an ease that occasionally troubled me.

My mother was so uninterested in me, so caught up in reading the social pages and the goings-on of her mother's family, that I doubted she noticed my voice, the way it quavered, in imitation of some girl I'd seen in a film, a girl with a voice pure and earnest. Only once had I suspected she was skeptical.

Weeks ago my mother almost caught me, and though I constantly lied about my whereabouts, this time I felt my appearance would be incriminating.

I had been standing in the hallway looking war-torn and dirty. I did not expect her to be home and dashed past her, so she could not see I was in a state of bliss. I'd never been so filthy and riled. Branches were in my hair; I could still feel the palms of the police officer who had pushed me off the concrete.

Fay was the one who had brought me into the tree. After school, she'd clutched my hand, whispering, *This city is about to explode.* Together we ran through the park, ignoring the whistles of men, ignoring the screech of pushcarts, ignoring the scent of chestnuts and manure. Behind us, Ava and Helen and Freida and Adelaide and Florence, Edithe and Rosa. We would have followed Fay anywhere; I felt honored to be chosen as her sidekick. In our navy dresses, a streak of blue between the trees, all of us eager to see the city erupt. *We are not schoolgirls,* I thought, *we are incendiary devices.*

We trusted Fay because we knew her mother was friendly with interesting people. Adele Lewisohn went about the city like a gracious searcher, keen-eyed and curious. She was not staid and timid like my mother.

When I was at the Lewisohn home, Adele asked me what I thought of the opera. *I've never been,* I said. Never been! she said, startled. *Never been,* I thought, *never been, never been.* On her table, I spotted newspapers, still wet with ink, Hebrew letters like precise code. Sickles and sunflowers. Symbols I longed to know the meaning of. I was introduced to Enrico Caruso, the tenor who sings Puccini at the opera. He sat in the drawing room, whispering as though his voice might cause a tremor. The blackest beard I'd ever seen, his broad chest swaddled in a lavish scarf of white silk. Enrico is deliriously in love with my mother, Fay said nonchalantly.

In their library, I looked at books brought back from Paris.

Inscriptions on the early pages. *For the lovely Adele—without whom this edition would not exist.* That a woman could know and help an author, a singer, was a marvel to me. I might have been in love with Fay, the kind of love I couldn't have known the words for yet, but I wanted to live the life of Adele; I wanted to live as she did, with art and adventure. Impossible, a voice said, you are too ordinary.

The cold air caused our ungloved hands to tremble as we climbed the trees. Fay and I took an oak tree; we were lithe and furtive. Helen and Florence fell into the clean grass; we heard their laughter below. My face became obscured by the cusp of autumn leaves; I might have worn a mask of foliage. Part of me knew I should hide. On this particular part of the avenue, the two mansions I now faced were owned by Guggenheims and Seligmans. My cousins were watchers. Isaac, scholarly and seventeen, obsessed with astronomy, might have looked out the window with his prismatic telescope. Fay had no such concerns. She stood in a bough, balancing herself in the crevice of bark. I sensed a shift in the air; I heard a noise, a rumble rising from the lower streets. At that moment, I knew. As I said, this might have been my only gift, this *knowing*. Even before I saw the women, I could sense the world was shifting, right then, on a chilly day as we sat perched in the trees like camouflaged sparrows.

THEN WOMEN APPEARED, first as a haze, a mirage—low clouds in the sky. As the rowdy parade moved up Fifth Avenue, I saw more clearly the unlikely sight of hundreds of women in white Victorian dresses on white horses. They

took over the street, waving violet banners, boisterous, forceful, despite their delicate dresses, ruffled and abundant. *A
poem more than a procession,* the newspaper would later say.
Girls not much older than me wore crowns and carried long,
golden scepters. A woman held her baby to her naked breast.
Little girls twirled in wrinkled pinafores. The sun turned the
sky pink; the slanting rays seemed to push apart the afternoon
clouds and coldness.

Men began to gather on the sidewalks, great lines of men,
in black overcoats and dark hats, framing the women like an
unwanted border. Men yelled insults; we could hear their
voices. *Go home, you harridans.* Four women held a stretcher,
ballot boxes on the canvas bed instead of an invalid. *Vote,* the
banners said. A woman dressed like a valedictorian, in a silk
robe and scholar's hat, raised her hands, and I imagined she
might have seen Fay and me, and her hands were gesturing
toward us, beckoning.

Can we join them? I asked Fay.

We must, she agreed, and we leaped from the tree, ran
from the park into the parade. How easy it was to march
alongside the women; we moved without fear that someone
might spot us and say, Aren't those the Jewish girls from Jacobi?

We marry you. Why can't we vote with you? a banner said.
Fay sang along with a song I didn't recognize; her voice
carefree and raspy. I swung my arms, striding in my narrow skirt. After a few minutes of marching, violence broke
out. A tussle, a spat. A young woman with a Wisconsin sash
pushed a police officer; he pushed her; I could not see the
precise movement of the fight, only the young woman falling

to the ground, and more police rushing into the parade. Fay screamed, Leave her alone. The surge of white dresses; the shoving and trample. I tripped, I fell forward, knees on the concrete, kicked by a hoof.

Then the parade calmed; the marches slowed. I saw a little piece of fabric, a strand of velvet, on the street, and I grabbed it, before standing. I did not know what it was, and it did not belong to me. I ran alongside a carriage, trying to find Fay. When I saw her, she was being pushed by a police officer; he was attempting to force her to the sidewalk. He placed his black baton under her breasts. She held her head high; her eyes flashed, and she spat. Startled, the police officer left her, as though sensing the crowd might turn on him for hitting a radiant schoolgirl with a hard weapon. I might have hit him myself if he had not left.

We embraced. Are you wounded? I asked her, my voice breathless.

What a brute! She laughed. I'm not wounded, Peggy. Did you see me spit at that foot soldier? Oh, it was glorious!

I don't know how you are so brave, I said. I thought of the baton, how it touched her body. I was too naïve to understand why the moment felt erotic, troubling. I knew though there was something lewd and stark and brute in the way he'd pushed his baton into the soft part of her body. Fay was aglow; she looked roused, feline. She might have been in such an altercation before; she wasn't the least bit bothered. She brushed the leaves from her hair and smoothed mine, pressing her palms into my cheekbones.

What have you found? she asked, pointing at the black remnant hanging from my hand like a tail.

It must belong to one of the suffragettes, I said. It's not mine.

It belongs to you, she said, and she tied it around my forehead.

It belongs to you, I thought, hearing her voice as I entered the solemn lobby. *It belongs to you.* My heart still raced; I felt revived as one does after diving into cold water. Did Fay love me as I loved her? Was that a confession? I thought of her hands on my face; the closeness; her breath, her starlet lips. *It belongs to you.*

Dizzied, hopeful, I entered the lobby of the Waldorf; I greeted Marcelo in the elevator. I did not look in the mirror; I was so swept up in ardor that I forgot to be careful.

In our apartment, the parade might never have happened. I could not hear the cymbals and tubas; I could not hear the roar and demands of the suffragettes. My mother sat at the dining table, counting the fluted glassware, inspecting the chiseled crystal. I felt a sudden sympathy for her. She would miss out on so much; she would stay confined in an old world; she would never see a banner rippling in the wind; she would never hear a discordant note or dance jaggedly. In Paris, an artist would stick a stuffed monkey to a board and call it a Cézanne, but my mother would never see such an absurdity. She would only gaze at the Old Masters.

This sympathy was momentary. She turned; she looked at me—her daughter in disarray. When she asked why I wore a black band, I paused. For a moment, I wasn't deft and clever. *It's just a thread I found from women who want to break the world apart. It's just a symbol I'm wearing in solidarity. Do you know of Durkheim's theory of collective effervescence, Mother? Your daughter*

has just been collectively effervescent on Fifth Avenue. Arise, awake!
You've now forever lost me.

Oh, I said, after some moments of fraught silence, it's part
of a costume. I've been asked to play Amy in the school's annual production of *Little Women*. Mrs. Quaife wants to introduce me to the theater director at Vassar. (This was true: I had
been asked to play the role of the cruel sister.) I told my
mother nothing of the wondrous afternoon. Had my father
been alive, I knew I would have told him. The majestic
women on horseback; the golden banners rippling and rising
in the wind; the way the word *vote*—a simple word—became
both chant and sword. I told my mother nothing of the moment Fay and I had become aloft, higher than my bedroom
window, precarious and giddy. Perhaps these omissions were
why my voice sounded flat, unconvincing.

My mother looked at me, as though it were dawning on
her that I might not be honest. I attempted to cure her disbelief. I rambled on about the play; I pronounced one of my
lines. *It's wicked to throw away so many good gifts when you can't
have the one you want.* I pressed my hands to my heart; I used
all the devices of melodrama. I let my voice be sweet and
cloying. She lost interest in her investigation; I'd persuaded
her with my ridiculous performance. In my bedroom, I hid
the headband. I brushed the dirt off my knees; I went into the
sitting room and found the cerise thread, placing the needle
into the muslin, knowing it would please her to see me busy
with embroidery.

———

BUT ON THE DAY I learned of the black birds, at the dinner table soon after she'd angrily rung the bell, I knew she was less likely to be persuaded; I could hear in her voice both disdain and certainty.

"And after school? You have been elsewhere since three."

I looked at Benita. I pleaded with my eyes, and ever empathetic, she spoke up. "Mother, I saw irises in the winter garden today—"

"Be quiet, Benita. I have not spoken to you *yet*."

"I was practicing a monologue," I said, "Mrs. Quaife asked me to read for her."

My mother looked at me with a faint smile, a look she often gave to those she found both stupid and worthy of pity. "Earlier this afternoon Solomon informed me that you were on the steps of the Lewisohns'."

Solomon! That traitor. Since he lived nearby on Fifth Avenue, he must have spotted me, lovelorn and eager, entering into his enemy's mansion. But why would he tell my mother? He'd long ago lost interest in our family. My father was dissolute; my mother was too proud. When we saw him at synagogue, he waved to us, his face wary and appalled, as if we might lure him into our tragedy. I keeled toward the table; I wanted to press my body into something sturdy. I could imagine the conversation, the tone. Concerned, *worried*. About Peggy. *I know she has been troubled. I know Benjamin did not care for his daughters as he gallivanted around Paris. I know he left you in a terrible state.* Though I did not hear the conversation, I was certain it contained this kind of condescension.

Right then, in 1915, I vowed revenge. Not in an abstract

way, not in a symbolic way. I understood that I must one day show these men that they were wrong about me, wrong about my father. If they believed we were errant and reckless, I would prove—somehow—that *we* were the ones worthy of admiration. Even then, when I was sixteen and volatile, I would not let him cause me to feel chastised.

BENITA KICKED ME UNDER the table. I looked at her and tried to understand what she hoped me to do. *Feign ignorance,* her eyes said, *play dumb.*

But I couldn't. Somehow the idea of my father's brother, Solomon, wisp-waisted in his tailored suits, savoring the chance to compare me to his daughters—three angelic and modest girls with Christian names and clean hair—set me off.

Yes, I said, I love the Lewisohns. Her mother is so kind. She says I'm a serious-minded girl.

But you are not, not at all, my mother said. And Adele Lewisohn is hardly a good judge of character. I wouldn't pay a penny for her opinion. She lets her own daughter run around like a savage.

She lets her own daughter live, I said loudly. She lets her own daughter join her parties where she entertains opera singers and *all* the intellectuals of New York.

My mother was unflappable. She would not be wounded. Nonsense, she said. More to the matter, I did not receive an invitation for you from the Lewisohns.

Women don't need to be invited anymore, I said. They go where they please.

It's true, Mother, Benita said. Calling cards—invitations—
it's been—

Benita, I have not spoken to you. And both of you are
behaving in a manner I will not stand. She told Benita then to
cease her romance with the "Cossack."

I giggled when she used that slur. Benita began giggling
too, a nervous, uneasy giggle, and for a while we both giggled while Bernadette cleared away our plates with untouched
coq au vin.

Our giggles must have incited the Threat. It might have
been in Mother's arsenal for weeks, but I hadn't heard it. In
the past, she'd threatened to leave our share of her father's
fortune to the Hebrew Home for Unwanted Girls, a plan that
swayed me not at all. They deserve it, I'd told her, I certainly
don't. I think that's a wonderful and noble idea.

Weeks ago, when I'd shaved off my eyebrows and painted
the toilet seat red, in an attempt to alter something, however
minor and merely symbolic, she'd erupted with horror. The
sight of my razored face—which was immediately copied by
all the girls in my school cadre—caused her to grab an armchair handle and tilt. If you cause my heart to stop, she'd said,
you will be left to be raised by Daniel, who will treat you like
an unseemly orphan. He won't hold the hope I have for you.

NOW SHE BROUGHT UP the Tarrytown School. Hazel was
boarding there and had been away from us since September,
an absence that only reminded me of how hollow and pale
my little sister was, how she'd always been a kind of absence,

a forgotten figure. Hazel was happy, for they had horses and
fields not far from the one she'd once hidden in. She sent us
drawings of the black pony to which she'd given the unlikely
name of Bol. (*Bol,* Benita said, *whatever does she mean?*)

Hello, my mother said, picking up the black telephone
perched on an inlaid table. It was not a working telephone,
and I was never clear why she kept it near the dining table and
assumed she had seen such a placement of an antique in a
magazine. She began to perform, with a clenched, firm voice.
Is there room for my daughter Peggy? Oh, that's wonderful.
She can attend immediately.

No, Benita cried, her voice soft as snow. You can't take
Peggy away from me. Mother, I will be so lonely without her
here.

I meant to apologize, to promise I would not spend another moment with Fay. Instead, I thought of Mrs. Quaife,
her earnest voice, saying, I believe the greatest of your many
rare talents might be your skill at persuasion.

What is really wrong with my friendship with Fay? I asked
calmly, as though discussing a spot of green on a piece of
clementine. Why do you fear my friendship with the family?

"Peggy," Benita said. "Stop!"

"Is it," I went on, standing up and affecting the manner of
a cloaked prosecutor, "because her grandfather bought the
mines away from our family?"

All of this is rot! I was prepared to say. I could be adopted
by Adele. I could move to a castle with Benita. I cared no
more. I loathed my mother for her belief in a world and a
time that was cruel, that was brute, a world that forced us
into dresses and dances so we could serve as camouflage.

The mines? my mother said. What in God's name are you talking about? You know I know nothing about men's business.

Well, you should, I said. They did terrible things. Fay told me. She knows. They sent young boys down into dark shafts. They beat up men who were striking so they didn't have to breathe in anthracite and die of black lung. They were bastards!

I thought she might slap me. Her face paled.

The reason I do not want you to associate with that family, she said, in a voice that seemed rather gentle, gentler than it had ever been, *the reason* is because they are not good. Not Good.

Benita began to giggle again. I believe I saw the black birds rise once more over the maple trees outside our window, a flock of birds, a dark spattering.

The Lewisohns, my mother said with great bravado, are libertines. Libertines, she said again, as though by saying the word twice, it would be all the more of an insult, all the more damning.

Afterward in our bedroom, I asked, laughing, what exactly *is* a libertine?

I don't know, Benita said, you are the one always reading.

I suppose I shall be heavily punished for my sin, I said, sighing. I don't believe I've ever seen her so angry. I'm still trembling. I defied her, I said. I didn't intend to—

Peggy, Benita warned, I've told you, you need to be more careful. Why don't you listen?

You're the one who is undressing for Count Litsky, I said admiringly.

How did you know? She was startled and rose from her bed to make sure the door was locked and the window too was latched.

I can just tell, I said. There's something new in the way you move your body.

He touches me, and I— Benita sighed.

I wanted to say, I know, I feel the same way when I'm near Fay. The body is not a body but all longing, a sudden sigh.

Promise me you'll be careful, she said. *I couldn't bear being here without you.* She began to cry, and I rushed to her; we held each other, sobbing. We were sixteen and eighteen; our sobs were those of girls awakening in their bodies, forceful and wild.

I couldn't bear to live without you, I said. I will stop being with Fay if it means I might be separated from you.

And Peggy, you must stop speaking with Helen Kastor too, she said. Mother doesn't approve of her family.

I will stop speaking to Helen, I said, thinking of the way Helen had promised to bring me a gift. I can get a knife engraved with your name, she'd said—my grandfather brought German blades to America, and then he invented his own machines. Good enough for the US Army, I swear to you. Kastor Blades can sever a limb.

Even Fay agreed. The Kastor factory was magnificent. To see the assembly of such gleaming, beautiful knives, row after row of serrated and sharp blades. You have to join us, Peggy, when we visit the knife factory.

When Benita was asleep, I wore a white nightdress and moved to the library. My father's dictionary, an ancient ivory object, was resting open on a pedestal. I often turned the frail

pages, afraid they might erode in my hands while I looked to
see the words he'd once underlined. *Cavalier, hydraulics, ballast.* The word *libertine* was unmarked; the definition somehow seemed stark and profound. Certain words evoke a desire
even when no longer a mystery. *One free from restraint; one who
acts according to his impulses and desires; a defamatory name for a free-
thinker.* I looked at the word as twins must look at one another, knowing, known. I'm not a schoolgirl, I thought, I'm
not a debutante, I'm not the daughter of the Silver Prince. I
whispered then; I said the verb like a vow: *I am—I am—I am
a libertine.*

—

MONTHS LATER, IN MAY, the RMS *Lusitania* liner sank near
the coast of Ireland. On the front page of *The New York Times,*
I saw the photograph of the doomed liner. It might have been
a painting; black of the boat; white of the sky. I could not
help but vividly recall the photograph of my father's doomed
liner three years before. How similar it was! And the same
dread and unease came over me. I took the newspaper to my
bedroom, fearful my mother might see it and also suffer from
the reawakened memory. I stared down at the photograph as
though it contained a code. As a composition, it might be
intriguing. If an artist had painted such a scene, I might have
admired the unexpected slant, the abandonment of logic or
form. But the method I often used failed me in May. I could
only see the truth of the boat's destruction and think of the
Titanic—the men mindlessly eating lunch and listening to the
orchestra when the boat began to tilt. I memorized the un-

likely image: the back of the boat swallowed up while the front rose and tilted out of the sea and toward the sky.

The *Lusitania*'s accident was not caused by an iceberg; it was not merely a rift. Germans had purposefully torpedoed the boat, sending two missiles from a lurking submarine. Stricken, the boat sank far faster than my father's. So fast, survivors would later say it seemed as if the sinking took ten minutes.

ON BOARD, OUR NEIGHBOR Alfred Vanderbilt attended the ship's concert. He wore a tweed suit; he listened to the pianist play the coda of Debussy's "Brouillards." He flirted with Lady Marguerite, noting the Cartier diamonds in her tiara, her absent husband, the way she pronounced the name of her Montreal mansion with an accent he found charming. Ravenscrag, she said, her vowels abrupt as a hitch, not the least bit plummy. I knew Alfred Vanderbilt had nearly boarded the *Titanic* because his son William Henry told me in the coatroom line at a dance. My father almost sailed on the *Titanic,* he'd said in a manner that wasn't gloating but was still tinged with conceit, but he canceled his ticket because *he* had a *premonition.* But in May, Alfred Vanderbilt found himself on the *Lusitania,* sailing to France for a conference of horse breeders. Alfred Vanderbilt was a railroad prince; he'd gone to Yale; he'd married in Newport; he was, the papers said, *a man of pleasure.* Still, he found himself like my father in his final moments, surrounded by the sea; adrift in dark water, flailing and shivering. He was not rescued; his body was not brought out of a cove or found adrift in Africa. His body would never be found. Like my father, he would be described, not as dead or missing, but as "lost at sea."

I lost interest in my studies at Jacobi. I could not appear on stage as Amy even though Mrs. Quaife had invited the head of the drama programs at Barnard and Vassar to witness my theatrical talents. I begged off, claiming illness. I might have pneumonia again, I said, I might have influenza.

I returned to the Yale Club and unchaperoned, in my wrinkled uniform, I carried five or six of the newspapers, looking foolish and bizarre, as I traipsed about, the papers hanging from their long, wooden rods: VANDERBILT FAMILY ALL BUT HOPELESS; WIFE OF LUSITANIA'S RICHEST PASSENGER HOLDS UP UNDER STRAIN OF NO NEWS. SEVERE SHOCK TO NEWPORT. *Colonel Emerson feels that a man of Mr. Vanderbilt's prominence would be recognized, if he was saved, even if he had been seriously injured.*

Soon the same myths—lies, I suspected—were reported, and the man was seen as possessed of heroism not hubris. He had refused a life jacket, as my father had; he tried to save others, strangers insisted. "He showed gallantry," a woman named Ethel Lines told reporters. "Find all the kiddies you can, boy," he'd said to his valet. I doubted these stories as I doubted those told by the strangers who once came to our hotel, pestering Daniel for reward money, insisting that my father had turned sentimental and trite, when his daughters knew he was rakish and reckless.

At school, I really had attempted earnestly to abandon Fay and Helen. I tutored the younger girls in Italian and Latin, which allowed me to avoid the excursions and adventures of my classmates. But soon after the sinking, Helen took me aside as I walked toward the room where I would tutor, a room with embroidered samplers and maps of the world.

Helen, in a finer version of our uniform, a white silk shirt and a blue skirt with a black leather belt, elevated by laced boots, with a sharp high heel, fragrant with Patou, said she must tell me *a very important secret*. Her voice was hushed and genuine. We were on the steps of school. In the spring, our uniforms became lighter, less stiff and woolen. Amelia had begun to wear a bow tie, while Fay wore suspenders. Some girls attempted the ghostly look of Theda Bara, lining their eyes in kohl. Fay, who continued to know more than the rest of us, had revealed that the femme fatale was Jewish. Her real last name was Goodman. But when we sat on the steps, the talk turned to the sinking. We huddled together by the stair-well near the wisteria. We smoked Coronets, we took off our stockings.

Do you think we will go to war? Amelia asked. Roosevelt said it is inconceivable that America should not take action.

Germany lied, Frieda said, her hands twisting about a string bracelet, her forehead furrowed. Frieda was a bit of a doomsayer; we teasingly called her Cassandra. There were two missiles, she said, that is why the boat sank so quickly.

Fay interrupted. She wore too much black liner; her eyes looked veiled and menacing. There was ammunition on board, she announced, with that Lewisohn confidence. No one will tell us that, because we are supposed to hate the Germans. But Americans always have ammunition on their boats. How's that for symbolism? Blown up by their own gunpowder.

Here Helen intervened. She whispered to me, *I know what*

you must know. She whispered to Fay, who looked intrigued. She slipped off her suspenders; they hung from her waist like riding whips. She unbuttoned her blouse, winking at me, while I looked at the paleness of her clavicle. We rose in tandem, left the other girls. We walked to the lake in the park, the same place where I'd once kissed the boy named Morse.

I have some confidential information, Helen said gravely. We looked idyllic and lovely under the curving branches of the cherry tree; the sky cloudless and a light, pastel blue. No one would have known we were speaking of anything other than romance. Helen, it turned out, had been in her father's office, looking for a fountain pen, when she spotted a telegram. An order for five thousand Swiss Army knives. From the US Army, she whispered. Fay nodded.

So we are going to war, Helen said. I wish I didn't know. What terrible knowledge. I felt like a spy must feel.

You are a spy, said Fay, lighting a cigarette. She put her arm around me, for she could tell I was frightened. We might have been virgins, lambs to be slaughtered, yet we knew what others did not: war was soon to be declared. Walking home, I saw young men on their bicycles, looking in wonder at the lovely weather, their faces radiant and naïve. Should we warn them? I asked Fay.

Oh yes, she answered, let's let them know they are about to be blown to smithereens. She spoke in a way that seemed hardened to me, cynical, sarcastic.

Helen began to cry. I wish my father wouldn't— She cried over her words.

You wish your father would stick to cutlery, Fay said, but he won't because there's money to be made in weaponry.

You sound like Cassandra, Fay, I said. You didn't used to be so dour.

I'm honest, Peggy, she said. Our fathers, our grandfathers are killers. Every last one of them. She kicked a stone, suddenly, with such force that it rose up and left a little cloud of dirt.

I liked her fury, then I watched her pick up some stones and throw them into the air. I forgot my mother's warning; I forgot Solomon might be strolling about. I kissed her, our lips touched. Pebbles fell from her fingers; we felt the blossoms in our hair as they fell from the branches above, and we let them fall, for once untroubled by the pinkness.

CHAPTER 4

Sulfur

1916

A T THE RITZ TEA ROOM, I DANCED PERFECTLY. MY MOTHER chose my first partner. His name was Edward Loeb; he was slim and twenty-two, with a tuft of blond hair. The blond hair kept falling into his eyes as he turned me about; we danced the Star Quadrille. We wove in and out of a maze of ribbons, we twirled under papier-mâché moonbeams; we exchanged banners with small lights, all in a choreographed movement in which we might look like bright stars. Mr. Erlesto smiled as he saw me, light-footed and graceful. My splendid student, he would later say. You taught me well, I replied, because I was willing to be polite for the evening. Really, I knew I'd not needed lessons; I'd always known how to bring music into my body.

I bowed before five hundred sons: I danced until my fingers were chafed and my legs ached. The corset clenched; black hooks marked my spine. I wore white tulle, white fox fur, my dark hair flecked with diamonds. I could hear the gasps when I made my entrance. How surprised my mother's friends were. *Oh my, is that really Peggy? I've never seen her look so beautiful.*

The black birds did not descend. I had decided against staging a destruction, either because I was kind or because I was cowardly, I wasn't sure which. In the end, I'd done nothing more than sketch the dark wings, a white page of paper full of black dents and slashes. I invented a newspaper headline and drew the words in Gothic letters: PEGGY GUGGENHEIM STARTLES THE CROWD. Perhaps that is enough, I told myself, trying to understand my timidity. Perhaps the image is as important as the action. Isn't that what art is? An idea, an image as important as an action.

I apologized to Fay a month before the ball. I don't think I can go through with it, I said.

With what?

Having dead birds rain down on the guests at my ball.

Oh, Peggy, she said, giggling. She'd cut a slit in her blue skirt; her eyes were red and cloudy. All night she'd been writing an essay on Baudelaire; it was her new goal to study English literature at Barnard. I never expected you to pull that off.

I could have, I said defensively. I certainly could have!

Where on earth would you have found the birds? Would you have killed them? She smiled kindly. Would you have collected pigeons in the park and given them arsenic? How would you have hidden them? There's no attic in the Ritz Tea Room. The place is crawling with inspectors.

I don't understand, I said. Why did you tell me about Ava Fairchild if you didn't want me to do something similar?

I thought you would like the symbolism, she said, turning

to her notebook, where she had scrawled lines from *Flowers of Evil*.

And what is the symbolism of the black birds? The old-fashioned ways are decaying? These pretty places are infested with death?

Nothing quite that complex, she said. When I heard the story, I just thought we are the black birds. Us Jewish Jacobi girls, we're stuffed away until we can't breathe. We can't fly about, and then people are disgusted by us when we aren't soaring about, pretty little things, carefree.

That makes me want to do it, I said suddenly.

Don't rush into it, she said as she passed me her cigarette. As if she were saying, *Don't worry, Peggy. You'll have plenty of time to cause a spectacle.*

MY MOTHER REFUSED TO invite the Kastors or the Lewisohns to my ball. Would they have attended? I looked about, as I tasted the icing, the apricot. Part of me wished they would barge in, sullen, in their rumpled dresses, with knives from the Canal Street factory. Their absence made the room seem gray and drab, and I looked at my cousin's stopwatch, wondering, *How much longer until I can escape?* The conversations were dull and silly. Mrs. Rose wanted to know if I would summer in Elberon. Mr. Warburg observed that the water in his glass was rather sulfurous. Sulfur, said his son, is an interesting proposition. As a matter of fact. As a matter of fact, we have found stockpiles of the stuff in our Athabasca mine, and it's far superior to what the Rockefellers are taking from the volcanoes in Sicily.

I closed my eyes while they spoke, feigning a whimsical
look. I thought of Fay, standing near the white goddesses on
her rooftop, reading aloud Baudelaire's poem about Paris.
Seething city, city full of dreams. I wouldn't have been surprised
if I'd been told then that Fay would one day marry a gangster,
a gambler, the second in command to Arnold Rothstein, the
kingpin of the Jewish mob. She would hold playing cards for
Meyer Lansky, whisper the ways to win; she would learn the
names of alleys in the Bronx, become inured to the scent of
gunshot.

Nor would I have been surprised to learn that Helen
would live in Paris, where she'd marry the son of James Joyce,
type up the pages of *Finnegans Wake*.

As I sat in the ballroom, I kept my eyes closed; I rested my
hands on my lap so I wouldn't be tempted to tear apart the
calling cards. I saw their names, Felix and Martin, the names
of men who, approving of my performance, my debut, now
requested *the pleasure of my company*. Once more, before I
danced, I thought of the black birds and how they might have
fallen. I would have to find another way; I would have to find
another way to destroy this world. I was not as daring or dangerous as Fay or Helen, I thought, but I wanted a future of
gangsters or poets; I wanted violence and beauty, but I
couldn't envision having the freedom to escape. When Edward found me, I was by the fountain, trailing my hand in the
cold water, looking down at the residue of wishes, all those
futile pennies.

There is my star, Edward said. It's time for the final dance.
I let him twirl me about, but when it came time to bow, I

whispered in his ear, Hide me now, and he did. He outstretched his arms and then lifted me up gracefully. *Coup de
grâce*—perhaps that's what it's called. The birds did not fall,
and instead, unaware of my dark heart, the bankers and their
sons gave me a rapturous amount of applause.

CHAPTER 5

Aviators

1917

THE WAR BEGAN THOUGH IT TOOK LONGER THAN WE expected. It was nearly a year after Helen Kastor saw the slip of paper on her father's desk that America entered the war. April 1917. By then, I'd lost touch with Helen and Fay and the other girls from Jacobi. Helen was at Barnard; Fay was at Vassar. I should have gone to college, I wanted to go and even wrote an essay on Romanticism and *The Raft of the Medusa,* but Benita had talked me out of it, saying we could travel to Europe together, and besides, she said, educated women were coarse and ruined. She insisted this was true. Ethel Warburg's baby was born with a missing hand, and the doctor blamed Ethel, saying she'd damaged her female cells reading nonsense at Radcliffe. So I found myself with a sister obsessed with babies and a mother fascinated by death.

Every day my mother read the names of the dead. *Oh,* my mother would say, *the Chafee boy was shot in Cantigny.* She wrote letters to the mothers of the dead, letters that were full of such sorrow. She softened, she became poetic when she realized she could offer what she had never been given as a widow—an ode; a tender sympathy. She lost interest in the season, the social pages, and Benita and I made the mistake of believing we were freed from her desire for alliances and dignity.

Dear Mrs. Chafee, she wrote, I know how it is to endure when every consolation is hollow and one's heart is only full of grief. She tore checks out of a heavy book and sent them to strangers, after speaking to her lawyers, who had made quiet inquiries and learned the names of widows in need of funding for a proper casket or voyage to attend the lonely burial.

———

PEGGY, MY MOTHER SAID, I can't stand your idleness. You must learn to be a nurse; you might be useful for once, tending to the boys with influenza.

I nodded, but I had other plans. I was eighteen and somehow even more restless. I had an inchoate desire that was physical; my body was suffused with longing, and some days I would lie on my bed and feel like a slim, moving flame. I had no language for this longing; I didn't even know it was erotic. I could only hold visions of floating in water, of being carried away by the current as I let myself writhe and ache.

The war started in April, and by June, our girlhood ended. We fell in love with aviators. I suppose it was inevitable, but it felt dangerous and odd. We met them in the park before they returned to France. Under the cherry trees, they lounged, chins tilted toward the clouds. Tell us what it's like to be inside a cloud, Benita and I begged. Blossoms fell on the men's shoulders, just as they had once fallen on Fay's. Now the pink petals fell against khaki. We sat in their laps, touched the rough cloth.

On these afternoons, we learned about battle. You would think war would be a fact as firm as metal, but somehow Benita and I would hear different things when the aviators spoke. This would lead to our first rift, one that would separate us like boaters who choose a different strand of river. Remember, I was the morbid daughter; she was the innocent. So I listened to the aviators and saw nothing romantic or glorious in their tales. War was a farce as absurd as my debutante ball, a spectacle, a sacrifice.

What are your planes made of? I asked, when they boasted about flying in the clouds.

The wings are made of linen, they said.

Linen! These men are in danger, I told Benita later, when we came home, our lips parched from their kisses. The wings of their planes are not made of metal. They are made of linen held together with wire, frailer than insect wings.

Benita didn't care. She trembled when they told us about soaring fifteen thousand feet above Chamery. Here's how I hold my Vickers, they said, taking her delicate fingers and curving them around the imaginary machine gun.

What happens when you're shot at? I asked.

We're strafed, they said, the plane goes down and we run like hell.

Benita was adoring and chided me for being cynical. She took a peaked cap and placed it on her clean chestnut hair.

I never thought I'd be so charmed by a New York girl, the aviator said.

This one was named Edwin. I didn't like the way he said *New York girl,* as though my sister might be sullied by the sewers.

Oh, are you truly charmed? Benita asked. I don't believe you are.

Her voice changed in that moment; she abandoned her elocution. She lugged at her vowels, like Edwin, who said *Chartres* as *Charters*. Could it be that I truly felt dread in the way she avoided the French pronunciation?

I'm damn charmed, he said, and offered evidence. He tore the metal button off his uniform; he handed my sister the American Eagle as a silver miniature. Keep it until we can marry properly, he said.

When we walked home, Benita held the button as though it were a sapphire.

I did not like that aviator, I said.

I'm going to marry him, she said.

No, you are not, I said. I forbid it. You're engaged to Count Litsky!

I no longer love him, she shrugged, and besides, he's unlikely to leave Russia now.

I knew this wasn't true, as he'd returned just before the war began, claiming he might be conscripted by the czar.

All the better, I said, we can travel to Moscow. We can escape! Mother's too maudlin to notice. We should leave before she's sent me off to tend to soldiers with syphilis.

Had I never known Benita to not laugh with joy at my daydreams? But she didn't laugh then, not even at the clever alliterations in my sentence—*maudlin mother* and *soldiers with syphilis.*

Count Litsky is depraved, she announced. He's decadent and lascivious. I much prefer Edwin.

Edwin's a brute, I told her, but she was already tracing the raised eagle with her ring finger. For the first time in my life, my sister ignored my words. She wasn't even listening.

My mother arranged for me to attend lessons at the Red Cross, but instead I signed up for a typing class after I spotted an advertisement in one of the newspapers my mother called *rags.* PRACTICAL LESSONS FOR LADIES, the ad said. SPEED, ACCURACY, TECHNIQUE. What could be better? I wasn't kind enough to be a nurse; I was bothered by scabs and jowls. If I were to become a secretary, I could perhaps work for a diplomat or a book editor. I dressed as drably as I could. I wore a houndstooth skirt and cashmere cardigan. I cleaned my nails with the knife Helen had given me. She was spending the summer in Cambridge and sent me letters now and then, filled with poetry. *Here in the gray gloom men recite morbid poems to me, and I often think of you when I hear these lines, darling Peggy. I was by the Thames reading Eliot when some pompous man named Rufus or Neville took the book from my hands and read this to me:*

Weave, weave the sunlight in your hair—
Clasp your flowers to you with a pained surprise—
Fling them to the ground and turn
With a fugitive resentment in your eyes:

When I first read Helen's letters, I felt idiotic and ashamed. *Fugitive resentment.* Such phrasing befuddled me; I sensed there were layers and ideas I was too daft to grasp. Thinking of Helen in London being seduced by reedy poets along the

Thames, thinking of how she possessed a compass that would always direct her to the liveliest scene. I dug the knife under the nail though there were no longer traces of filth.

Lately, I couldn't be bothered to take a bath. Benita was either in the bath or off with Edwin, and I didn't want to be on the cold tiled floor listening to the pipes hum while like evidence in a mystery, my sister's collection of Parisian perfumes and face powders left stains and traces. In a week, Edwin would return to battle, and I hoped she would forget about him. He treated me as though I was "pesky." He'd taken to calling me Pegleg, a nickname that infuriated me. I brushed my hair with the boar's-head brush until it shone. Oddly, I'd become prettier when I turned eighteen. My hair now held a shine and was less wayward.

My eyes were bluer; my features less rough, though my nose was still repulsive. My seamstress said, you have a beautiful figure, and I nodded, yes, *at last I do*. Stupidly, before attending my first typing class, I put on my fur coat. It was summer, but I tended to shiver inside the high buildings where men had their offices. My mother insisted her chauffeur drive me to typing class because she considered the location, 33rd Street and Madison Avenue, to be N.G. The streets were a ghastly color that summer; I don't know why. The sky and the streets seemed perpetually washed out and gray. I rolled down the window, and the sky smelled like arsenic. It seemed on every other corner, there were Red Cross nurses in their white hats, white dresses, and dark capes, holding signs that said HUMANITY CALLS YOU. WHAT IS YOUR ANSWER?

Miss, Henry said, as he maneuvered the Rolls-Royce to the edge of the sidewalk, here is your address. He handed me a piece of paper as though he suspected I might flee. I knew he'd likely been instructed to observe me, to ensure I entered the proper building. So I did. I entered into a pale gold lobby with flickering lighting, took the elevator up two floors, with a girl wearing unlaced boots and carrying a purse with a broken clasp. Are you here for the typing class? I asked.

I am, she said, are you? Are you? She sneered at my fur coat, and I felt as if she'd run a scythe over my entire body. Even then, I didn't understand how my mere presence could arouse such hostility.

Let us take the left hand, the teacher said. Fourth finger is 2 q a z. Second finger 4 e d c, first 5 r t f g v b.

We sat at scratched tables, side by side, like workers in a factory. The other girls wore necklaces with dangling crosses, plaid dresses and woolen knee socks. They wore their hair in loose buns, and they yawned constantly. Their hands moved deftly.

First finger, Miss Guggenheim, the teacher said sharply. The figures blurred, and I pressed the keys too tentatively. What if I hand in a row of black holes? I thought. There was skill alone in knowing how hard to press, how to create a delicate impression upon the page, and I did not have this skill. I pressed too hard; I looked about helplessly.

First finger, Miss Guggenheim, the girls said in the hallway as, in sync, they all clenched and unclenched fists. Though I knew it was merely exercise, a way of releasing the cramp from their fervent typing, I watched with awe, thinking it was rather beautiful, the symmetry of so many fingers.

I don't know how you do it, I said, you all type so quickly. You'll catch up, a girl with freckles and a floral scarf said sweetly. But the girl I'd shared the elevator with hissed. Oh, you need help, do you? she said. Why don't you ask your chauffeur?

AT HOME, BENITA HAD left me a note to meet her in the park; she would be with Edwin. Instead, I lay on her bed and wrote a letter. *Dear Count Litsky, Benita misses you terribly and wonders when you will return. She is being courted by a man unworthy of her. He is timid and ordinary. I trust you will soon return to New York where you will be met by your devoted admirers, the Guggenheim sisters. I can often foresee shifts in the future, and I can promise you many more men will die so I advise you to avoid service in the Russian army and hide in the Winter Palace if possible.*

Then I practiced typing for two hours until at last my fingers found the right places without my eyes scanning the keys. Ever restless, ever lonely, I put on my suffragette's band and a summer dress of crisp cotton with a low bodice. Fabric flared from my hips: I wore a boater hat of white straw with grosgrain ribbon. Men whistled as I walked along the green. How strange it was to suddenly find yourself a lure. A siren. I pondered the poem. *With a fugitive resentment in your eyes.* I kept the knife in my pocket like a promise.

Benita was in our favorite spot, by the Dodworth Building at the Met, right by the room where men watched over the first object, the Roman sarcophagus. The ground slanted, and there was a ludicrously resplendent maple tree. Benita lounged against Edwin, her shoulders soft against his uniform, his chin touching the top of her head. Anyone might have thought this was a protector's posture, but already I

knew Edwin was not my sister's savior, and I knew he never
would be. He winced when he saw me. Benita jumped up and
hugged me with a warmth that made me dizzy. She did not
ask after my typing class; months ago she would have waited,
knowing she might need to comfort me.

Pegleg, Edwin said dryly, you look extremely morose.

That I am, I said, morose, morbid, mordant.

I gazed through the window and saw a handsome young
man in an aviator's uniform looking at the bones of the dino-
saur.

Edwin is being sent to Italy, Benita said, next week. They
exchanged a furtive, knowing look.

You must visit Dante's grave, I said.

Hard to be a tourist when you're in a plane being shot at,
Peggy, Benita said. He's in battle not the Grand Tour. Really!

The handsome man waved at me through the glass, and I
left my sister then. I went into the museum. We found each
other on the steps. He was lanky and looked like he had a
furious heart; he looked like he could hurl a machete. He
gave me his card. Howard Wessel, it said, US Army.

What is it like when you're in the sky? I said. Can you see
the texture of clouds?

We don't have parachutes, he said, lighting a cigarette.
Parachutes slow you down.

I wondered if he had somehow misheard clouds as parachutes.

So what happens when you get hit?

He shrugged, blew smoke over my shoulder. The
Germans—what they do, I know this now, is they aim at
your propeller. So my thinking is, if you get hit, best to just

fly your plane into the sea. Your plane of linen and wire. Fly
it right into the sea. Parachutes are for cowards.

I admire your indifference to sensible descent, I said. *Parachutes are for cowards.*

What about you? he asked. Can I take you to tea tomorrow?

Tomorrow I'm going to the Westchester Dog Show. I
laughed; I even giggled. It sounded so trite after hearing his
war story. My sister and I— Here I pointed at Benita, who was
a few feet away on the grass, with her blue hat slightly askew.
Our dog Twinkle is in competition. Look for us in the papers.

Well, he said, you look to me like a champion.

Of course I liked him then. I didn't even mind if he was
being facetious.

Who had said that to me before? *You look to me like a champion.*

Benita spotted me and suddenly waved. Edwin waved as
well. I might have told Howard how I hated Edwin even
though we were all supposed to love aviators. Some sense of
recognition lit up Edwin's eyes; he flicked his ash and looked
into my eyes for the first time. Do you want a warning? he
said.

No, I thought, *I do not want a warning. My whole life has been
one of warnings.*

No, I said aloud.

Well, champ, I'll give you one anyway. He sounded like
he was imitating a movie star; some actor who rode sidesad-
dle and started fires with two stones.

I'm a little worried about my friend Edwin, he said, now
putting his hands on my knees.

If your sister breaks his heart, he might just do something stupid.

He already has done something stupid, I said. She's far too good for him.

Well, anyone can see that's true, he said. I've tried to tell him, but he's in love. I'm worried, he said. If she hurts his heart, well then— Well, then.

Howard Wessel, he moved his hand from my knee where it was resting nicely, and he turned his hand into a gun. Thumb to the palm, finger to the sky. Finger to his temple. *Pshaw, boom,* he said loudly. He hurled his cigarette to the grass, just as perfectly as I'd imagined he might hurl a machete. I liked the way it arced and soared, the brunt in the blue sky.

Then he kissed me. What a strange way to kiss a girl, I thought, right after you've pantomimed your friend's suicide.

THE WESTCHESTER DOG SHOW was at Willets Mansion, near the green field where our sister Hazel had once hidden like Houdini. HEIRESS DISAPPEARS. Had she enjoyed the fuss, gig-gled at the sirens, the footsteps of the search party? Or had she felt a kind of bewilderment, amid the green fields? My sister *was* bewilderment. She lived in that state. I could not believe she contrived her own absence. Even later, when she did such a terrible thing, I still held on to this image of Hazel as a girl who wandered away, an innocent astray.

Benita and I both dressed fashionably, but more modestly than we did when we were with the aviators. We knew we would be judged as much as our moppish, perfumed animal. I wore a silk dress, pale green and paisley. A white bodice

with buttons and a ruffled border, and ruffles at the edges of
the sleeves. Benita wore an ivory blouse and a skirt only a
few shades darker; she might have been camouflaged were
it not for her scarlet hat with a big velvet bow. We wore
spectator pumps and white stockings and must have looked
at least winsome as we walked our dog—all obedience and
propriety—around the sandy ring. We had not invited the
aviators, and it seemed as if our old alchemy returned; we
moved in tandem; our shoulders touched; we knew, without
words, when to pull on the leash, when to stride so as not
to reveal the quickening pace of our pet. I remember—will
always remember—Benita in the warmth of sun that day, her
shy smile, slight disbelief, as the crowd clapped.

We were used to rebuke and correction from our mother,
but there on Gedney Field, we heard applause and saw delight
in the judges. Flora Whitney is smiling at us, Benita whispered, and as Twinkle knelt into a neat, soft shape, I saw flint
in my sister's eyes. Was it only the applause? I could see her
raise her lovely eyes and consider the crowd. She waved, with
only a slight movement of her hand, as if afraid she might
seem too showy.

I, of course, was less modest and smiled directly at the
three judges, then turned about to acknowledge the claps
from the crowd behind me. The glint in Benita's eyes, the
way she laughed as Twinkle nipped at her ankles. She must
have felt emboldened, for she looked suddenly more assured.
I can do what I want, she seemed to realize, I can bend the
world and triumph. I knew her so well that I didn't need to be
told of her epiphany; I sensed it and I knew—with a start—
she would be the one to escape.

We were sent to the photographer but were told, though we had won first prize, that we would need to wait until the other winners, in categories such as Grooming and Great Danes, were photographed. Benita shrugged, her shoulders suggesting resentment and impatience, perhaps suspicion that it was because we were the only—*the first*—Jewish girls to win at Westchester. Without a word, she wandered away from me. She held her long skirt up so it wouldn't trail in the grass. I followed her, letting my dress hover near my ankles, not caring at all if I kept it clean.

We lay together, near lilac trees. Around us, the fields of a farm in Westchester appeared endless, such an untrampled, vivid green.

How I hate the city, Benita said. How I hate the concrete.

I LOVED THE CITY and had begun, after my typing class, to have Henry drive me about so I could look for strange sights. I did not have a camera, but I memorized certain corners.

This is the Willets Mansion, I said. Can you imagine Hazel hiding here? I can't believe she had the nerve. The grounds seem opaque, overly tended. How did the sheriffs even search for her in such even, empty fields?

Perhaps it was wilder then, Benita said, perhaps they've razed a forest.

We rarely talked of Hazel. She was still at boarding school. I suppose we will need to invite Hazel to our weddings, I said, sighing.

Benita petted Twinkle tentatively. High on her cheeks, there was a sudden circle of pink.

Benita struggled with secrets. Her skin betrayed her. She found purpose for her hands.

I won't invite Hazel, she said. She's likely to forget anyway, or just show up on the wrong day.

I'll invite her, I said out of sympathy. But you will be my maid of honor.

She looked at me then, and whispered as though we were in a crowd. Peggy, promise me you won't say anything cruel . . . but I think I may need to marry Edwin very soon, before he leaves for Italy. He says if I don't marry him, he'll commit suicide.

Though I knew this, though I'd been warned by Howard, it still startled me.

That's terribly manipulative of him, I said. He's taking advantage of your sweetness.

I do love him, though. And I couldn't bear it if he went back to war with a broken heart. But he's very impatient. He doesn't want a large wedding. He wants to marry simply, at City Hall.

Mother will hang you.

Can you imagine her rage? What do you think she can do if I present her with the marriage license, if I say, "Well, I've done it. I'm off now. Good-bye."

I sat up, raising myself from the grass with such alacrity that Twinkle barked, a piercing pitch, tuneless and pained.

But you can't really marry him, I said.

Edwin and I are engaged, Peggy. Why wouldn't I marry him?

I'm engaged too. This was a slight exaggeration, but Howard *had* hinted that he wanted me to meet his family in Chicago. It's a lark, I said, dallying with aviators; it's great fun. But you can't actually marry one.

She leaned back, nestled Twinkle on her chest. I love Edwin. He's marvelous.

He's dull, I told her. He's far too dull for you.

And what about Howard Wessel?

I imagine he'll get shot down, I said, fashioning a grass cigarette. I am not being morbid or silly. I believe this is inevitable: all our aviators will die. They'll tumble from the clouds. Bullets in their hearts, linen wings aflame. Even Quentin Roosevelt will die. I think it's rather nice to have that certainty. Unlike with father. I'm perfectly prepared for Howard's death.

You are turning into such a nihilist, she said dismissively. Do you really think Edwin is dull?

He's terribly dull. He may be handsome, but he's handsome in a flashy way. I don't like how he talks to me.

But you provoke him. You use that utterly ridiculous voice you picked up at Jacobi. You bait him. It's as if you want me to realize he's stupid. Why would you ask him if he'll go to Dante's grave? He's not bookish like you. It only humiliates him—not knowing who Dante is.

He was boasting about being stationed in Italy.

She pulled a ring from her pocket. Pale green jewel and a band that was tinny.

Benita, you must not marry Edwin! I'd never raised my voice to my sister. I'd never been furious with her before. Benita, I said, my voice now frantic and pleading. Why don't you give the count another chance? You could have trained tigers at your feet, sit upon a crown in the Winter Palace instead of being with someone beneath you who only cares about sports and battles.

You are as snobbish as Mother is, she said, turning hastily from me. What do you mean? You believe he's not good enough because he's not extraordinary, because he doesn't remind you of a character in a novel, and she believes he is not good enough because his father does not have a fortune.

Well, my reason is intelligent and hers is inane.

I'm just exhausted by all the effort we put into showmanship. I've trained and I've tried and I—I feel like Twinkle here; it's all for show, all to impress, and then did you see how Mrs. Whitney wouldn't even wave to us? And why do we so want to be inside the Christian blond world when they're all so frivolous and cruel?

I don't want to be inside, I insisted, but she flicked the gold ribbon I'd pinned to my waist.

They give out ribbons to our dogs, she said, her voice harsh. All these balls, all these parties, all these dresses, all these contests . . . all so we can pretend we're no longer peasants, we're no longer despised. I like the fact that Edwin doesn't have grand dreams. Look where those grand dreams left Father, tumbling about in his dinner jacket, forever on the bottom of some sea. I'm not like you or Father. I'm like Edwin. We have no grand dreams.

But Benita, we have an obligation to do something extraordinary.

I don't believe I do, though. I want to be fat and kind, with five children. I will be perfectly happy living in Iowa looking every day at my field of corn.

Five children, I said, and my voice wavered.

She rubbed her stomach. Even then, I sensed death in her desire. But before I could warn her, we were called back to the fairground. A photographer seated us together on a small stool. He must have sensed the tension between us, because he asked if we would prefer to be photographed separately.

No, of course not, I said loudly, as though our position on a stool could prevent her abandonment.

Are you two identical twins? the photographer asked, laughing like a fool. His camera extended, an accordion arm. He stood with a batter's stance.

I stared at the lens, wondering if one day I would be photographed by someone who knew how to distort the image.

Closer, he said, let your shoulders touch. We shared a stool; I bent my left leg back and hooked it onto the stool so I would not collapse. Benita steadied Twinkle; her smile was serene, while mine was aslant. The prize ribbon was under my breast; I felt like a cow at the county fair. No one would have known my sister and I had just quarreled. Was this portrait then a lie?

I wished suddenly that I could be photographed by an artist, by a magician, by a person who could capture an idea not an object. Benita and I should be severing not intertwined. We should be nude, improper, and brazen. Right there, on the field where my younger sister had once staged her own vanishing, I vanished into the daydream of a new style.

Right then I dreamed up Dada. I was only eighteen, but I soothsaid; I Cassandra'd, I closed the door on the Old Masters. Future photographs would shimmer and disturb. I could not have known that in a few years I would be in a studio with Man Ray, but I foresaw that one day my likeness would be distorted. A violin-like figure on the naked back of a woman, teardrops like ice droplets under an eyelash. A snake curved around the shoulder bones of a socialite. Did I foresee these photographs? Did I will myself into a world where they could exist?

I stared at the dirt while the shutter sounded like a clarinet, while the man's head hid behind a black cloth. *You haven't captured us at all,* I wanted to say. *Your photo is a lie. You capture us as we appear to be, not as we really are.* Truly, I would rather have had a photograph that showed us as X-rays, revealed what we carried inside. Black and white blurs. Benita's womb had a fetus that might be a bomb. I had a stick of dynamite that might be a daughter, or a gallery.

CHAPTER 6

The Sunwise Turn

1920

I PERSISTED WITH TYPING SCHOOL UNTIL THE GIRLS TRIED to murder me.

By the end of the month, I would find a new place, a new purpose; my whole life would turn into a dream. And that wouldn't have happened if the girls hadn't done what they did.

It's funny because, at the time, as they left notes on my desk, Jewish stars with blood drops, doodles of me, a girl with a grotesque nose, like a yellow bulb, an overgrown summer squash. I wasn't the least bit bothered. Truthfully, I felt I deserved these attacks. Why shouldn't they hate me? Why shouldn't I be warned? Imagine, I thought, if they knew of the vast sum I'd inherited on my twenty-first birthday, just a few months earlier. They put it in a trust where I couldn't touch it. At least Benita will be prudent, my mother said to her lawyer. We must establish a protective system for Peggy; she is like her father, and she won't know how to behave wisely *with such a vast sum.*

I planned to—I couldn't plan. I couldn't envision a financial element. I hadn't had so much as an allowance. I did ask for a small sum of money so I could drive across the country—and even then, on the road, it was constantly surprising to learn the price of things. We had grown up in a world where the cost of things—from an apple to a necklace—was not discussed. My mother insisted on being shown dresses with the price tags cut off. Take it away, she would insist, if a valuable item was brought to her with a cost revealed. Numbers were gauche; numbers were gaudy; numbers were to be taken care of by men.

A woman, Mrs. Willerton, arrived weekly and filled our cupboards with jars of mustards, preserved cherries, grosgrain ribbons, milled soaps, figs, Vapo-Cresolene. We were not to ask for anything beyond what was brought by Mrs. Willerton. We were not expected to be frugal, but we also were not to express interest in material items. It was one of the few values I shared with my mother and her crowd, a belief that economics were an abstract, opaque system, and to find satisfaction in spending was really an empty pursuit, an illness of sorts; it was too easy to become a perversity, a caricature, the hook-nosed demon, despised for their superiority, their avarice.

Soon, twenty-one, I would no longer be called a Goog; I would have as much wealth as a queen. I could buy an island in the tropical faraway, a throne of gold; I could commandeer an army. But this "vast sum" was, as, Mrs. Kohn had taught me, unfair and undeserved. All I could do was give the fortune away and perhaps live, as my father wanted, in a hidden house in Saint-Cloud. But the girls must have sensed that I would not spend my life typing for obese men in airless offices, and that I was learning a skill not an occupation.

One day, a month into my course, I heard a hiss in the keys. A hiss, then a slithering, as a snake emerged. I did not scream. I merely picked it up and put it in my purse and returned to the exercise. Did they expect a spoiled girl would squeal and flutter like the rich, stupid girls in movies? I was nonplussed. I'd seen a dead baby, I'd dreamed of my father's corpse covered by sea slime; a snake did not terrify me. As I put it in my purse, I considered turning to the girls and saying what Raskolnikov said to his accuser, *But you shall not trifle with me; you shall not torture me.*

Instead, I silently typed the next exercise, number 33. Punctuation. *Dear Sir: Dear Madam: My dear Sir: My dear Madam: Gentlemen Yours truly, I am Yours very truly, we are Very truly yours.* The exercises worked like numbing agents on the brain. Not entirely unpleasant. I'd perfected my skill, become quite adept and rapid. I was certain I would receive honors on my certificate.

Perhaps I should have spoken up, because two days later, as I passed the girls, in their brown, bland dresses and tarnished silver crosses, they hissed. Peggy. *Sssss.* A chorus of hisses. Did they think I was the devil? I teared up but kept walking. I heard giggling behind me; a rustle in the coatroom. I should have kept my purse with me.

When I sat down and started typing, eager to disappear once more into the mindless hum of my exercises, the letters were so faint on the page, they were almost invisible. Once I pulled out the ribbon, I realized someone—could have been anyone, or all of them—must have replaced the good ribbon with a used one; but I was too embarrassed to ask for another.

So I feigned my work that day, unwilling to create a fuss. Not wanting to give them that satisfaction. I typed, and rather enjoyed the appearance of absence on the paper. I hit the keys hard, but no letters appeared. It was perfect, a sheet of futility. I sighed loudly, I said aloud, Oh, this is the most beautiful page I've ever seen.

I flounced off, ignorant. I left class early before the teacher would see; I couldn't risk her chastising the other girls. Henry was not there, so I walked up Madison Avenue. Near the Yale Club, I heard someone yell my name. *Hello, Peggy!*

I rushed into his arms. Harold! He was my favorite cousin, the son of my father's sister, the only one who held my hand at the memorial. Now he wore a newsboy cap, his bangs tousled and thick, below the tweed rim; he wore a patched blazer and tennis shoes. He looked rumpled and charming. He'd been at Princeton, he'd learned to box; he married suitably— Marjorie Content, of the Contents, whose name seemed to have been fortuitous, for whenever I saw them at the Waldorf-Astoria or in Elberon, her father was joyful and dancing. He was the stockbroker for my uncles, as well as for the Morgans and Harrimans. Marjorie was asked to attend Miss Finch's, a much better school than Jacobi, my mother liked to say. I'd be content to be with Marjorie, my cousin Isaac had said at Benita's ball, a silly pun that I would go on to hear endlessly. Of course, I thought, proudly, Harold was the one to win the heart of the beautiful girl whose last name was a synonym for pleasure.

When he looked at me, I felt naked, as though he saw

under me, saw my skeleton. His gaze was too intense and knowing; I flushed and began to babble.

I've just come from typing class; I had to leave early because the girls stole my ribbon.

Whatever do you mean, silly?

He put his arm around me. I suddenly wanted to cry, to tell him everything. Benita had left me! She had told me not to go to college so we could travel Europe together, but then she had eloped with Edwin, married at City Hall. I'd stood there, her maid of honor, holding a bouquet of such splendor, Queen Anne's lace, lilies, roses, all fragrant, bright and ivory. She wore a simple, forgettable dress. The whole event had been planned as though under a pointed gun. Hushed, urgent. We brought the flowers and dress home hidden in canvas bags from the seamstress. There was a grim, forced feeling at the ceremony. The official said my sister's name as though she were ordinary.

For a moment, I thought my mother was right. Benita should have married in grand style, if only to hear her name spoken with a flourish, if only to hear a symphony, instead of footsteps and coughs.

"I hear your sister caused a little scandal. Didn't know she had it in her."

"Neither did I!"

"I thought *you* were the family rebel."

"Well, Benita has stolen my crown. Harold—you should have seen the uproar! Mother was furious!"

"Is her husband a fortune seeker?"

"He's too dull to be a schemer. He is Jewish, there's that, but from *Iowa*. It's not just that—it's that Benita eloped and

deprived Mrs. Guggenheim to have a splashy wedding for the
new Mrs. *née* Guggenheim. Mother lives for us, you know. I
wish she'd remarried. All she's wanted for the past twenty
years is to orchestrate the wedding of the century."

"I suppose Florette brought in the lawyers."

"She brought in her cavalry, not your father, or the brothers, but these beady-eyed barristers."

"Beady-eyed barristers!" He laughed warmly; he had the
kind of laugh that made you feel clever and adored.

"She tried to annul the marriage. They ran down a list . . .
is he impotent, is he deranged. She brought in Eleanor Roosevelt's 'assistant'—the one who figured out who was sending
FDR love letters, and that was exciting."

"Detectives often are, aren't they?"

"Yes, but he tried to rope me in. Said I should give him
evidence of Edwin's ill intentions. Honestly, I wanted to . . .
I know all kinds of things, Harold, because I'm the one Benita loves. And Edwin blackmailed her into marriage, said
he'd kill himself, said he'd use his army rifle or crash his plane.
I could never help a lawyer, though. I hate those men. Not
you, though. Harold."

"I'm not a lawyer, Peg."

"But weren't you studying law?"

"No. You've confused me with the other Loebs. I'm
against moneymaking, not in general, but for myself. I want
to do something else, even if it promises little or no return.
Brokers, lawyers—they use a dead language, you know. A
dead language in a dying country."

"I know."

We looked at each other. Traffic rambled down the avenue. How rare and wonderful it was to have someone find the words for an inchoate dislike. *A dead language in a dying country.*

Harold leaned closer to me, whispering. We were right to be careful. Fortunes fell or grew on our whims.

"I'm leaving the Guggenheim Brothers," he said softly, as though revealing treason. "Just like your father did. I'm about to make a break from this world."

He carried a satchel of books, and showed them to me. "In here, I have the manuscript of my novel. It's called *Professors and Vodka.* A little *roman à clef* about my torrid times at Princeton. And I've just invested in a bookstore, this tiny avant-garde shop about to collapse. These spinsters own it; they have no idea about finances. Not that I do, but I can help them I think."

"Oh, I must go. Give me the address!"

"It's in the Village—I doubt Florette will let you go down there."

"Oh, I have my ways."

I opened my purse, to get my pen and notebook, but I'd only glanced into the silk inside when I gasped. The used ribbon. Clearly, it had been tampered with. It was bleeding ink, and there was a ticking noise. I picked the danger up; it bled blue all over my gloves. I screamed and hurled it far away. It felt like fire, heavy and hot. It landed on the concrete like a vicious grenade.

"They could have killed me," I said. I began to weep.

"What was that? Jesus."

"The girls at my typing school; they hate me. I should have told them not to trifle with me!"

"Those goddamn assassins," he said. "What witches."

"Do you think they put spitting pins in there, or a little bomb?"

We looked at the ball. It was spinning on the sidewalk, the steel letters intact, but still, it seethed. It sparked. It may have hissed.

Harold took my hand. Come with me, Peggy, he said. I will cheer you up.

Where? How?

"We're going to the bookstore, he said. I'll introduce you to some artists. Show you some photographs. Stop crying, please. Let me inspect your purse. Be sure there's no other explosives."

I loved him then. Harold, my first rescuer. We began to run down Madison Avenue, him in his sneakers, me in my little crocodile skin heels.

To the Sunwise Turn, he said.

The Sunwise Turn, I echoed, already knowing the name was prophetic; he was taking me toward a brightness, and I ran faster than him, despite the fact that he was a boxer, a bullfighter, a man who would later be written about in a novel by Ernest Hemingway.

THE MINUTE I SAW Madge Jenison, I decided I must be her protégée. She competed with the shop for my attention, and at first, I glanced about as though my eyes were avid, starving. I felt I'd fallen into a fairy-tale setting. The walls were the brightest, burning orange. Banners hung from bookshelves, fabric dyed into streaks and black lines. Batik, I would later learn, was the name for the design. A cat, calico and limping, curled up on a ledge next to a ceramic pot full of marigolds. And the books! On the floor, in piles, in shelves that tilted, on tables, propped against a stained-glass window.

Amid this brightness, this clutter, sat a thin woman, in a loose linen tunic, low waisted so it fell over her hips, over a pleated skirt. This—the abandonment of hems and belts and cuffs—the sway, the draping of her dress—startled me. She must be a mystic, I thought, naïve to the flapper fashions that were in the Village, she might be the daughter of a sultan. She offered us tea; we drank it from chipped glasses; it tasted of ginger.

"You must hire Peggy," Harold announced. I'd noticed my cousins, the men who'd gone to Yale or Princeton, affected a vaguely British accent and spoke solely in assertions, as though every sentence were a salvo, an invitation to debate. I found it condescending and tiresome; I wished he would let Madge speak before he told her what she *must* do.

Madge set down her glass; she let her hair out of a chignon, so it fell in soft waves. "Have you had a job before?"

"I haven't," I said. I looked at the floor. I wished I wasn't an heiress; I wished I could have said I'd worked as a secretary. Was it evident? Three months ago, when I'd turned twenty-one, I'd inherited my share of my grandfather's fortune. Could this lovely, wise woman tell I was given $250,000 for no deserving reason? The money was all in a trust; I couldn't touch it; I'd let the lawyers convince me to do so. But only after I'd asked for enough to drive across America.

Could Madge see it in my eyes—I'd attempted to fix my ugly nose in Cincinnati; I'd attended a rodeo in Texas and lay

under the stars with a cowboy named Red Ruxton. Could
she see the starlet in California who stole my diamond watch;
the dry plains our train crossed, the vast sky in Idaho, the
palm trees and flickering screens in cinemas. I'd learned I
didn't like movie people; I didn't like dry heat and deserts; I
certainly didn't like doctors in Cincinnati who put a blade to
my bone and said, It's hopeless. I've never seen such a stub-
born bone before. I had asked for, as Tennyson might have, a
nose tip-tilted like a rose. Perhaps the surgeon had needed
more practical instructions.

I wasn't sure I even liked America; I'd hoped the trip
would make me fall in love with the West, the hope, the out-
laws and sunrises. Instead, I'd only learned I didn't like the
dust and the desperation, the suspicion and hostility. In Chicago, I'd met Edwin's parents, and they'd told me I was too
opinionated. Outside Reno, I saw a chain gang, men shackled
in a line, sweat on their skin, their faces contorted by the sun's
glare. I hoped Madge could see this in me, for I saw it in her:
I am not certain I belong in this country.

"She hasn't had a job, but she's read more than anyone I
know," Harold said protectively. "She read Browning when
she was six; she's read *all* the Russians."

"Do you like any modern writers?" Madge asked me. She
leaned back in her chair, assessing me. My white gloves were
smudged from the typewriter ribbon; I wore a cashmere hat
with four violet feathers; I wore a coat with ermine trim.

"I do," I said earnestly.

"Freud?" she said. "Gurdjieff?"

I looked back at her blankly. "I would like to read them,"
I said. "There's nothing better than discovering new ideas. I

am desperate to find new writers, new ideas. I'll work for free, Mrs. Jemison. I would consider it a kind of apprenticeship, and an education—"

"Well," she laughed. I could see my enthusiasm appealed to her. "I wasn't planning to pay you. I don't pay any of my clerks. A bookstore is a fragile enterprise. Bookselling is a lost cause. The big ones, you know, Brentano's and the like"— she said Brentano's dismissively, as though saying sewer or Satan—"only survive because they sell stationery. We will not sell stationery. We need to sell sixty books a day to survive, and you'd think that would be easy, but it is not."

"Madge, I can tell you are about to start a sermon," Harold said. He lit a cigarette. "Is she hired or not? I have to go meet with my editor."

"I'll see how she does," Madge said. "It's very boring work. You have to pay bills and run errands and that type of thing. Often girls of your upbringing aren't used to such tedium."

I nodded. I felt an electric charge in the slanting rays of sun. Harold kissed me on the cheek, and I barely felt his lips. I could have left with him, but I felt too enchanted by Madge. I asked her to tell me my duties so I could write them down and memorize each task before tomorrow.

"Come here," she said. She handed me a stack of books. Lola Ridge, Lytton Strachey, Tristan Tzara, Bertolt Brecht. "Here are a few of my favorites," she said. "We can discuss them if you'd like, when you've finished your work. I do owe Harold, you know, he saved the shop from inevitable death. But that's not why I want you here. Do you know why I want you here?"

I looked in her eyes; I couldn't imagine what she saw in me, besides the fact that I came from a family with enough money to buy sixty books a day.

"No," I said, smiling. "I truly can't imagine what you see in me. I haven't been to college. I haven't held a job. My nose was recently butchered by a plastic surgeon so I'm even uglier."

She laughed. "I can tell you're not sentimental."

"That is true," I said. She swept by me, opening the door. Her skirt moved like the sea, her hair caught the sun and showed flecks of silver; she seemed to be wholly fluid, lacking bones or strictures. "It is suicide to be sentimental," she said, pronouncing it like an edict. And as I walked past her, back to the world of my mother, she said it again. Behind me, I could hear her repetition, the sentence like a line in her prayer.

It is suicide to be sentimental.

ON MY FIRST DAY, I wore my moleskin coat with rose-pink chiffon lining, and wore my hair as Madge wore her hair, in a chignon. My first day began with errands; I brought a letter to Mr. Houghton, the publisher, and successfully suppressed my desire to read what Madge wrote. I went to a little dusty store called Sal's Everything & All on 30th Street and sorted through the wooden bins for the items on my list: thumbtacks, picture hangers, two mousetraps. I began to sort through the large and disorderly pile of receipts and requests Madge had left on my desk. When I brought her the supplies from Sal's, she looked at my coat and smiled, a smile that seemed bemused.

"What a lovely coat. Pink chiffon! I hope you can get the dust off."

"Sal's is a bit dusty," I said. I coughed, and then said, to distract her from my coat and my cough, "I love the colors in this shop. I've never seen anything like it."

"Sit down," she said. "You have been running around all day. Did you know that these colors—they're not merely decorative; there's a theory behind them. When we started this shop some interesting artists were experimenting with color—there was, of course, the Post-Impressionist show of 1915—"

"Oh yes," I said excitedly, glad I could at last seem to have some understanding of her sophisticated, unknown references. "Gauguin, Seurat—"

"Exactly. And the Sunwise Turn was this country's first attempt at an adventurous color treatment." It was strange to hear a woman speak in a way that might be considered boastful, to hear her claim she was the first. I leaned closer, nearly knocking my knees into the teapot she had placed precariously on an ottoman.

"Orange is said to be a selling color, thus this—" She pointed at the walls behind her. "And then we used other colors from the prism. It makes it so much more alive and complete than only a few contrasted colors. Your cousin described it as if we had 'flung a pot of paint into the face of the public.'"

Flung a pot of paint into the face of the public. I thought of dust and color; I thought of the image of Madge flinging paint into the crowd. I had no epiphany, no longing, and yet later, many years later, when I was in Paris, I would do the same thing, as though she had given me a purpose on that perfectly ordinary Monday.

"You look delighted," she said.

"I do like the idea of you flinging paint—I mean symbolically—"

"Of course," she said, winking.

"I should go back to my desk," I said, noting the time. "But—would you tell me about the shop's name. Is it from a poem?"

"It's from an old seaman, a captain I think, who visited the shop. He said the wind and the weather, they move sunwise. And there's the idea in *The Golden Bough* that a key turns sunwise, the screw turns sunwise, the clock hands turn sunwise. But could it possibly be the name of a shop? It sounded more like a poem in *The Atlantic* or a cottage sitting squatly at the turn of a strange, twisted road. But I liked what it meant, and someone once said to me 'meaning is what we live by.'"

I believed her, of course, and nodded effusively. Later, back at my clerk's desk, I went through the receipts, tabulating the monthly costs of light bulbs and ginger tea. This desk was set on an open balcony, so I could be observed, but more important, I could look down on the life of the shop. Chimes rang, a metallic, melodic clink, when anyone entered. I'd turn from my boring job, only for a second, to glimpse the arrival. Almost always those who came in were not customers but friends of Madge "dropping by," and always I found their faces fascinating even from the vantage of my high perch.

Marsden, from Maine, with his white scarf and frightened eyes, carrying a canvas. A gift for Gertrude, I overheard, I shall carry it to Paris. Slashes of paint, a landscape purposely

reduced to color. Post-Impressionist, Madge would later explain to me. Haven't you heard of him? She was appalled by
my ignorance. You haven't heard of Marsden Hartley? You
haven't heard of Gertrude Stein? A girl, the daughter of a
French historian, arrived in a plaid coat with her red hair in
two plaits. I heard her ask for a book about the Latin Quarter.

Two boisterous men, not much older than Benita, entered,
one carrying a silver flask, one carrying a clarinet. Darling
Madge, they yelled, we've come to serenade you. Swaying,
they sang a song they said was sinful. A silver lining, they
sang, before one toppled, nearly crushing the lilies I'd arranged so carefully. No one talked of war; no one talked of
society. I thought I must learn this language, their language.
Words came into my dreams. Latin Quarter, Gertrude Stein,
sinful, serenade. On my last day as a clerk, Madge dispatched
me. Go talk to the Armenian rug man, she said vaguely, tell
him I'm tired of his rats in my garden.

OF COURSE, I COULD not have an enclave, an escape, an Eden,
without one of the prosperous Guggenheims entering. Enter
my aunts, into the Sunwise Turn, on a spring day, when the
ginkgo trees on Minetta Street were in bloom, the sidewalks
covered with little fruits that were the color of apricots, but
smelled like fragrant rot. Madge, I think, was impressed by
my diligent ways, by the mistakes I'd found in the accountant's reports. When I confessed I could not understand *Tender Buttons,* but I loved it anyway, she embraced me. I quoted
from the poem as I watered her plants: *A seal and matches and a*

swan and ivy and a suit. Why don't you try and sell some books? she said. You've done enough trudging.

I was rather good at selling; it unsettled me how easily I could sense what books strangers would like. Still, I rarely sold more than a few books each day. Most of the artists were too poor and preferred to read the book while standing in the shop. While tidying up a trail of tobacco, I saw the Daimler drive up; it parked by the doorway, immense and glossy, a shiny bear. Then before I could dash away, Cora and Claudine entered, swinging their Italian handbags, reeking of Patou. Woo-hoo, Peggy, they yelled. Woo-hoo.

Aunt Cora, I whispered, what are you doing here?

We've come to buy books, of course. She sneered at me. You are covered in dust, my dear; your hair is a fright. Why don't you lighten it?

Claudine, my mother's sister, was less ferocious, less critical, but she still looked around the shop and grimaced. *I'd heard it was charming, but really.* From her bag, she produced a tape measure. Help us, Peggy, dear. We need six feet of books. For the library. She might have been buying curtains.

Cora was strutting about the store, pulling out random editions, commenting on the colors of the spine. I do like the mauve, but I need more of a red tone in my living room.

I stood there, attempting to look amused, but I wanted to weep.

Books aren't decoration, I said at last. Why don't you buy wallpaper or antiques?

Because we want to help you and your little shop. And we will read the books. We are not philistines. It's just important that they are of the right color. Why don't you help Claudine? Go get her a cart of some sort.

A wheelbarrow, Claudine insisted. She'd climbed up the ladder and was dropping piles of books, letting them fall onto the rug.

I recalled a wagon in the rug man's garden; I went out and retrieved it, eager to satisfy my aunts so they would leave before Madge returned from her lunch with Amy Lowell. Their insistence on subjecting each book's cover to an aesthetic test—too dark, too worn, too odd, might have amused me, but I could only stand near the register trembling. I began to ring up the books, ignoring their attempts to create a spectacle. They might have been at Gimbels, insisting on a pewter candleholder. Do you have any more crimson books? Do you have a few books with gold pages?

I don't know, I said. I can tell you what the books are about, or what books contain poems. Why don't you read *Tender Buttons*? It's wonderful and it's new.

To myself, I muttered *a seal and matches and a swan and ivy and a suit*. This ridiculous scene went on for some time, and when they had finished, I handed them the slip with the sum owed. Eighty books, my aunts bought that day, more than the shop had sold in the last four months. Still, I could not thank them.

You're very rude, Peggy. You're wan.

You should get some air; the dust in here is outrageous. Who is that man in the corner? Is he a bohemian?

Cora, I said at last, I need to make a delivery.

She winked at me, as if aware of my ruse, and I fled upstairs. They were garish, I thought, they were ludicrous. Yet

Madge was elated when she returned. She saw the check with the name of Guggenheim; she saw the sum; she took in the empty shelves, the entire seven volumes of *Medieval History* now absent, along with five editions of Edgar Allan Poe's now unfashionable poetry. She danced as though she were a child. You must have more of your family visit, she said.

Oh, you wouldn't say that if you'd been here.

I certainly would, she said, and she looked at me directly. All the effort I'd put into becoming a person she would respect seemed worthless. Now I was merely the wealthy niece, the source of extravagance. I might have quit then: I might have found the meaning I desired futile, but I did not. I decided to pretend my aunts were ghosts; spectral, elusive. I decided to continue to eavesdrop and scrawl down the names of streets in Paris to which I sent packages or received letters. *Rue Saint-Victor. Rue Hallé.*

I returned to the shop, stalwart, infatuated, devoted. Such persistence brought a reward. Only a week after the near disgrace of my aunts' visit, Helen Kastor came into the shop, bringing with her the man I would marry. I couldn't recognize him as my fate at first. But then again, you never can.

CHAPTER 7

Hooligans

1920

LAURENCE VAIL SWUNG INTO THE SUNWISE TURN. SWUNG, swaggered, swayed. He was all motion, all color and force. I'd seen all kinds of artists and poets by now; I'd been at the bookshop for nearly a year. Men in burgundy velvet capes reeking of a smell I thought was chestnut; an aristocratic woman wearing a dress made of newspapers; a painter with a snake coiled around his wrist; a painter's model, nearly eighteen, nude under the borrowed smock slipping off her shoulders. But Laurence Vail startled me. A wolf might have walked into the dusty shop; a clear cannon shooting out stars.

What was his most distinct feature? He was composed solely of distinct features. His hair a pale red, streaked with gold, rippled down to his shoulders. Never before in my life had I seen a man without a hat. The careless, unhidden hair alone seemed illicit, vaguely sexual. His nose was Roman, heroic, so narrow and stern. He had lovely, watery eyes, a faded lilac color, and a boyish smile, at odds with his carved, haughty face. He wore an absurd outfit; a coat of sailcloth, a crimson color, and wide corduroy trousers, tailored, but with a torn pocket.

He was very tall, over six feet, and when he walked by me, the papers on the counter rose up and fluttered into the air. Such was his energy; he roused the stillness. He strode in a certain, meaningful way that seemed athletic and significant. What was the sport, I wondered, that trained a man to move in such a way? Later, I wasn't at all surprised when I learned he came from a family of mountain climbers and, in fact, his mother had been the first woman to make it to the top of the Matterhorn.

All afternoon it had rained, and the bars had closed because of Prohibition, so I wasn't surprised when he walked into the shop with an open umbrella, and two friends, one a woman in a dark dress. I didn't recognize her at first, because I looked at the floor, determined not to stare at Laurence, who clearly expected to be stared at. Like a wild magnet, I thought. I collected the receipts and notes he'd rustled. A familiar voice said, Peggy, in the voice we used to use when we were girls at Jacobi.

Helen, I said, with doubt in my voice. *Was it Helen?* Her time abroad had changed her; she looked far older than I did; she wore a silk scarf, tied around her neck, the knot pronounced and oddly askew. Her lipstick was very dark, and she wore tortoiseshell spectacles, damp with rain. Under her gaze, I felt unformed, messy. But she smiled so warmly and apologized. *I'm sorry I didn't answer your letters. I went from London to Paris and met these hooligans.* She motioned toward the back of the store where Laurence now stood in conversation

with another man, an ordinary man, who was nervously dangling the dripping umbrella. I suppose you heard I married,
she said.

I didn't hear! Helen!

It was very informal, she said. We married on the Rue de
Camille, much to my mother's chagrin. I'm now Helen
Fleischmann, doesn't that sound dreadful?

Helen was one of those people who said something pro-
vocative and then acted hurt if you went along with it. I
wasn't certain what to say. It did sound dreadful, I thought,
Fleischmann, the name of the family who lived at 649 Madison. The yeast fortune. It angered me for no real reason. She
was no longer Helen of the Knives; and perhaps because of
this, she truly seemed to have less shimmer.

Leon, come here, she ordered, her voice soft but com-
manding.

I couldn't lift my eyes; I was aware of the presence of Laurence as one is aware of a fire. My heart moved and ached; a
reminder with a rapid beat. The shelves and the window
blurred.

Introductions were made. This is Peggy, my dear friend
from high school. And this is my husband, Leon.

Is Madge here? Leon asked briskly, not looking at me. He
had the umbrella in his hand and kept swinging it about in a
distracting way. *I'm good friends with Madge. Let her know I'm
here, Leon Fleischmann, of Boni and Liveright.* I nodded; recog-
nizing the name of Madge's favorite publisher. He enunciated
the name in such a way that I was tempted to giggle. He said
the name as if it were that of a British lord or an exported
delicacy. Liv-ahh-right.

Certainly, I said, heading for the staircase. I might have
expected Helen to defend me, or even to wonder why I was
behind the counter at the bookshop, but she seemed to take it
for granted that I was a dutiful secretary of some sort, which
was perfectly reasonable since really, I *was* a dutiful secretary
of some sort. I must get Madge to read *Gaius Gracchus* or the
Trotsky, Leon said to Helen, who merely murmured in reply.

But to my surprise, I did not end up announcing Leon's
arrival to Madge. By the shelf of new plays, Laurence stood
before me. I attempted to walk around him, but he moved as
well, and I laughed at the way he formed a gate, his thin arms
outstretched. Hello, he said, laughing, as well, I'm hoping
you won't leave until I've met you. He spoke with such ease
that I could no longer feel nervous; it was as if I'd been invited into a warm place. I looked him in the eye; I said my
name; I brushed back the loose braid in my chignon.

Oh, Peggy, Helen said. She'd swept up beside me. You
must meet my other hooligan.

Is that your name? I asked, not wanting to return to the
coldness of the counter. The other hooligan?

Before he even had a chance to answer, Helen said she was
ravenous and I must join them for dinner. How could the sky
be so warm when the rain lashed all around us? Helen hopped
over puddles on Greenwich Street; Leon held the umbrella for
me, as though it were an object of apology. Only later, when
we were very drunk, I would learn that his name was Laurence Vail but he was never called by that name in the cafés of
Paris. Everyone, I learned, called him the King of Bohemia.

———

JUST AS I KNEW the aviators would fall in their forlorn planes, I knew that sooner or later Laurence would kiss me. Still in our rain-soaked coats, we sat at a tavern, one of those places with sawdust on the floor, gingham tablecloths, stained wallpaper with water coming through the many small holes. Helen ordered steak. The scent of blood; the scent of sawdust. Away from the bookshop, I felt adrift; I felt as though I'd fallen through a trap door and landed in a horse stall. But Laurence was very entertaining, and nearly every person who entered the tavern waved at him or stopped by to say hello.

I learned from his stories that he'd grown up in Paris and lived there still in his family apartment near the Bois de Boulogne. His father was a painter from Brittany; an *academic* painter, he said with contempt. *The kind of man who paints little girls with enormous hairbows in their hair and boats with white sails on the horizon.* (How Helen and Leon laughed when he said *little girls with enormous hairbows.*) And I thought of the Lembach portrait of my sisters and how I loved it still and I always would even if it was unfashionable. His mother was American, a Puritan, old money, DAR, a champion mountain climber. You can imagine, he said, the clash of values, and having as a child to choose between snowshoes and turpentine. His sister, Clotilde, was his savior. So is mine, I said, hoping to let him know I understood the bond.

Oh, but it's not the same, Helen said, you and Benita aren't scandalous.

The rumors aren't true, Laurence said, nonplussed. I don't know why people think we're sleeping together.

Oh come on, Leon said, putting his arm around me. No one cares about incest.

I tried to look placid. The conversation moved on to Laurence's play, the reason he was in the Village. The cast was abysmal, he said, too earnest, no sense of humor.

I thought of his sister. *Clotilde,* I thought, what a beautiful name. I imagined her in Parisian dresses, the finest silk, Peter Pan collars. Thick eyebrows, Macedonian cigarettes, velvet slippers. Their slanted childhood, "enough money to live on, just enough." Moving between the Alps and galleries. Clotilde was, in my daydream, an artist's model, her body existing in replicas all over the Left Bank. Clotilde in clay, Clotilde on canvas. Laurence would accompany her to the portrait sessions, sitting in a corner, working on a play, or perhaps a painting, then taking his sister to a bistro, where they shared a single plate of oysters. There was no room for me in these vivid imaginings; yet I thought: *I want to enter into his life:* which, for some reason, I could not cease seeing as a film in my mind. Clotilde in an overcoat, in men's pants, her long blond hair pinned up and hidden under a beret. Though I hadn't heard yet that she was a singer, I imagined her singing. On the walk from the Seine to Batignolles, she was like a female Pied Piper, attracting idlers and students, solely with her voice, the fierce melody of it. By the time they reached the Café de la Paix, the gang was motley, exhausted. Some left; some sat with Laurence and Clotilde, curious to know if they were a couple, lovers, or a duo from the stage or cinema; Laurence constantly explaining that Clotilde was his sister, his best friend.

In my imagining, he would always choose the table closest to the sunshine and sit in the wicker chair, settling into a spot where he would spend a day. Coffee and omelets were brought to him, while Clotilde insisted on candy or pastries, anything, she said, that was not once an animal. All day Laurence would talk to painters and poets, without pretension or mockery. He wanted to hear about color and texture, a painting that might have been of a cloud, might have been of the sea, but was a mystery, a fragment, anything but a portrait, anything but a sailboat in the harbor. Clotilde sang; she borrowed thread from the waitress and sewed the hole in her slipper, using a part of her earring as a needle. When a man asked if he could paint her, she said too many men had painted her; it was like plagiarism or grave-robbing. When the man asked her name, she said it as though it were a rare flower.

I'd never thought of having children before, even when Benita begged me to discuss with her the possible names for the children she so desperately wanted. But there in the tavern, I thought with a sudden clarity: I want to have children, and I want them to grow up like Clotilde and Laurence. I want them to have vols-au-vent from a bakery painted blue: I want them to sing on the sidewalks without reprimand; I want them to know the scent of turpentine, to have clarinets and goblet drums; to make a peculiar music before they sleep; I want them to have chapped hands in a Swiss valley, to ski past the goats, to learn to traverse glaciers.

Thinking this, I looked over at Laurence who was still talking about the play, the actress, her lisp, her lack of vitality. I looked at him with determination; he might have thought it was desire. Were they really any different? At the end of the evening, I watched how Helen subtly steered the tray with the check toward her palm, like a magician with their handkerchief over a playing card. Neither man made any effort to hand her money. Out on the street, the West Village sky was cobalt and rainless. Laurence said he wanted to take the subway; he was vague and affectionate as he kissed Leon and Helen good-bye. Only when I was in a taxi did I notice he had slipped a note into my pocket. *You looked very bored this evening. I'll make it up to you tomorrow if you will meet me outside the Turn at 5. I promise I won't bore you.* He'd crossed out *won't bore you* and above the words written: *will take you somewhere fun.*

HE SHOWED UP, PROMPTLY, at five. Walking beside him, I felt as if I were next to a strong wind. He wore a tailored seersucker suit, and by coincidence, I wore a navy dress with a rounded collar of white lace. He smiled at me approvingly. I won't bore you today, he said. I promise we'll do something amusing.

I wasn't bored last night, I insisted. By nature, I'm a very quiet person until I'm acclimated.

Oh, I hope so, he said, but that's sweet of you to say. Shall we go for a climb?

He tried to hail a taxi, long-limbed and alert, waving his hand high on the empty street.

Where were the mountains in the city? I wondered. Where were the cliffs? A delivery truck of some sort stopped, and Laurence spoke to the driver for only a moment before he grabbed my hand and lifted me into the open truck. We sat amid tea boxes, wooden and lined with battered copper; the faint scent of jasmine.

At 125th, we took the ferry to Fort Lee and walked to-

gether along the river. The wind kept lifting my hat so I gave
it to Laurence and said, would you throw this in the river? We
laughed, watching as the hat floated away from us, lifted by
waves, like a memento of a missing body.

The cigarettes he smoked were called Egyptian Prettiest;
thin wisps of brown paper and a harsh taste. Tobacco caught
in my throat.

Have you ever been climbing? he asked.

In Elberon, I said, when I was very young. But nothing
like you've done.

Does it frighten you?

Not in the least, I said. You'd be surprised at how nothing
frightens me.

Nothing?

I tried to think. Others might say spiders, rats, snakes, any
creature that suggested rot or curses. I was only afraid of living forever with my mother, or of losing Benita, but I couldn't
find a way to explain this to such a carefree stranger. Nothing, I replied. I've never understood why anyone would be
afraid of heights. I boasted; he was the kind of man who
made you want to boast; I sensed he'd become impatient if I
did not carry myself with a certain bravado.

We reached a rock sticking out like a shelf from the Pali-
sades' main cliff. High above us the rock was worn white on
the edge where the waves must have touched it during gusts
or tornados. He began to climb, and I followed him, setting
my toes into the footholds. He clambered up, hands into
crevices, his feet swinging off the cliff. The sky was light, pale
blue, a promise.

Clouds lilted; I clawed forward, as though I might reach

them. White wombs, I thought, white parasols. Only once I swerved, reaching up, touching air when I'd already taken a step. I swung, precarious, a minute of thinking, this is how I might die, falling into the Hudson, before I grasped a ledge. When I reached Laurence, he looked at me, with my hair wild, my stockings torn, and his expression was so tender.

Riviera weather, he said as I sat beside him.

It's beautiful, I said, lying back on the grass, looking at the skyscrapers across the way.

I'm always cheered up by elevation, he said.

I'm also delighted by ascent, I said, laughing. I sat up, kept my eyes on the clouds, not wanting to be reminded of the city, the malice of skyscrapers. Who in his circle would want to paint us, here on the rather ordinary cliff, an image too romantic, too idyllic? I'd never felt so soft, blurred, blissful, as though I were no longer with blood or bone but only a ribbon, a river.

He kissed me, and I lay back down on the rock, bringing him over me. He kissed me too gently; he held his hands on either side of me, as though to keep me from swaying.

We stayed on the cliff, only kissing, until the sky began to darken, and on the ferry home, he said he was leaving for Paris in the morning. We'll have to meet there, he said, at another elevation. He suggested we meet at the Eiffel Tower, a month from Sunday.

CHAPTER 8

Eternal Wound

I MIGHT NEVER HAVE LEFT AMERICA HAD I NOT RECEIVED a letter from Harold, that fateful winter after the war ended and the mayor declared that no alcohol would be served in New York City. The bars moved underground; the soldiers came home, and I saw them seeming to fall through the streets when they went down the steps to the hidden speakeasies. Edwin returned and began to work for J. P. Morgan. Benita was always reading magazine articles, looking for tips. Drink elderflower, take afternoon naps. Motherhood eluded her. She began to wait by the window of her apartment, so she could begin trying with Edwin before dinner. Lonely, I carried the letter with me as I stacked books into shelves, as I added up the sums of receipts, as I watered Madge's plants and collected frail spiders from the windowsills.

Dear Peggy, I still see you in the Sunwise Turn, your delicate cusp. Marjorie and I are living in a small apartment but spend all our time in cafés. I have started a new magazine called Broom. *As in sweep the old out. Sweep it away! I*

*have asked the Uncles to help out but they refused, saying they
see no chance for profit. And why breathe, I know they believe, if there is no chance for profit? I don't mind. I'll perse-
vere. I met someone who is smitten with you. He is young
with an attractive, noble, and wild face. He arrived at Le
Canard last evening with several beautiful, engaging women.
The entire night everyone wanted to discuss them and couldn't
stop looking their way. When he heard me speaking of the
Sunwise Turn, he nearly launched himself into my lap. Do
you know of a young lady named Peggy? he asked. She is my
cousin, I said, and he wanted to know if you had plans to be
in Paris; he mentioned your climbing skills. (Your climbing
skills?) As directed, I am passing along his request for your
visit. Something about the Eiffel Tower, but I am not sure
you would want to go there for it was the ruin of your father.*

It wasn't that I went to Paris for Laurence, exactly. More
like he gave me a destination. Put a face on my hope. For
what? For another kind of life, far from the one I'd been born
into. A life among artists. Where people bought books for the
author, not for decoration. Where I wasn't hounded, at every
turn, by the thought of our family as something cursed. Always I could see the ghost of my father, dropping that coin in
the middle of the museum, saying, *this is death.*

BENITA AND I WERE both surprised when Hazel showed up at
my going-away party. Our sister is here, I whispered. She
wore an ill-fitting dress; it clung to her new breasts and
cleaved in the back, buttons undone. She was with one of the

girls from her boarding school and must have borrowed a dress. She'd been accepted to Barnard and was spending the summer at a riding camp. Despite the dress, she looked hearty and freckled; lovely in her own way. Since I had induced my mother to take me to Europe, I saw everything in a golden light, even my troubled sister. What did it matter? I thought. I was leaving in the morning for France; I was sailing away on the SS *Normandy*. Like my father, I promised I would return. Like my father, I suspect, I had no plans to.

That evening I noticed Hazel was more patrician; she spoke with a northeastern manner; a little pinched.

Here we are, I thought, three sisters who have grieved and grown up with that hard stone in our hearts.

Hazel moved about the party, waving indifferently at our uncles. Have you forgotten me? she said to Uncle Solomon, when he gave her a look of distressed scrutiny. I'm your brother's daughter. I'm the one who begged him to come back for my birthday.

Solomon nodded; he turned to and began to speak about his collection. Even then, I hated the word *collection*. It made my skin crawl, as though art were not a living thing but something to encase. I noticed how he used the mention of a Chagall to ignore a haunted sixteen-year-old girl.

I went to Hazel's side. Your dress is rather tight, I said.

You sound like Mother.

I don't mind, I said, I just wondered if it was purposeful.

She looked down at the fabric. Her expression was faraway. She touched the fabric and looked back at me as if to say, *What is this dress and how did it find its way on to the wild branches of my body?*

When I saw Laurence in Paris, I wanted to be wearing
weasel skins. Red lipstick in a shade called Eternal Wound. I
wanted to enact every move and contortion I'd found in a
book of illustrated frescoes from Pompeii. Legs on his shoulders, then intertwined, then a handstand. I would be the first
of my kind. A daunting virgin. Again, he would say. I've
never done this one either.

Seventeen Vuitton valises stood in a row by the locked
bedroom window. Each valise contained a lock; each one
contained a different wardrobe for a different city. Each one
was engraved with gold letters, an etching, a warning, Miss
Peggy Guggenheim. I packed the valise for Paris, but I let my
mother fill the others. You'll need this for Rome, she said,
adding sandals with thick straps and a pearled buckle. You'll
need this for the healing waters, she said, folding a gingham
bathing suit with bows on the hips. I nodded; I obliged, but
when she spoke of any city other than Paris, I was not truly
listening.

II.

SURREALISM

———

"Why should one not love beauty?"
—EMMA GOLDMAN

CHAPTER 9

The Silver Princess

I WENT TO MAN RAY'S STUDIO FEELING LIKE I WAS HIDING a bomb. I could not feel the baby kicking yet, but I knew she was there. I'd not been nauseous, nor did I show any of the other early signs: smoother hair, golden skin. Still, I'd woken that morning with the sensation of carrying something soft and feathery. Laurence would laugh if I said these words out loud: *a sensation, soft and feathery.* But when I knocked on the door of the studio, instead of saying hello, I almost blurted out this secret; I almost said the word *daughter.*

It was an October morning. I was twenty-three. On the way to his studio, the sky was sunless and gray, but I did not shiver. My heels clicked along the cobblestones. How wonderful it was to be able to move with alacrity. I'd lost the gait of a girl restrained by insults and corsets. I hurtled toward the wrought-iron doorway of a building on the Rue Campagne-Première.

It's next to the club, Laurence had said as he kissed me good-bye, where we watched those women dance with peacock feathers.

My first winter in Paris, I thought, I'll see the city transform. Laurence warned me the city became sullen and bleak,
enough so that every winter his father tried to commit suicide. *We'll have to go to the mountains of Switzerland,* he said, *I
can't bear Paris without the beauty.* I did not enjoy skiing with
the Vail family. Nestlé coffee and pea soup. His father barking
at me: a mountaineer does not look at the mountain. I imagined myself feigning disappointment. *I won't be able to join you
this winter; it would be too dangerous now that I am with baby.* Even
now, on the chilly morning, I doubted Laurence's prediction
of Paris in the winter as a grim place that would provoke despair. Looking about, I saw only lovely, determined slivers: a
few blossoms on the barren chestnut trees, a woman in a
patchwork coat, carrying a bright green glass vase.

I went to the studio hoping I would be done by the afternoon. I felt too restless and elated to sit still. I wanted to return to the apartment and make love to Laurence again. Again
and again. I wanted to drink Pernod with strangers, ask their
advice on a name for my daughter. Whenever I was truly
happy, I pictured black birds falling from the ceiling, my father's body turning in the waves. How had I defied the curse?
I was married; I was in Paris; I was soon to have a baby. Surely
there would be a reprimand from the forces of my father's
family. *Dear Peggy,* Daniel had written me, *we are saddened that
you did not attend your aunt's funeral. We do hope that you will not
confuse the "thrill of the new" with a life that is cheap and tawdry.*

Since our wedding, I was rarely still. The last few months
my life had become even more of a whirlwind. If there was
a lurking American man in a raincoat, with checks from
my uncles in his pockets, he would not have been able to

keep up with me. Every evening I was attending a party, a
dinner, a performance. At a rehearsal for Satie's *Relâche,* I
watched as dancers twirled with light bulbs strapped to their
nipples; as hundreds of mirrors on stage refracted blinding
light.

In the mornings, I sorted through invitations addressed to
Madame Peggy Vail. I could no longer imagine being a girl
called Goog. I began to believe that I belonged to this city
with the dark rivers and the scent of anise. Never once had I
regretted deceiving my mother, and I had no desire to return
to New York. Nothing could bring me back to a city that
now seemed cruel and corrupt. I did not go back for Hazel's
wedding or for my cousin John's funeral. *I am sorry I cannot
attend,* I wrote on pale blue stationery borrowed from Clotilde. Only Benita would bring me back. *Peggy,* she wrote,
Please come back to me.

———

MAN IS BRISK, TACITURN. In his black-walled studio, he
coldly asks me to wait over there, on the bench. Already, I
begin to worry that I've overdressed. He must regret having
invited me.

Already, he is likely thinking: *Of all the designers and artists
and intellectuals in Paris, I have to spend the day with this silly girl.*
Perhaps he's thinking of Kiki's breasts, how he posed her in
front of a window and the shadows on her breasts looked like
stripes on her skin. More zebra than woman; he cropped her
face out of the photograph. Thinking of Kiki's perfect breasts,
her naked back later to be painted to resemble a musical in-

strument, he must sigh: *Of all the beautiful models in Paris, I am stuck with this flat-chested bore.*

Wait over there.

What else can I do? I lift the long metallic skirt, the shining fabric pools around my ankles. I do not want to be photographed on a bench, seated and docile, a still life. But what can I do? Often I can charm my way into what I want, but Man seems intractable.

So I watch him fiddle with lights, wrapping the cords around his wrists. *Berenice,* he calls out. Saying her name like it is a reprimand. A young woman emerges from the darkroom. She's freckled, light-eyed, with her bangs cut into the shape of a *V*. She helps him untangle the cords, silently. When I smile at her, she looks startled. The two of them begin to talk in a language I can't understand. Exposures. Silver gelatin. Rayograph. He stands behind a contraption that looks like something from vaudeville.

Accordion-like, the glass eye extends.

"I'm very honored to be photographed by you," I say, when the silence becomes too tense. "I'm certainly not as interesting as Joyce or Cocteau. I'm not even certain why you've invited me. I hope it's not for one of those *Tatler* articles on socialites abroad. But I have brought a dress by Poiret. It's rather extraordinary. Gold and turquoise. Beaded, I believe. So at the very least, the dress will be interesting."

He turned a meter or a dial. Laurence had told me not to be intimidated. He's a Russian Jew from Brooklyn. His real name is Emmanuel Radnitsky. I watched him and thought sympathetically: he's dropped the *nitsk,* the *uel*. When he was a boy, he'd stolen tubes of paint from the stationery store and

felt not the slightest bit of guilt for this thievery. Why not?
an interviewer had asked him. I was obsessed with color, he
said, and so my conscience did not trouble me.

———

AT THE END OF my Grand Tour, and soon after Laurence proposed, my mother wired me from her hotel in Milan. DO NOT
MARRY HIM. I tacked the telegram to the wall of my room at
the Plaza Athénée. Next door I could hear Valerie Dreyfus
listening to Boccherini, String Quartet in E. I lay in bed and
thought of Laurence, on his knees, on the 367th step of the
Eiffel Tower. *Will you marry me?*

I was too startled to answer, but I must have said yes for he
insisted we wed soon—immediately—as though *I* were the
one who was fickle and temperamental. Tomorrow let's just
go to the civil registry in the sixteenth, he said.

Oh, but I want my sister here for my wedding, I said. We
must wait for her.

When I heard Valerie's music stop, I knocked on her door.
For a month, we'd been roommates. I was not much of a
chaperone, but I did my best because I'd become very fond of
Valerie. She was eighteen and somber; I liked her serious
manner, her lack of complaint. In the mornings, we'd take
the subway to the Louvre, our eyes ringed with kohl. We'd
pick a floor randomly, and I'd give a lecture on one of the
paintings. I chose one of the paintings I had loved when I was
her age—the Manets and Uccellos—even though these works
no longer had such a powerful effect on me. These lectures
were always interesting to Valerie; she was rapt and fasci-

nated. Often we were followed by touring groups. Once the leader of a group of Eton schoolboys asked if her charges could listen to me talk. *You do a much better job of explaining the paintings.*

On the subway back to the hotel, Valerie would tell me stories about her life. I learned her grandfather was also a bastard. He'd been found selling wheat of *a very low quality* in his warehouses, lying to the Department of Agriculture about the source. He said he'd imported the wheat from Argentina, but in truth, he'd bought it from Winnipeg, at a loss, because it had been burned in a fire. He may go to jail, she shrugged, he may go on trial. She wanted to stay in Paris. *I can't bear listening to conversations about Cartier watches and wheat production rates.* Mrs. Dreyfus said—perhaps—she could take classes at one of the art schools if she was cultured enough by August. Valerie schemed up her own plan; I was merely a pawn in it. In August, she would present her mother with a book-length series of neatly typed essays on *The Art of the Louvre.* So when we went back to our adjoining suites, she sat at her stern desk, writing these essays, carefully referencing the notes she'd taken on our visits. I'd brought with me hundreds of records, and Valerie would borrow *La Sylphide* and listen to it over and over again until she had completed a draft of her essay. I know I'm a flapper, she said one day, but I don't really like jazz. I'm nervous enough.

While Valerie wrote, I spent the afternoons with Laurence. We'd reunited almost as soon as I arrived in Paris. How easy he was to find. I asked Harold where the American poets went, and after he gave me the name of some cafés, I wandered down to the Left Bank and found him sitting at La Closerie des Lilas. As soon as my mother left for Milan, Laurence began to visit me in the afternoons. We would roll about in the bed, laughing at how it felt as if we were on ship, the canopy waving about like sails in the wind. I showed him the drawings from Pompeii, told him how eager I was to at last lose my virginity. I almost feel it is my mission, I said, now that I'm with you in Paris.

He said he couldn't make love to me at the Plaza Athénée; it was too stuffy and claustrophobic. He worried my mother had paid off the porters to keep watch on my chastity. He was tired of using the servants' stairwell; he couldn't be himself in such grandiose surroundings, and when we were in bed, he would envision my mother storming into the entryway, while he hid in the armoire. So one day we went to a small apartment he had rented, a bleak yellow room with one of his father's landscapes on an easel. I exhausted him; I recalled the drawings, the lifting of legs, the bending of knees. If I bled, I didn't notice. You must slow down, he said, but I loved the way I sighed; lying down across him, not moving, but feeling as though I were rising on a perfect river.

—

THEN, THOUGH HE DID not know about my father, he said to me, Didn't we once make a plan to meet at the Eiffel Tower?

Yes, I said, while I twirled a straw in a glass of cold lemonade.

And you stood me up, he said, laughing. Why don't we go now?

I almost said no. For I feared that once in the tower, I

would be overcome with a sadness about my father. So far I had kept my father's dreams secret from Laurence. I had never mentioned how he lost millions on the enterprise of elevators. I wasn't certain why I had not told Laurence beyond some inchoate sense that he would feel competitive or envious, even though my father was a ghost and Laurence was the fortunate one, beside me, living.

Laurence hailed a cab. He had chipped his tooth the day before, while pulling a cork from a recalcitrant wine bottle, and the slight mark charmed me. I thought he'd never looked more handsome. When he smiled, I would look at the little indentation in the row of white teeth, the tiny wound in a face that was otherwise perfect. He wrapped his arms around me in the taxi, mispronouncing the name Settignano in a way I also found lovely.

We won't take the elevators, of course, he said. Those rattling contraptions of doom.

I'm not sure I can walk the whole way, I said. Truly, I was intrigued to ride in a careful cage, but he said he knew I was a true mountaineer.

Don't look down, he said, and don't look at the sky. Look only at the step ahead of you.

Still: a sensation of dizziness; the blurred trees below. I recalled how my father once told me how he sat on a railing with Edison, when the scaffolding on the tower stretched into the clouds. He sat with the inventor, swinging his feet, drinking coffee. *What a magical feeling,* my father told me, *to feel the city become a miniature.* I willed myself onward. Laurence finally swept me up in his arms, seeing me teeter. My hat swung off and his did too, borne away in the same gust, such a beautiful symmetry. He seemed emboldened by this imagery. Our hats became birdlike; he brought me to the highest landing. Before I could even balance myself, take in the color of the sky, he was on his knees. Peggy, will you marry me?

What a strange way to feel, so calm and yet unsteady. The ring he handed me was a simple band with a small sapphire. I wondered if it was borrowed from Clotilde. It appeared tarnished, perhaps found in an antique shop next to a Napoleonic scabbard. I found it so touching when he pulled the ring from his trouser pocket, where all morning it must have stayed wrapped in a napkin, as one might carry around a child's tooth or a breadcrumb. I sat on his lap; I kissed him. I told you I am not the type to cry, I said, and he laughed, because I was sobbing. I insist, I said, I am hard-hearted and I never cry. Cry away, he said tenderly, as tender as I'd ever seen him before. Truthfully, I wondered if I was crying because of the ring or because, each step up the tower, every step—I had thought of my father and how joyfully he spoke of his dreams. He would want me to be here, I thought, seeing the same sliver of sky.

Then I turned myself toward Laurence. How long could I make a nest of my grief? Treating life like straw and hay, to burrow in, to have some cradle that was truly a coffin. Yes, I will marry you, I said, if you're certain. I'm really not sure why you'd want to marry me.

You are silly, he said. I've been wanting to bring you up here since you arrived in Paris, but it was impossible to get you out of the bedrooms.

So this isn't spur of the moment—a whim?

It's very deliberate. I even planted this here, he said, putting his hand under the platform and bringing forth a box of marzipan candies, a champagne bottle wrapped in white tissue. Not a whim, he said.

We drank champagne from the bottle; he put his head in my lap, and I stroked his hair. "Aren't you going to put on the ring?" he asked.

"Oh, is that what I do?" I blushed. "I wasn't sure if I put it on at the wedding . . ."

He looked at me quizzically. "You seem faraway," he said.

And I was. I suddenly had the most vivid memory. I remembered my father saying if you went high enough above the city, you began to believe you were part of the sky, so clear is the air, all signs of men gone, everything bright and so heavenly.

LATER, WHEN I TOLD Benita, she squealed. "Didn't you dream this very thing? You would meet him at the Eiffel Tower!" I imagined my sister clasping her hands together, on her toes, then twirling on her Aubusson rug. She sighed; she said with a tone of apprehension and glee: *Did you feel Father's presence when you were in the sky?*

"I did," I said. "Benita, I felt him in the clouds. I felt him on the ascension, on every flat step. I could imagine him with his measurements and machines. A wired contraption. He was in the sky, I'm certain. And Laurence didn't know! I've never once told him about the elevators. He just chose that

spot to ask me to marry him. Doesn't that seem like a good
sign? Do you think it's meant to be?"

"Oh yes," Benita said, "I do."

———

A FEW DAYS AFTER his proposal, I found Laurence in a terrible
state. Lying in bed, his face wan and tense. By contrast, I was
radiant as a saint. At the front desk of the Plaza Athénée, I'd
wired my mother in Milan. I WILL MARRY LAURENCE VAIL. Then
I bathed in rosewater, pulling petals from the arrangement in
the hotel lobby. I wore a chemise dress from Callot Souers,
with a low waist and a belt below the hips; the seamstress had
not stuffed cotton balls into my corset. Instead, she had said,
Oh, you do suit the Garçonne silhouette.

Why do you smell like roses? Laurence asked when I arrived.

I put some petals in the bathwater.

I must confess it's not my favorite scent. He said it in a sullen way. It surprised me. Yesterday he'd been singing to the
clouds, saying he'd love me forever. Did it only take a day for
his doubt to set in?

He paced around the room, while I sat on the bed and put
a cigarette into my anthracite holder. His Adam's apple was
bobbing about; halfway up his neck, then down below his
collar.

What flower do you like? I asked. I'll pull those petals off
if I can.

I don't have time to think about flowers, he said coldly.

Well, what do you have time to think about? I asked, my heart already heavy. I knew the answer before he said it. *I think about how I don't want to marry you. I think about what a mistake I made yesterday.* I kept smoking, dropping ashes into my palm because I felt if I got up—if I so much as reached for an ashtray—he might chastise me again. *You dirty Jew,* a man had whispered at me a month ago when I bought the newspaper near Le Pigalle. I'd pretended not to hear him, but that evening, I noticed my potato nose had swelled up, ever redder and more grotesque, from a day in the humid air.

Laurence sat in a wicker chair, next to an empty easel. He brushed his hair away from his noble forehead. How could a forehead be so erotic? How could I love his forehead, so wide and noble, more than his eyes, more than his voice?

"What do I think about? Well, after our trip to the clouds, I've been thinking about our future."

"It will be thrilling," I said brightly. "Everyone thinks so."

"Who thinks that? Who have you told? Half of Paris, I presume."

"I've told nobody," I said. "I was just remembering how the Viscount Stewart-Castle—he married my cousin Eleanor—he told me that when I was in London last month. When I visited him, Stewart-Castle at his castle. He truly lives in a castle!"

Laurence did not laugh, though I thought the repetition was quite funny. "Did I meet this man?"

"No, he was referring to *my* life. He said he was certain *I* would have a thrilling life, and since you're to marry me, I'm

sure you will share in the thrills. I don't see why you should
start to worry."

He paled when I said "to marry me." His Adam's apple
began to bob about again. Was this a tic? The protrusion, the
rapid exertion?

"Look, I'm not certain we should marry," he said. "If you
must know—the idea makes me nervous."

"I didn't think you were the type to get nervous. You've
stood on the Matterhorn in the midst of a snowstorm, when
you were *eight* . . ."

"I know. I've never been nervous. It's a very strange and
unpleasant sensation. And it's not because I don't love you,
Peggy."

"Well, why have you changed your mind?" I asked,
though suddenly, with that cold water clarity, I knew.

Clotilde, we both said at once. *Clotilde, Clotilde.*

"I don't think I can bear not having Clotilde in my life."

"But I adore Clotilde," I lied.

Clotilde loathed me. She made no effort to hide this loathing. She said *my brother* constantly when talking to me. My
brother is working on a murder mystery. Has my brother read
you his new poems? My brother said you've only read Dostoyevsky. Didn't you attend college? Oh, you didn't. How
odd. I thought all the Jewish girls went to Barnard and Vassar.
My brother does have a weakness for Vassar girls; that's why I
thought you went to Vassar. He doesn't think you are ignorant, just a little uneducated and sheltered. If I knocked on the
door of the Vail apartment, she would not invite me in. Oh,
my brother is not home. You might find my brother at the

cafés. A door shut; sometimes I saw a sliver of one of her father's landscape paintings. And at the cafés, she'd ignore me, waving to her friends or strangers, never acknowledging me.

I envied her symmetry. Her even eyes, her slim and perfect nose. Her legs, always bare, always perfectly poised like a dancer. Men flirted with her constantly, enthralled by her full lips, her cruelty. Once Laurence threw a bottle of wine at a man who had merely asked her to dance. Glass shards on his shoulder. I didn't pay enough attention when Clotilde said, *Oh, Laurence, not again.*

Now he looked at me, his face oddly tense.

I would very much like it if Clotilde could join us on our honeymoon.

On our *honeymoon*? I asked. I nearly laughed aloud. Laurence had proposed we honeymoon in Capri, rent a villa on the Tiberius side of the island. We can rent sandolos, he said, we can dine at Morgano's with the fishermen. He said he would introduce me to a count who was a distant relative of Marie Antoinette's lover; he promised I would meet a marchesa who roamed the island with her leopard. I'd day-dreamed about little else since he described the enchanted place.

Clotilde with us? I couldn't think of a more absurd idea. I imagined a string of screwball situations. "Madame Vail," the valet would call, and we'd both go running. "Telephone for Madame Vail," and we'd bump into each other under a grandiose chandelier.

"Well, I suppose that's fine," I said. "Could I bring along Boris?"

"Who on earth is Boris?"

"He's my Russian friend. Boris Dembo. He's been teaching me Russian."

"You won't need Russian if you're in Italy."

"No, but you'll be busy with Clotilde so I'll need company."

"Have you gone mad? I don't want Boris Dumbo joining us on our honeymoon."

"*Dembo,* don't be mean."

"Look, it's just a vacation, really. We can be alone together for a few weeks, and then Clotilde can join us. First Capri, then St. Moritz. She's so fun to travel with. You'll see."

"I suppose it will be fine. But don't you think people might think it's a bit strange?"

"And why would I care?"

"No, of course, you wouldn't care."

"If you can't accept Clotilde, I don't think we should marry."

Clotilde can't accept me, I wanted to say. Instead, I said, "I do understand, Laurence. I feel the same way about Benita."

His face softened; bright color returned.

"Can you tell me about the marchesa?" I said, because I wanted to think about something sprightly, a loping savage on the white sand of a beach. I needed this unlikely image to focus on as I felt as if a taut wire were wrapping itself tightly around my heart.

Laurence kissed me on the forehead.

Tell me about the leopard, I whispered. I went to sit on his lap; I wrapped my hands around him and took his pen from his hand. Took out a notebook. Pretended to be a BBC reporter, put on a fairly convincing British accent.

"What can you tell me about the leopard in Capri? Is it true the beast belongs to the Marchesa Casati? Has her skin been torn? Does the leopard sleep in her bed?"

Laurence took the notebook from my hand. It was the first time I felt he was irritated with me. Disappointed, bothered. He kissed me in a perfunctory way.

AND THEN THE NEXT afternoon, his Adam's apple still bobbing about, he brought up my childhood. My skills. I barely knew how to boil an egg. What would I do without servants? Without Belgian ponies and chauffeurs and strawberries brought from Barrytown.

I don't know where you are getting these ideas, I said. I don't care about such things. If I did, I wouldn't be in Paris, I said firmly.

You're swanning about at the Plaza Athénée, he said dourly.

I thought back over the nights I'd spent with him in his bleak apartment. Had I ever complained about the grime in his teapot, the cold bathwater, the black spores on the bathroom curtain rotting out the fabric until the linen looked like a body ringed with bullet holes?

"You are young," he said, "and I'm sure poverty is a mildly amusing experience. But what happens when we have children and I can't set their nurseries up with velvet curtains and the sun comes blasting through and they wail?"

"I had velvet curtains: I had all of that, and I was a miserable, lonely child. Stifled. It's the lack of curtains I want. We will have friends who will paint murals on their walls; I'll cut up my old dresses and make lampshades from tulle. I want them to hear music and have books and learn to fish."

"It's not romantic. You think it's romantic, poverty, and it won't be romantic. It will be grueling and pathetic."

"I used to dream about the gulags when I was a little girl, that's how awful living like a princess was. I don't want you to be nervous about this. If you don't want to marry—if it's because I'm not very intelligent or talented or beautiful—"

"Oh do stop, with that," he said. "Let me think about it. I'll go away for a few days."

"Where will you go?"

"I can't tell you."

"So you're running away?"

"I suppose so. I might come back. You should go to the civic office next Wednesday. As we planned. I'm sure I just need to get this out of my system. Don't worry."

Maybe I don't want to marry you, I should have said. Instead, I blinked back tears. "It's rather difficult to plan for a wedding if you won't be there."

"I'll be there," he said. "I mean I think I will. I might not be, of course."

"Would you mind letting me know beforehand, so I don't show up and humiliate myself?"

"Yes, of course. I am a gentleman, you know."

"I'm not going to bother getting a white dress," I said.

"No, you probably shouldn't."

"I don't like white dresses anyway; they remind me of when I was a debutante."

I lit a cigarette and threw the newspaper into the fire. I watched the flames jump through the screen, and then I looked at Laurence with a rather cold stare. "Have a nice trip," I said.

"This isn't easy," he said. "I do want to marry you, but—"

"Yes, yes," I said. "Good-bye." I hurtled out of the room like the proverbial scorned heroine and heard him yell after me, "I'll have my mother call you," he said, his voice rather formal and distant. "I'll have my mother call you if I decide not to attend the ceremony."

"Well fine," I said.

It was strange because I had my own doubts. For as long as I could remember, I'd never had a fervent desire to be a wife. Why not be lovers with Laurence? Truthfully, I might have been relieved, except as soon as *he* had doubts, I became more set on marrying him. I strode down the boulevard like a furious mare. I trampled on the green. Why marry a man who was in love with his sister? To think he had wanted her to join us on our honeymoon! I walked by the cafés, hoping to see Mary or Helen or Caresse, so I could laugh at the entire Vail debacle. *Can you believe the nerve of the man who wants to spend a romantic tryst with his sister and his bride?* I saw only the usual faces—Andre, Yves, Leon, Alexander. The American men living on allowances while their parents begged them to come back to Ohio.

An artist is not a serious profession, my mother had said when she learned about Laurence. It is not a profession of virtue. Perhaps she was right.

Where were my friends? Most likely they were working— Helen was helping a blind man type his novel about night, Mary was placing Japanese papers tenderly onto the spine of a book. The men were gossiping about pederasts and bordel-

los. I waved to a few but crossed the street and walked alone
by the river. I did not yet know of the nickname the men had
invented for me. Perhaps they hissed or muttered the words
while I waved. I was wounded enough; I was lucky not to
hear.

Near to the river, I looked below at the summer tableau of
so many lying on the concrete, idyllic, serene. One could not
truly be angry in Paris, I realized, the beauty was too elating.
I could feel the joy of others, as though by osmosis; I absorbed their delight. I walked down the stairs to be closer to
the river. People were basking, their faces turned to the sun.
An easel, a trumpet—these signs of carefree action. I could
not be morose amid the glimmers, the laughter. I felt as if I
were walking into a painting. I'll stay in the city, I decided,
even if I never see Laurence again. He was a lure; a ruse. But
now I'm here; I can be struck by the sudden moments: the
charcoal slant on a canvas, the emergence of a drawing of
Notre-Dame; a young girl in braids, with a boat made of
newspaper, wading into the water with the certainty of a captain. How she giggled when the boat began to move upon the
dark river. *Mon bateau, Maman,* she said, twirling and pointing, *mon bateau.*

When I returned to the hotel, the concierge looked at me
nervously. He would not meet my gaze. I should have known.
I want to send a telegram to my mother, I said. To the Hotel
Hassler. Could you wire or call her? The marriage is off.

He looked at me, quizzically.

My boyfriend has decided not to marry me, I said, *c'est la
vie.*

But Mademoiselle Guggenheim has arrived, he said.

Florette Guggenheim?

Yes, he nodded. Should I ring her?

Please don't.

I tiptoed down the hallway, holding my heels in my hand. I found a lace scarf in my handbag and wrapped it around my face like an outlaw's veil.

I knocked on Valerie's door. Poor Valerie, she was ghost white. Your mother is terrifying, she whispered. You didn't warn me.

I thought she might have changed, I said.

She came into my room and started going through my drawers, as though I were hiding opium. She talked about how she shouldn't have trusted a Dreyfus, that everyone knows we are crooks. I know she's right, but the way she said it, Peggy, I've never felt so worthless.

She's a master of disparagement.

I think she went to the Blue Star offices. She wants to get you on the next liner to New York. I heard her asking for a chauffeur to Le Havre. You should probably hide, Peggy. As for me, I have spent all summer working on my book about the Louvre and what will that matter when she tells my mother I have abetted your waywardness. I'll be sent home; I'll probably never see a painting again.

Valerie, I said, I do know how to elude my mother. Let's have some tea.

Your cheeks are sunburnt, she said, it's rather charming. Were you on a boat?

I walked at least five miles by the Seine. I've never seen so many people in splendor, just idle and happy, merely from the warmth of the sun or the gold shimmers on the river. I don't know why I haven't strolled down there before. So much nicer than walking on the street.

You look like you've been crying, Valerie said.

Before I could tell her about my spat with Laurence, there was a loud bang on the door.

My mother and the abashed concierge walked in. He took an envelope from my mother and slunk away. Another betrayal, I thought, before looking at the face of my enraged mother.

I forbid you to marry Laurence Vail, she said.

And why is that?

I don't have any references for him. I haven't met his family. I am making inquiries, but until I have received those, you shall not marry him.

What are you hoping to find? That he murdered someone while he was in the trenches or at Oxford? That he has syphilis?

Valerie began to giggle nervously.

I've heard about him in Rome, Peggy. I knew before you wired me. Leon Fleischmann came to see me. *It will be a catastrophe,* he said, and now I've had the word in my head for days. I do not want your life to be a catastrophe. And Dulcie Sulzberger visited me as well.

Dulcie?

Yes, Dulcie offered to marry you. I'll do anything, he said, as long as Peggy doesn't marry that man.

But I don't want to marry Dulcie.

He said you could live with him like a sister. The Sulzbergers are impeccable, the most revered family after the Seligmans. It has always been that way, even when I was a girl. And Dulcie has been in love with you since you were four. His sister Marion adores you too.

At the mention of the word *sister,* I began to feel dizzy.

Mother, Laurence has left Paris. So you can stop acting like a terror, a true witch, and apologize to Valerie, who has been such a dutiful and sweet charge. Read what she's written on the masters of the Italian Renaissance while I rest.

My mother looked perplexed. Why on earth, she said, would he leave Paris after proposing to you?

He's nervous about our future, and he wants to think it over.

Well, think it over, think it over, think it over. I intend to have you on the next sailing. We'll leave in the morning.

That's fine, I said. I will pack this evening.

I've arranged for your things to be packed. I couldn't bear to be in your room. Heaps of lingerie, cigarette ashes. What on earth are those drawings on the wall?

The Pompeian frescoes.

She covered her eyes. Why are my daughters always running off on me? Deceiving me? I could have run off with one of these fortune hunters from Milan. But I was devoted and loyal to you girls, even when you clearly despised me.

We didn't despise you, Mother. You're very intrusive. Why would you want to investigate Laurence and bribe the concierge to surveil me? Why not be happy that your daughter is in love with a fascinating, adventurous man?

Half of Rome has told me he's a terrible playboy, that he's temperamental and volatile.

Dulcie and Leon are just jealous; they're both in love with me.

It's perfectly normal for me to investigate his background, particularly if his family have not bothered to invite me to their home and introduce themselves.

What if he investigated my background? What if he learned my uncles sent eight-year-old boys into mines where they died of asphyxiation?

Not that again, Peggy. There were no children in the mines. Your red teacher was merely trying to get you to give to her charity when she told you those tales.

There are entire books about us. They call us swindlers.

Those books were funded by Henry Hilton. My father sued him when he was forbidden to stay at the Grand Union Hotel. Hilton called our family vipers and snakes. Can you imagine how it felt to be a little girl, and in the newspapers Hilton published a statement saying the "Jews had brought public opinion down on themselves by vulgar ostentation and a puffed-up vanity"? I still remember those phrases, Peggy, from 1877! *Vulgar ostentation* and *a puffed-up vanity*. He declared that the Seligman Jews had almost ruined his fine hotels and the best of American society with our obtrusiveness, which was apparently frequently disgusting and always repulsive to the well-bred. This is what he said about my father, the most dignified, gentle man. Then he destroyed him with these books and rumors about sending children into the mines. You really have no idea about your grandfather, no idea at all.

Well, maybe I'll write a book about the case. Now that I have no wedding to plan. The Hilton-Seligman Affair.

The Sensation in Saratoga, my mother said wryly. What do you think of the title?

A bit lurid, I said, but intriguing.

You are good at intrigue, Peggy, my mother said. I'll give you that.

Shall we take Valerie to dinner? I said.

Yes, and I will apologize.

The Vail Debacle, I said when we were in the elevator.

Valerie chimed in at dinner, surprisingly clever. We ate coq au vin, drank cognac. Valerie turned the title-making game to her own biography. The Sorbonne Siren, she said.

I like that, I said, drinking some of my mother's cognac while she put on lipstick with the help of a hand mirror.

The Sorbonne Siren and the Silver Princess.

Whoever is that? I asked.

You, Peggy. I've always thought of you like that. Not because of your father's nickname. But because of the Poiret dress. Have you seen the Poiret dress, Florette? It's magnificent. Peggy causes a sensation whenever she wears it, and when I look at her, I think she looks like that, like a silver princess.

I waited for my mother to sneer. But perhaps she felt sorry for me. Forsaken, abandoned, deflowered, spurned. Yes, my mother said, I shall commission a statue, like one of those you see at the Panthéon. I shall place it in the entryway of the apartment I purchase for Peggy and Dulcie. What a gift! Oh, Peggy, I am joking of course, but you do deserve a statue. Look at you holding your head up. You are more of a shining warrior than a Silver Princess.

Mother, I've never heard you praise me before.

I praise you all the time, she said, but your head has been so full of poetry and nonsense that you haven't been listening.

—

I WORE THIS SILVER dress to be photographed by Man Ray. Laurence had helped me pick it out when we went to the atelier of the man who made dresses for Russian ballerinas, the man who was credited with the end of corsets. Instead, his dresses were draped on the body, without buttons or darts, without any kind of obstruction or enclosure.

Later, when the portrait was hung in the Smithsonian, a curator will call me. What material is your dress? What type of fabric? She will ask me for details. Why is this important? I asked her. I'm asking for selfish reasons, she said. I want to find a dress like this. I'm rather obsessed with it. It summons up the Roaring Twenties. The fun you must have had!

Oh, it wasn't so fun, I told her. It certainly wasn't roaring. I don't know who came up with that inane adjective.

The dress had beaded jewels on the bodice, silver and turquoise, arranged in circles, so I appeared to be wearing delicate armor, a breastplate. The skirt also shimmered, pooled around my ankles, so I looked elongated, serpentine. In bed, when I'd felt the baby kicking, when I'd gazed at Laurence's heroic forehead, feeling such joy that he had, in the end, returned from Rouen to marry me, I'd kissed him on his chin, on his eyelids, on his knuckles. He awoke, grinned with mischief and even lust—when he saw me in the dress.

Perfect, he said. Better than all those boring ladies in their suits.

It's not too extravagant?

You have to stand out, he said. You have to create a memorable image.

I nodded. He was using a professorial tone with me, as though I needed an instruction on how to conjugate verbs.

Why don't you wear the headdress? he said. The one from Vera.

I found the turban, wrapped it tightly. This was a clever idea, I thought, for now I looked taller. The line extended. I would insist on standing; I would be a long, thin line, as if one could straighten lightning.

You look Egyptian, Laurence said. Like those mummified kings we saw in Egypt.

I do, I said, like King Akhenaten. Should I hold my cigarette lighter?

Of course, he said, the black thing in your lips, very sexy.

We colluded in the bedroom; we might never have been more in love. He ran his hands over my body, pleaded to make love.

I don't have time, I said. I'll mess up my persona.

I can't wait to hear about it, he said. You must memorize Man Ray's expression when he sees you. He'll be like a startled deer. And don't let him persuade you to wear something more ordinary.

He's hardly going to do that. He photographed Nancy in a top hat and an armful of bangles.

But that was a *costume,* he said, this is your real style. This is modernity. The new woman. You'll scare the shit out of him, he said. I'm sure of it. And don't let him change you. Just remember he's Emmanuel from Brooklyn.

———

AFTER A WHILE OF waiting, Berenice came to take my coat.
She gasped when she saw the dress.

Is it too much? I asked. Is it too theatrical?

He can decide, she said quietly. But I think it's beautiful. I
don't think I've ever seen such a beautiful dress.

Stand here, Man said, pointing to a place on the black and
white tiles, in front of a plain wall. Rough vowels, the guttural rasp.

You're from Brooklyn, aren't you? I asked him. And your
parents came from Russia?

I am Man Ray, he said, as though his history were a taboo,
an erasure.

Yes, I said. I do understand the impulse to change one's
name. I would do anything to be rid of Guggenheim. Do you
know what they called us in New York? The Googs.

He didn't laugh or look amused. Berenice looked rather
uneasy, as though I were veering into a discussion of voodoo
or mesmerism, the illogical.

Please sit on the bench, he said. Turn to the side. Fold
your hands in your lap.

I think you should photograph me moving, I said. I took
a step or two so he could see the drape of the dress, the way it
shimmered when I stepped.

Oh, you do, he said. And why is that?

Because you are inventive and rebellious, and I think the
portrait could be as well. Those portraits of society women
sitting by a vase of flowers, they do tend to look false. There's
sort of a contrived placid state. I don't think most women feel
that way. I certainly don't.

Do you know about photography?

Berenice winced; she retied a string on her apron.

I've been trying to learn. I do like the work of Atget and Stieglitz. I know it's very technical, of course, and I know you've been trying to experiment with light.

But you don't know about photography, he said. Knowing the name of a photographer is not knowledge.

I do know about moving, though.

Do you know when the body moves in front of a camera there can be no focus?

I shrugged. I think it's a perfectly good idea, I really do, I said.

Stand still, he said.

I really did try. I watched him hold the camera, take it from the black stand; I watched him move a lamp about, first below my knees, then on a hook. After some time, I noticed his lens was pointing not at me but at something beside me.

I'm interested in the shadows your body creates, he said. You make a beautiful shadow.

Berenice and I exchanged glances; I seemed to know she understood; she approved my desire for movement. Stealth-like, I raised my hand. When he didn't protest, I turned to the side. I glared at the camera. I moved again, crouching slightly, so I wouldn't look so stiff and docile; I would look like I was pouncing. I've never glared so willfully; I felt as if I were forcing him to capture my defiance. What control did I have, though? He could crop away my head as he'd done with Kiki. He could place the bright light on my body so the dress became translucent, until I was bones not silver. He continued to take photographs with his camera aimed to the side of my body.

Are my shadows more interesting? I asked with feigned curiosity.

Your shadow is your shadow, he said.

Berenice and I once more looked at each other.

Bernie, he said, leave us be.

She can stay, I said.

Not when she's flirting.

I hardly think she's flirting, I said. She seems very intelligent. I'm sure she is a wonderful photographer. You know how you can tell when someone is talented? There's compassion and an observant way—

Oh no, Berenice said, I am not a photographer. I don't even have a camera. I'm helping Man in the darkroom.

She's an angel in the darkroom, he said curtly.

I could tell I'd upset some unspoken boundary. I'd been so excited about the portrait, but now that it was happening, I felt disappointed, as though the longing for the experience had been stronger than the actual moment. It was a bit like my marriage. Before the marriage, there had been such suspense. Others called it cruel, but it worked on me as a kind of gravity. It was as if I ached for something that seemed so desirable and elusive, but once I achieved it, I lost interest. What if longing was the true, heightened state of being? I must not desire so much, I thought, then I won't be disappointed. And yet even now, while he clicked away, I wondered about the absent Berenice. As soon as she left the room, I decided I must befriend her.

Do you have a father? I would later say, and she would shake her head. He died by suicide.

Are you bored, Miss Guggenheim? Man said. I wished I hadn't told him about the Googs because he now pronounced my last name with a sarcastic emphasis on the first syllable.

I am a little bored, I said. But not by you. I am interested in your ideas.

Which idea? I have so many.

I like the idea of the accidental encounter you spoke about in *The Review*.

Nothing is more beautiful than the accidental encounter.

I agree completely, I said, and he seemed to warm up to me. He lowered the camera so it now appeared he was trying to capture my face.

I thought about how my life with Laurence, my life in Paris, had become really a series of accidental encounters. At cafés, at parties. I might leave the studio and meet someone wholly fascinating and genuinely kind. The city was full of New Yorkers who had fled the police inspecting flasks, the lack of rivers, the desperate men in front of Grand Central begging to shine, their fingers black with polish. I might bump into Berenice tomorrow, buy her a camera, allow her to leave the darkroom where she perfected a cruel man's photos. Even last night, at one of our parties, a woman named Thelma had bent to her knees. You are a vision, she'd said, you are part bird, part woman.

Man said, Peggy, let's try a few photographs on the bench. I can see how it looks when there's a different shadow.

I let him believe he was capturing something of significance. Even though I thought it was futile, his focus. Let him try, I thought, but I know he'll fail. Though I wasn't an artist, I knew I would be brighter than the dark shape, the dull shadow.

—

WHEN I RETURNED HOME from Man Ray's studio, I was relieved it was not Sunday. On Sundays, Laurence and I held parties. The custom began soon after we returned from our honeymoon. We told people we were "at home"—it was a kind of code. This way we did not have to bother with invitations or planning. We would merely run into a friend and say nonchalantly, *Oh, we will be at home this evening*. I'd buy crates of wine, violet candies, mismatched plates I found at Les Puces. Clotilde sometimes brought Louis, her latest boyfriend; his face full of pimples; he left grotesque clots on the bathroom towel. Strange things happened at these parties. Tristan stood on our kitchen table and announced he would present the first performance of *Symphonic Vaseline*. He chose ten people to sing *cri* and ten others to shout *cra,* and this was surprisingly beautiful, *cri* and *cra* alternating and ascending all evening.

Coming into the living room, I told Laurence I didn't care in the least about Man Ray. He was impossibly rude. He treated me as if I were a branch with a rather fleeting but interesting icicle.

What a loaf, Laurence said, what a prune.

You can't imagine how boring it is to pose, I told Laurence. When I was a little girl, I was always with Benita. I've never been in a portrait by myself before. How I wish my sister had been there. I might have behaved better.

Our apartment was on the Boulevard Saint-Germain with large windows and French doors facing the balconies. I liked to boast that it was very Proustian. Though I had never been to Proust's apartment, I'd read about the green lampshades and rustic furniture. We had a small courtyard with hawthorn blossoms winding up around the brick wall. On the top floor, there was a skylight, which seemed to be less window and more part of the sky. This will be for my daughter, I thought when I returned from the studio. I felt relieved, as though I could shed a reptilian skin. I took off the dress and lay under the skylight in only mended lingerie. Because I knew I would not see Benita, I donated most of the lingerie I'd bought for her to a celebrated author Helen was trying to help set up in Paris. At first Helen wouldn't tell me her name. She doesn't want it known that she's asking for charity. But she likes fine things; she is penniless but likes Darjeeling tea from Harrods and black lace stockings from Madame Blanc.

Don't you think she'll be insulted if I give her some garters and bras? She's an intellectual, isn't she?

Trust me, Helen said, she likes to type in negligees. I would too if I had her beautiful body.

Oh, I told Benita on the phone, I am so glad I don't have to host a party. I've spent the day with the most pretentious, arrogant man, and I'm exhausted.

Mother seems to love your parties, Benita said. She's always talking about them.

I know, isn't that strange? She's amused by the antics.

Benita had settled down with Edwin in an apartment my mother bought for them on Park Avenue. She seemed quite happy, though I noticed she was careful to answer my calls

only at certain hours. I suspected Edwin forbade her to speak
to me; the black sheep, the inciter. Nothing had yet caused
our bond to break; I was certain Benita would never be persuaded by Edwin, despite her mystifying adoration of such a
dull man.

It was Hazel who was the one who married with my
mother's permission. At the Ritz, to a banker, the son of a
Jewish millionaire. She was the one who achieved what Benita and I had not. But her obedience, or her acceptable
choices, did not seem to impress or satisfy my mother. Hazel
was only nineteen when she married; she waited until August, the summer of our Grand Tour, believing my mother
and I would both have returned.

You must attend your sister's wedding, my mother said.

She didn't attend mine, I said.

Because you married in the most willful, impossible way.
First Laurence changed his mind, then he ran away to Rouen,
then he was back. A big tizzy! I was not invited, then I was.
Then I wasn't. So how could Hazel have possibly known
when to arrive? There was no announcement. No headline.
No invitation.

Benita managed to be there, I said tartly.

Well, in the end, you had a wonderful wedding, my
mother said. The champagne, the dancing. Poor Boris Dembo
in tears.

All those men you tried to marry me off to were crying, I
said.

Haze's wedding was odd, Benita said. It felt as if we were
all wrapped in plastic. Poor Hazel, she looked lovely but lost.
She stumbled over her vows. And then at the dinner, Sig-

mund kept cornering Edwin and asking about sex. *How far do I go in? How fast do I go?* He wanted a diagram of all things. And Mother looked like she wanted to yawn throughout the ceremony.

After the wedding, she said, "Well, I'm glad to have Hazel in the care of the Kempner family. She is too much of a handful for me." *A handful.* What a thing to say about your own daughter, Benita winced. And then she went on and on about your wedding, how Laurence's mother invited the American colony and how Laurence invited all his bohemian friends by writing them *petit bleu* notes inviting them to a party, not mentioning that he was marrying. And how all the French Seligman cousins came, dressed to the nines. And how Laurence's mother was a lovely hostess, and how she was friends with King George whom she met in St. Moritz. I think Mother told that story a hundred times.

I don't think that's true, I said, but it certainly won her over.

When I thought of my wedding day, I always recalled how I'd worn a pale lilac suit, so convinced Laurence would not arrive. Helen had picked me up at the hotel, and we'd silently taken a tramcar to the *mairie* of the *seizième arrondissement* at Avenue Henri-Martin. I expected to enter an empty room, promptly turn around, and hail a taxi. But Helen had insisted Laurence would arrive, and as we walked toward the building, she pulled blossoms from the trees and arranged them in my hair. Arriving, there had been a circus-like atmosphere, with the prim matrons and the pickpockets and musicians and my cousin's children with their rolling hoops and sailor suits. My mother had conspired with Mrs. Vail to bring

in crates of champagne, and after the ceremony, we gathered
on the sidewalks and danced to a band Laurence had hastily
arranged. Even Clotilde had been gracious, twirling me
about, slurring the word slightly, her voice bubbly and can-
died. *My sister, my sister.*

What a charming family, my mother said. I don't know
why you didn't introduce me to them earlier. Laurence is so
charming, she said. It's so rare to meet someone who makes
you feel better about the world.

IF SHE ASSEMBLED A dossier on Laurence, she never mentioned it. Later, I would sometimes wonder if she'd learned
anything about his violence. Would she truly have forgiven
him everything merely by learning that he'd met with King
George in St. Moritz? It was easier to believe the detectives
had provided her with a few pages, a mention of opium, three
women at a bordello, a fistfight at Oxford, a stolen oar after a
rowing rivalry.

Come with me, Benita said, as the partygoers began to
dwindle. Three in the morning, we walked—I staggered—to
a single pine tree marked by a gingham ribbon. A black tarp
resembled a horse, the same silhouette. But when Laurence
lifted off the dark covering, he gasped. What a gift, he said,
his voice trembling. The motorcycle looked bright as fire,
glistening red. Something transformed in Laurence's face; he
seemed to be experiencing a new sensation—gratitude, hum-
bling. He hugged Benita, who winked at me, as if to say,
Now, you can really have the volition, the propulsion. Not
a mere idea of modernity, but an instrument with a motor

instead of a heart. You can be part of the moving world, the flying machines, the orchestras of Satie, Isadora Duncan and her dancers all leaping in tandem, without pause or grace. It was so unlike my sister to give a gift so fiery and decadent.

I won't tell you to be careful, she said, smiling, but do be careful, at least tonight.

Laurence straddled the seat; I thought he might leave without me.

Do go ahead, I said.

Peggy, you fool. Get on. You're my wife.

This is how our wedding day ended, then, because of my sister. Not in tears, not in a fight. She must have believed Laurence would show up for the ceremony, that I was somehow alluring and hopeful enough that he could not persist with his flight. This alone touched me more than any vow or gift. I sat behind him, wrapping my arms around his waist. All Helen's blossoms fell from my hair; I watched them turn to white blurs. The moon was pale and immense. We wove past cars, with the sound of applause still in our ears. Who was applauding? How many weddings were there on that summer night? We rode like we were leading the cavalry, racing ahead of some imagined bulwark. Somehow I knew where he would take me, and so I closed my eyes, felt as though I was in flight, until we reached the steady entrance of the Arc de Triomphe.

WHEN I'M LYING, LOOKING at clouds, I can count the months I've been away from America. I do this often, a kind of ritual akin to collecting matches.

Do you think the curse is over? I asked Benita.

What curse?

I've told you. I have this belief that we were cursed when we were born. The three sisters of the Silver Prince. First, the father will die, and then one by one, the sisters.

You are the most morbid woman alive, Benita said.

Well, I think it's over because here we are, all married, all fine. Freed from Mother, freed from the curse. And after what happened to John.

Oh, Peggy.

John was the son of Simon; he'd died at Exeter after a strange mass appeared by his left ear. None of us were certain how the red protrusion caused death. John was the boy all the Guggenheims had wanted. Blond, wide-shouldered, all-American, handsome. Simon had tried for ten years to have a child, and when John was born, he was brought up like a holy saint. We heard from Simon only when he called to announce news of John. *He has been accepted to Harvard. He will work in Chile to learn the mines.*

After he died, the golden son, Simon refused to have a funeral. I will not bury my son, he said, and my mother sobbed when she wrote one of her genuinely gracious condolence letters. We were not allowed to speak of John. An ear infection, a doctor told me, unprovoked. *Very sad that your cousin died of an ear infection. Such a promising boy.*

I wonder if the curse has moved to the sons, I said. Because I hear David has been suffering from melancholy, taking too much interest in guns.

Maybe you should consult your fortune teller about this, Benita said, since you are so gullible about sensory perceptions.

I just feel the curse has lifted, I said, even when I was being photographed by Man Ray, I could feel this charge move through my body, as though I might finally be confident.

It's a terrible thing to talk about our cousins as though they're doomed, Benita said. We have eccentrics in the family, like Washington, with his charcoaled teeth and mistresses, and Delia, with her dirty dresses and singing in public. All families have eccentrics, even the Astors. I don't think there's some legacy to dread; you just feel you should be punished because you feel guilty having a fortune.

Perhaps, I said. Just then my daughter kicked again, the kind of kick that was bracing and tender at once. I told my sister everything, but I could not tell her this. I would seem gloating, having what she most wanted. I would wait until I was certain. I looked up at the sky again, thinking soon the church bells would chime; I would wash off the kohl, the dark lipstick.

Peggy, Benita said, it's the strangest thing, but while I've been talking to you, I've felt this tiny kick in my stomach. She began to exhale, as though she had been holding her breath for years. Peggy, I think you are right about the curse being lifted. Because I've tried so hard. And you know I've lost two babies, but this—

I felt a kick again but stayed silent.

You must come visit me, she said, you must come back to New York now that I'm pregnant.

CHAPTER 10

The Interloper

1923

COME HERE, I CALLED MY MOTHER. SHE MUST HAVE heard something nervous in my voice; her heels clicked against the parquet floors. Her voice was full of concern. *Are you all right, Peggy?*

Laurence was in prison. The police said he was there for unprovoked assault and resisting an officer. Laurence would shrug and say, *I was only protecting my sister.* When he said that, I got stony, faraway. *Next time try not to throw a bottle at a decorated soldier.* When he drank, Laurence was gregarious, then vicious. The violence came into him like one of those Gothic ghosts. He still couldn't understand his arrest. Arrests. His cell was in a former cave in the fourteenth arrondissement; he'd named the spiders Quill and Quick. I brought him *The Double,* worn copies of Dostoyevsky.

My mother insisted she stay until he was released. *If you won't even let me hire a governess. You can't be alone with Sindy.*

Sindbad. Born in May. My daughter turned out to be a son.

In this way, my mother and I were once again living together in a sunlit apartment. But we rarely battled; instead, we found an easy camaraderie. I didn't believe she was there merely out of motherly concern. Benita and I believed she had a wealthy beau in Milan, a duke of some sort. On weekends, she would say, would you mind if I dashed off to the Villar Perosa to see some hummingbirds with Contessa Ranieri Campello della Spina?

You wouldn't even recognize her, I told Benita, she's not the least bit matronly. She's aging in reverse. There must be magical waters in Turin.

Gone were her bustles, her parasols, the black lace shawls, the girth, the grayness.

That morning I'd woken up before my mother, a rarity. Restless, lonely, I decided to take Sindy for a walk. My mother refused to call him Sindbad. *Sin* and *bad,* she said, what were you thinking?

He's the sailor in *The Thousand and One Nights,* I said, it's the most beautiful fable. *Who seeketh pearl in the deep must dive.*

Nevertheless, my mother called him Sindy, and I began to as well. Who names their son after a sailor? a philosopher might ask, and I would reply, a mother who lost her father to the seas. Unsurprisingly, Laurence and I had battled over the name, once he recovered from the disappointment of not having a daughter. For a few days, I'd wanted to name my son Gawd: a handsome Dadaist poet, Jacques-André Boiffard, had suggested it at one of our parties. If he's a boy, you should name him Gawd. *Can you imagine how amusing that would be? My son is Gawd. Good morning, Gawd.* Flirting with him, saying, what a perfect idea! Gawd Guggenheim, he said, oh, but you must. I didn't have the heart to tell him it would be Gawd

Vail. Gawd Vail sounded dreadful when I said it aloud. Laurence liked the name Cedric. Mary liked the name Cedric as well because she'd once been in love with a painter named Cedric Morris. What about Michael? I said. Why not give him a name that is nice and safe?

By this time, I was in a heavenly daze, sleepy from the chloroform I'd asked for at the end when I'd felt as if wild horses were dragging me apart. *I cannot endure it anymore,* I'd pleaded. The nurse Laurence had brought to the room was a dragon. *Just try a little more.* I'd never hated a woman more in my life. I might have killed her if she hadn't put the muslin cloth over my nose. *Michael,* Laurence said, baffled, is the most boring name imaginable. I like it, I said, isn't that enough? Oddly, we didn't consider Benjamin. Later, when Hazel would name her son Benjamin, I would think enviously, why didn't I think of naming our son after Father? So in the end, he was named Michael Cedric Sindbad Vail. He looks more like a Sindbad, said Laurence after a few days, looking at the baby, all red-faced and plump, protruding ears, dark black hair. When our son wailed, Laurence rocked him, singing, *Who seeketh pearl in the deep must dive.*

Now I tousled his dark hair, wrapping him in sheepskin. We slipped out together, onto the quiet street. I maneuvered the pram, a woven wicker bassinet on thin wheels, over cobblestones. Sindy started to cry when I waved to the baker, flour dust on his hands, drawing down the green awning. My son was surprisingly operatic. I loved how he insisted on roaring despite his delicate features. I no longer felt my heart turn with worry when he cried; I no longer felt as if a wire were set to tear my heart out of my body. I wanted to move quickly, so the motion would lull him back to sleep. It was always impossible. The wheels stuck in the crevices, then the entire carriage would tilt to the left; I'd kick the wheels and hear the metal springs squeak and clench. You don't notice the rutted sidewalks until you are a mother; you really don't.

The sun bore down as though it were already midday. I was still hungover from the party the evening before at our apartment. Because Laurence asked me, I kept holding the parties on Sunday evenings. It seemed to me there were more strangers than friends at the soirée last evening. Who was the man asking me if I happened to have some Turkish spiced lamb mince? Who was the woman wearing a necklace that looked like a leash? It took me forever to get the guests to leave. I'd swept up afterward, gathering the bottles, wishing I could go look out the skylight, show Sindy the moon. I was certain I had not heard strangers moving about beneath me. I was certain I had locked the door. Sindy was feverish. I held him to my breast, hoping for his forehead to cool. It surprised me how much I loved nursing. It was a kind of communion. I loved watching my son's face soften, how tilted his cheek, sated and blissful.

I careened along; I stayed off the boulevard. I wanted to avoid the cafés that faced the Seine, the terraces, the morning dew on the cane chairs. I didn't want to be seen looking so ridiculous and graceless, pushing the pram like it was a rhinoceros. Recently, I'd started to avoid cafés in the afternoons as well. *Where have you been?* Caresse wrote. *I haven't seen you in weeks.* I suppose I didn't want to be asked when Laurence would return. How is LV? Will we see him before May?

As well: I feared hearing my nickname. My nickname was

Miss Moneybags. I'd learned this only a week before while sitting with Helen and Giorgio. Miss Moneybags, I'd overheard. The words like a hiss, like a cruel ether. Now, not wanting to hear anything but my son's silence, I turned back toward the apartment. I clung to the handles of the carriage. How precarious it was, motherhood. This vaunted state.

Benita would never complain about the streets, the carriage. My sister was still childless; she'd lost, since I'd moved to Paris, five babies.

The doctor told her to stop trying, my mother said. Her body can't handle the strain.

How fortunate I was, but I envied my sister for not having to live with such precarity. It never went away, I suppose. My father taken by the sea; the suddenness of accidents. Here I was, worrying over a nickname, instead of lifting the wheels up and over the curb, carefully. My grasp could falter for only a second, and the pram could be crushed in traffic. I envied my sister for not knowing this terror, this end of walks—days, weeks, years, even—in which it was fine to be a bit careless. And then, not wanting to think of Miss Moneybags, or accidents, I vowed to find a governess, and until then, a smoother street. *Tomorrow,* I told myself, *I'll take Sindbad to the Parc Monceau and show him the obelisk.* I thought of a passage from Proust. It came into my mind like a hint to a puzzle, and I felt suddenly cheered by the thought of Swann *inhaling, through the noise of falling rain, the odor of persistent and invisible lilac trees.*

AFTER THE WALK, I went into my bedroom. I'd spent the night in Sindbad's room instead of my own because he'd been so feverish. All evening I woke fitfully, finding my son's forehead in the dark, through the bars, though he was no longer hot and there was a peacefulness in his breathing.

I placed my earring on a hook. I was about to select new earrings, a gift from my friend Mina, blue velvet triangles, when I noticed the unmade bed. For a moment I wasn't certain if I was in a dream or a haze. It startled me. The rumpled sheets, the pillow on the floor. This alone would have felt uncanny, but the smell was even more disarming. The smell was so pungent; familiar and foreign. I put my hand over my mouth. I was too used to the smell of my own milk. Spoiled by it. It changes you; I can't describe. The smell from your own body; then slightly sweeter, in the breath of a baby.

Come here, I yelled, and my mother came rushing. I'd never felt such longing for her presence, brisk and stolid. I tried to unlatch the windows; I pushed back the thin curtains. How could a smell seem like a threat?

When she came in, my mother grimaced. For God's sake, open the window.

I'm trying.

She didn't retch, but she made a retching noise. Push it harder, she said.

It's full of sap, I said. Then she stood beside me and put both her hands on the window, pushing with all her force. Then it opened, then there was a breeze.

My mother began to giggle. Giggle! It was the sweetest sound. Like a children's whistle, like canaries. I giggled as well. We stood there, giggling.

After some time, she picked up the pillow. Tell yourself it's the callery pear tree, she said.

We don't have a pear tree.

Tell yourself you do.

It's sperm, Mother. It's semen.

I know. But one can pretend.

How did it get in my bedroom? I said. It's truly a mystery. I slept upstairs. I wasn't in here once last night.

Well, it's obvious, she said. During the party, one or a few of your guests took the liberty of fornicating in your bed, she declared. How. Dreadful.

It is dreadful, I said.

She seemed surprised at my echo; it was so rare we agreed.

It really *is* dreadful, I said again. I open my house to these guests; I give them endless wine, and a place to dance and talk, and in return, they—I didn't want to say *fuck* in front of my mother—they fornicate in my bed.

And several times, she said, by the smell of it.

A thought seemed to occur to her. She whispered. She pointed at the armoire. *Look in there.*

You look in there, I said.

As though in a screwball film, my mother lifted a wrought-iron poker from beside the fireplace. She handed me the slimmer tongs. I expected her to start shimmying, the Grizzly Bear, the One-Step. She took an unafraid step forward, put her hand on the crystal knob while brandishing the poker in the air, so it was poised to hit whoever emerged. It seemed to me that she *wanted* to kill the interloper, the ejaculator. That possibly her whole life she had been waiting to kill him. I tried not to giggle. Her eyes were brighter than they'd ever been.

Doves rose in the sky, and the clouds darkened. What if

my mother's obsession with manners and society had been a ruse, a ploy? All this time she'd been dreaming of murder. I was suddenly sure of it, and I'd never loved her more. My husband was in prison; encouraging me to throw open the doors of our home to strangers, so he could retain his title. King of Bohemia. I nearly spat on the floor. He would offer the interloper a drink. He would say, *Come right inside*.

I stood behind my mother. I raised the dark tongs. HEIRESS KILLS INTRUDER. COPPER KING'S WIDOW VALIANTLY FENDS OFF PARISIAN CRIMINAL. She opened the door, a denouement. In the armoire, there were only bed linens, neatly folded, a mohair blanket with a note, *to be mended*. My mother clasped the lavender sachets we had sewn on our stay in Provence. We threw them on the bed as though they were amulets.

I can still smell it, I told her, it's stronger than lavender. Maybe one of the guests spent the night masturbating in here. Moving around, choosing different places.

Well, I suppose that happens when you encourage debauchery.

I am not encouraging debauchery, I said. How easily we ceased being allies.

What do you call it then, what goes on here?

A salon, a party. It's true that lately more strangers are showing up. But Laurence believes the door should be open to everyone. . . .

I'm going to get the Lysol, my mother said. She'd always believed in chloride. When we were girls, she would scrub our skin after we went to the circus. She insisted the maids bleach the towels, even when the soft cloth stiffened, chafed our skin.

She started dousing the walls.

Mother, I think it's on the floor.

You're right, she said. How on earth did it get on the floor? She knelt. Poured the entire bottle onto the rug.

I began to cry. I blamed the odor. It's too harsh. You've overdone it.

I'm sorry, she said. I have overdone it with the disinfectant. Let's go get some flowers. We'll fill this room with the scent of lilies. Please don't despair, Peggy.

I sat cross-legged. I put my head in my hands. She brought herself to my side. I'd never been so close to her.

I don't care about this, I said, waving, I don't care about the smell of Lysol.

Then why are you in tears?

I shouldn't care in the least that some stranger fucked in my bed. But *I do care*. It's proof, I suppose. I'm not a true bohemian.

Well, good, she said. You won't end up a wastrel. She said this so affectionately, it almost felt like praise. She wrapped me in her arms. I was twenty-three; I had never been held by my mother, even at my father's funeral. She stroked my hair.

I'm too prim to be bohemian, I said. That's just the truth.

If you are prim, I am to blame. She winked. It was a kind of collusion. Don't worry, she whispered, I won't tell anyone.

Let's put our weapons back, she said cheerfully, after a few minutes passed. Sindy had started to cry from another room. She lifted the tongs from my hand. She put the poker back by the fireplace, almost reluctantly. She took her hand off the dark iron; she dusted dark ashes from her hands.

CHAPTER II

The White Envelope

1923

THAT SAME MORNING I DECIDED TO STOP PRETENDING to be a bohemian. I considered the detritus in the kitchen: crates of empty wine bottles in the dark corner; a rag doll slashed and stuffed with Egyptian cigarettes. A Guerlain lipstick in the cutlery drawer, a corset in the bathroom. I gathered up the wineglasses from the evening's party and began to wash them, before throwing them in the trash as well. It suddenly seemed like madness to me. How much of my inheritance had I spent on these parties? Who among the strangers had ever thanked me? The Seligman silver had been pilfered. I had tried to be a woman who did not care about possessions. I *was* a woman who did not care about posses-sions. But I thought of Nana Rosa, with her large, dark eyes, undimmed, handing me the box engraved with her maiden name: Content. I hope you will be content, she said, smil-ing, showing me the silver she had carried with her from Baiersdorf at seventeen.

When I saw Modigliani's portraits at the Salon d'Automne, I was struck by a portrait of a woman who looked like my

13

grandmother at seventeen. Those gray-green eyes, slanting and serene. Fifty francs, the owner said when I inquired.

Instead, I'd bought cognac and champagne for party guests, likely the same ones who had slipped some of the silver into their trouser pockets. She doesn't need it, they'd likely said, she has her daddy's millions. Madness, I thought, to pretend I wasn't brokenhearted that this gift from my grandmother was gone. I smashed some glasses. I dropped them into the trash with a purposeful *clunk*. I listened to the sound of the glass shattering with all the discordant beauty of a Satie symphonic drama. I did this for quite some time. Thinking, *Now what will I do with my life when I'm no longer a bohemian? Who will I be if I'm not the woman throwing parties?* Then I shoved the morning edition of the paper into the bin so my mother wouldn't see the shards.

I can't be a hostess anymore, I thought. I truly can't.

I felt stifled in the kitchen. I found my wallet; I always locked it in the Venetian cabinet during the parties. I'm going to meet with Laurence's lawyer, I told my mother. I'll be back soon.

Put on a proper dress, she said, you look frightful. Socks and sandals!

I'm too tired, Mother. Sindbad kept me up all evening.

I've offered to hire a governess.

Yes, I will take you up on that offer, I said. That's very generous of you.

Don't forget I gave you the Daimler, which, I have noticed, you never drive. I don't know if Laurence should drive such a car. He drives like a lunatic.

I didn't tell her I put the car into a garage in a distant

neighborhood. I would have been mocked mercilessly if I'd driven it around Montparnasse. Besides, it frightened me when I read it was the auto favored by King George in Sweden and Grand Prix drivers. I preferred my yellow Citroën.

Laurence isn't here, my mother said. So I don't see why you need to stow my gift. You do know you're the only woman in Paris to have a Daimler? It's quite an honor. You and King George. You can't show up at De Monchet's office in your lumpy Citroën. Why don't I go with you? You have no idea how to talk to such men.

Unscrupulous showboats?

Eminent legal experts. You're lucky to have an introduction. He can get Laurence out of prison. Étienne promised. There's no better man. But you must bring the white envelope.

Yes, I have the white envelope, I said. I waved it at her. Every time I held it, I felt a fissure in my spine. It might have been a hawk's corpse; a severed toe.

—

I AM NO LONGER a bohemian, I said out loud, as I went out onto the sidewalk and set off down the Boulevard Saint-Michel. I was always making these idiotic and simplistic declarations.

I am a libertine. I passed the tables of the various cafés, set out toward the pavement. Someone called my name and I kept walking. *Peggy, Peggy, wait*. I passed the newsstand and paused to see if they had American papers. Lately I read everything I could about the attempts of airmen.

FLYER HEADS NORTHEAST, FOLLOWS ARC OF EARTH'S CURVA-
TURE. I had a craving for something sweet. I went to the patis-
serie and asked for three éclairs. *Merci, mademoiselle.* It occurred
to me that I should visit Man Ray's studio as he still had not
invited me to view my portrait. We'd had a falling-out; he
was angry because I'd bought his assistant a camera, and now
she was a photographer in her own right. Bernie: I could tell
she had an eye, right away. Perhaps he hadn't let himself notice. He hadn't forgiven me for showing him.

Already I was late for the meeting with De Monchet.
What an endless morning. Scrubbing semen off the rug with
my mother, nearly toppling my son out of his carriage onto a
sewer with loose grille. I wasn't in the mood to discuss bribing a police officer. I suspected that was what the meeting
would be about. Bribing a police officer, bribing the accuser,
bribing a judge. Now that I'd accepted I was not a bohemian,
I could be more certain that I was not willing to be a part of
some bribery scheme. We all do it, my mother once told me,
when we must. How do you think Daniel got that horrible
woman Ninette to stop selling her stories about your father
to the press? Was that so wrong? Your uncle protected his
brother's reputation, and you girls didn't have to grow up
reading about your father's dalliances.

I don't enjoy turning to you like this, Laurence had said, when
I first visited him in his cell. The prison was near the Palais de
Chaillot, a dreary stone building with a dank underwater
scent. Laurence said he'd befriended his jailor. It took some
time, he said, but he laughed when I said *his leather boots were
hardly dancing slippers.* Now he's stopped kicking me in the
mornings.

The cell is half-toilet. The thing flushes itself on its own every few minutes, covering the floor in an inch of water. Fortunately, beneath the window, there's a ledge I can climb onto and doze on. The guards spit in your face if you even ask for a glass of water. But I've made friends with this one, he's decent enough.

I'm sure you'll have all the guards coming over to play cards with you by the end of the month, I said.

This fellow, Ferdinand, offered to help me, Laurence said. He knows the game. He told me if I didn't injure anyone, they may let me off with only a fine and a few months. If I didn't resist arrest, I may get out of here in a week.

But unfortunately, you *did* injure someone, and you did resist arrest, Laurence. My voice sounded very flat and far-away.

Listen Peggy, I realize lately we have not been very kind to one another. But still, *in the end,* I know you are very dedicated to me. I am your child's father. You will not fail me, I hope.

No, Laurence, I will not fail you. I will be sure your friends have a place to revel—fill their empty cups with cognac and champagne.

Oh, come on! You know that is not what I am asking you for. I don't give a fig about those foufs. Have any of them come to visit me? Only Breton. We had a nice chat about how lacerating life can be. I'm to write an essay for him—about this dung pit.

I looked away, looked at the bland wall. It was a rather strange feeling, feeling like he was the needy one.

You know, darling, he said once more. *I do not enjoy turning to you like this.*

SEVERAL WEEKS BEFORE SINDY was born, Helen Kastor had used the same phrase, but more graciously. We went to tea after an afternoon at the Louvre. Like schoolgirls, we darted inside when the rain began. We walked through the galleries, arm in arm, gossiping. She wore a peach chenille suit with a silk blouse; her hair newly cropped. We waited for the sun to appear, betting on the hour. I won; the sun bore down at four o'clock, and Helen handed me a few francs. We were not nostalgic. We did not miss New York. We did not plan to attend the reunion at Jacobi. I must appeal to you, Helen said, taking my hand.

I winced, an instinctive impulse. Was Helen leaving Leon? Was she penniless? Did she need my help setting up a pied-à-terre?

It was not that I wouldn't help her. She was my oldest friend. Without her, I would not have had the courage to come to Paris. I only winced because of the phrasing. I felt like I'd been hearing it my whole life. A red-haired boy in breeches in the Waldorf-Astoria, claiming he'd witnessed my father's last words. Miss, Miss, I must appeal to you.

But of course, Helen was too sensible to implode her own life. She seemed to live as she dressed: neatly, with an admirable restraint, full of careful and exacting choices. From her handbag, she took out a thin pamphlet, with a black ink drawing. Nothing particularly erotic about the drawing, but

I looked at it closely. It looked like a Beardsley, stark and clever. A woman wrapping her legs around a snake. *The Book of Repulsive Women*. Helen said the book was morbid and sexual. You'll love it, Peggy. I want it back, she said. If you lose it, I'll kill you. There are only eighteen copies of this in Paris.

Do you want me to help you publish it?

No, she said. I want you to help me bring the author to Paris.

Who is the author?

I can't say. I can't tell you.

Why not?

I just can't. She has an assignment for *McCall's*. To come to Paris and write about women who marry aristocrats. And she's mortified. She's a serious journalist. She writes about the suffragettes, for God's sake. She writes about boxers. But she's far too talented to be a journalist. James thinks *she's* the one who will change literature. So I don't want her to have to beg and scrape to get to Paris and then spend her time here writing about fluffy fortune hunters. When she could be writing gorgeous smut like this. She pointed at the pamphlet. Maybe we should publish it! I always thought you would be a wonderful editor.

I put my hand on my immense stomach. Pregnant again. I looked like one of Brancusi's eggs. A stick figure with an orb.

I'm not sure I can get involved with this when I'm feeling like an elephant.

Why don't we just get her a nice hotel room? So she can stay in Paris. I really do think she should be writing novels. God knows we have enough journalism. What if a woman wrote *Ulysses*? What if we had a lesbian version of *Don Qui-xote*?

Your appeal is wholly appealing, I said, laughing. How much should I contribute?

Is five hundred francs too much?

I shook my head; I wrote her a check, while she politely looked away at the barges on the Seine. She folded it neatly and squeezed my hand. Oh, I suggest you don't mention this to Laurence, she said.

I won't mention it to Laurence, I said, though I wasn't sure he would mind. He was always telling me I had neither brains nor talent, so I should give my money to those who did.

—

NOW WITH THE NEWSPAPER in my hand, I moved along the boulevard, thinking how lovely it would be when I could bring Sindy to the Seine. I thought of picnics, the way he'd sit in a sailor suit, waving at the boats. What a darling he was, even if I had so wanted a daughter.

A church bell rang. I checked to see if I still had the white envelope.

In ten minutes, I was to walk into the offices of a lawyer called De Monchet.

—

VIOLENCE, LAURENCE SAID, IS *a significant gesture.* A significant gesture—his Surrealist friends believed in staging sig-

nificant gestures. They believed these gestures should replace
Art.

Breton wrote: *The simplest Surrealist act consists of dashing
down into the street, pistol in hand, and firing blindly, as fast as you
can pull the trigger, into the crowd.*

A few lines from a poem in *The Book of Repulsive Women*
simply read:

> *We'd see your body in the grass*
> *With cool pale eyes.*
> *We'd strain to touch those lang'rous*
> *Length of thighs,*
> *And hear your short sharp modern*
> *Babylonic cries.*

———

I WAS NOT ENTIRELY sure that violence was always a significant gesture.

Once, on our way to a party, Laurence flung me into the
street when I refused to take a taxicab. We shouldn't waste
our money, I said, we're five blocks away.

Says the woman in a fur coat the cost of a small island in
the West Indies. Yes, let's save a few francs and show up soaked
and looking like a pair of drowned raccoons.

My mother bought me this coat.

I know what you've been doing with your money, he said
in the most malevolent way. I know, he hissed. I warned you
not to give an allowance to Djuna. All you've done is give her
the means to become a full-fledged, full-time alcoholic.

You're funding her ruin. The Guggenheim Award for the most loaded lesbian in Paris.

You told me to give my money to those who were talented. And I listened to you.

I also told you not to mix yourself up with Djuna. But she seduced you. I heard the whole tale. Modeling lingerie for you, your Sappho awakening. He smiled at last. You might have invited me.

Laurence, I said. Let's just walk under the awnings.

As we did, a large—very large, the size of an urn—gust of filthy rainwater fell from the corner of the awning and landed in Laurence's open mouth. A preening lady at the table under the awning burst into laughter. A mouthful of rainwater, she said. You should have ordered the wine.

Then he pushed me into the street. Lights fled by, and I leaped out of the way. Laurence, I screamed. Are you trying to kill me?

I am, he said. He stalked off, leaving me in the street, my heels surrounded by sad, dark pools, the smell of urine and cinnamon. How had he taken my purse? The push—his palms on my back—had been so sudden and disorienting. I was the bottle he hurled; I was the slim, rich bottle he wanted to see crash and splinter.

Laurence, I called after him, bring me back my purse. How humiliating. Miss Moneybags without her Moneybag.

Laurence, Laurence, don't leave me here. A taxi went by, and I dashed out of the street; my dress covered in gray streaks. I walked into a brasserie, where we'd dined, and saw Caresse. I've just been robbed, I said. My purse snatched right away from me.

Oh, you poor dear. She handed me her wallet. *Take what you need*.

I could feel the force of his palms on my skin into the night, all evening. Certainly, I would have bruises on the blades of my shoulders. I lay in the bed trying to—trying to what? To will myself back into my own body, not the one he turned into a bottle. I undressed and looked into the mirror, seeing the pleasing symmetry of my small breasts, the softness. I turned, peered over my shoulder, but I couldn't see a bruise, not a slight, ruddy mark, yet the flesh felt dented and sore. I sat down on the bed and wept for some time. He stole my purse, I thought, the source of his hatred for me. Who had told him I was writing checks for Djuna? What if he'd discovered my correspondence with the banker? You can live on the interest alone, for it's been a very good year for the aeronautical industry. Be advised we have reversed all your losses by our strategic investments. As instructed, we have set up a trust fund for your daughter, and as instructed, we have not named her father as the executor despite the fact that this is a deviation from the standard practice for marital assets.

He pushed me into the street; he said yes, when I asked him if he was trying to kill me.

I swore to myself that if he touched me again, with that savagery, I would divorce him and declare him an unfit father. I found some cognac and read *The Idiot* until he came home as the morning sun rose. I feigned sleep, and when he woke in the morning, he handed me my purse, neglecting to look me in the eyes or even mumble something something sorry.

You hurt me, I said. I don't think you know your own strength.

You were being silly, he said, making me walk in the rain and laughing with those bitches when the waterfall landed on my lips.

I certainly did not laugh at you.

You certainly did, he said. You are so cheap, Peggy. It's infuriating. But I am sorry. Just listen to me next time and don't cause a scene.

I think I'll go to the Luxembourg today, I said, standing up. This was how I would handle his petulance. I would dress and eat and walk as though I were deaf.

I wanted to see Manet's *Olympia,* to let her bold gaze meet mine. To steal a bit of her resolve. At the museum, I parked myself at her feet. When a man paused beside her—squinting, appraising—I said, She's posed like Titian's *Venus of Urbino,* only she's a whore.

He turned around, astonished. But I wasn't finished.

She's looking straight at you, I continued. Which means you're the john.

He actually glanced over his shoulder, as if I could be talking to someone else. I don't think—

Do you know she was a painter, too?

Who?

The naked woman. The one he painted.

He shook his head.

None of her work is here, I said, laughing lightly. Surprisingly enough.

After he left, I felt cheered—either by the painting itself

or by his discomfort, it was hard to say. I took out a grocery list, the only piece of paper left in my bag. Erased the word *eggs*. The word *beef*. The word *flour*. Wrote a question, *What became of the woman holding the flowers?*

Once my legs began to cramp, I took myself to the gardens. I admired the toile dress of a little girl who walked by. It featured the scene of a shepherd: deep greens, flecked lambs.

What a lovely dress, I said.

Her dad whispered, say thank you to the lady, but the girl turned from me and began to chase after the pigeons. The gray birds soared up into a flock, and she yelled, come back, come back, oh you gray *birdees*.

FOR MY MEETING WITH De Monchet, I was to dress in an imposing manner. I'd done so, wearing a stiff-collared dress and high boots, when I met with my mother's friend last week. Étienne.

I have brokered this meeting with the help of my Italian friend, she said. I do miss Laurence so. The poor boy. Rotting in the Catacombs.

He's not in the Catacombs, I said. He's in a nice prison.

A nice prison, she said. You really are something.

Well, it's only for drunks and *poules*. If he's found guilty at trial, then he might be sent somewhere more medieval.

This is why you must meet with Étienne. He knows how the magistrate dismisses cases. He knows this whole system.

Off I went, obediently. *The devoted wife, dressed imposingly.*

Étienne was ruddy-faced, flippant. Peggy *Goog*-en-heim! It had been so long since I'd heard someone put such emphasis on the first syllable. I knew the type. Behind my back, he would call me an Israelite. He wore a Liberty silk tie and Plom shoes; he sat on the edge of his desk. He talked in a quiet voice; he closed the velvet drapes. Some kind of silver instrument flickered from between his fingers. Was he cleaning his nails? I wondered. Was he flicking out the dirt while he talked to me?

I sat primly. (This was before I had accepted my primness.) I could see him assessing the value of my handbag and dress. I could see him noting the gold letter on the strap of my boots, which were from a man my mother met named Salvatore Ferragamo. The instrument glistened. He placed it in a drawer and said, I will explain the plan to you.

The scheme?

The course of action.

I will not tamper, I said. I am not interested in tampering.

I appreciate your integrity, he said. I will note that De Monchet is from one of the oldest families in Paris. If you would like, he will help you with your husband's release. He understands these bar fights happen every evening. Absurd they've charged your husband. It's really very simple. A beautiful young woman such as yourself shall visit De Monchet. You have a young son named Michael, your mother said. Not yet six months?

I nodded.

Terribly sad for the boy, I imagine. Monsieur de Monchet will make some inquiries as to how this matter has progressed. He'll speak to the magistrate on your behalf.

I was told we could not have a lawyer at trial.

That is true. He will not be your lawyer at trial. In some

sense, he will not be your lawyer at all. You might even not speak of him as an acquaintance. He will be a legal adviser before trial. He'll talk to the magistrate, as I said, only if by chance they meet at their club, and he will casually mention the case of Monsieur Vail—a descendant of the Vail family. His great-grandfather was friends with Lafayette. Franco-American relations are on the line. Lafayette was, I believe, very fond of the Vails.

Who told you this? I asked, laughing.

We have looked into the family history on your behalf. Your husband went to Oxford, did he not? He could have pissed around London, but he returned to Paris and joined the French army. His sister, Clotilde, is engaged to an officer in the army. You can discuss this with De Monchet. He'll straighten it out; I can assure you there will be no trial. As he is not acting as your lawyer, you will not be required to pay him a fee. His desk is rather messy, but when he goes out for a cigarette, you may find an open spot on which you can leave the white envelope. I have not mentioned the white envelope. I must leave you now, he said curtly.

What in God's name is the white envelope? I asked my mother. A bribe?

There is no white envelope, she said, handing me a white envelope.

I don't know if I want to do this, Mother. You know how clumsy I can be. What if he doesn't go out for a cigarette? What do I do then? Do I hand it to him?

You absolutely, absolutely do not hand the envelope to him, she said, unless you want to join your husband in prison.

Laurence threw six bottles at those men, I said. There was

one man, with a scar by his lip, who was nearly blinded. He had to have a shard of glass removed from his eye. I don't see how we can get around that.

Don't be naïve, she said. You have to know who to trust. That's the secret of life. And the man you need to trust now is De Monchet.

AT ONE O'CLOCK, WHEN I should have been in a lawyer's office, I walked away from the busier cafés and strolled toward the Stryx, which was most often empty.

Before I even reached the terrace, I saw her sitting by herself, reading a newspaper. Her hair was a dark red, pulled back tightly. Her lips were painted into a Cupid's bow, an even darker red, especially in contrast to her pale skin. I felt terribly frightened just looking at her. She seemed not to be a mortal. *The most brilliant woman alive,* Helen had said. She tilted her chin in a haughty way, but there was something lonely and forlorn about her as well.

She must have spotted me, for she stood up and called out. Her voice with a rasp, without the desperate French accent. Peggy, she called.

I walked toward her; I hoped I was not trembling.

Will you join me? she said. She called for the waiter. I've been here a month, she said, and I've figured out how to avoid the pretentious crowds. I see you have too.

I do like this café, I said.

I wondered how she recognized me. Had she been at one of my parties? I never drank, so I couldn't imagine that I'd been dazed when she'd been in my home.

Oh, I recognized you from Man Ray's studio, she said. I saw your portrait on the wall. I asked who the beautiful woman was. All in silver, the slink. Fantastic, she said. And I heard from Bernie that you bought her a camera. I think she's in love with you.

I laughed at her frankness. When people were polite, I felt faraway, but when they were direct, even blunt, I was perversely comfortable.

Was the portrait boring? I haven't seen it. He's furious with me for buying Berenice a camera. And asking her to take my portrait.

Oh, it's sensational, she said. I'll steal it for you the next time I'm there.

She took my hand. I've been wanting to thank you. Helen said you wanted to be a private donor, but she slipped up. Said your name. Peggy this, Peggy that. I've been meaning to write you a letter. It was incredibly kind of you. I wouldn't be in Paris if you had not helped me. I had one hundred francs to my name. Pitiable. I'm a pitiable wench, she said, laughing.

You don't need to thank me. I'm a tremendous admirer of yours. I read the article after Helen mentioned you would be arriving in Paris.

The article, she said, with a slight bite. I've written four hundred articles.

Oh, I'm sorry. I know you have. I mean the one about force-feeding the suffragettes. How terrifying. To go on a hunger strike.

It was dreadful. They really did stick a red rubber tube down my throat. Spray my nose with cocaine and disinfectant. *You either swallow or choke.* One should have the right to die for their beliefs, I would say. But what good did I do? They're still torturing those women in Britain. And people said it was just a stunt. For attention. As though I'm a circus act. I investigated; I intruded. Enough of that, she said. America doesn't want the truth.

Not at all, I said. I don't have the faintest desire to return. You should not return. How is your hotel?

It's fine, she said. I don't want to complain.

Are you not comfortable?

Not particularly.

I'm sorry. Helen is usually so careful.

It's rather cold and small, but as I said, I don't want to complain. It's very hard to write when you are in a depressing atmosphere, I'm sure you understand.

I do, I said. Well, I can look around if you like.

Where did you stay?

What do you mean?

When you came to visit Paris.

I blushed. Oh, that was long ago. I stayed at the Crillon. It's very stuffy and old-fashioned.

I'm sure I'd be quite happy there, she said. But you and Helen have already done so much. I'm quite parched. Should we order a Pernod?

I suppose, I said. She spoke so quickly, with such certainty. It was dizzying. I wondered how much of her briskness was a facade. Helen said: *Oh, her father was a monster, and a lot of terrible things went on in that family.*

Are you thinking about my father? she said.

I laughed. I felt unclothed, suddenly. But it was exhilarating; a kind of seduction. I ordered Pernod. I must be careful,

I thought, or I will have handed her the white envelope by the end of the evening.

His name was Wald Barnes, she said, and his mother was named Zadel. Polygamists from Albany. My brothers were named Saxon and Shangar. He changed my name several times. First, it was Djalma, then it was Djuna. The only gift he gave me was a French horn. I ran away when I was seventeen. That's all you need to know, and you shouldn't feel sorry for me.

I hardly feel sorry for you, I said. You do know that everyone worships you in Paris. They have sold out of your book of poems.

Peggy, I only published eighteen copies.

But still, it's whispered about everywhere.

Oh, that's sweet of you to say. Is it true you are married to Laurence Vail?

Yes, I said.

And you're realizing it's the greatest mistake of your life? She smiled.

There was a hum about her, a *frisson*. When I drank the Pernod, I noticed she was staring at my lips. It was the strangest thing. I realized I'd never had someone stare so brazenly at my lips, certainly not a woman. *You're naïve,* my mother had said. I lit a cigarette, and she took it from my lips. She inhaled and said, Open.

Pardon me, I said. I don't understand.

Her knees were touching mine. The branches were empty from yesterday's rain. The bark black and bare; the sidewalk strewn with white petals.

Open your lips, she said. I did so, and she put the cigarette in my mouth.

I do love Laurence, I said. But he can be volatile.

He is wonderful in bed, she said, knowingly.

I thought you—

You thought I was a lesbian, she said. I am not. I am only in love with Thelma.

The sculptor?

Yes, she's the other reason I want to stay in Paris.

I was dizzy now, from the drink, from the sensation of being twirled about.

You are unfairly maligned, Peggy, she said. You're more intelligent than they realize. They underestimate you.

I believe they do, I said, smiling.

They most certainly do, she said, and she took the cigarette from my lips. When she leaned toward me, I thought she might kiss me, and I felt a sudden longing to twist myself up in her body. We must have stayed there for hours. The moon was low, shaped like a shell. We decided to try to see how the pattern turned once the moon hung low enough to transform; to be a reflection in the river. But once we stood, she declared she was very tired. Would you like to meet in the morning? she said. She wrote her address on the white envelope. We can look for lamps, she said. I want an antique lamp I can place by my typewriter.

We can look for black velvet capes, I said, tilting so that she steadied me.

I've always wanted a velvet cape, she said. How did you know that, Peggy?

I can see you with the cape tied around your neck.

Let's forget the lamp then.

We can get a lamp, I insisted. I had to bite my lip so I wouldn't say, We can get whatever you want, lamps and lights and capes of the darkest velvet.

CHAPTER 12

An Imperious Urge

1923

Once Laurence was let out of jail, I decided we should drive to the sea. It was an impulsive decision. I promise this was not one of my schemes. I never imagined we would end the day buying a villa by the sea and leaving Paris. But it happened as if in a dream, this stumbling upon Paradise.

We drove away in the Daimler, leaving Sindy with Adele, a new governess. Her parents were professors and assured me the daughter was studious and at ease with babies. I had no idea how one selected a governess, only that I did not want to put them through a series of tests as my mother had done with the long line of girls she hired to show us the kindness she could not.

We sat in the garden. I brought her clementines and mint tea. Adele was eighteen and very poised, with curly, dark hair framing her wide face. I liked that she did not cover her freckles with powder; she was very freckled—I'd later see the little spots on her shoulders as well, the spattering—slapdash— gave her a slightly feline quality. One of her eyes was brown;

the other green. When we sat in the garden, I realized how peaceful our apartment felt since I'd stopped holding parties. I'd dusted and swept the entire place to prepare for Laurence's return. Waving out a bright Provençal tablecloth while standing in the garden, setting it across the table, smoothing out the creases that remained even after ironing. Oranges in a wooden bowl, a few candles. I bathed Sindbad—his hair was now an odd blond—and dressed him in a sailor suit Benita sent with a note: For your king of the sea. I thought how wonderful it would be when he could speak instead of offering a series of gurgling noises.

Papa, I said, Papa is returning home.

Try to teach him the word, I said to Adele.

What word? she asked.

Papa, I said.

She looked at me with something I suppose was sympathy. She helped me hang my jubilant banner. WELCOME HOME, I'd painted, before having Sindy walk over the paper with his paint-dipped feet. His little toes left crests and half-moons, dappled, a burst of blue dots.

———

I PROMISED MYSELF I would keep the conversation with Laurence light and pleasant. We must not bicker again, I thought, for bickering couples were boring. Every time Helen and Leon bickered, I felt they diminished themselves; they seemed tawdry and weak. I suppose if I'd grown up with a mother and father, I would have been more accepting of marital spats. But whether they were mine or another couple's, the battering of words bothered me, like a mosquito banging against a windowsill. How pathetic: nagging, berating, whining. A pathetic form of discourse. I preferred silence or accidental poetry. Alliteration, a pun.

Since I'd been spending time with Djuna, I'd noticed how she often spoke in a precise and unusual manner; her Elizabethan sentences, her careful rhythm. *The running waters wept for thy return,* she said once, when I opened the door to her apartment. *And all their fish with languor did lament.* I knew the poem, of course, but wasn't sure I could deliver the line with her intensity. She raised an eyebrow, looked at me. I kissed her on the cheek. My life's sole bliss, I said sweetly, my heart's eternal treasure.

My life's sole bliss, she whispered, twirling in her black velvet cape, *my heart's eternal treasure.*

I wondered what Laurence would do if I suddenly began to speak to him with lines from Spenser. I'm not certain why, but since he'd been released, I'd felt like we were at grave risk, that there was a chance our life would fall apart spectacularly if I did not salvage it somehow. But how? The drive seemed the first step in staving off some rupture. And he did seem to like the Daimler. He placed his hands on the steering wheel with a firmness I remembered from when he touched my body.

My mother won't shut up about how King Edward has this auto, I said.

It feels remarkable, Laurence said. I suspect they've stolen the design of the Mercedes engine. Do you know they call this engine the Silver Ghost? Remarkably quiet. I can't even feel the pavement. How fast can it go? Should we try?

Of course, I said.

He spoke about six cylinders and the sleeve valve principle. I suppose this was a kind of poetry. A sly smile on his face as he passed the other drivers, one by one. I gazed at the cedar trees on the side of the lane; the signs with their arrows. Calais, Lille. Soon the air would become fragrant with lavender and the roads would grow narrow. Soon we would drive up the circling roads cut into cliffs. We would wash off the dust of Paris in the sea.

But now we were still passing through a row of gray houses, parched grass, the sky black with exhaust.

Do you like the girl Adele? I said, chewing on my nail. I'm trying not to be nervous leaving Sindy with a stranger.

She seems fine, Laurence said flatly.

Apparently, she's learned a great deal just from reading *Villette.*

So you hired her because she's read Brontë?

Yes, she can be our own Lucy Snowe. Minus the Christian prayers.

He tousled my hair, and the car swerved. Feeling his hand on me, I thought, *Oh perhaps he isn't furious at me.*

We drove silently for some time, until he turned and asked me where we were going. Rather accusatory, as if I was having him motor about with no specific destination. Where are we going, Peggy?

To the sea.

I don't want to swim. I'd rather climb.

You can climb, Laurence, I said gently. You can do whatever you like. I just thought the sea would be warm and clean—

I can't just wash off prison. You have no idea. I was beaten; I was starved. A little dip in the Mediterranean isn't going to cleanse me.

It might.

It won't.

I really think it might, I said, trying to cheer him with my conviction. Think of how blue and warm the sea will be, how you'll rock back and forth with sun on your skin. I think you *will* wash prison away.

What about you? he said snidely. Anything you want to wash off?

I wasn't certain what he meant, only that his tone was suddenly piercing.

I know what you've been up to, he said, gripping the steering wheel tensely, as though it were taking all his will not to smash into the Citroën ahead of us. It gave me a chill. I would rather he raised his voice. The whisper felt too controlled, too considered. *I know what you've been up to.* Eerie to hear him speak so softly, but coldly, as if he could no longer muster an audible sound, let alone tenderness.

I think we should take the turn to Calais, I said.

Instead, he drove into a field. The smooth car rattled for the first time; a lurch. He braked so abruptly that my head nearly knocked into the windshield. Dust rose from the dirt. I blinked the grit out of my eyes and retied the scarf around my chin. How hopeful I'd felt tying the silk scarf around my face in the morning. *You look so chic and adventurous,* Adele said. *Like Marlene Dietrich.*

Get out of the car, Laurence growled, so I can look you in the eye.

What have you been up to? he asked, while we leaned against the green enamel of the car. He turned my body with his hands, so I was forced to face him like two chess pieces, while the lumbering, dented cars—the ones we'd earlier felt quietly superior to—kept driving by.

Visiting shops. Visiting people. Nursing Sindy.

I've heard you were carousing around every evening. Having a grand old time. While I was in an infernal hellhole—black spiders were my only companions.

Oh, I did get drunk, I said. You're always drunk. Your friends are always drunk. I thought I might as well get drunk too. So I got drunk, and you know what? I loved it.

That's not what I'm talking about. It's something else. There, I can see it in your eyes and face. Oh, I can tell what it is.

Laurence seemed to become more wild and upset as he spoke, while I felt suddenly calm and cold, like a stone in clear water.

You've been with someone, Laurence said.

That's a lie.

It is true. I can see how you've changed. Even now, this isn't you, Peggy. With this haughty little smirk. He imitated me then, *I did get drunk, and I loved it.*

I closed my eyes and thought of another line from the Spenser poem. *That us late dead / Hast made alive again.*

Eventually I'll find out, he said. Don't worry, I won't kill you.

I don't know why I smiled; I wasn't the least bit happy, but I smiled.

You're enjoying having your little secret, aren't you? he

said. Just like you enjoy having your little checkbooks and your little banker boys. You like secrets. That's why you fell in love with me. Because I had to be a secret.

There is no one, Laurence. I have a terrible headache. I want to go somewhere and have my hair washed.

Your hair washed! he screamed. She wants to wash her hair! he yelled at a driver in a Citroën, an oblivious man with a tweed cap, a ginger mustache, likely wondering why are those two lovers screaming at each other when they are beautifully dressed and have such a beautiful car? Why is that man's face red with rage? Who has she murdered? *Oh what has she done.*

I will keep you here until you tell me, he said. Or I will leave you here in this field and go back to Montparnasse and ask around until I hear who you've taken up with.

Listen, Laurence. I confess I *did* have a wonderful time with some friends while you were gone. I've never felt more like myself. They're all lesbians so you don't have to worry about me being with a man. We had conversations about Dada and how silly it was and how we must try to break off and invent something new. I can't talk like this with you and your friends, so I felt rather understood and liberated. And drunk.

Oh, he said. He looked chagrined but wary. He looked into my eyes as though they were trustworthy, as though I hadn't been a wicked liar when I was a little girl.

Let's go for a swim, I said.

Yes, he said, putting his arm around me. Let's go find the sea.

—

WE FOUND EDEN. I promise we did, though it might not seem possible in the midst of this dull marital spat. Always, it seemed that beautiful places were arriving to save me from whatever life I'd made for myself.

We found it because I felt a momentum in my bones; I felt a direction, a certainty. I might have navigated the car had he let me drive. But as it was, I was the one. I was the one who had never carried a compass but had sudden moments of knowing exactly where I must go. My suspicious husband, my brute lover. I brought him there.

After a night in a small hotel in Marseilles, Laurence seemed to have slept off his hostility.

My first proper sleep in six months, he said cheerfully. I took it as a good sign that he did not mention the broken toilets or two black spiders in his prison cell. The sky was bright; shimmering with heat. We bought straw hats and espadrilles from a hardware store, drank some bitter and burnt coffee. As the roads began to curve, to wind, I felt the dizziness of a sudden ascent. Below us, the sea was breathtakingly beautiful. Red roofs against the blue sea, I said, recalling a letter Cézanne wrote while painting *The Sea at L'Estaque*.

Stop here, I said, when we passed a wooden sign planted high on a pine tree.

MADAME OCTOBON's, the sign said, with a whimsical drawing of a fish and pears.

Have you heard of this restaurant? Laurence asked. Why not wait until we reach Cannes?

Truthfully, I did not want to drive farther, to the noisier part of the Côte d'Azur. I was eager to swim, my skin rippled with sweat and the sensation of burning. A woman came to greet us as we parked under the palm trees.

How strange it was, I thought, to still be in France but feel the landscape transform so drastically. The red tiled roofs, the palm trees, the turquoise shutters.

The woman looked as you would expect Madame Octobon to look. Burly and Romanian, with a thick neck and headscarf. She wore a white caftan with embroidered flowers and loose buttons. What a beautiful couple you are, she said. Have you come from Paris?

I nodded. Laurence began to speak to her, tenderly, graciously. It was interesting to watch him win her over with only a few sentences. What was his magic? I wondered, seeing this slightly rough woman look at him hopefully, hoping he would smile at her joke. He wins over women, I thought, that's what he does. She barely looked at me. When she brought us water and bread, she nearly bowed.

It bothers me, her obsequiousness, I said.

It's because of the Daimler, he said. She probably thinks we're royalty.

You're flirting with her, I said, even though I know you don't mean to.

I can't help it if I'm charismatic, he said. I can throw a bottle at her if you'd like.

Let's see how long you can go without throwing bottles.

A noble challenge, he said, laughing. I can't help it, you know. I loved hurling the bottle at those pompous men. If you must know.

Why is that? I asked.

It satisfied my natural urge to dominate.

Hmm, I said. I suppose I have that urge as well.

But you can satisfy it, because you have buckets of money.

Djuna satisfies it with art.

Oh, Djuna again, he said. She really has you wrapped around her clitoris.

Could you satisfy your imperious urge here? I said, pointing at the garden, the white cliffs, the green sea.

Yes, he said. I will try to climb that. He pointed to a high rock, set off above the cliff. A towering but broad expanse. Closer to the sun, he said, sighing. This sun!

This sky, I said.

The sun, the sky, the green sea. And look at this tree, he said. We were sitting at a long table facing the sea. When he leaned back, he lifted his arms and brought down a branch, plucking a lemon. I did the same, only to pluck a yellow puff. Put the mimosa behind your ear, he said, so your skin smells like honey. Around the villa, a wild garden was so jagged and vivid, flourishing without a clear pattern. We wandered over and tried to identify the jumble of plants.

Artichokes, Laurence said. He snapped some branches. He handed me some herbs. Thyme, he said. Rosemary. But these blue plums, he said. Quetsche. My grandmother used to make little tarts with these. Perhaps my girlfriend can make us one. He split the plum, handed it to me.

I put the wet oval in my mouth; how lovely, I said, wishing for more of the violet fruit.

We are acting like such city fools, I said, giggling. Look, a chestnut! Look, the tiny plums!

But why shouldn't we be awed? Much better than the piss and cigarettes of Paris.

I could lie down here and die, I said. I mean it is too heavenly.

Let's lie down and make love in that lavender, he said, pointing to a faint purple field in the distance. We held hands and began to walk through the garden: I felt a longing for him like when I would wait in the burgundy bed at the Plaza Athénée. He whispered, I can't wait to fuck you again; I would rather be inside you than float on the sea. I stood on my toes; the ground rose unevenly; I needed to lift myself to meet his lips. I kissed him without tenderness: I kissed him as though I were a creature wanting to tear him to pieces. Lust was a form of forgiveness. Fucking might be a reparation, a salvation.

When we lay in the lavender field, in the dirt furrows between the stalks, he thrust into me so deeply, I thought I might shatter. I love you I love you I love you, he said, with a hint of surprise. The petals stuck to our damp skin; we lay there, flecked, fragrant. Sparrows flew above. I watched him pull a plum from his pocket, bite into the blue flesh. The sun beat down on us; he put his head against my shoulder, and for some time, he slept.

FOR LUNCH, MADAME OCTOBON brought us braised rabbit on white beans, still simmering in a terra-cotta pan, a platter of orange carrots, a salad with greens, and bowls of red muscat grapes.

Soon after, Laurence borrowed a rope from her and changed from his espadrilles into a pair of walking boots. He's a mountaineer, I told Madame Octobon, when she looked up at him, admiringly, as he tied the rope around his waist, after he used my treasured knife from the Kastor factory to whittle a branch into a walking stick. He's learned wonderful advice from his father. Never look up at the sky. Never look down at the ground below. Only look at the step ahead of you.

Please don't fall, she said flirtatiously. I have baked you a magnificent dessert.

I don't think he's ever fallen, I said. He climbed the Matterhorn when he was eight.

I have never fallen, he said, kissing me. I expect you ladies to wave to me when I've reached the summit. I'll bring you back a piece of cloud. He set off.

Thank God, I thought. I closed my eyes and let the sun beat down on me. It was the strangest thing because every time I closed my eyes, I had visions of Djuna, like little fragments of a film. The cigarette in my lips, her lace corset. The way she'd looked at me when she told me I was unfairly maligned.

It wasn't erotic, my fantasy, but it was arousing: I fantasized about her striding through the cafés of Montparnasse, dressed in the velvet cape I'd bought for her. Like a toreador, the flounce of the fabric between her shoulder bones. I will slap you if you call her Miss Moneybags, she said to one of the poets, perhaps Louis, with his pimples and slicked-back hair. She is undeserving of such an insult. What she has done with her wealth is likely to change the world once I write the novel of the century with the comfort and security she has provided. And you, you worm, you sit here drinking wine and mocking her while you bleed all over her towels and leave repulsive pus behind as your sole contribution to modern art. Pus and pimples, Louis, that is all you are to me and Peggy.

I must have been smiling. Madame Octobon roused me from my daydream.

What is it like having such a handsome husband? Is it difficult for you? Every woman must want to sleep with him.

Fortunately, all my friends already have.

And you don't mind?

It was before we were married. He has very good taste in women. He likes intelligent American women. They all adopted me when I came to Paris. One of them, Caresse, has a canoe and goes riding down the Seine. I would never have met a woman like that if Laurence hadn't been a cad.

I see, she said, but she looked disappointed that I wasn't the least bit bothered by her worship of him. Did she want me to break down in tears?

I'm quite attractive myself, I said. You may not think so, but I was recently photographed by Man Ray. For *Vogue,* I think. Or *Tatler.*

I see, she said. That must have made you very happy.

Not particularly, he kept photographing my shadow. He's quite an ass. But I liked his assistant, Berenice, and I bought her a camera. I think I'll invite her here next time.

I hope you won't bring up the Paris crowd. They tend to ruin a town.

Yes, I said, laughing. What do you call this town, by the way? Could you show me on a map?

We're not a town, just a village. She wiped some sweat from her eyes, which were surrounded by deeply etched lines. I do everything. Run the post office, deliver the newspapers. The nearest train stop was forty minutes away, in Toulon. Yes, she said, I do everything.

I told her she was marvelous. I decided to befriend her even though she was one of those women who hates women. I flattered her for some time. I wondered what she would think if I told her Laurence had been in prison, after being dragged around Paris streets by furious police officers. Don't kill my brother, Clotilde had cried out. Peggy, don't let the police kill my brother. I thought she'd be mortified because she seemed like the type of woman who loved police officers and priests above all.

Are you friends with the priest? I asked, because I recalled a tiny white church we'd passed, with a high white cross and a small cemetery with scattered, tilted gray graves.

Oh yes, I bring him breakfast four days a week. Père Jacques.

Then as though my mention of a religious man invoked some grace, we both lowered our heads, nearly in prayer. I felt the wind through the trees, and the loveliest breeze. There must be a geographical element to the air in this region, but I was not a scientist and knew nothing about the reasons for the purity. But such purity. Had I been doused in the water, baptized, it might have felt this revelatory. I tried to hold the breeze inside my body, as though such a form of beauty could be contained. The scents—the scents around me: mimosa, jasmine, musty cork. In Paris, I was so often reeling from the rancid smells, the sewer water in grates, wine on Laurence's breath, urine and horse manure in the concrete. The smell of rot when I sat by the stone walls of the cell on the night Laurence had been brought in by the savage police. The scent was forever linked to Clotilde bawling, "Please don't murder my brother." Clotilde pleading, "Peggy, contact your family, call your senator uncle, send a telegram to the ambassador, but, please, my brother must get out of here."

Pleading and rot, and Laurence bloodied, half-conscious, sloped against the wall. (And I did call Simon; I did call the ambassador; three in the morning, and I listened to the official silence while watching blood from a bullying officer's boot slide down Laurence's beautiful forehead.) Suddenly, it came back to me. The strangest thing. I must have blocked it from my mind. When I signed him out of prison, I'd been told firmly by the prosecutor: he will be on probation for six months. If he harms anyone, if he gets in another brawl, he'll be sent back to prison. If he stays out of trouble for six months, we will consider him released. Six months.

The thought came back to me like a spark.

Had I signed a paper attesting to this deal? I must have. He must have. But I had been overwhelmed by seeing him walk out of the barred room, gaunt and ghostlike. A faded photograph, a tarnished medal.

Surely, I was in a daze when I wrote a check and promised silence. We won't mention the beating, I agreed, we won't speak of Officer LeGrande, who kicked Laurence in the jaw.

Above, I scanned the faraway cliffs as though I might make out my husband's form.

Instead, I saw an arc of scarlet.

Are there any homes for rent in this village?

Far up that hill, she said, nodding toward the scarlet color
I'd spotted, there's an inn called La Croix Fleurie. Quite a
place. Cocteau used to stay there. It's in complete disarray, I
believe. The owner closed it several years ago, and it's just
been abandoned. But he might rent it.

Could we go see it?

I have the key, she said. As a matter of fact. I keep an eye
on it for him. But Monsieur Vail couldn't live there—it's very
run-down. Certainly, *you* would find it primitive.

Let's go see, I said. I flattered her again. How wonderful
you have the key, Madame Octobon. You really *do* do everything!

We found Eden this way, scrambling through weeds, tear-
ing leaves from our damp skin, breaking branches, struggling
to find the former path. My skin was lashed; I tripped on a
loose rock. Push through, Peggy, she said. Her body was a
bulwark, so wide and firm; I think she secretly enjoyed seeing
me swatted and barred.

Oh rose thorns, she called out giddily. Watch your silk
dress, Peggy! You should never wear silk to the South. Dress
like the peasants. Next time wear linen.

She was right. My dress was destroyed by the time we
reached the door. At one point, I'd fallen forward into a palm
tree; the fronds slashing my face, the bark ripping the silk.

How often do you visit here? I said, laughing.

I suppose I've lapsed in my duty, she said. Don't tell Monsieur Beaufort. Look at you, she said, laughing. Ravaged by
the wild path.

Oh, but once we were through the wildness, I gasped, the
villa seemed like something from a dream. How often have I

said that? If I've said it before—about a bridge in Venice or New Jersey, I was silly. *This* was the dream I'd had since my father's last letter: *I have found a house for you and your sisters and Mummy in Saint-Cloud.*

With a strong certainty, I knew I must live in this house, even as I stood outside the entrance, in the blazing sun, with this odd, mercurial woman.

The interior was even more run-down, with grime on the windows and walls, but I liked the winding staircase leading to a second floor in which every room opened up to the terrace. The view was extraordinary, only the sea, the sea extending to a distant high rock shaped like a bison.

We must be forty feet up here, Madame Octobon said, I'm not sure it's a safe place for children. You said your boy is almost one? Soon he'll be crawling about, and you'll have to put up bars or—

She made a motion with her hands. I'd think of it later, of course. The motion: hands rolling around hands, the miming of tumbling.

We don't fall, I said. You heard Laurence. Besides, there's the sloping land, and we could build up a garden, an orchard.

Yes, she said, I think it's one of the highest homes in the area. It's quite rare to be this high. Come see this.

She took my hand, brought me to a small room, with ivory walls and a remnant of toile wallpaper. Above an indentation, likely a bed, a looping drawing of two men in an embrace, grapes and leaves sprawling across their feet.

I love his drawings, I said. I bought *Dessins* when I worked at a bookstore in the Village, all those drawings of *le mauvais lieu*. I thought it would be simple to copy them, but of course, it's impossible to create that feeling of sex like he does. My imitations were very flat. I did learn to sketch a nice penis.

She laughed and looked at the drawing closely.

The owner would want someone here who appreciates Cocteau. The last person wanted to paint over it, and so he refused to sell.

I won't paint over it; I promise. Maybe I'll invite him here to do more. Not that I know him, but Laurence does.

Yes, she said. I imagine Laurence knows Jean. Let me see what I can do. But there's no electricity, and there's no hot water, and the owner won't spend a cent. You'll have to take it as is.

I nodded. I went out to the terrace and envisioned gardens, a path between the pines. I envisioned palm trees by a table, a grove, white roses, a red tiled floor, a corner bench, more white roses, terra-cotta planters full of jasmine and lavender.

Oh, she said, I forgot to mention— She hesitated. I thought she might mention something gruesome. Cocteau's lover's overdose from opium; a cellar full of rats. Ravenous hawks, a child's corpse.

There's a beautiful beach, she said, it's private, impossible to reach. Enclosed by the cove, very tranquil. I don't know if you like beaches, she said, but this one is more beautiful than you can believe. White sand, the water perfectly turquoise.

I do like beaches, I said. I told her we could walk down to see it when Laurence came back, but once she spoke of a secret, warm enclave, I was wholly convinced: Cocteau's painting on the wall, white sand, fifty acres of forest, rooms where my children's lullabies could be the sea.

I would like to meet the owner now, I said, if that's possible.

Don't you want to show your husband?

Yes, I suppose I shall. He will love it. How could one not love this spot? It's Paradise.

But won't you be bored? You will have none of the excitement of Paris.

Paris is full of tourists now, I said. Tour buses pull up to Le Dôme and boys from Boston stick their faces out the windows hoping for a glimpse of Hemingway. I hardly recognize anyone I know these days. *And Laurence drinks too much and strangers fuck in my bed and I might be deeply in love with the most incredible woman. If we go back to Paris, my husband will end up in prison again and might never meet his daughter. And I want my daughter to be raised by the sea, because if I had been raised that way, my life might have gone so differently. And I've failed at being bohemian, so what can I do with myself, if I can't be a genuine member of the world of artists?*

To my surprise, she seemed to have taken a liking to me, and when we were back at the restaurant, I could hear her on the telephone, trying to persuade the owner. A beautiful couple, she said, art lovers. A darling child. No, she won't. I'll ask her. Yes, calm down.

She slammed down the phone.

What an odd man, she said. He'll let you buy but on one condition.

Yes?

You may not turn it into an inn.

Why would I run an inn?

I tried to tell him. You have to sign a contract. You have to remove the sign. Those are his conditions. The price is not bad, she said. She wrote it on a napkin. I thought it was strange that the price was so extraordinarily low; I saved the same amount nearly every month. I wouldn't even need to call the bothersome men in New York who wanted nothing more than to chastise me for being indulgent. I took out a checkbook. I felt deliriously happy.

It must be nice to buy whatever your heart desires, she said. Not with rancor or envy. With astonishment. Djuna had said something similar. You must understand how un-usual your life is, she said. Most of us spend so much of our time denying ourselves: denying ourselves drink, denying ourselves stockings and shoes; denying ourselves a second course, denying ourselves a seat at the cinema. You've never known what that does to your soul. Denial of desire. It cor-rodes your heart, she said mournfully. That denial is cor-rosive.

I hope we will be safe here, I said to Madame Octobon. I wasn't intending to correct her, to show her that I wasn't merely buying the house on a whim. I'm buying this house as a fortress, I said. I am no different than Joffre or Pétain.

You're planning to stave off a mutiny?

No, of course not, I said, staring into her eyes, staring her down.

I don't think she knew I possessed such will. She fiddled with a loose thread on the tablecloth. She blotted tea from a saucer.

Look at me, I said. And she did. She raised her head; she stopped fiddling about. She did listen to me when I told her that I knew I must move above the sea or my family would face a reckoning, or a rift. Listen to me, I said, when I tell you I am trying to stave off a tragedy.

When Laurence returned, he was sunburnt; his hair flat with sweat and dirt, but somehow he was radiant. I watched Madame Octobon bite on her bottom lip, as if not to gasp. When he turned toward the window, I saw a black line of dirt down his back.

Did you fall? I asked.

Just a little backward fall, he said, nothing I couldn't stop. You look majestic.

The conquering hero, Madame Octobon said. She winked at me.

He began to sing; he offered to cook for us. A tart with herbs.

I wish he could always be like this, I thought. What if it's as simple and primordial as movement in nature? In Paris, he became a caged animal. He had no choice but to be furious, coiled up, cruel. Now he was utterly calm and joyous.

It was wonderful up there, he said. There's a medieval castle, one of those perfect ruins. And cork. I brought you a little bit.

He handed me a dark piece, dagger-shaped. It sprang under my fingers, like some living animal.

Could you still see the sea?

I could, he said. The air was clean as clouds.

The sun was not yet setting; it was the part of afternoon when the day seems to peak before its end; the sky turns pink and fragrant.

Peggy, Madame Octobon said, aren't you going to tell him?

Tell me what? he said, again with such a calm tone. It was hard to believe a day before he'd screamed at me in a field, half-mad with the idea that I'd committed infidelity.

Let's go for a little drive, I said.

She slipped the keys into my pocket; she winked at me conspiratorially.

You lovebirds go venture into Paradise, she said, and I'll cook some concoction with lamb and mushrooms.

On the way to the car, he picked some wildflowers and put them behind my ear.

My heart is still pumping blood, he said, I haven't felt this alive in— I think I was dead in that prison; a bloody ghost. Put your hand on my heart, he said. And I did, though I did not need to. I could tell his heart was revived, but pressed against my palm, I could feel the burst and pulse; I could feel how newly it was beating.

This time the path to the entrance was less arduous. Because Madame Octobon was heavy-bodied and stalwart, she'd been able to create a true path. I took his hand and led him up the stairs. The only sound was distant, the waves against the rocks, the lulling sound.

This villa is for sale, I said. I thought it might be nice to live here. What do you think?

Live here? he said. He contemplated. The silence, the two terraces.

We can build you a studio there, I said, pointing to a higher field. You can finish your novel.

He nodded. The breeze lifted and brought with it the scent of oranges and pines. To my surprise, he pulled me to

his side, ran his hand over my hair, and then placed his palms
on my stomach.

Will you go swimming naked? he asked.

Every morning, I promise.

And sunbathe in the nude?

Every morning.

Then let's live here, he said nonchalantly, as though decid-
ing to order a boiled egg with toast. I'm getting tired of the
whole damn circus in Paris. But you have to promise.

I'll be golden as a goddess, I said. I'll swim once in the
morning, and twice in the afternoon.

We'll swim in the evening, he said. We'll swim under the
moon. Always.

He lifted me so that my knees were against the terrace
wall. I promise you, he said. Every evening we'll swim together under the moon's light.

CHAPTER 13

The Dangerous Month

1927

IN BENITA'S APARTMENT, MAIDS IN WHITE DRESSES MOVED about silently. Every mirror gleamed. Benita sat on the sofa with her remarkable posture, resplendent in pink.

Don't get up, I told her when I entered, for it felt as if any movement might doom her, even an embrace.

You're sweating, she said. I'll have Delia bring you some cold tea.

It's horribly hot outside, I said. I forgot what it was like—New York humidity.

You don't have this heat in France?

We live by the sea. There's always a breeze.

We called our home Pramousquier, after the closest train station. Mother nicknamed it Promiscuous.

I know I tore you away from Paradise and brought you to this infernal city.

Anything for you, I said. The silent maid brought me a crystal glass, with ice cubes and sprigs of mint. Benita looked no different than when she was a girl. Her features were softer, her hair pulled back off her face into a high crown of curls. But there was a slight sadness to her; her skin was too pale, and her smile wasn't as carefree. The dress disguised her body; there were pleats and layers; I was disappointed, as I wanted to see the largeness in her body, a pregnancy.

She handed me *Tatler*. Isn't that you? Peggy Guggenheim. Man Ray. Wild parties.

Oh my, I said. I didn't notice at first. Then I did. He'd done some kind of erasure. To hide my pregnancy. Would you look at that, I said. The pattern of my dress went from a pattern to a white blur. He took away my pregnancy. There was my son.

I wouldn't have noticed, but now you point it out. Well, that's a horrible thing to do. You do look beautiful, though. So glamorous. What happened at these wild parties?

How could I tell Benita? Oh, there was dancing and singing, and Laurence's friends, I always felt out of place. I prefer conversation, and you can't really talk when there's dancing.

I do miss dancing.

You will dance again, I'm certain. After a pause, I added, Did you know Aunt Gloria waited ten years to have her two sons?

I know you think that's inspiring, but I can't wait a decade for a baby.

I just wanted to tell you that so you wouldn't feel alone or odd. It's one of those secrets kept from us. I only found out when John died.

How is your tea? she said.

Lovely.

How was the walk here? Is it as you remembered?

I found it odd. Everyone was looking at the clouds, and I

thought, is this the new fashion? To walk about with your chin—here I imitated the people I passed, peering at the sky, their heads tilting. Then I realized it's because of Lindbergh's flight. Is he supposed to arrive today?

Oh yes, she said. We should go outside—I think it will be fine.

I don't want you to move if the doctor told you not to move, though you know I think he's silly. And don't tell me what an eminent gynecologist he is. I can't see the harm in walking.

She looked chastised. I thought of her spending her days here, in this quiet silken prison. I thought of how I ran to the beach, with my two children frolicking in the sand, lifted by the waves. And here was my sister, in this sweltering city, in a Park Avenue apartment that felt like an imitation of a doll-house, holding her hand on her stomach, the only motion allowed, the heartbeat. How could I have been so lucky? What would I have done if I'd been warned that I was in a dangerous month? If I'd lost five babies. I would have given up. I would have thought, it wasn't meant to be.

It was worse than she knew as well. The eminent gyne-cologist had told my mother the previous miscarriages had damaged her cervix, and if she did give birth, she would need a team of doctors to keep her from bleeding.

Let's go look out the window, I said. She rose delicately. The maid looked fretful, but Benita fairly floated across the room, graceful and swanlike under the chandelier. Beside the windows, there were two oil paintings of the Lake District, in speckled gold frames. For a moment, I was distracted—were they prints or postcards? How lifeless and bland. I peered closer to see if there were brushstrokes. By then, Benita was stepping as though over a rock path in the lake. I took her hand, and we stood side by side, looking out through the glass. I wedged open the window and looked up.

Do you see him? Benita said. But the air was so still and damp. We placed our faces against the glass. How long we waited for just a glimpse of Lindbergh.

Long enough that Edwin returned and said, Benita, whatever are you doing? You should not be standing.

Good afternoon, Edwin, I said, turning.

Yes, Peggy. I see you have arrived to break some rules, par for the course.

We're merely looking for Lindbergh's plane, said Benita, so politely. My sister could calm a wolf. I thought of how her voice betrayed no acrimony or annoyance, no sarcasm or sourness. What if I tried to talk this way to Laurence; would our conversations not devolve into abrasive spats? I will try to speak to him as Benita speaks to Edwin, I vowed.

Oh, in that case, Edwin said, suddenly cheerful. Lindbergh's plane! Does it land today?

He came to stand beside Benita, nestling his face into her hair. He adored her; he cherished her; he forgave her for her forbidden movement. Like that, instantly.

We haven't glimpsed it, but there—look—

When we saw it, it was such a glimpse of steel and magic. We squealed. Above the Central Park reservoir. We'd later read of his triumph in the paper: DARING AMERICAN YOUTH DE-SCENDS AT LE BOURGET FIELD AFTER 33½ HOURS.

Oh, Father would love this.

You see, I think this is a message from him, that we must believe in the new—the soaring.

Here's to soaring, Edwin said, patting me on the back, with his first show of affection.

The streets began to fill with people. We could see them below, in summer dresses and children in sailor suits. A chant began, Lindbergh! Lindbergh!

Here's to progress and to this damn brave American, Edwin said. The nerves of steel on that man.

Nothing compared to Benita's! I said.

Sitting around waiting for a baby, she said, hardly a triumphant world-changing event. Do you think we'll be able to fly to visit you in France?

We should name our son Charles, Edwin said. He will have my aviator genes. What do you say?

You know it makes me nervous to discuss names, Benita said lovingly.

Women screamed on the street. Men threw their hats into the air. Edwin brought over champagne, and Benita and I turned from the window frame, only for a second, to take the glasses of crystal. Take a photograph, I wish I'd said, take a photograph of the two of us. Had I only. If only I had the photograph of that day, the last time I— The last time.

Or did I ask? And did Edwin say, oh I can't photograph you now—now that you've been photographed by Man Ray. Yes, that was why I didn't protest or plead. Just the way he said it, as though he thought it mattered to me, as though I was a snob and a celebrity.

Man Ray's photographs make me look so sad, I said. So

skinny and melancholy. Why don't you capture me now, when I'm at my best, with my sister, the only one who can make me smile?

Yes, take it, Benita insisted. But after what happened, I could never find the courage to ask Edwin. It would take me many years, but by then he'd stopped corresponding with my family. Oh, but I would give it all back, the Man Ray portraits, to have the photograph with Benita on the day we saw Lindbergh's plane and all of Manhattan came alive to sing in the street for the man who did not go down or disappear.

Edwin insists I loll about all day long, Benita said. She said his name fondly. There was no hint of irritation or disillusionment. She spoke cheerfully about his job working with Waddill Catchings (Waddill Catchings? I asked, and she nodded, without even the hint of a giggle), the VP of something or other at Goldman Sachs.

What do you do with Waddill Catchings? I said when he returned to the apartment, rushing to Benita's side as if I might have marred her beauty with my breath.

I work in futures, he said brusquely.

I've always wondered what that means, I replied. Futures. It's very complicated.

Well, what did you do today, just as an example?

I read a report on the production of cocoa in Zaire.

Oh, I said. And you try to foresee if that's promising?

Peggy, Benita said.

I'm truly interested.

Yes, he said. I look into if it's viable. What does your husband do with his days?

I suppose it's some of the same, though he's looking at his own sentences.

I said this earnestly but truthfully. I felt terrible right after I spoke, seeing Benita's downcast expression. What could I say to be kind to Edwin? I knew if he bet on cocoa in Zaire, there would be twelve-year-old boys getting switches on their backs if they didn't peel the leaves back quickly enough.

LAURENCE SKIPPED DINNER, of course. When he returned from the White Horse Tavern, he tiptoed skillfully into my bedroom. Even when he was drunk, he was agile.

All the American poets have been missing me terribly, he said. I learned about the electric chair at Sing Sing. I think I'll add it to the novel.

Which character ends up there? I asked. The husband or the wife?

You'll have to see. How was dinner with Mr. and Mrs. Boring Bores?

He is boring, I said, I will give you that, but he is taking care of Benita.

By knocking her up every week?

It's what she wants.

At a certain point, you have to accept the limits of your body.

Says the boy who climbed Matterhorn when he was eight.

I didn't faint from the blood. Even the doctors warn her.

How did you know that?

The Florette Society Column.

Well, I'm here now. Maybe she can absorb my strength.

And how would she do that?

I don't know—osmosis, spirits. We have this bond.

At Sing Sing, do you know what happens when the body doesn't take the electric charge?

Oh Lord, Laurence. Promise me you won't talk about this at dinner with Benita tomorrow?

He reached over and put his arms around me. I thought he might say something kind about my sister. A Protestant's stoic advice. I thought he might run his hands over my body. But he began to shake my arms and legs, while making a hissing noise. Five thousand volts, he said, that's what it takes— imagine that, coursing through your body.

I BROUGHT SOME OF Mina Loy's table lamps to a store on Fifth Avenue. The latest in Paris, I said. The last time we were in New York, her jaded blossoms had gone over famously, all the rage: those carefully layered and painted petals. She thought of them as a kind of Cubist still life. All the women wanted them for their living rooms.

Now I was selling her lamps: shades crafted from spun glass and a thin sheet of cellulose, wine bottles for bases. When I told Mina that Bergdorf and Macy's were mad for them, she said she only wanted them sold to boutiques and galleries. But the women were persistent. They said, We'll take them all, and didn't even ask the price. They wanted more. I could have sold hundreds.

Benita was still in the same place on the sofa when I returned. It was like seeing a painting, only her dress was differ-

ent, but her expression was placid. Once again I was brought
cold tea.

What shall we do to keep this visit interesting? she asked
me. I know Laurence thinks I'm a bore, and you can hardly
find sitting beside me entertaining. Should I invite some of
your friends over?

I just want to stay with you. I'm not the least bit bored.

Can you stay until I have the baby?

Of course.

Suddenly, she looked so vulnerable. How were your births?
She whispered the word, as though it were a fierce and shame-
ful act.

Who could look at Benita and feel she was a bore? I suddenly hated Laurence. Her face was suffused with feeling and
desire. Willing to have her body torn apart and her intimate
parts probed and inspected by men who told her their theo-
ries of membranes and cells.

When I gave birth to Sindbad, I took the Twilight Sleep.
So I don't remember a thing. It was rather lovely, waking up
as though in a cloud, and there was this tiny, tiny creature.
But with my daughter Pegeen, I decided to follow Lulu.

Who's Lulu?

Our sheepdog.

Oh no.

I educated myself; I studied Lulu. It was a kind of education we aren't allowed to have. I tried to find paintings or
books on the subject, but I couldn't. And one day Lulu just set
herself down on the kitchen floor, grunted a few times, and
squealed. And I thought, I'll do the same thing.

Oh no, Peggy. On your kitchen floor?

Well, no, we were in Switzerland, so the child couldn't be drafted into the French army, but if I could have given birth on my kitchen floor— Anyway when the time came, I decided to start squealing and grunting. Laurence was mortified, but what could he do?

I didn't tell her that the pain had gotten too intense for me. In the end, I'd begged for their drugs. I didn't tell her that the night before, Laurence and I had gotten into an awful fight; he'd thrown a plate of beans in my lap. Broken a chair in our kitchen.

Instead I told her, That's my advice. Think of yourself as a sheepdog. Instead of all these doctors telling you that you are delicate and precious and endangered.

But I am delicate.

Show me your stomach.

Oh no, Peggy. I couldn't. Do you even look at it? It's rather frightening.

She lifted up her dress, and her face flushed. It was rather startling. The nudity. I couldn't tell her I'd had Berenice take my photograph when I was seven months pregnant, completely nude. We were more unalike than we'd ever been. She seemed frightened by the strangeness of her own body, where I loved looking like an urn, a volcano.

So grunt a few times, and then howl and lunge.

I'll prefer the chloroform, she said, laughing.

As if on cue, the doorbell rang. The doctor came in. After he inspected her, he took me aside.

Benita should not try to have this baby, he said. I've told her I think we should— I've advised her against trying, and I've told her husband, but he wouldn't heed my warning.

You told him?

Yes, in no uncertain terms.

When Benita came back, I did not repeat his stern and frightening words. Benita, your body can't bear the strain. You might die. You mustn't listen to Edwin. But she was radiant and hopeful. Come here, she said, and when I sat behind her, she let out a low, gentle bark.

No, I said, like this, and I let out a howl.

I wished I'd known earlier. Once again, a secret kept from me. But even if I'd known earlier, who could discourage someone from the thing they wanted most in the world?

LAURENCE ARRIVED DURING DINNER, rather drunk. We must go, he said, I have Florette's Rolls-Royce. Hart's invited us to the country. Not every day am I summoned by such a man. He's out of his mind, but he wants us there this evening. I brought your bags.

I have no desire to go to the country. Not now. It's late and—

He'll drink himself into a state if we don't arrive soon. We don't have time to bicker.

Before I could answer and say, You go without me, I need to be with my sister, the strangest thing happened. Like the black birds I'd once dreamed of. From the ceiling, there was a vibration, and then clatter. Crystal beads on the chandelier began to click and tremble.

The neighbors are having a séance, Edwin said. They pretend to summon spirits, but they've rigged up the table legs.

Edwin left the apartment, left me with Laurence, as

though the spirits in the parlor above us were worth attention, when I was the one in danger.

Benita was far away. In the distant bedroom of her endless
apartment, long as a city block, she was under a canopy.

We're going to the country. I have your bags. We must go.

No, I said.

Edwin said, Excuse me, but why don't you discuss this in
the parlor?

In the par-lour, Laurence said.

Benita had lain down to rest, missing supper.

Do not fight with me, I said. I'm not leaving.

And why is that? Because you truly love this world—he
pointed at the scalloped lamp and silver sunburst mirror—
rather than a cabin with jazz and Cuban rum?

No, because I promised my sister I would stay with her
until she has the baby.

It's quite fine, Edwin said, I think you are actually disrup-
tive and upset Benita.

What?

You're encouraging her to act savage, knowing full well
she can't howl in the hospital.

We were kidding, my sister does have a sense of humor.

Laurence had found my coat and draped it around my
shoulders. I took the coat off and sat back down into my dining chair.

I will not leave my sister, I declared. I promised her I
would be beside her when she has the baby.

Howling like wolves, I suppose, said Edwin dryly. I wished
he would defend me. When Laurence was drunk, I usually
ignored him and kept at a distance until he was sober. He

had a tendency to throw bottles, though I had kept this from
my sister. Other things I never told her: Sometimes when he
flew into a rage, he smeared strawberry jam in my hair. Or
he would step on my belly, as if he hated the parts of me that
were most a woman. He once made me stand beside an open
window, in wet clothes, in the middle of winter. There was
an element of humiliation that always caught me off guard; a
meanness that was not otherwise in his character. Leaving me
with bruised shoulders because I wouldn't take a taxi.

All this to say: when he took my hand—took, clutched,
seized—I didn't flinch. Here I go, I thought, I am about to be
hurled.

Edwin simply walked out of the room, without a word, as
if the vision of a marital spat were too distasteful. The cocoa
in Zaire was of more importance; I was certain he would
study the sales all evening.

I grabbed the table, as though the mahogany would hold
me here, in the posh and tidy home of my sister. He nearly
ripped out my arm, separating me. His breath was flowery, all
Pernod and vanilla rosettes. He pulled me past the sofa, past
the armoire, past the painting I had bought Benita in Posi-
tano, a blue Delft-like portrait of a little girl with a high lace
collar and a spark of mischief in her eyes, like moonlight
glinting off seawater.

I moved across the floor like a lowering sail. Occasionally, I
would reach out to try and get hold of anything with an edge.
He was remarkably strong; he took his long steps while pulling
me behind him with a hostile urgency. When we neared the
doorway, a maid darted away; I thought she might shield herself with the velvet curtain. I did not want to upset Benita,

who was resting in one of the pale and quiet rooms. Only as he let go of me to put on his boots did I call out. Benita, I must go visit a friend of Laurence's, but I'll be back tomorrow.

She must have heard the urgency in my voice; we were sisters; we knew the way we disguised fear. And if I was afraid, who was I afraid for? The one who'd been warned, the one in the dangerous month.

Trying to comfort me, she sang out from a faraway room. Don't worry about me, she called. I did not think this sentence would be the last I'd hear. I would return; I would be back tomorrow. I slapped Laurence when he put his hands around my waist and began to sever me from my delicate sister. Don't worry, she said with her beautiful voice. With a child still in her, with a heartbeat monitored via stethoscope. *I've never been so calm and happy.*

HOW DISTRESSING IT STILL is to realize I could be dragged away from Benita for no reason other than Laurence's latest infatuation. I've thought of this abduction often, this turning point.

Nothing would ever be the same after the evening when he pulled me past my sister's voice from the bedroom. Why didn't I threaten him, wrangle my way out of his arms? Roll down the window, refuse to pay for gasoline?

To say, oh, he was stronger than me, oh, he was my husband—now sounds pathetic, but I was naïve and frightened, for I wondered if I was pregnant again: I worried he would throw me to the ground and stomp on my stomach relentlessly.

But you had all the money in the world.

Couldn't you have called Daniel who dined at the Yale Club with the district attorney?

Instead, I sulked. Laurence drove my mother's car along the darkening roads. *I am not ready for repentance, nor to match regrets.* I could hear the envy in his voice as he recited another man's words. His own poems lacked this spark. I was tempted to say, This is a good poem, so it must not be one of yours, but I didn't want to reveal I was listening.

When did he become a thug? I wondered. Kidnapped, I counted telephone poles. In the morning, I told myself, I would drive the car back to Park Avenue.

It is to be learned, this cleaving, this burning.

What a line, Laurence says. *This cleaving, this burning.* You will like him, darling. Why are you sulking? I rescued you from the most boring people alive, and I'm taking you to meet perhaps the greatest living poet.

I've met him, as a matter of fact. He used to come into the bookstore, quite often.

But now you'll meet him as a poet's wife, not a salesgirl. I thought he didn't like me, rivalry, et cetera, but he remembered a review of Pound I'd written, and we hit it off. He's got a crate of rum he brought back from Cuba. We'll have a roaring good time. He said the word *roaring* with sarcasm. It was an ad man's word for our era. When he saw advertisements for the Roaring Twenties, he would mime a tiger, bare his teeth. There are two men that matter right now, Duke Ellington and Hart Crane. Wouldn't you agree? Wouldn't you agree, Peggy?

I pressed my face against the glass. I looked for road signs, for breadcrumbs. Soon we'd be in a forest; I could see ahead the jagged shapes on a ridge, black-green. I thought of fairy tales. When I was a girl, I would confuse the girls, for I found it too frightening to focus on their faces. The girl in the oven, the girl in the wolf's bed. Oh don't cry, Benita said, when she read from *Grimm's Fairy Tales*. Years later I realized she'd changed the endings, invented new events on the spot. Gretel was given a wand of ice; the trees turned into a chariot. Hansel found a pie in the oven, warm rhubarb and plums. Don't cry, she'd say, don't look at the drawings. My sister deceived me with her sweet, improbable endings in which the forests held no danger, in which parents didn't disappear, and children were forever discovering moonbeams and sugar. Once I remember she used French pencils, turning a wolf's fangs into gold and violet candy.

WHEN I WAS AWAY from Benita, I felt diminished and cold. I thought of Mina Loy's lamps like spun sugar, and how I would not have a chance to return to the shop and find out if they sold.

When I'd told Laurence of the interest in her creations, he'd said: You do have the peddler genes.

Do you think I could open a little shop, I wanted to ask, to sell the art of my friends? But I didn't ask, because I feared his answer. That he would dismiss the idea as silly, or else embrace it so quickly it would seem an indictment, somehow, of my character.

Now we drove in my mother's Rolls-Royce on a blazing hot summer evening: unrolled windows, the scent of pine.

Blues is better than ragtime, Laurence said, the saxophone far superior to the trumpet. Hart wants to bring me to Harlem to hear Ma Rainey. *I don't want no man to put no sugar in my tea.* Sing it with me, Peggy. He was exhilarated, at his best. When he came alive like this, theatrical and with so much energy, he was so attractive, and I found it hard to be bitter and angry. I didn't know the song; I could not make my voice staccato and gravelly.

But I sang along anyway, as the roads became narrow and bordered by towering pines. I don't want no man to put no sugar in my tea, I sang, while Laurence leaned away from the steering wheel, letting the car veer. He put his arm around me; I rested my head on his shoulder, and he found the road again, found my forgiveness.

You'll enjoy Hart, he said, if you sit still and listen. He does like to talk to me about poetry, which might bore you, but you know nothing about modern poetry so you'll find him quite fascinating, I'm sure, and if it is all too confusing, I'll explain it more simply, later.

More simply?

Yes, he nodded. He still believed I needed to be taught.

But that evening something shifted, and I no longer wanted to play the role of his obedient student. Had he not heard me? Hadn't I told him I knew Hart Crane and understood the use of broken lines in his poem about a building? Perhaps the question wasn't whether he was listening, but how I'd convinced myself he ever had been.

Laurence parked my mother's car on a dirt path, and we walked toward a structure camouflaged by trees. There's the toolshed, Laurence said, but where is the house? He gazed around the dark property.

The toolshed must be his house, I said, and I walked ahead of Laurence. The door was rotting wood, filled my fist with splinters when I knocked. A voice beckoned us in, and we walked past shovels and rakes, terra-cotta planters, bags of dirt and sand, a nest in the rafters.

Hart stood on a rickety table and showed us the samba.

Dance, Peggy, Laurence said. Move your hips.

A crate of rum from Cuba was covered in a wool blanket. I tried some in a teacup; I danced beside Laurence, exaggerating my hip movements, making both men laugh. Outside, the rain fell on the frail roof. I found it hard to believe there were cities—Paris, New York—when we were surrounded by the silence of the country. I curled up into an armchair, while the men kept dancing.

What do you think of the rum? Hart asked. It's pretty strong stuff.

I recognized in his voice an apology. It's a certain tone I've heard since I took the typing class. Defensive, but also ashamed. As if I were enduring an offering, as though I were a queen being handed something tarred or tawdry. *This is probably the smallest apartment you've ever been. I'm sorry I don't have an iron and these napkins aren't clean. Have you ever taken the subway? I'd offer you dinner but it won't be prime rib and artichokes. Did you have a butler when you were a girl? Was his name Mervyn Bunter? I'd offer you wine, but I'm sorry it's rather commonplace.*

These apologies always seemed genuine, though I would

have understood if they were sarcastic or mocking. I always did my best to reassure that I'd love whatever I was offered, but I often felt observed. It became tiring, to never show disappointment or discomfort.

Even now the rain had stopped, and several black flies were clustered around a broken window screen. The sound of their wings, their hum, their relentless battering.

The rum is delicious, I told Hart Crane, I've never been to Cuba. You must tell me all about it.

Wonderful place, I've been telling Laurence we must go.

Let's go, Laurence said. Let's leave in the morning.

Hart came down off the table and sat beside me. I brushed a fly away from my face, and as if on cue, he said, I'm sorry. You must not be used to insects buzzing about. I'm a bit feral up here.

She's stoic, Laurence said, not a princess type. You should see the rats in Paris, the spiders. Grotesque rodents in the sewers. Then the spiders fall out of the ceiling when she's washing her hair. Never once heard her scream.

It was so rare that Laurence complimented me; I felt wonderful hearing his praise. I leaned back into the chair, while Hart drank rum from the bottle. He was a brawny man, with the body of a boxer. He appeared to be scarred—I thought of scars later when I left him—but he really didn't have any scars; his skin was just pockmarked and ruddy.

Laurence joined us, sitting on the hardwood floor. Tell Peggy how long you've spent on *The Bridge*.

Hart groaned. Would you believe seven years?

You see, Laurence said to me pointedly, poems take time.

I wanted to say, *Well, yes, but I'm certain Hart has pages. Your poems are invisible.*

Hemingway writes quickly, Laurence said, ten books a week. If you want to write simply . . .

I want this poem to be like jazz, Hart said to me. That's why it's so difficult. How do you do that with language?

I'm trying this too, Laurence said. (News to me.) Bloody impossible.

I play with the breaks, to get the syncopation. But then I want to write about fucking some stranger in the bathroom with Elizabethan diction. Messy.

Messy, Laurence said sympathetically.

Soon their words began to slur, and the talk turned to their misadventures. I suppose I should have been flattered that they could talk as men talk without fearing they'd upset me: I asked the sailor if I could suck his cock, and he hauled off and beat the shit out of me, but then next thing I knew he was on his knees—turns out he just wanted to be the one asking. Sailors down by the harbor, East River. One time I went with this—

Do you have a telephone? I asked, for I was suddenly fearful I might fall asleep. I would very much like to call my sister.

"Peggy has a Siamese sister," Laurence said. "It's hard for her to be separated."

"That is true," I said. "I've been bereft since the operation."

"I may have a phone, but I have to pay the landlord for every call. Perhaps I could drive you to the post office in town in the morning?"

"It's only that she's pregnant. And her doctors—I've just learned she's in a dangerous situation."

Hart took my hand and brought me toward a hallway. It's on the desk, he said.

I found the phone, next to his typewriter. He'd begun a diary entry. Met Laurence Vail, with his wife. Asked if she might fund *The Bridge,* but she said that's her uncle. That's the other Guggenheim. Still might be worth the ask. I've heard she's beautiful but not too bright. Laurence said he can bring her to my shack and she'll see how I live like a hobo.

I turned away from the words. I felt sorrow on seeing it, that this man felt such desperation. I wished I could be Simon then, handing out great wads of money, for I could see Hart was unwell, behind the bravado, the kind of sadness that was tangible, a heaviness.

Five years later he would fold his coat neatly and throw himself off the boat in Mexico. *This cleaving, this burning.* When that happened, I would feel great regret.

You could have helped him, Laurence would say. If you weren't so selfish. You spent that whole weekend moping about. Imagine if you'd bought him a home instead of Djuna.

Didn't I dance that weekend? Even though you'd dragged me away from Benita.

You could have helped one of our great American treasures, he said. At least I know I did my best.

But then I only wished I could leave the shack, before he made the request for *just a little donation to tide me over.* His sadness was palpable; I could feel it in the paper, in the walls. Why was it up to me to save the poets from their own despair? Why had Laurence brought me here to face this desperate man? *I hear she's beautiful but not too bright.* I unrolled the paper. I took up his pen and crossed out "not too" and made the editing scrawl. Transpose, I believe it's called. So the sentence would read: "I hear she's not too beautiful but bright." The cup of Cuban rum gave me strength; I never would have tampered with his sentence otherwise. I left it on the table, like a taunt or a dare. Pretend it's Dada, I thought, an intervention, a playful rearrangement.

No clock in the room; I thought it must be ten in the evening, though perhaps it was later. I called Benita and listened to the staccato bursts. Counted them. One, then twelve. Why did Edwin not answer? What if she had gone into labor? I tried again. I forced myself to envision my sister and Edwin entwined and asleep on crisp linens embroidered by Spanish nuns. His hands resting on her stomach. Phone unplugged so she wouldn't be disturbed.

I thought of Benita's breath, when she lay beside me, when we were girls and used to fall asleep to the sounds of the violin in the airshaft. The dark sky and the portamento; the sound of the slide from one string to another. I could hear it in this frightening house with black flies and drunk men. Far away, 740 Park Avenue, the hushed rooms and drawn blinds, the silent rooms of Park Avenue—I never prayed, but I then prayed for some force inside those rooms that would cherish my sister.

I walked up the stairwell and saw a cot—a medical cot, the kind used in wartime. A flimsy, metal contraption with a Pendleton gray blanket. I lay down and closed my eyes, and wasn't the least bit comfortable. Why was I here? I heard the music from the room below, and I knew exactly what would happen in the morning. Laurence would say, Let's go get more rum and records. Let's go to Havana, where the hummingbirds are the size of bees and we can climb hills of sugar.

IN THE MIDDLE OF the night, I woke with such an intense dread. I could hear someone—Hart or Laurence—typing. I crept as if into the forest road. First I tried the Rolls-Royce. Though he'd left the door open, the keys were not inside. I considered the scene it would be if I went inside and demanded the keys. Through the dark tangled trees, their long-fingered shadows, I saw a light on the road. I wandered toward it, though I was in a pale slip and a raincoat I'd picked up off the floor. I was barefoot. My feet went into the mud. The auto was gone by the time I reached the clearing.

I sat on a stone bench. I watched the sun rise. When the next auto came by, I planned to race out into the road. I'd wave, hail the auto until the driver stopped out of concern. Please, I'd beg to the stranger, take me back to Manhattan. *Take me back to my sister.*

INSTEAD, LAURENCE WANTED TO return to our house by the sea. So we did. Pegeen's hair had turned from black to blond when we returned. I brought her dolls with hard eyes, and my own childhood books. *Arabian Nights. The Wind in the Willows. Just So Stories.* I talked to her more than I had before I left; I asked Adele to let us be.

The house felt fecund, ripe. Teeming. But things were not right. I brought Sindbad a train set, but he was morose. He'd begun speaking with a bit of a British accent, picked up from the gardener. My daughter's room was the coolest in the house.

Mina's mad at me, I said, cross-legged.

Why, Mommy?

She didn't want me to sell her beautiful lamps, I suppose she thought it was dirty. Some people think money is dirty, and I suppose they're right.

It was ridiculous discussing capitalism with a three-year-old, but Pegeen looked sympathetic. Her eyes were a lovely color.

Is she a bad person? she said.

This would later become my daughter's obsession, when we watched noirs in theaters, when she learned her nanny was in the Hitler Youth, but it started that day, looking at drawings, trying to figure out—as I was—how someone who could draw so beautifully could also be cruel. Bad person, she said. Had she overheard this? It wouldn't surprise me if the servants spoke badly of me or each other.

She's not a bad person, I insisted.

Back from Manhattan, I'd mailed Mina a check for five hundred dollars. *The lamps were a sensation,* I wrote. *I could have sold hundreds more.*

"They weren't decorative," she wrote back. "They weren't meant to be sold like lingerie. I didn't make them for women in the Social Register. Now they'll never be in museums; and I have heard they are selling lampshades with papier-mâché sailboats and flowers at Gimbels and Galeries Lafayette! Thank you for the check, and your efforts, but I do believe we should end our partnership, and I hope in time we can resume our friendship."

I wrote her a letter of endless apology and offered to pay for a lawyer to sue those who had stolen her ideas. But she did not reply, and soon after, in the first weeks of July, I began to hear that in the cafés of Paris, Mina was speaking ill of me to anyone who would listen. She called me a schemer. Though I had never kept a penny from her work and had, unbeknownst to her, paid her landlord for a year of rental of her studio, Mina had taken to denouncing me as both a stingy miser and dangerous. It was Djuna who repeated these slurs to me, with unsubtle glee.

Knowing how it would wound me, she saved the cruelest insult for last, saying it emphatically. She calls you a *profiteer*.

ON THE BOAT HOME, I'd barely spoken with Laurence, instead striking up a friendship with a tall, red-haired man who was studying cell production. Doctor Knicker Knacker, Laurence called him. This detente continued when we returned home.

Are you mad at Daddy? Pegeen asked. Is he a bad person?

Will you forgive me? Laurence said. I don't know what got into me. I have these enthusiasms and passions, and it seemed then that you must help Hart, and if we didn't leave that evening—really, I can't bear the silence. I miss your witty bons mots.

To distract myself from this conflict, I thought, I should find something to do. All-consuming, challenging. It seemed simple, particularly after the harsh letter from Mina. It wasn't only Mina. Djuna was ungrateful and vicious. I'd failed at being bohemian, I'd failed at being a happy wife, I'd failed at being a patron.

In this way, an idea arrived. I would take up painting. I would take lessons from Gilbert. If you let me paint your portrait, he said, I will teach you.

Laurence was envious. First Professor Knicker Knacker, and now this?

Am I supposed to never speak to men?

You look at them with your large eyes.

I want to learn something. Perhaps I'd be good. Instead of being behind the artists, I could be the artist.

He looked skeptical.

You don't believe I have talent?

I think if you had talent, you would have been compelled to paint. It's not something you take up like studying Japanese tea rituals.

Let's see. If I don't do this, I will kill you. I turned away.

Please, Peggy, he said. I can't bear your silences.

I picked up the brushes, set them out on the table. Gilbert will be here at one, I said, you can work in your studio.

I must say I'm inspired by Hart. I've started trying to make my sentences sound like jazz. Could you tell me if they have that rhythm?

IN AN ODD COINCIDENCE, Hazel had begun to paint as well. She had divorced young and married again, a journalist named Milton. Now they had a little boy, and she was due again soon. She was living in Paris and taking painting classes at the École des Beaux-Arts; I could only imagine how much money she paid for the privilege. We spoke occasionally, but recently, her voice was less gauzy. I explained to Gilbert, she's always been very conventional. But I feel she wants to copy me, come to Paris, meet artists.

When she called, it was to pass along praise from her teachers. Wouldn't it be ironic, she said, when you've spent years boasting about your artist friends and all the important artists you know, if I was the one to receive a gallery show.

I only wish her the best, I told Gilbert. We painted in the mornings. I must say, I wasn't very good. It galled me that I could not create the image in my mind. You can tell me I'm dreadful, I said. I suppose it's good for me to understand how truly hard it is. And I've read all of Berenson, but I can't paint a sea. Is that a balloon? Pegeen had asked.

Was it better to be idle or disappointed? When Hazel showed up—that's when I gave up. I couldn't stand for my sister to be better than me, though that wasn't it.

Let me see your painting, she said.

I've given up on that, I said. I'm much better at writing.

It was true that I'd asked Djuna, How do you start, could you tell me how you begin?

In her notebook I'd seen a single sentence. An idea for a story. A woman sees a bird on the hill. She follows it, and it leads her to an abandoned child.

Why do you ask? she said. Why don't you write about your own life? That's what people want to know. What happened to your father.

Oh, I couldn't write about that.

What about your ancestors? Everyone loves an origin story.

Truthfully, I couldn't see what I had accomplished to merit an autobiography. But Meyer, my grandfather, was objectively fascinating. The American Dream. I asked my mother to send me his obituary.

Why ever would you want that?

I don't know if I know his story accurately.

Did you know a journalist comes by every day or two, wanting to write a book about the Brothers, but the recent one, I suspect he's going to write about the scandals. The obituary was lovely. Your father would have been happy.

It was rare she mentioned my father. Did he like his father? I always assumed he didn't since he left the company.

Oh no, he adored his father. Worshipped him. But why would you want to excavate this? I thought you wanted to only live in modernity.

I sighed. The maître d' came out and waved to let me know my five minutes were up.

How is Benita? I asked.

She's heartbroken you left her. I am too. She said Edwin was horrified by how brutish Laurence was to you. Of course, I've never seen Laurence be anything but gentlemanly. Except when he drinks, but hardly *brutish*. I told him not to start the rumor that my daughter is married to a brute.

How is Benita? I repeated.

She's quite pale; the doctor is worried. She doesn't want them looking at her, poking about in her lower body. But the dangerous month will be terrible. I'll be worried every moment.

I thought the dangerous month was in May.

Perhaps it was, but now it's July.

That makes no sense.

It makes perfect sense. They didn't expect her to be this

far along. Now she is. So the dangerous month is July; I don't know why you always have to be so contrarian. The closer she gets to birth, the more the danger increases. Do you understand that?

I don't agree. She's made it past May. For once in your life, could you be optimistic.

It has nothing to do with optimism. I'm a great optimist. It has to do with basic logic.

I was so tired of being told I was stupid or did not understand that I handed the phone to the maître d', along with a hundred francs.

Apparently, I don't understand basic logic, I told Henri.

How about a Pernod? he said. And some oysters? When I nodded, he winked. You certainly understand basic logic, he said, if you've ordered something from the vines and something from the sea.

LIGHTNING STORMS WRACKED THE sky, and when I walked along the beach in the morning, I would find mysterious fragments tossed about: crab pincers, African cigarettes, a small sandal blue as the flower of chicory. The lightning terrified the children, and so we invented sources for the cracking flashes. It's a signal that a queen is in the sky, I told Pegeen. The clouds must be having a party, Adele told Sindbad. Are the clouds born from God? my son asked, in a wistful voice that made me feel as if my heart might separate from my ribs.

The time with Crane had buoyed Laurence, and he announced he would finish his book that August, before we left the stifling heat for the mountains in Switzerland.

In those days, my husband and I observed a kind of distant détente. Secretly, I was furious at him for taking me away from Benita. I told myself he was only envious of how much I loved her, but still, I could feel the stirrings of loathing. Sometimes I wondered if this anger at him, for taking me away from her, was also the way I let myself get angry at him for everything else: His rage. His derision. The way he spoke with reverence of all the poems he hadn't written; while all the while treating me like a dilettante.

Rather than bicker, we avoided each other. When we spoke at all, it was in terse, blanched tones. I was restless and lonely, and I thought, I must do something to take my mind off my worries about Benita. *She is not looking well,* my mother wrote me. *She walks with a pained limp, and her skin is far too pale.*

What I decided to do was write my autobiography. I set up a writing table in one of the guest rooms, the small room with French windows facing the sea. The heat was inescapable, so I wrote instead sitting on the window ledge, where palm trees and bougainvillea framed the shutters and provided a pleasing shade.

I began with Meyer, my grandfather, arriving in Ohio from Germany at the age of fourteen. *He began selling shoehorns, spectacles, shoelaces, glue, hens, cigars. Soon he invented a kind of stove polish; soon he was selling uniforms to the US Army. Jew, Sheeny, Jesus-killer! Christian men stoned him; threw him into the dirt.*

As I wrote, I imagined men like Hart Crane snickering. They would be soused, spilling wine like watercolors on my white pages. Who would want to read about my ancestors

who built a fortune by going down into the dank dirt of
mines, underground, filth?

*Even after they called him a Jesus-killer, Meyer would not give
up. He was very determined.* Oh, it was awful. It read like a text-
book for high school students. How much better he deserved,
my grandfather. But I couldn't find the brushstrokes to capture the wave.

THE NEWS ARRIVED AT the end of July. Mary Butts was staying with us for a few weeks, working on short stories I found
intriguing, full of spooky women made of jade and furs and
dirty rags. But she was also an addict who once swallowed a
fresh bottle of aspirin after she had used all her opium. She
swooned about the house, devouring the novels of Trollope
and Forster all day. She ate almost nothing, but with a great
sense of urgency. I'm craving a lemon tart, she demanded, as
if they grew on trees. And shortly after it was procured for
her, I found it discarded on the counter, barely eaten. Holding Pegeen, I let her stick her finger into the ravaged remains—
testing her tongue against her own finger, tasting the curd.

That glimpse of Pegeen with her finger jammed into the
pastry was part of the world before. Then the news arrived
from New York, and all those memories felt as if they lived
on the other side of a door.

The telegram was sent to Laurence, but I was the one who
opened it. Sindbad and Pegeen were in the garden with Adele.
I could see them from the kitchen window. Sindbad, determined and assertive, bent down and dragged his hands
through a plot of dirt. Pegeen, nearly two, moved more ten-

tatively, but then she let out a loud, uproarious noise. A sound
of pure glee. I had never heard her make such a sound before,
and it jolted me back into the kitchen, with the cast-iron pans
hanging in rows and the scent still of yesterday's coq au vin.
Then they were all running wildly toward the house, deliriously happy and racing, even Adele. Her black Italian hair
rising in the breeze. I smoothed my dress; I sliced an apple. I
found myself arguing with Djuna in my head. *Don't you realize what I've done for you?* Be maternal, for God's sake, I told
myself, you are fortunate to have these wood fairies flourishing in the violet light.

I placed the apple slices in a porcelain bowl. I glanced at
the day's mail, which always arrived in a bundle tied with
blue-and-white-striped twine. I noticed this, the mail, but I
must not have recognized the yellow paper. WESTERN UNION
above a watery, purple ink.

The children came in, talking cheerfully, and showed me
some black spiders they'd trapped in milk jars. What is this
one, Maman? Sindbad said. I went and found a book called
The Life of Spiders, and together we began to flip through the
pages.

Spid-a, Pegeen said. Spid-ah.

I read the entries in the book aloud.

The hobo spider is reclusive and makes a web near the ground.

*The noble false widow has white markings and can look like a
skull.*

A breeze came through the window, and Pegeen kept
glancing around the counter, as if another tart might appear
where she'd found the last one.

We stayed like that, reading about spiders, until Adele

took them to dress for dinner. I lifted the mail, and it was then I recognized the telegram. It was addressed to Laurence, but I did not see his name: I saw only the simple lines of letters typed and pasted to the paper. I thought, at first, it must be from my mother, announcing a visit or some cousin's engagement.

When I read the words, at first they were insensible.

Please gently inform Peggy that Benita has died in childbirth.

I read this and continued with my tasks. It was as though the words had no meaning. I went to the garden and found some tomatoes, pulled them off, pulled some roses from a prickly spine.

Where is Laurence? I asked Adele, when she returned to the kitchen.

Writing, Adele said.

Could you ask him to come in? I said, but she didn't seem to hear me, and I wondered if I was whispering or if I hadn't spoken. I sliced the tomatoes and left the pulp and seeds on the wooden board, a vicious red. The smell nauseated me, and I took the roses and crushed them with my fists until the scent of petals sweetened my skin.

Lulu came in smelling of the beach; she shook herself; droplets of water, and she licked sand from her paws. Upstairs, the children's laughter was piercing and sharp as birdsong.

I read the telegram several times, hoping the words would change.

Please gently inform Peggy that Benita has died in childbirth.

A sharp blade might have come down and cut me in two. It felt as if I had lost part of my physical being.

I should have been there, I thought. I should have stayed; I shouldn't have let Laurence take me away. How could I have been so meek and timid? If only I'd stayed, if only I'd stayed beside her. But I didn't. I deserted her, and she died.

Mr. Vail will return for supper, Adele said, and I nodded but walked outside. I carried the spiders in the jar and set them free. I looked at the clouds, ghostlike and low over the sea.

I WALKED TOWARD LAURENCE'S studio on the path we'd once called Swann's Way. Sometime that summer, while I was with Emma, it had become untended and overgrown. I pushed through thickets; I heard the fallen pines crunch under my feet. The wildness comforted me. I wept as I walked and as branches cut into my skin.

Why was I walking toward Laurence, I wondered, when he was the last person on earth who would comfort me? The forest was kinder; the caring leaves and the silent green. I pawed the ground. Hours went by. The moon disappeared. My face was strewn with leaves and dirt when Laurence found me. He held me in his arms and shook me gently, saying, *You still have me*.

I COULD NOT EAT or sleep. I could only listen to the Kreutzer Sonata. I couldn't stand to look at my children. Benita was the beautiful, good one, and it was Benita who deserved these beautiful, good children: these carefree beings who climbed trees, who built turrets and moats out of white sand.

After a week of this, Laurence said I must pull myself out

of this suffering. I tried several times to be cheerful and talk-
ative, but the effort exhausted me. The sensation of being
severed returned to me, and I often felt as if my heart were
beating at half speed, as if I were walking with one leg. In
that week, more ghost than person, I learned more about her
death. A case of placenta previa. A hemorrhage. Polite, use-
less words for saying she bled to death.

I learned the baby died as well. They buried Benita's
daughter beside her in a casket lined with ivory.

Edwin was inconsolable at the funeral. I obviously could
not attend in time. Even if I'd been able to come, I wouldn't
have wanted to be there when my sister's body was lowered.

Edwin, my mother said, nearly spitting out his name, her
voice steely and vengeful. She *never* should have been allowed
to have the baby.

We commiserated, my mother and I. For the first time, we
spoke constantly. The telephone connection was often static
and fraught. I warned Edwin, my mother said. *I warned him it
could kill her. He only thought of himself; he only thought that he was
owed a child. I will have him fired. I will take the apartment away. I
will set my lawyers upon that man and have him charged with homi-
cide.*

She paused. Though she'd never asked my opinion, she
now said, Peggy, what should I do?

Please don't speak of lawyers, I said. Please don't mention
those kinds of men.

You're right, she said, and we listened to each other's tears,
and she said, *Have you spoken with Hazel? She's not taking it well.
Of course, she blames herself and says she feels guilty for having two
healthy children.*

I must have heard from Hazel, but I don't remember a word she said.

The lawyers informed me that Benita had left me her share of the fortune. I must have sat there, numbly, while I read this news. Somewhere a man on Madison Avenue with the last name Wyeth said, *She wanted you to have everything.*

A WEEK AFTER THE telegram, the children and Laurence returned with buckets of flowers. I had asked for flowers, imagining a prim bouquet. They took the train to Toulon and gathered every flower they could find, in the stalls that lined the train stations and markets. The three of them did this for several days, leaving at breakfast and returning at dinner with huge buckets of sunflowers, roses, branches of mimosas. The house became fragrant. The children placed flowers in mysterious places, so when I opened drawers, there would be a frail piece of twine holding together baby's breath and lilies. Beside my bed, on the terrace, vases and milk jars were full of sprigs and purple petals, yellow centers.

Maman, Sindbad said proudly, we found all the flowers for you. I know you're very sad but we have brought you all the flowers in Toulon.

IN AUGUST THE HEAT became unbearable. Clotilde stayed for several weeks and moved lightly through the house. She helped me cover my bedroom walls with photographs of Benita. She never seemed surprised to see me crying. She could understand my grief, I think, because she loved Laurence so much. She understood the impossibility of living in this world without the one who'd helped you survive it. But she didn't stay forever.

On a day so hot it was difficult to move, we went to one of the little fishing villages to find parasols for the children. Though I was the one suffering, Laurence was the one who did not look well. His hair, bleached by the sun, looked stiff as straw. His high cowlick, which usually gave him a distinguished look, had receded over the past few months, and his forelock fell messily into his eyes. He was bloated, paunchy, and his skin was spotty, with rough red patches that would emerge, suddenly, when he was angry. My hair was dirty; my dress slipped off my shoulders; I must have been no more than ninety pounds. We walked through the fishing village like sallow, shipwrecked vagabonds.

In an antiques shop, he left me and went into a room of rare clocks. I found a nice edition of *Treasure Island* and two parasols with wicker handles.

Laurence wanted me to buy him a Prussian clock. I looked at the tag and said it was absurdly overpriced. *Why do you need a clock when you have no concern for time?* I said, and he stormed off, while I calmly paid for the children's items.

Walking on the cobblestones, the heat was dizzying, and I thought I might faint. I could see the shimmer of the fishing boats and the blue of the sea lit up with sun like sparks. I headed to a fountain; I planned to splash some water on my face. I could recognize Laurence's footsteps behind me, but I ignored them. He caught up with me and shoved me from behind, pushing me toward the fountain. He pushed my face under the water for several long seconds, then lifted me up, and tossed me to the dirt, kicking me as if I were a sack of filth. By then, a crowd had gathered around us, and I reached for my handbag and gave him my wallet. Go get your clock, I said.

He took from his wallet a bill—it was one hundred francs—and set it on fire.

A couple in white straw hats and gingham scarves gasped, not at me lying there, with wet hair, and a bleeding forehead. They gasped at the money on fire. Monsieur, someone called out, and Laurence stood still, until the paper had turned to ash and his fingers were black and singed. When the police came, they rebuked him for burning money.

Is it a crime? he said.

As a matter of fact, they said, it is.

I fled. I found the car and drove alone back up the rugged hills. The air had become static and heavy. I hoped they would put him in prison. This time I would not rescue him. I lay atop the white coverlet, looking at my sister's pretty face, her calm eyes, her openhearted gaze. My skin was still wet, and I thought, Is this from the fountain or did he spit on me? I felt mangled; unruly. I examined the scrapes on my shoulder bones, dark and filthy as railroad tracks. I found some calamine and rubbed it into a bruise that was so blue it might as well have been black.

Move away from the beast, Peggy, I heard my mother's voice, suddenly. I'd been thirteen and lying on the tiger rug, dangling my fingers into its dead mouth. *Move away from the beast, Peggy.* Like that, my mother's voice came back to me.

———

LAURENCE WAS DRUNK, very drunk, when he came home. I could hear him stumbling about. I had asked Adele to take the children to the abandoned cork factory. It was in a nearby forest, and I knew they would spend hours exploring the hills and discovering mysteries in the building; they would not be back, I hoped, until late afternoon.

I heard Laurence on the stairs. Was there a way to lock the door? Should I push the desk against the door or should I give up, let him kill me?

When he walked into the room, he was livid and unashamed. I'm sorry, he said tartly. But your stinginess is unbearable. I don't think I can take much more of your incessant penny-pinching.

I said nothing; I got out of bed and sat on the floor, staring up at the photographs of my sister. Then I covered my face with my hands. So I didn't see at first; he did it rather quietly. I heard the rip of paper, and I saw he was pulling the photographs off the wall; he was throwing them about; he was shredding them into bits small as ticker tape. I tried to grab his arms, but he flung me to the bed.

Please leave, I said calmly.

I did not want anything then but his absence.

Once he was gone, I gathered the photographs that were still whole. I returned them to the wall. I found a fragment of a photograph, Benita's ringlet, her cheekbone, and I pressed it into a locket. In the morning, he said he was taking the children to Switzerland for some alpine air. I smiled numbly. I suppose I was glad to be rid of him.

CHAPTER 14

Bird Bones

1928

THE SPRING AFTER BENITA DIED, I BROUGHT THE REVO-
lutionary Emma Goldman to live in the South of France. We
set her up with a little cottage in Saint-Tropez called Bon Esprit. It had a view of the Alps, a garden full of fruit trees.
Pears and cherries. Little mirabelle plums like candies in your
palm. The idea was that she would hunker down and write
her memoirs.

For quite some time I'd been running a fund to help support her. It had started with a letter from my friend Howard
Young, wondering if I would consider starting a fund to release her from financial insecurity. *She has been hounded, ha-
rassed, and beaten by police for forty years,* he wrote. *She has been
imprisoned and forced into exile by the American government. . . .*
But something shifted that winter, after Benita was gone; on
a gray day, the thought came to me like a spark, *She is the one
who should write her life, not me.* I could help her do it.

So Laurence and I had driven her down in our little silver
Hispano-Suiza, quick as a flash of lightning but always on the
verge of exploding.

Once she was settled, I drove the rutted roads to Saint-Tropez to see her. Her cottage was on a high hill, beside a small vineyard. Down below us, fishing boats listed and never seemed to leave the bay. White roses grew wild in the garden, and the flowering fruit trees grew wayward, unpruned.

At a small iron table, Emma was seated alone with her typewriter. Her gray, wiry hair appeared to have been grabbed carelessly into a loose knot, and she wore a sort of smock with heavy woolen socks and rather ugly sandals. She was fifty-eight. I was twenty-nine. I was a wife; she'd spent her whole life avoiding the title. Now she looked like a sober grandmother. It was hard to imagine this was the woman who had once incited riots in America, found a new lover after every speech, been compared to dynamite and powder kegs.

But when she talked to you, she was charismatic. I couldn't keep my eyes off her.

"P.G.," she said, "have some of E.G.'s fish."

"I'd love to," I said, and I watched her shuffle into the house, her gait slow and arthritic. I felt suddenly self-conscious in my silk dress, the kind I always wore that summer, with a rope belt and slanted pockets on the hips. People had begun to tell me I was "worrisomely thin." I wore lipstick and espadrilles. Would she lecture me about my ancestors? Would she blame me for their crimes? Well, so be it, I thought, and was glad when she came back with a bottle of muscadet. Fisherman's champagne, she said, cheerfully. She carried a ceramic tray with a white and lumpen fish, which smelled vinegary.

"Where on earth did you find gefilte fish in Saint-Tropez?"

"I made it," she said. "You've had it before?"

"We used to have it at my great-grandmother's home in Elberon, I can't say it was a crowd favorite."

"Try mine," she insisted. I did, and tried not to wince. It was the texture, rather than the taste. Filmy and gelatine.

I turned my face from hers, glanced at the ledge beside us, where she'd placed tiny pots of sage and thyme. "You've made this place even more charming," I said.

"I'm so grateful to be here. I haven't had my own room in ten years. And I know it wouldn't have happened without you, even though Howard Young did try to take all the credit."

"He did spearhead—"

"Let me praise you," she said, "I really am grateful. Howard may have told you I was whoring myself all over Toronto." She laughed. She said it really was a kind of whoring, giving speeches when your heart wasn't in it, when your ankles were aching.

It was funny to sit there talking to a woman I'd once regarded as mythic. As children, my cousin Isaac and I were obsessed with her, this girl terrorist, somewhere between heroine and demon. Nights, we imagined her spectral, stalking through our hushed rooms, taking away the treasures we knew we did not deserve. We imagined her living in a tenement at twelve, sewing corsets in cramped, fetid rooms. And then at seventeen, falling in love with the anarchist and assassin Alexander Berkman. *They say she bought the gun,* my cousin Isaac told me. *Bet she would have better aim; the boy couldn't even shoot to kill.* We imagined her as a teenage vigilante with her coarse lips and high-collared blouses. If she had sought to shoot Frick, who like my uncles hired Pinkertons to bash striking miners with black sticks, blinding them with tear gas, what would stop her from coming into our homes?

She might come disguised as a maid, I told Isaac. *Do not trust any new maids!* She might hide her handgun in the white bones of the corset she's sewn. We reenacted the crime. I would always play Emma, while Isaac would imitate his father, Daniel, striding about, before I held the mock handgun to his temple. *Get me all the copper in Chuquicamata. Shoot those lousy strikers in Perth Amboy!*

Time passed. Frick survived unscathed and went on living in the mansion next to ours. Berkman was sent to a penitentiary in Pennsylvania. He plotted his suicide. He told Emma to bring him cyanide capsules. When she arrived to visit, masquerading as his sister, he was stunned that she did bring the requested poison.

Now she was sitting in a garden in the South of France, serving me her gefilte fish. She told me she woke every morning at six, wrote for three hours, and then went to the market in town.

"Every time I buy a tomato," she said, "they ask, is it for painting or eating?"

She laughed, a loud, deep laugh, and she went on. I listened rapt. I'd spent so much time with the children, or in familiar arguments with Laurence, I'd forgotten how it felt to hear someone surprise you with their sentences. She told me that, in a strange coincidence, her great love, the assassin Berkman himself, was also living in the South of France. Sasha, she called him. In Nice, with his girlfriend, Emmy Eckstein.

"Emmy Eckstein!" I said. "What is she like?"

"She's pretty, in a way, but she never says a word, and she's very much under Sasha's thumb. She has no personality."

"Nice is dreadful," I said. "You must come visit us at Pramousquier."

"Yes," she said. "If you promise me there will be real champagne."

"There will be real champagne," I said, and then I found her embracing me, her body warm in a way that I thought might bring me to tears.

She embraced me again, as I stood near my automobile. "You seem suddenly nervous," she said.

"Oh, I suppose I am. It's only—the drive is a little dangerous—"

"Stay. Stay here until the morning."

It was strange to have a sudden child's thought. *What if I stay here? What if I run away?* I could not tell her that I was nervous because I dreaded returning to Laurence, who would undoubtedly be angry about: the color of my dress, the time of my arrival home, the Yiddish words I heard again from Emma, the money spent on Emma, on Bon Esprit, on a Bolshevik (*She's not a Bolshevik, she's opposed to the— She's a bloody Bolshevik!*), about my affection for her, about her white, not pale pink roses (*Not Durham? Not Bourbon?*) about her book *Anarchism and Other Essays,* now on my bedside table, now in my lap, now in my hands, because (tossing the book about) politics are *such a bore.*

Before I went into the car, she said, "You must have this, P.G."

Winking, she handed me the parcel of wrapped fish. Into

my hands she pressed this, the fish that was chosen because it was believed immune to the evil eye.

FROM THAT EVENING ON, I drove often to her cottage, though the drive along cliff edges would cause me to be startled by the force of my fear. Driving back home, in the night, I would often hear the waves and then feel a slight surge under the wheel, as though the black road were an undertow. I would right the wheels; I would steer the car back toward darkness, I would think, *how easily I could have careened into the Mediterranean.*

Still, I went to see her four or five times a week, perhaps simply because I liked her company. Laurence wondered why I'd forsaken all my friends in Paris. I'm tired of their gossip, I said, I'm tired of hearing about their silly affairs. When my friends called, saying the city was stifling hot and smelled of urine; the bread was stale; there were so many Americans; you couldn't get a table at the café; oh if only they could swim for an hour or so, I lied and said, We are swamped with guests; we are all about to leave for Switzerland.

I would walk through the garden in the late afternoon, knowing she'd have completed her day's writing. She often dictated to her secretary, a quiet and intense girl named Emily, who brought Emma the same breakfast each morning, at the same time: toast so black it crackled under her knife as she spread the butter. After returning from the market, Emma worked for another four hours in the afternoon, without a break, and then arranged her typed pages on the table. I would read them aloud, or she would read them to

me, and then she would often insist on cooking dinner for
me. She cooked chicken over charcoal in the red Provençal
oven; she made pudding and served it with a sauce of grape-
fruit. She never said, Oh, you're so thin, it's worrisome. Instead she cooked these rich meals for me, which I ate, until I
became plumper, hungrier, often excitable from the conversation and sustenance.

One day she cooked a rather sallow kugel, and we laughed
at how the cinnamon looked like ants floating in the curded
cheese.

"Did you eat *this* in Elberon?" she said, laughing.

It was the first time she'd ever mentioned my wealth or
my ancestors, and I suddenly feared that she had been waiting
for the right moment to berate me. I sat there quietly, then
said, "It is very kind of you to always cook for me."

"I used to cook for the girls in the penitentiary," she said.

"What were they like?"

"There was Aggie, one of the sweetest and kindest, but
the poor woman was withered at age thirty-three. She'd been
condemned to death, for killing her husband. There'd been a
boardinghouse row, over cards, and a young man hit him with
a fireplace poker, then turned state's evidence and blamed it on
Aggie, the new bride. Then you see, you have the stupidity of
the law who come along and stamp Aggie as a hardened criminal. Another poor one was Mrs. Schweiger, a devout Catho-
lic, whose husband sought distraction with other women. She
desperately wanted a child, but was too frail and unhealthy,
and so, lonely and always weeping, she emptied a pistol into
her husband. Homicidal melancholia, *you* might say, but here
in the horrible halls, *they,* the officials of the state, called her

every ugly name. I remember confronting the head matron, a vicious beast, after she called Aggie 'The Bad Woman.'

"Most of the women were in prison for prostitution." She paused. "The crime with two participants, and yet, interestingly, only one criminal.

"I almost became a prostitute," she said, grinning when she saw my startled expression. "So I understood those girls. There's a law that says you must not lure men. And then there's desperation. Desperation is more powerful than any law."

"Why did you—"

"I needed to raise money for Sasha. I tried to get sewing work, but I was known in the factories as a troublemaker. A notion came to me. I recalled *Crime and Punishment,* which I had read over and over when I was fourteen."

"You thought of Sonya."

"Yes! I thought of Sonya, trying to raise money for her dying consumptive stepmother. I thought, if sensitive, sweet Sonya could sell her body, why couldn't I? But the first man I spoke to gave me ten dollars and told me to go home. And I did go home. I used his ten dollars to help buy Sasha's gun."

"You must put that in your book."

"Perhaps I will," she said. She leaned back in her chair. She seemed someone incapable of fatigue. "You never talk about yourself," she said.

"I'm not very interesting."

"I doubt that's true. Was your father—"

"My uncle Daniel," I said quickly, "you probably know, my uncle Daniel Guggenheim was as terrible as Frick. He ordered four strikers shot in Perth Amboy."

"But what does that have to do with you?"

"Everything, I suppose."

"Or nothing whatsoever. You can't be blamed for his ruthlessness and greed."

"But I've been given that money, from those mines, from that copper."

"And look what you've done with that money," she said, pointing toward the garden and her typewritten pages. "I've lived my whole life in near squalor, and I've lived with purpose and meaning. Why shouldn't a revolutionary have a moment of beauty and leisure? Not to mention that you've made it possible for me to write this book. I'm not a president or a general, but there I'll be, perched beside them in libraries, a little stick of dynamite."

She confessed that she'd actually seen my father's home, years before I was born. Her boyfriend had brought her to Fifth Avenue. Took the train from the tenements and sweatshops. They stood on the sidewalk and looked through the windows, envious and disgusted. She couldn't help seeing the flowers in neat boxes, the tulips on Madison Avenue. She knew it was the spoils of exploitation, but she felt a tinge of despair. Why had he shown her such magnificence? To see it starkly, the contrast between the robber barons and the workers: the immaculate streets, the girls in pinafores, compared to the fish in buckets, the widows black with charcoal. Somehow I wondered if I had ever seen her, back then—or at least felt her gaze, if I looked out the window, and saw her tattered clothes and disdain as she spoke with her boyfriend.

Let's throw rocks, Benji, she might have said to him.

You seem taken with it all, he could have replied. But you don't want to live like that, do you?

Why shouldn't I? Why shouldn't we all live like that?

Because you can't live like that unless you make a profit.

Now, nearing sixty, she was living like a queen in her cottage by the sea, summoning distant memories of the tenements where she'd been raised.

She told me that an old friend had seen her at a club in the Riviera, dressed in a fancy embroidered robe, and asked what had become of her.

"This is why we have fought," Emma said. "For happiness and joy for everyone, including me."

WHENEVER I RETURNED TO Pramousquier from Bon Esprit, I would be in a heightened state, my mind racing from our conversation, Emma's stories. It often took me some time to return fully to my own life, to change my tone, to focus on the tamer details. I tried to hold on to the warm feeling Emma gave me, her kind words, before Laurence returned and said something snide and critical. This loathing felt almost physical, as if a stranger had begun to enter the house, making the intimacy between us even more impossible.

Into the guest bedroom, I brought my clothes and the books Emma had sent me with a note, which I will quote because her exact words are dear to me: "You have meant so much to me, you always will whether you know it or not. All the gay times under your hospitable roof, your visits to me in Saint-Tropez, your brave drives back and forth from Pramousquier. My love to you, Peggy dear. . . ."

When Laurence knocked on the door, I would say, I'm sleeping. I turned up the gramophone. I fell asleep to the sound of violins and woke an afternoon later when four swallows flew into my room.

Things with Laurence had only gotten worse since Benita's death. He seemed to hold it against me, how much I grieved for her. For a year, he'd taken my grief as an insult. As if it were a rebuke to him, a way of saying he wasn't enough for me. That my love for her had been, somehow, *more*. Of course it had.

He once hauled me into the sea still in my dress, stockings, and shoes, then, before I could dry out, made a fuss about seeing the new Al Jolson film at the cinema. I sat there shaking with a chill, watching Jolson fill the theater with the jaunty sounds of his piano, glad for the noise so no one could hear my teeth chattering.

Emma was the first person I confided in about how bad things had gotten with Laurence. She said, you can't live like this. It's not worth it.

Driving to Saint-Tropez, after a bad fight, I breathed in the jasmine and felt for the first time a hunger. I remembered the route with a sudden clarity. When I arrived at Bon Esprit, Emma looked at me, with my scraped cheek and gaunt face, the loose dress I wore so there would be nothing chafing my injury. She embraced me. Peggy, she said, it's terrible how he tears you to pieces. She told me to lie down and brought me a broth with mussels and carrots.

"Would you like me to read to you?" she asked, and I nodded. She cradled my head in her heavy arms and read to me from *Crime and Punishment*. Though she did not know I'd also loved the book at fourteen, she chose this book to read to me. Her voice became more Russian, throaty and vigorous. *He did not know,* she read, *and did not think about where he was going; he knew only one thing—that all this must be ended today, at once, right now because he did not want to live like that.*

ON JULY 21, EXACTLY a year after Benita's death, Laurence said we must go out and dance. I was not sure if he was being wise or perverse. In a rare moment of confidence, I decided to outwit him. I wore a silver Lanvin metallic dress with a low, draping back, low enough to reveal a long line of bone. I pressed a blue cloche cap onto my hair, tilted it slightly, and wore shoes of the same electric blue, with stacked heels and thin straps crisscrossing my ankles. Rouged my cheeks; kohled my eyes, traced my lips with a Cupid's bow pattern. On my neck, and between my breasts, I daubed Patou, letting the wet rows dry before I added more.

We drove to a club in Saint-Tropez; Laurence wanted to hear the band from Harlem famous for their version of the Chaplin Rag. No one plays it faster, he said, the trumpeter is extraordinary. We drove close to the cliffs. The sea was silver. Gulls rose over the white rocks. Closer to town, the roads became busy, and we had to slow down, idle behind the Bugattis. Yachts cluttered the sea, wide as warships. Saint-Tropez was no longer ours alone. Look at all the vulgar interlopers, Laurence sighed, as though reading my mind. To our surprise, Saint-Tropez had become a desirable place for starlets and aristocrats. You'd see them parading about the beaches, their servants carrying their gramophones and parasols. If we'd left Paris when it became too hectic with Harvard boys and perfectly blank-eyed artist models, we might now leave the fishing villages as they became playgrounds for men who threw about their money in the turquoise casinos. A Rolls-Royce cut in front of us, and from the window, a young girl with bleached white hair laughed as she hit the side of our car with her diamond-wristed hand. *We will have to move elsewhere soon,* I wanted to say, but I could not get that word to leave my lips. The word *we*—I could not say it to him, especially now on this particular evening.

"Will you dance?" he said, resting his hand on my knee.

"Oh, I will dance," I said, and I grinned, then covered my lips, so he could not see my grin didn't match the way I felt. My heart was stealth; my heart was cunning.

Laurence was right; the band was terrific. They stood on the stage, solemn and sleepy-eyed, in seersucker suits with white bow ties. The trombonist was lithe, with a sly smile that seemed to mock the crowd. Their music was lithe too; it snaked about the room, as sultry and languorous as one feels after a shot of morphine.

I left Laurence and saw the trombonist wink at me. My grief overcame me, and I felt despondent, and I began to dance with abandon. Hands on my knees, hips swaying in time to the rag. Soon, I was on the banquette, then a tabletop, dancing beside two girls who moved like Mistinguett at the Moulin Rouge. The girl beside me, her hair was bright red, impossibly shiny; she wore only a bandeau top and net stockings, and when the trumpeter played alone, she lifted her hands and suddenly, joyfully, shook her body spasmodically.

When I was dancing on the table, a man came up to me, out of the crowd. He looked like Jesus. His hair was long and lanky; he had a broken tooth. He offered me his hand, helped me down, and once I'd stopped dancing, he said, *Emily is looking for you*.

I looked around eagerly for Emily. It was hard to imagine her at this nightclub, for she was boyish and serious, in the pleated skirts and cardigans she'd worn every day since she started working as Emma Goldman's secretary. But we'd become friends, of a sort, and she'd given me volumes of the Romantic poets, her textbooks from when she was a student at Wellesley. After I told her about Benita's terrible death, she gave me her tattered books with all the sentences she'd underlined, lines about grieving. She was only a year younger than me, but she seemed much younger, so wide-eyed and intense, talking earnestly about Truth and Poetry.

Where is Emily? I asked the man, but the music was very loud, and he could not hear me. Once again he took my hand, and he led me outside. My ankles were scuffed, so I took off my shoes and dangled them by the straps while we walked together toward the sea. The sky was indigo; the only light was from the red moon and the ships, stilled and blinking.

"I liked watching you dance," he said. He lit a cigarette, and I lifted my chin to watch his slow, mischievous smile behind the spark of the match. He spoke with a British accent, which didn't seem to belong with his ragged shirt and ruffian manner.

There was a crackling energy moving through my body that night, as if I could conduct the grief like an electrical current and pass it somewhere else. Perhaps that's why I wanted to touch him so badly.

"I lied about Emily," he said, still grinning. He offered me a cigarette. "She's not here. You must know darling Emily would not be *here* in this decadent morass. But I saw you with her in the market one day. We used to be lovers. Well, friends. Sometimes lovers."

"Well, she's lucky then."

"You think so?"

"Certainly."

He leaned down; he was very tall; he leaned down and kissed me. The sensation startled me, for it had been so long since I'd felt that roughness; I'd become so used to only the touch of my children's lips, the tender, swift brush of their constant kisses. I let my lips take his; he put his hand on the naked part of my back and slipped his fingers down behind the silver, briefly.

"You were dancing like someone in distress," he said after we separated.

"My sister," I started, but he took my hand before I could finish, and we walked toward a hill, a forest. When the hill sloped, he stepped ahead of me, with a kind of pouncing gait, agile as a cat.

I caught up with him, and we kicked through the pines, ascended the stone stairs of a turret. The hills were full of these kinds of stone towers, remnants of the Moors and their battles, but I'd never been inside one before. As we walked up the stairs, he told me, with a kind of offhand ease, as though the information were too trivial to really matter to me, that his name was John Holms; he was vacationing in the Côte d'Azur for the rest of the summer; he knew Emily from London. She'd written him a scathing letter about his review of

To the Lighthouse in *The New Statesman*. You must be very dim to not appreciate all the vitality, she'd written. She ripped me up rightly, he said, and I thought, I *must* meet this girl.

"And she fell madly in love with you," I said teasingly. "I bet she was swooning."

"She was. But Emily falls in love once a week," he said. "She is marvelous, though."

"Isn't she? I'm a bit in love with her myself," I said.

By now, we were perched on the open vestibule. Below us, we could see the fields and vineyards and sea. "This is where the Moors shot their artillery," he said, lifting his hand out, to mimic the motion of a gun. I feared he might begin to talk about the Moors or battles, so I moved closer to him and kissed him again.

He wrapped his arms around my shoulders, pulled me toward him, again slipped his hand down beneath the silver.

"Do you think you could be a bit in love with me?" he asked.

"Perhaps a bit," I said. I slipped off my dress, and we moved together toward the heavy stone wall. He shielded me from the rough stone, turning, so it would be his skin that grazed the dark rise of castle. I felt his warm skin against me and sighed, as though at last I'd let go of a plank of sorrow. I thought of his name, *John Holms,* and then I remembered. He was the one, Emily had told me, listing her many lovers, who had killed six men.

"YOU ARE LIKE A child playing with dynamite," Emily said, when I told her of the castle and the evening.

She giggled, though, that particular American giggle, sweet, a little nervous. We were sitting in Emma's garden, and between us was the finished manuscript. It seemed unbelievable to me, after years with Laurence, slaving over a novel that never seemed to materialize, to see Emma complete her work so quickly. To celebrate, Emma was cooking an omelet with thyme, Boursin cheese, and very thin slices of sausage. I had contributed three bottles of what she deemed a "very fine Chablis."

"Don't tell Emma. Please," I said. I leaned back in the chair and felt as if I might at any moment levitate.

Emma came out with the meal, and as she sat down, Emily began to giggle and clasped her hands together. "Peggy is trysting with the very dashing John Holms!"

"Oh, it's nothing," I said.

"It's nothing? Look at you. You're blushing like a new rose!"

"Well, why shouldn't I feel something instead of sorrow? Why should I shut off all desires—"

"Of course, you shouldn't," Emma said, with her gentle authority. "Laurence is a fool and a jackass. God knows, you deserve some affection."

"Affection," Emily said slyly, pouring herself a glass of wine. "I can promise you that John will give you lots of *affection*."

"Let's celebrate the book," I said. I turned my gaze toward Emma. She was looking rather stunned as she held up the manuscript. She'd titled it *Living My Life*.

In the morning, Emily and I would drive with the manuscript to Paris and hand it to a young publishing assistant who would carry it, disguised as a cookbook, on the voyage to New York, then to Emma's editors at Alfred Knopf. "They want it to be two volumes," Emma said, without the least bit of modesty. "I will be the first woman to have a two-volume autobiography."

"Two volumes," I said, and we clinked glasses and tore into the omelet.

"Peggy's ravenous," Emma said. And I was. I ate nearly all the omelet, then went into the kitchen in search of a baguette. When I came back, Emily and Emma were turning the pages. The first page was blank. "You don't have a dedication," Emily said.

"Let me fix that," Emma said, and she took out her pen, and on the white page, she scrawled, *For Peggy.*

BY THE END OF summer, we were fully in love. John was a strange creature and a genius. He was always climbing trees. He was tall and slim and moved like a feline. His beard was dark and pointy, and he really did look like Jesus, even in the sunlight. I wasn't the only one who thought so. Sometimes, as a kind of party trick, he would scurry around on his hands and feet. He could do it quite quickly, in fact. He loathed walking, found it dull and ordinary.

He was a man of letters, but in his case that meant he was always talking and rarely writing. He was never without a notebook full of sentences and fragments scribbled in pencil that he never allowed anyone to read.

Both of us were married, or something close to it. I was married by law but already convinced I needed to leave my husband. John traveled with a woman who wanted to be his wife so badly she already used his last name. Dorothy. It didn't take her long to sniff out the animal energy between us. He was crazy about me but had an allergy to making decisions. One of his friends called it "a complete impairment of will."

That previous spring a fortune teller had predicted I would soon meet the man I would next marry. Perhaps I would not have taken her so seriously if I had not been looking to be saved.

Emma lent me and John her cottage for an afternoon; he was nimble and attentive but eager—as ever—to give instruction. As if I hadn't had enough practice. Emma left a bowl of blue quetsche plums with a note on the kitchen table. *Please replace the sheets.* I don't think she particularly cared that we were falling in love; she just wanted to help me escape.

Around her, who had never been a wife, I felt sheepish about certain tendencies, certain patterns. Needing Laurence to save me from my family, then dreaming of another man to save me from Laurence. The man the fortune teller had promised.

Don't listen to that nonsense, she said. You're better than that.

MOSTLY, WE MET OUTSIDE. In the incredible August heat of the *midi*. John would be cross-legged, waiting, under a canopy of pines. He would mark the tree with a scarf, so I would know where in the forest to find him. He would be in a thin white blouse, with rumpled olive shorts. Whittling a branch, whistling, drinking whiskey. Flask in one hand, knife in another. He'd gaze up at me, tramping through the trees, in a sundress and straw hat.

I would sit on his lap; I would bend to my knees. A constant desire had returned to me. For years, I'd thought I had lost this need, as though it had been absorbed by my children, as though it were something they took, like milk or lessons. For years, I had thought of my body as something mechanical and practical, a device for others, a collection of limbs and breasts that soothed and fed. But on those August afternoons, with John, my body returned to me. In those afternoons, with him, by the blue waves, on the warm sand, by the pine trees, the trees that he'd marked with scarves, so I would not have to search or be misled but could find him easily.

HE DOVE OFF THE high cliff, dove like a bird, as if his body were slight and winged.

We swam together, but I could not sliver the water, as he did, with quick strokes that somehow did not cause the waves to ripple.

Lying on the sand, our hair wet and sleek, skin dappled with water, the golden clouds, and the sound only of nightingales . . .

"Emily thinks if Laurence finds out, he will kill you."

"I'll kill him," he said blithely, turning on his side and tapping my nose. He said he didn't mind the ugliness of my nose; he liked to watch me move, said I moved like a quick sprite, suddenly like a bird.

"I will kill him," he said again, in a matter-of-fact way that I suppose I should have found chilling.

"Have you killed anyone before?" I asked, acting as though I had not heard the number from Emily. I didn't doubt Emily; John had a watchfulness that felt almost biblical, like those men in the Old Testament who have been charged with the lives of their tribe. He had that physical acuity, a coiled, clever way of moving his body.

"Six times," he said, kicking up some sand.

"Six times?" I said, laughing. "Was this some street brawl?"

He tapped my nose again. "Bird Bones," he said, using the nickname he'd taken to calling me, after seeing the frailness of my naked body, "you can't be that naïve."

"Tell me," I said. "I'll still love you even if you were an assassin."

"It was during *the war*," he said, and he sat up and gazed in the distance. "I was eighteen, and I was put in charge of a company. I'd been to Rugby, then Sandhurst, so I suppose they thought I was of some *superior quality*." I'd never heard him speak with sarcasm, and it unsettled me. I could not understand how he could look toward the sea, with the sun's glare, but he could, and though he seemed to not want to talk, he could not stop.

"The Germans made an attack; they came into my trench. I was absolutely terrified. Just sheer terror. I was alone; my men had been sent out without my orders. I just ran down the trench, killing them. I killed them by hitting them on the head with an iron stick. I must have hit them very hard. I am very strong. Later, when I found they were all dead, I broke down and cried."

He lit a cigarette, kept talking, with his body turned toward the sea.

"They gave me the Military Cross for that. It was the first time my father was ever proud of me. After that I found out all my men, all of them, had been killed. I was so furious that they'd been sent out without my orders. I couldn't forgive it. I had to command another company and march them thirty hours without food toward God knows where. Some of the men fell, and we left them. We left them and we marched on like dunces. I believed in the army, but I could not bear it. When we reached God knows where, somewhere along the French Somme, we were taken prisoner by the Germans and put in a prison camp."

"For how long?"

"Two years," he said, taking out his knife and drawing a circle in the sand. "That was better than the trench. For some reason, it was all Oxford boys in there. Hugh Kingsmill, others. I learned from them, about literature. I read every minute of the two years. It was so cold that we were in bed most of the time. I sent to England for books and educated myself during that time. I read all philosophy. I could out debate all the toffs. I must have been insufferable. I thought I was Socrates. Because I was an officer, the merchant marines allowed me to have liquor, but food was scarce. So scarce. You'd find a piece of bread or chocolate, and you'd divide it into as many pieces as there were men. I climbed to the top of the enclosure one day because I could no longer stand it in the coop. The guards began to shoot me, but my friends got me down. Everyone was homosexual. I was not. I did not want it. I have had none of that, not out of any distaste or cowardice, but I just—"

He turned back to me, and his eyes weren't tearful but looked wary and paler; he lay near me, then on top of me, putting his head beside my shoulder. "I like your shape, Bird Bones," he said, and he ran his hand across my hip.

"Emily thinks we should all move to England in the fall," I said, after we'd made love and dusted off the sand with our hands, brushing off the knees and necks of our intertwined bodies.

"Oh, I know," he said, "She thinks we should live in a castle on the moors in Yorkshire. She has this daydream, of us, all living there, and writing like devils, like the Brontës."

"Would you want to go back to England?" I said.

"I suppose it depends who is with me," he said. Then he swooped me up in his arms, swung me around until I was dizzied. Swinging me, he grinned, as though he hadn't just described his worst moments of suffering. He imitated Emily's girlish, excitable voice, "*We could write like the Brontës!*"

"AND WHERE WERE YOU?" Laurence said when I returned. I'd been careless that day, staying longer than I should have. When I began the affair, I would be sure to return while I knew Laurence would still be in his studio. I would have time for a bath, time to dress, and compose myself. But lately it was difficult to leave John. I felt a physical resistance, and I'd come to stay longer and longer on our outings, until this time, when I came home in the early evening.

"Emma's," I said bluntly, and I walked by him. Sand was in my hair. I had a long bite mark on my neck.

His eyes were red-rimmed. He seemed to always be looming about like a rag doll hovering over children's heads at some macabre puppet show.

I still became uneasy around him; my body, even in a lulled, content state, would suddenly prickle; my heart would race. I knew I could no longer share my life with him. Our fights were turning more brutal. I suspect he sensed my betrayal. Only a week before, he'd pushed me down the stairs when I knocked on the door of his studio, then set fire to my scarf and sweater. He'd stepped on my belly four times until I feigned fainting.

Now I walked by him. "You look tired," I said. "Why don't you sleep? I'm going to check in on the children."

I had no idea what time it was. I felt like I was acting from some blind force that drove me on and on. Adele was very strict about the children's bedtimes, and I feared I might have missed them. But when I walked into the room, they were both sitting up, in their side-by-side beds. Sindbad was in blue pajamas my mother had sent; they were made of broadcloth and should have been ironed, but as we had no electricity, this was not possible. I imagined my mother's mortified face, seeing her grandson in his wrinkled pajamas, and her granddaughter, with her hair tangled and unbrushed, naked, holding on to a doll that appeared to have been amputated.

"Rascals," I said, and they hopped out of bed and ran to me.

Soon after meeting John, I began to be able to look at my children again. I'd looked at them with guilt after Benita died, but now I saw them as though they'd come out of the shadows. Their skin seemed suffused with lightness. Pegeen showed me a drawing she had made. She was three, but already she could draw recognizable figures. A reindeer, she said, with apples from a tree on the moon beside the river and with some blue bubbles.

"Magnificent," I said. "I'm going to send this to Paris. This is much better than the dull, old work in those stuffy galleries."

Sindbad, who was becoming a bit of a tyrant, said, "I don't like bubbles."

Pegeen teared up, and I offered to read them a book if they were kind to each other. I climbed into Pegeen's bed and thought, Am I really hiding in the children's room? Could I be any meeker?

Then I thought, I don't give a damn if Laurence finds out. I read them *The Children of the Frostmoor,* and I thought, Let him come in here and strangle me while I read to his children about a moon of frost in Sweden.

THE NEXT MORNING I told John he could stay in our guest-house. He's a literary critic, from London, I told Laurence. Perhaps he can advise you on your novel. He's friends with Emily.

When John arrived in the early evening, toting only a canvas bag and a few magazines, I introduced them briefly and watched Laurence assess John: his wide shoulders, his fine chest. *A clammy handshake* was all Laurence had to say, as we walked back to our home. *It was like touching a dead fish.*

"I'm very tired," I said. "I think I've had too much sun."

I went into the guest room, I lay down. Through the window, I could see the light in the guesthouse. When Laurence's light goes out, I'll be over, I'd told John.

I walked through the pine trees in my white nightgown. I could see John at the window, looking down through the trees, and we raised our hands in the same moment, waving in sync.

"Isn't he terrible?" I said, of Laurence. "Can you see why I despise him?"

"Is he French? He has an odd accent."

"His mother was American."

"He's emanating insecurity."

"Well, I've probably done that to him. He was the King of Bohemia when we met, swaggering all about."

I lay down on the bed. The pillows and sheets were covered with a fabric of embroidered flowers. The rugs were Persian and worn, the walls were painted a wan gray. "This guesthouse has no harmony," I said, "I'm sorry. I've spent the past year in a fog—"

"I couldn't care less about the decor," he said. I sat in his lap and pulled his wallet from his pocket. "Do you have a photograph in here?" I said. I knew so little about his life. He'd told me he hated his father, who had been the governor-general of India. In the wallet, there was only one photograph, a yellowed portrait from Sandhurst; John was handsome, full-lipped, serious, in his uniform.

"What was Sandhurst like?"

"Rigid. Lots of sons of Sirs and Lords. Would you like to hear their names?"

"I would like to hear their names."

"Lie on the bed and I'll tell you."

He lay beside me and began to whisper, *Osbert Beake, Peregrine Cust.*

"No," I said, laughing. "Tell me more."

He slipped off the shoulder of my nightgown, ran his hand around my collarbone. *Tufton Beamish, Hercules Wedgewood.*

We were both laughing; I leaned over and clutched the side of the bed to keep from rolling off. "Is it really that funny?" he asked, grinning.

"Tell me more—"

I was still laughing so I didn't hear the door open; I didn't hear Laurence walk in. John sat up in the bed and looked at Laurence, nonplussed. I recognized in Laurence the certain physical traits that would occur before he lashed out at me; his flushed cheeks; his quickening stride. So it surprised me when he lunged at John, pulling him off the bed. They began to push each other about, with such force that I could not bear to watch. John placed his hand around Laurence's neck; Laurence kicked him with a sudden swiftness, and then once John let him free, he darted out to the living room and returned with a wrought-iron candelabrum. I ran outside and saw Joseph, our gardener, who must have been woken by the sounds of men bashing each other about. "They're going to kill each other," I said.

Joseph, who was nearing seventy, went into the house, and something about his manner, pleasant, calm, even slightly amused, must have shamed both of them. Laurence dropped the candelabrum and walked out the doorway, pushing past me, with a look of contempt. John slung his bag over his shoulder and collected his magazines. He didn't seem the least bit upset. He kissed me on the cheek and whispered, "I'll get a hotel for us in Avignon."

That night I slept next to Pegeen. I listened to her breath, sweet and even. *It is over now,* I thought, *there is no going back.* I felt a sudden relief, then nothing but fear. In the morning, I woke to see Pegeen staring at me. I had suspected she was unusually sensitive, as all children are. But that morning I felt as if she saw me with a sudden, unearthly comprehension. Before I went to find John in the forests, she would feign stomachaches. *Maman,* she'd say, *how it hurts. How it hurts!* Whenever I returned from my time with him, when I'd go to tuck her in, she insisted I push her sheets farther under the mattress, tighter than the maids did, as if encouraging me to perform an act of enclosure. Now she put her small hand on my necklace. Abruptly, silently, I felt the soft touch on my throat. She found the tiny clasp and began to pull it. Maman, off. Maman, off. She said she wanted to wear my necklace. So I helped her. I took her in my arms and showed her how to open the clasp. Her hands touched my hands, and we helped each other with this, this undoing.

THAT AUTUMN PEGEEN AND John and I moved from town to town. In Marseilles we stayed near the harbor, where the streets smelled like bouillabaisse and salt wind. Pegeen loved the bright laundry strung above balconies, snapping in the breeze. In Aix she ate so many *calissons* that she groaned with a stomachache all night, and for weeks the smell of almonds or icing made her sick. John was gentle with her, surprisingly patient. For a time it almost felt like we were a little family.

But trouble found me eventually. It always did.

When I opened the hotel door and saw a tense, officious man in a London Fog raincoat, I assumed he was a private detective, hired by Laurence to find me. This was October, in Lyon. I'd been gone from Pramousquier two months.

Might we talk? he asked politely.

Are you here to bring me back to my husband?

I pressed my head against the white doily, poured myself some tea. In the next room, Pegeen was still in her pinstriped pajamas, playing a game she'd invented called Names. On one page, she had written the alphabet and asked me to circle my favorite letter. Then she kept herself busy, trying to write as many names as she could summon. That morning it was R, and she had already filled the page—Rosalie, Ruth, Rachel, Rifka, Rita, Rosalind.

Your husband, the man said, is not my concern.

I told him he might take off his raincoat. It does make you look like a detective.

He laughed then. Suddenly, he looked younger, only thirty or so, with the high cheekbones and intense gaze of a film star.

Are you a detective? I asked. I couldn't understand why he was here, especially if he wasn't sent on behalf of Laurence. *Find my wife,* I could imagine him saying, *find my daughter.*

I'm not a detective per se, he said. But I am here with the hope you'll help me with an investigation.

Oh, I said, and I paled. Are you with Fleet Street? Were you sent by Dorothy? I don't want to end up in one of those tawdry stories. FLIGHTY HEIRESS SEDUCES WAR HERO.

You seem caught up in romantic drama, he said with slight distaste. That's not why I'm here. Surely you know why I'm here.

I truly do not. He handed me a card. Pierre Voss, Operations, France, Guggenheim Brothers.

My uncles have sent you, I see. Daniel or Simon?

They're all terribly concerned. We need you to make some kind of statement in support of your sister.

My sister, I said. What do you mean?

He looked rather terrified then, a shadow from the sconce's light fell on his face, like a dark slash.

You haven't heard?

I haven't spoken to her in ages.

I don't want to be the one to tell you, he said. But your mother—and your uncles—they've been calling you frantically for days. Because, you see, there's been— He bit his lip.

I'd been in such a frenzy, I hadn't read the newspapers, listened to the radio, checked for telegrams.

The Metropolitan Police would like to speak to you, and I've been sent to bring you to the interview. Of course, the brothers want you to tell me what you know before you speak to the detectives—

What has Hazel done? I interrupted. I thought perhaps she had stolen jewels as a lark from one of the riding girls' nemeses. Harmed another innocent animal. This was the summer James Joyce's daughter was acting up, setting her hair on fire, sleeping in cemeteries. But Hazel was not young

and tormented; she was matronly and living in London with
her second husband, Milton. Her life seemed to be about port
and Chaucer. Occasionally she would send me paintings she'd
made of their library or her sons.

Her sons. Pierre said the words as I thought of them. The
sons, he said, have both passed away.

But how is that possible?

He sat down on the settee, and I noticed his eyes were
damp, his long fingers trembling. He said Hazel had gone to
the penthouse of a friend, and the children had fallen from
her arms. Thirteen stories, from the Hotel Surrey.

Fallen from her arms? I don't understand. I have to speak
to her.

She's safely hidden at the moment. She couldn't even leave
the building without reporters and detectives.

So they've stashed her in a sanatorium, I said, Solomon
and Daniel.

Yes, on Park Avenue. One of those unmarked buildings.
She's in terrible shock, as you can imagine.

And why have you come here? To tell me to hide as well?

It seems you have done so.

For other reasons.

Could you come with me now? It is rather urgent. I'll take
you to Paris.

I have my daughter here.

We can bring her back to her father.

No—you see—we can't. I was about to say more, then
didn't.

Instead, I said, What—I don't understand—if it was an
accident, why are the detectives involved?

We can tell you at the station, he said. All that condescension, all that distaste. It came back to me how Daniel once told me I was not well with my penchant for picking up matches. Concern or contempt, either way I was clearly troubling, an obstacle.

A complicated situation, he said, patting me on the back and steering me to the door.

Adele arrived, thankfully, I'd called her in a panicked state. I'll need you to bring Pegeen to Emily. When I watched Pegeen pack her duffel bag, I tried to think of something cheerful to say. One calamity—the fight between Laurence and John—had led us here, where we now faced an even greater wreckage. And then my daughter looked so wan and resigned, as she held the handle of her bag, the resignation like a rebuke. *Once again I'm being moved about,* she seemed to say, *and how I hate it.* Who could blame her?

On the drive to Paris, I was nauseous. I asked Pierre to let me out of the car, but he refused. I won't make a run for it, I promised him. You must understand, after what you've told me, I feel full of bile.

I'm sorry, he said. He handed me an envelope of some sort, and I spat in the fold. I thought of my mother then, how she must have desperately tried to reach me, and what if Laurence had returned her messages? *Your daughter's run off, the slattern.*

The synchronicity of our disappearances struck me, Hazel's and mine. I knew of the sanatorium she'd been sent to, for occasionally girls from Jacobi would be sent there for "cures"—nurses brought them into beds with pale muslin canopies, soft, gauzy, overly serene. A door closed, and you were undressed. I couldn't remember who had recounted their stay, only that once you arrived, you were nameless. Patients were given small ribbons and for days would be coldly identified as the color of silk. Mauve, Turquoise, Ivory. Their scandals were minor but consequential. Pregnancy, theft, opium. Rosa, a grim girl with a bitter mien, posed on a sheepskin ring, her legs parted, in the lavish drawing room of the Frick mansion. We tittered; we speculated. Why is she walking through the white door? The girls always returned, until they didn't. Vivian had been sent to Neuchâtel; Helen's aunt—we were told—was given raw meat and strychnine, for her condition. The rest cure, said Helen, torture for the upper crust. When my aunt came out of the white door, she was timid and thin as a rail. I couldn't look at her—it was as if she'd been blanched. A blank, Helen said, and we all trembled in our black dresses and unkempt hair. It served as a warning. If we went too far, we might be sent to *rest*. It was imperative that we keep our misadventures secret. We calculated risks, determining that nude photography and exhaustion were the most likely crimes.

Now Hazel was in that place. Surely, if she'd lost her two sons, she needed consolation, solace. I thought of her wounded stare, the way her expression could turn filmy and faraway, as though she was seeing the world through the thickest fog.

Oh, I said to Pierre, I really must speak to my sister.

IN A ROOM OF GENTLEMEN, Pierre exchanged greetings and was congratulated on procuring Peggy, the middle daughter.

Now that there were only two of us, I was, in fact, the older sister.

My sister was stricken with shock, I was told. She was refusing to speak to detectives.

Why would she need to speak to detectives? The boys fell from her hands. Have you ever tried to carry two young children? They're scrambling and kicking, and Hazel has always been clumsy.

Has she?

She has.

Well, it's rather complicated.

Pierre had mentioned the Surrey. I asked why she'd been in New York at all.

So he gave me the bones of the story, and I imagined the rest. On a fall day not so long before—a day I'd spent with John in fields of lavender, grief-stricken but still, unbelievably, innocent—Hazel had woken in her London flat. Late, as she often did. My sister was not disciplined or punctual; she had never been concerned with appointments; she had never owned a watch; she often fell asleep in the afternoon or woke to read in the late evening. But recently it had become something more pronounced. Harder to dismiss as quirk of personality or indolence. Something darker. A kind of creeping lethargy.

On that morning, Milton, her husband, wanted breakfast, a neat napkin, a boiled egg in a Tiffany's cup—the blue speckled duck. He searched for the cup—a wedding gift from me, as it would be, only to find the slim white side lined with yellow yolk, a piece of shell clung to the duck's beak. Milton was not fussy, but the single disarray on his Sunday morning set him off. What was wrong with the woman? he thought, her manners, her cleanliness wavered. He wasn't certain how long the egg should remain in the boiling water; the revolting day-old yolk remained despite his repeated scrubbing. Was it then he thought he should divorce her? It was more, of course. He wouldn't divorce her over a lump of yesterday's egg yolk.

But he thought to himself, *enough*. Enough of the dress unbuttoned, the pram unlocked. How it had slid down the hill in Hyde Park, while he sat on the bench reading Chaucer, how he had run after the runaway pram with his two sons inside, wailing. How Hazel had looked at him blankly. Why ever are you screaming at me? she'd said. These things happen.

You certainly weren't paying attention.

Why must you always be *scholarly*? She'd said the word with disdain, as if he were a gravedigger or a mystic, engaged in quackery. She was the one who went to fortune tellers, came home with wildly nonsensical predictions. I'm to meet an important figure in Tuscany. Why do you sneer? Benji will fall in love with a lovely Nordic woman, have five white-haired children.

The nonsense didn't bother him as much as her sincere need to believe in the nonsense. She was hollow, he thought. She craved wonder and the fantastical.

When he'd met her, she'd spoken of Barnard, how she enjoyed her studies with Professor Devison. To meet a woman who was awed by the little-known Devison—his professor at Columbia as well—intrigued him, and she came along to the

British Library, before the boys were born, taking the slips, with their long numbers, saving him from burrowing in the stacks, the claustrophobia of all those volumes.

When he told her he was divorcing her, she stared at him blankly. You do know I have the fortune, she said. How will you get by?

It felt craven and sad, the way she thought his love for her had merely been a form of comfort, when he was not like her sister's husband, who, when visiting London, had insisted on going to Savile Row, buying pipes and fedoras and narrow pants, Harris Tweed, mohair, Spanish cologne.

On the day I had found a guesthouse for John, perilously close to Laurence's writing studio, my sister was more careful with her betrayal. She hired away the neighbor's governess, after insisting she did not want or need a *servant,* and told her husband she was taking the boys to Devonshire. He had announced the divorce in such a cold way, as though he were mentioning a wisdom tooth's removal. It's time we divorced, he'd said, I won't hear any arguments. I simply don't love you. That's the fact. I don't know that you love me either. We can chop off the gangrened limb before we both become miserable.

Gangrened limb, she thought. He thinks of me as something rancid and fleshy. She filled fourteen valises with the boys' clothes, their toys, their birth certificates. On the liner, she was asked for her tickets. I have no tickets, she said. I didn't have time. I left rather suddenly.

For a moment, the steward looked at her as though she might have climbed up from steerage. Her uncombed hair, the indifferent governess, the two boys wailing.

Oh, she said, loudly, making a statement that would become evidence. There was evidence in the egg yolk, evidence
in her insistence to the porter that she was not a gangrened
limb. This is Benjamin Guggenheim, she said, pointing to her
son, with his blue eyes, glorious and bright. I am Hazel Guggenheim, mother of Benjamin, daughter of Benjamin. You
must believe me, she said, as she searched for the birth certificates. I am not Mrs. Waldman. She tore the marriage certificate rather placidly.

The passengers had moved away, already whispering of
omens and signs. *You know her father went down on the* Titanic.
I'm not surprised she's having a nervous breakdown. When Hazel
found her wallet, she seemed to gain composure. Oddly, the
wallet was also a gift from me; I had bought it in Milan, at
Furla; I was always buying Hazel gifts that seemed rather
dull, as though I intended to help her have what she often
lost, those things that were common, practical.

She wrote a check to the bewildered porter and leaned
back, letting her little Terence settle himself into her lap.
Terry, she said, let's look at the ocean together.

Later, a kind woman on the boat would tell the *Telegraph*
she seemed to care about her sons. She made mention of
going to the deck, she said, but she gave no indication that she
wanted to cause trouble. I felt sorry for her, to be honest, she
seemed very frazzled; she wasn't sobbing but she seemed to
be sobbing, if you know what I mean. I told my husband, *I've
never seen a woman look so lonely.*

The men at the police station kept telling me the story of
my sister. Her unspeakable tragedy. After settling herself at
my mother's apartment, she went to visit our cousin.

Do you know Rosa? one of them asked.

Yes, I said, she's our cousin. She lives on Park Avenue. She's married to a man who collects rare porcelain and naval equipment. I don't mean to be flippant. I just don't understand why Hazel would visit her; they aren't very friendly. But I suppose she needed someone to confide in. If her husband was leaving her, that's not something she could tell my mother.

It was funny being interrogated. I felt the need to explain my own sense of Hazel's movements, as though I were the one under suspicion.

She went there, and Mrs. Lake was out getting ice cream. She showed up early.

Yes, she struggles with time. It's a quirk of sorts. She often shows up on the wrong day. In the South, I waited on her once for seven hours at the train station.

But she insisted on going into the apartment, and the maid let her in. The boys were causing a ruckus, and Hazel said she needed to give them water.

Yes, I said, I'm sure she did.

But then she went out onto the penthouse roof. Do you know why she would do that?

Because it was a hot day—because she wanted to feel the breeze. Or see the park. Or get away from the maid, who was likely rather unfriendly.

The odd thing is, when she went outside, she went over to the parapet. She might have sat on the swing or chairs on the terrace. But Hazel walked right to the edge, where there was no gate or railing. Why would she walk there?

I don't understand why you are asking me. Surely my sister can explain.

Your uncles thought you could help us with your knowledge of your sister. It would be very helpful because the story is rather confusing.

She hasn't been arrested, has she? I mean, certainly if it wasn't a terrible accident, she would have been arrested.

That's an issue. Many people believe she should be arrested. If a woman walks to the edge of a fourteen-story building, and her two sons end up dead on the concrete.

I don't—I don't believe that would happen. People believe she—

I couldn't even say it. I put my head on the table. Somewhere Pegeen was dressing her dolls and Sindbad was reading a comic book. I could already imagine Pegeen's scratchy voice, her hair falling across her eyes, asking, *Is she a bad person?*

I have my own children, I said. I should be with them.

That's when I remembered Benita gliding around her apartment; how carefully she'd tried to take care of what was inside of her. When I thought of her, I sometimes felt I had no right to have any children at all.

EMMA INVITED ME TO stay with her at Bon Esprit. The wind was already prickly off the sea, but she was planning to stay through winter. We wrapped ourselves in blankets when we sat in the garden. We pulled the last late plums from her trees.

Stay as long as you like, she said. I've sewn curtains for the guest bedroom. She brought me tea and cinnamon cookies.

She was always trying to feed me; this was a side of her I hadn't quite anticipated; certainly not when I'd imagined her as a dashing young revolutionary smuggling cyanide into the prison.

When she sat on the bed, I realized I'd never seen her with her hair down. It made me think of pigeons in a Venice square: the same gray, a somber shade. But she looked earthen and real, a sage, with lines of wisdom. How lucky I was to be with her, I thought, instead of my own mother. Though her company also made me miss Benita. No one else's presence had ever brought me as much comfort.

I was in love with John, but I didn't exactly find him a comfort. And he was having trouble leaving Dorothy. In fact, it looked like he was going to marry her. But he couldn't let me go. I think he wanted to mold me. He could see two different parts of my soul—one passionate, the other trivial—and he wanted to feed the first one until the second disappeared.

Also, he was not making much progress with his writing, and I think he wanted a pupil. Everyone thought he was brilliant. But he could be quite full of himself. Djuna once told him he was like "God come down for the weekend." ("*What* a weekend!" he'd said.) He wasn't who I needed. Not right now.

Emma sat beside me and took my hand. Not trying to make me anything but what I was.

What do you think happened? I asked her.

I believe her, she said, reading the article to me. One baby began to fall, and when she reached out to grab the baby, the bigger boy fell. She said it happened so suddenly.

Emma kept reading the article. I wanted her to stop but did not know how to ask her.

You see, Emma said. They are going to use this against you.

Oh, I know. The gossips, the girls from the synagogue will say I loved Benita more, that I screwed up Hazel by ignoring her.

Emma looked as if she might say something, then did not.

We were always hated, I continued. They called us the Googs. A widow with three daughters, a father who had brought his mistress on the liner. Now Hazel will be one more reason to despise us. The Medea of Park Avenue, that's what they're calling her. It's the old curse. Won't let us go.

The curse?

We've been cursed since my father's death. How long do curses last? Am I next? I suppose I am.

I don't want to hear about this nonsense. Fairy tales. You've survived. You are the survivor.

When you said they would use it against me, I said sharply, who did you mean?

Here it was then: a message delivered by barristers. Tomorrow, while the burial of my nephews took place, I was to go to Nice to the offices of Graunstein and Halbert, my presence was requested at three o'clock, Laurence Vail—*Vail vs. Vail*—filed for divorce and custody.

I plan to attend, Emma said, taking my hands. I will not let these men destroy you.

She was true to her word. She helped me fight for the children, then stand my ground when I'd agreed to give up Sindy and he wanted Pegeen too. She wrote him a telegram in all caps, her words so forceful I remember them exactly as they appeared on the thin paper: HER FEAR THAT IN MOMENTS OF VIO-LENCE YOU MAY DO TO THEM WHAT YOU HAVE DONE TO HER.

If anyone needed witnesses, she said, they could ask any café owner in Saint-Tropez.

She tried another tack, telling Laurence I was in a fragile state, which was clear enough for anyone to see. I hadn't been eating properly for months. I was a bouquet of nerve endings, cinched together by a belted dress. I told myself I would eat when all this was done. *All this*. Which would be when?

After our *conciliation*—that's the legal term in French; a sweet word, I thought, for the joint declaration of our intention to separate our lives—Laurence and I left the judge's chambers and went to the first café we could find. He drank Burgundy. I drank whiskey. He stained his mouth red and gave me earrings. I pushed across the table a sweater I'd knit myself. For you, I said, then we began to cry, together.

III.

MODERNISM

"It is nice to bloom late in life;
I think maybe one appreciates it more."

—PEGGY GUGGENHEIM

CHAPTER 15

Borrowed Bedroom

1937

NEARLY FORTY, I RETURNED TO PARIS WITH A DREAM AS strong and strange as my father's. I was not fleeing board-rooms and greedy brothers, or chasing the embrace of a girl with sultry eyes and peacock feathers in her corset. I never had my father's gravitas; I was not dashing. The newspapers often described me as *delicate*. Bird Bones, he'd called me. Now even remembering the phrase made me ache. I still felt, sometimes, that his death had been my fault—letting him go in for surgery when I knew how much booze was in his system. And then his heart just gave out.

I was thirty-nine when a white-suited man walked me down the slanted plank of the *Queen Mary*. On the ship, I'd done my best not to be recognized—wearing dowdy plaid dresses; traveling with Milanese leather suitcases bearing no initials, no monogram. I found ways to hide my eyes so no-body could tell that they were solemn. It was a kind of disguise, that shabbiness. No one could say what they used to say when I first came to Paris at eighteen. *There she is, the American, the heiress.*

It was December, almost Christmas. My mother was dead.
I was going to start a gallery with the rest of my inheritance.
They could call me a dilettante if they wanted, as they always
had. I would simply shrug and say, *Look at this strange, crooked
painting. Doesn't it make you feel something that you can't quite
name?*

The white-suited man, an employee of Cunard, handed
me a numbered card with the name of the driver. Even he,
aware of my last name, couldn't guess why I'd come to Paris.
Maybe he thought it was to attend to ateliers and select a
spring wardrobe; or perhaps he imagined I was like my sister
Hazel, on the hunt for a bewildered aristocrat. So be it.
They'd been wrong about me since I was fourteen. I could
use it. If they thought I was love-starved or frivolous, they
wouldn't get in my way when I took my father's name and
placed it where it had always belonged: in the clouds, above
the mortal world of motion and industry.

When people heard the word *Guggenheim,* I didn't want
them to think of my father's drowning. I wanted them to
think of vicious colors and strange beauty, of how I wrecked
everything that was proper and timid—in myself, and in this
city.

THOUGH I ASKED FOR nothing that first night at the Crillon,
they brought me a silver tray: clementines in a crystal bowl
and a gleaming tea service: lid off, it revealed a nest of floating, fragrant mint. They delivered a box of blue paper and
envelopes, engraved with the Crillon crest. Already, they had
embossed my name on the envelopes. *From the room of Peggy*

Guggenheim. It felt forlorn and unnecessary, this stack of paper, tissue-thin.

When we were young, my mother always used to demand her own stash of stationery. She would insist that my sisters and I spend an hour a day writing letters to America. *What will we say?* said Hazel, who often floundered with my mother's stern assignments. I wrote elaborate letters, embellishing adventures or referencing Baudelaire. I needed no prompting, no encouragement. Benita wrote of the fashions on French girls, she wrote of her *delightful days* in her neat, careful script. *What shall I say?* Hazel persisted. Tell them you've been to the Louvre, my mother said bluntly. Tell them what you've learned about Marie Antoinette. Though she had little interest in history, my mother's voice always grew tender when she spoke of the terrible queen. It thrilled her that the Crillon always gave us the suite once occupied by Marie Antoinette. She played that piano, my mother would say, pointing at the dark, heavy object that seemed to loom about, too grandiose, in the music room.

I hadn't asked for it, but I drank the tea. I'd caught a cold on the Atlantic crossing. Six days I spent in my cabin room, studying Herbert Read's *Surrealism.* I'd turned down invitations to dance from a Yale boy with a frail mustache who must have thought I was twenty-five; and a Swiss journalist who said he was suspicious of anyone who genuinely enjoyed the novels of Hemingway. As we crossed the Channel, rocking on the dark waves, I circled a sentence from Hugnet and still remember it precisely: *Surrealism aims at exteriorizing all men's desires, all his obsessions and his despairs; it gives him the means to free himself, to venture forth.* He was exactly right. Surrealism simply confessed the fires that already burned us up. The part of me that took solace in these paintings was the same part of me that had loved to lie on my father's tiger; that had felt strangely peaceful in its savage fur.

In the evenings, on the boat, my quiet evenings of reading were sometimes punctuated by snippets of trumpet, or the riff of a French horn, some moment when a single instrument was louder than the symphony. I stayed with my Surrealists through meals, then sometimes felt suddenly, shockingly hungry, thrust back into my body again, wandering about the levels, finding the restaurant doors locked for the evening. With such habits, shut away in my room, I could not understand how I'd arrived in Paris, hoarse and red-nosed, with an ugly cough, this itchy sort of sneezing. Then I remembered; I was not always honest with myself. Some nights I'd gone out onto the deck in a thin nightgown, very late in the evening. I'd stood against the rail, with the wind and the waves, standing near the ocean's darkness, just weeping.

EVEN BEFORE I HAD the dream of a gallery, I'd met some of the Surrealist painters in the rowdy crush of London cocktail parties and openings. Their paintings were witchy and beguiling, like stepping into another person's dreams. Strange and rude. Oddly compelling. Some of them got stuck in my head as if they were my own untraceable memories. There was a bust with rabid blue eyes, perched on a stark and lonely expanse, hissing a kind of fevered steam. It made me uncomfortable, but I was getting more interested in my own discomfort. Breton, the one they called their pope; he said

Surrealism wanted to *multiply the ways of reaching the most pro-found levels of the mental personality.*

When I thought of opening my gallery, I imagined the critics saying, *Oh, Peggy Guggenheim, she's nothing but a wallet.* Saying that Surrealism was just the latest fad, and I'd fallen for it. But sometimes when I looked at these paintings, I got a shiver that let me know they were on to something—a sensation like what I'd felt with my father years earlier, trying to find language for that Braque, *It's meant to seem like something beautiful he stumbled upon, perhaps by accident.* That sense of having stumbled onto something, or into it—I felt that often with the Surrealists, as if you'd lost your footing and fallen through a rift in the earth.

In London, I'd met Roland Penrose. His hair was almost black; his eyes were almost blue. He seemed nearly hand-some, but there was this *almost* quality. His wife was named after a holiday or saint; her name was Valentine. He told me his grandfather was named Baron Peckover. *Oh no,* I said, laughing.

It's true, he said, touching my elbow. He was a wealthy banker, though, of course, not as wealthy a banker as your grandfather.

I don't think anyone was, I was tempted to say, *except for Rockefeller.* There were always these men, the sons of bankers or lawyers, and they sought me out, as though we shared some forbidden ritual.

It seemed strange to have met Penrose only two weeks ago and to now be looking at his painting in this volume. It was a portrait of a woman. The shape of her head was familiar, but her skin was blue, wings covered her eyes; small orange fish

protruded from her lips. I was studying this painting, wondering why it didn't create as much unease as the others, why
it didn't hold me close with that crooked gravity, but trusting
that difference, that my eye still *had* something, as it had with
my father, all those years ago—and then there was a knock at
the door.

It was a woman in a light mauve uniform. She bustled
about, lifting up the white webbed orange peel. She seemed
familiar with me; she moved about with the comfortable
manner of a neighbor. *Où sont les enfants?* she asked.

Les enfants, I said, laughing. Pegeen was ten; Sindbad was
nearly thirteen.

I explained that the children were in Switzerland with
their father. Skiing, I said. When she looked perplexed, I motioned with bent shoulders; I mimicked the lifting of poles.
She nodded and seemed to be considering another question. I
did not want to be rude, but it was not a subject I wanted to
discuss. *Où sont les enfants.*

I returned to staring at the painting of the blue woman,
now noticing the thorns around her neck, a single peony, petals drifting toward her breastbone. Some time went by. I did
not hear the steps, her departure. When I looked up, she was
standing as she'd been, near the silver tray. She was standing
perfectly still; she looked transfixed and terrified. Then she
began to cry, a quiet tremor, which she interrupted, bracing
her back. I'm so very sorry, she said, with such kindness, her
voice pure and feathery. Before I could comfort her, she fled
the room. Before I could comfort her, she said, *I'm so sorry
about all that has happened to you.*

What had happened to me? My mother had died, yes.

But years earlier, the deeper grief: Benita. Perhaps the great love of my life. And I had been the one to tell her, *Don't let them tell you that you're in danger. Just grunt and howl.* There was Hazel. Her boys falling from her arms. And my own boy, lost to me for years; Laurence took him in the divorce. We split the children like King Solomon splitting a baby. Sometimes the smallest thing would make me think of Sindy— spotting the peppermint candy he liked in a shop window; or the sound of another boy's polished shoes, clicking on the sidewalk; and I would feel my own body had dissolved into particles that might simply come apart. Pegeen stayed with me, but I worried for her, too; it often felt as if there were not enough skin between her nerves and the world. Sitting on a rickety chair could give her vertigo. She'd cry and cry.

For a time, John had made me believe that I could bear it. He was the smartest man I ever knew, and he taught me so much. But I was always his pupil, and in the end, he had trouble turning his genius into anything. He wrote only one poem during the six years we were together. And when he died, I knew in my heart that I'd killed him. We'd been fighting, and I wished that I might never see him again—and then the next word from the surgeon was *He's gone.* I was a fool to let them operate. I knew how much he'd had to drink the night before. Once he was gone, it was hard not to feel—not persecuted, exactly; but that the pattern of my life would always be loss. *I don't want to hear this nonsense,* Emma said. *You are the survivor.* Still, the old curse lingered. I could face it, or I could run from it; but either way, there it was.

———

ON BOXING DAY, THE Crillon was too quiet. I walked into the music room and found a few records to play on the phonograph: Rubinstein's Melody in F, Schumann's Träumerei. By this point, the cusp of 1938, my friends and I had all stopped turning on the wireless. In my little flat in London, I would sometimes forget and, from habit, switch on the news. On the BBC, the announcer's voice became terse, a tone I would later learn to recognize as aversion. *Today in the Reichstag, this afternoon in Munich.* A lurching voice would enter the air of my kitchen. His angry voice, with the harsh German syllables and everything an exclamation: *Abgeordnete! Geschichte Europas!* Then the calm Oxford mien of a translator would come over the airwaves, a passionless reiteration of the words of the madman. *The members of a foreign race must not be allowed to wield an influence over our political, intellectual, and cultural life. We refuse to accord to the members of a foreign race any predominant position in our national economic system.* It all sounded quite logical, delivered by a faraway and proper voice. But then, later, I'd be cooking dinner, watching Pegeen sketch in her schoolbook, and I'd think: *A foreign race.* Well, that's just a general phrase. He means us, of course.

I knew if I kept listening, he would soon be more specific and brutish, so I turned off the radio, suddenly, as one might grab at a fast spider. Crossing the Channel, I'd heard his voice in the *Queen Mary*'s salon, ranting about *Yiddish gabbling* and *poor wretches* and *the Bolshevist onslaught of the Jewry.* He's quite bonkers, isn't he, the hairdresser said, as she dyed my hair Abyssinian black. He's a madman, I said, please turn it off. She did. We all did. It seemed enough; it seemed sensible to turn off his voice and listen instead to the sounds of a symphony.

———

THAT NIGHT I WENT to a dinner Joyce was hosting at Fouquet's. I hadn't seen this crowd for years: Nora and James holding court, and my dear friend Helen, once married to Leon, now married to Giorgio, their son. The restaurant was dark and noisy and boisterous, right off the broad shoulder of the Champs-Élysées, that road broad and regal, a muscled flank. Inside everything was lush and glittering: sleek wood, black velvet banquettes, a beaten gold bar. It was a place where it felt good to be drunk and wealthy. To know your place in the world.

It took me some time to navigate the crowded bar and reach their private room; and once I found their little party, it made me sad to see how weary they'd become. James now had an eyepatch and a cane, but he still had the towering, dignified quality. He'd always been very kind to me, when I knew him years ago, when I was a young wife. I never knew why. Helen always said, James just adores you. That night, he was wearing a suit tight as a corset, and beige tennis shoes, with the charming air of a casual king. What a hug he gave me!

Nora seemed stern and amused, and it was difficult to tell if her gaze was skeptical toward me or just toward the crowd who always surrounded him. I couldn't imagine what that would be like. Both my husbands thought they were geniuses, and I spent most of my time prodding them, placating them, while here she was, with a man so brilliant, and everyone knew it. Everyone knew he was taking forever on this book about the evening. Seven years it had been, and it still had no title.

His son Giorgio, Helen's husband, was always very flirta-
tious, and he was always overdressed, like an Italian playboy,
with the fluff of a cravat, spats, the uncertain smile, like he
was never quite sure of approval. Where is the daughter? I
wondered.

Helen herself looked tense and worried, though she was
beautifully dressed, in a coppery sheath, with her hair in fine
curls, and a fur wrap. She was one of those women others
called impeccable.

I took the only empty chair, by the group of acolytes who
always surrounded James. His slaves, his assistants, his sons.
Helen was very fond of them. They dressed like miniature
models of James, in the same round glasses, the same slicked-
back hair. When he crossed his knees, they crossed their knees.
When he said something even vaguely witty, they threw
back their heads and laughed as though he were the most delightful person in the world. Which of course, he was. I was
always struck by how people reacted around genius. It was so
different from how they reacted around me. They gazed up at
him; they looked as though they could be saved.

But they didn't see his sadness. I sensed it coming off him
like steam. Where is the daughter? I thought again. Lucia was
her name. Then I remembered that she was in Switzerland. In
a sanatorium, Helen had told me. For a fire in the brain. I'd
met her once, years earlier. She had a beautiful figure and a
fierce way of dancing—pushing her breasts forward, and her
legs. Shameless. Somehow free. She reminded me of a fish
jumping out of the clean, sunlit water.

Pegeen was in Switzerland as well, but on the slopes, with
her father. She was delicate, our daughter, but mostly I still

believed she'd live a beautiful life. Sometimes I watched her cling to Adele, though, screaming and screaming as she was being sent into a lesson—for tennis, or dance—and I wondered if there was a primal footing she lacked; a way she had not caught her balance in this world.

Though we had not seen each other for years, it was easy to catch Joyce's eye. I did not worship him, like the others. I could see he needed solace. I felt such sympathy for him, thinking of his daughter, I reached out and took his hand, and he held it for a while, while all around us, the guests dined on the food that Helen was most likely paying for.

That's when I noticed Sam. A kind of shock went through me; I might have shivered. He was sitting with his back closest to Joyce, lighting his pipe. I liked his high cheekbones, the green eyes, the distracted air as though he'd wandered into our party in the midst of a dream. Where have I seen him before? I wondered, because he looked familiar in that way a person can, someone you've known or know already that you'll love.

He didn't look my way; he didn't return my stare.

Five years earlier I might have accepted this as defeat and moved on, assuming I was rather ugly, rather brash, with the worn eyes of a mother; or found some other flaw. But now, as I felt my life starting anew, I couldn't look away. Even when it made him uneasy. I could see how he winced under my gaze. I thought of looking at those paintings in London; looking at him, there was the same strange unknowable element, something chaotic and rude.

Who is that young man? I asked Helen, when she came over to borrow a cigarette, leaning back.

Beckett? she said, raising her eyebrows. Bit young for you, no?

She told me he wanted to be a poet. He'd written a little chapbook on Proust that quite a lot of people liked. For now, he worked for Joyce as a kind of secretary. Then she lowered her voice. Lucia had been mad for him, she whispered. But he'd broken her heart.

I kept staring at him. I noticed the way he held his body stiffly, apart from the others; and how he never really looked at anyone. He often appeared to be pondering a complicated question that he would probably never tell you about. His clothes were awful, French and too tight. He owned a single blue dinner jacket I'd eventually learn he was unaccountably attached to.

How nice it would be to be beside a man who rarely spoke, I thought. All the men I'd been with—Laurence, John, even Humphrey, whom I'd been sleeping with of late, who'd been giving advice about the gallery—all these men spent most of their time taking the attention, talking relentlessly. I would run to the garden and read Tolstoy just to hear my own voice.

Bold as I was, I didn't have the nerve to reach over, to introduce myself, to even say hello. But I kept staring at him, as a kind of dare, Will you look my way? I'm sure I had a slight, devilish smile on my face, and someone watching me might think, well she's trying to collect him, the way she collects sculptures that are odd or crooked.

WHEN THE MEAL ENDED, we went to Helen's apartment on the Rue Scheffer. It was very bourgeois, with a grand piano,

a tray of tiny cakes appearing suddenly like stowaways on the
sideboard; and Giorgio got up to sing. Beckett was there too,
and I thought he was looking at me at last. Only when I
started gathering my things did I realize he must have been.
He cornered me in the cloakroom, when I stood by a stack of
furs, finding my own. His voice was so musical and soft. It
didn't seem to belong on him. Behind us, Giorgio was still
singing, and the rest of the room joining in, and this chorus
of belonging, of gaiety, felt apart from us, in a way that
brought us closer without having to speak at all.

We were alone in the silence, and I sensed I should not
speak. I simply looked into his eyes and smiled, with a slight
pursed lip, as if to say, *I knew you would come my way.*

He smiled back, as if he'd always known too. Then nervously, though there was no need to be nervous, when I was
clearly intrigued, he said, May I walk you home?

BACK AT THE CRILLON, I invited him up to my room for a
digestif. I had an apple brandy I was fond of, a deep golden
brown; you served it with a kind of large glass eyedropper. I
found myself imagining the work it might do on this lanky
man, with his stiff gait; how it might loosen him. It had been
hard to drink properly with Laurence and John. Because they
both drank so much themselves, I felt I had to hold myself
back. But now I was coming back to its charms: the loose, sly
collapse; the fire in my throat.

In my regal suite, Beckett barely knew what to do with his
body. I gestured at the stern white couch: silk-upholstered,
unyielding. Sit down, I said, turning my back on him to fix

our brandies. And when I turned back again, I saw that he'd lain down. Stretched his body across the whole thing. It made me laugh: his feet jutting over the edge. That ridiculous blue jacket. He looked so improbable.

Then he said, Please rest here with me.

I hadn't been expecting this: his open desire, or the way he expressed it. But I liked being surprised. We ended up in bed and remained there until evening the following day.

The only time he left was in the early afternoon, to fetch us a bottle of champagne. He wasn't a man of decisive action, except when it came to bringing champagne to bed. That was one of his specialties.

The only reason we didn't stay in bed for days, in fact, was that I had a dinner scheduled with Arp. I couldn't postpone because there was no way to reach him. He didn't possess a telephone. I invited Beckett to join us, but he shook his head quickly. He almost seemed pained by the idea. He left my room rather abruptly, saying only, "It was nice while it lasted."

I hadn't been expecting this either. His curtness. Almost cruelty. Those were his exact words. Who could forget them? They stung, but in time, as I got to know him better, it came to seem entirely in character. He always had a fatalistic way of seeing things.

In the moment, I told myself that his departure was a gift. Or at least, a test. I had my work, now. My gallery. I had myself to fall back on.

Arp was expecting me at eight. It seemed fitting that I had left a man in bed to meet an artist. This was my work. I smoothed my hair and chose a dress.

———

JUST SIX WEEKS EARLIER, I'd signed a lease in London for a space on Cork Street, right in the heart of Piccadilly. It had once been a pawnshop. The first time we visited, we left with dust on our shoulders. We were calling the gallery Guggenheim Jeune.

It was Wyn's idea. I wouldn't have had the nerve.

Wyn Henderson was my secret weapon. She was big-boned, the mother of two teenage sons. She was rather like a bull, a good-natured bull, with the manner of someone who had spent years bossing about her boys. I didn't know where the father was. When you met her sons, they were tremendously polite, without the insolence, the rolling of the eyes, the cocked hip and constant sneer, of most boys their age. She wore plain, beige suits of a coarse fabric. I just picked this out when I went to get groceries at Marks & Spencer, she told me. Everything went like clockwork with Wyn. I was always sleeping in or forgetting appointments, and often I'd have to force myself out of a kind of fog that I'd been living with the last few years, when, as the maid put it, *all those things happened to me.* Wyn wouldn't tolerate my disarray, and I knew, if the gallery were to have any chance, it would benefit from the fact that I was a little terrified of her.

No nonsense. Chop-chop. Move along. It took Wyn less than a day to find the space on Cork Street, and she bargained the landlord down to an absurdly low rent. To pay this, I would need more than what was left in the trust I had been living on and giving away since I was twenty-one. There was very little left. *You must stop giving your money to lesbians and anarchists,* my mother said. *You must marry a man with property. After all you girls have put me through, I'm likely to leave my trust to the Warwick orphanage.*

But she had not. Now her trust would make it possible: the gallery I'd never told her about. I'd vowed not to tell her until the gallery became public, I couldn't bear her fury, and then she died before it did. I couldn't bear that either. Even near the end of her illness, doctors kept it from her as though she shouldn't know of her own disease. When it spread to her lungs, they deigned to show her an X-ray in which her lung was a white mass. It looked like a full moon.

When I signed an eighteen-month lease, Wyn and I drank sherry at a pub with tigers' heads. The lease began on January 1. "That's rather soon, isn't it?" I said. "When should we have our first exhibit?"

"Already scheduled for January 24," she told me, and rubbed her hair, which was very red and matched the roses on her dress from Marks & Spencer.

"That's barely a month away," I said.

"You better get to work, then," she said, in such a cheerful way that I was tempted to roll up my sleeves right then and there.

When I worried about the gallery, and I often worried about the gallery, I tried to summon my father. What were his tools? He knew very little about engineering, and yet he'd been bold enough to attempt a feat of levitation: those impossible elevators straight into the sky. Perhaps he'd carried blueprints, a scroll tucked under his arm, as he walked up step after step, to meet with Thomas Edison. Half the city thought the tower was an eyesore; the other half a miracle. This art was like that, too. But there were no blueprints for art; there were no instructions for propulsion, for carrying the correct amount of electrical energy.

Over sherry with Wyn, I forced a confidence I didn't have. "I'll go to Paris and talk to Brancusi," I said, as though I did this sort of thing all the time. "Marcel will give me an introduction. Brancusi's sculptures are magnificent. He's quite revered in Europe, but no one in London has heard of him."

"*I* haven't heard of him," Wyn said. "As I told you when you interviewed me, the only living artists I know are Dalí and Picasso."

"They're both supposed to be egomaniacs," I said. "Marcel told me they're both devious bastards."

Wyn didn't believe in gossip; I could see her wince. "My point," she said, "is that the gallery must not just hang work on the walls. We must be a place for discovery. If we get to work, and take this very seriously, then on January 24, all of London will know Brancusi."

"I don't know about all that," I said, laughing.

"I've put together a list of journalists," she said, rearranging the cherries on her mousse. "Did you know there are seventy-four arts reporters in London? I intend to personally call each one of them. I suppose we can emphasize the novelty element, the first woman in London to open a gallery for modern art et cetera, and then, of course, there will be a certain *frisson* among the society rags, *Tatler* and so on, because of the name."

Wyn had suggested the name the first time we walked away from the empty space, which still needed a bit of work. When I'd tried to open the window, flakes of paint had fallen into my hands. "Guggenheim Jeune," she said, "like Bernheim-Jeune, on Rue Laffitte. It's not so *jeune* anymore, but they were the first to show Vincent Van Gogh. It's still very chic. It has a nice, smooth sound to it, doesn't it? Guggenheim Jeune. And you are young, compared to all these old rotting-teeth gentlemen with their hunting parties and Impressionists."

"Really, Wyn. You have no idea. When people hear the name Guggenheim, they think of banking and mustaches and burnished mahogany."

"Well, they won't anymore," she said derisively. *They won't anymore.*

We were standing on Cork Street, waiting for a tailor's truck to move away from the curb. There was rain on the streets and a fog lifting over the Thames. A small jolt went through me: I realized then that I'd wanted revenge on the Guggenheim Brothers since I was fourteen. They'd regarded us with such condescension and contempt after my father's death—after his squandered fortune, our fall from grace. It made me want to dig a nail into my own skin, just remembering those days, all my cousins speaking to us in tones of strained sympathy.

"Will you come out?" my cousin Eleanor asked me once, as if she were on a charity assignment. "If I were you, I wouldn't want the fuss of being a debutante. It's really terribly dull, but if you want the party, I will ask my father if I can loan you my dress."

"I'm going to have a flock of birds hidden in the ceiling," I said, "and when they release them, they'll have died from the lack of air. It will be wonderful, a sea of dead birds descending on you and your sisters. You'll be covered in black feathers."

It was a lovely thing, seeing the look on her face when I said that.

By this time, I was sixteen and I had taken to calling myself Raskolnikov after the killer in *Crime and Punishment*. Eleanor did not loan me her dress.

Revenge, I thought. It was a tawdry word and not wholly accurate.

What was it I wanted? Honor, a throne, a triumph. When people heard the name Guggenheim, I did not want them to think of Solomon, with his Park Avenue collection of Old Masters, or Simon in his senator's office, standing next to the president. Perhaps they might think of me, an almost-young woman in an entirely dark dress, my hands on a sculpture that wasn't winged or feathered but still somehow looked like a bird in flight.

AFTER THAT FIRST NIGHT with Sam, I wasn't sure I would ever see him again. I certainly wasn't expecting to bump into him while crossing the street in Montparnasse. But when it happened, it didn't surprise me: his lanky silhouette against the fierce dusk sunlight, his dry smile, as if he'd been expecting this. As if I'd simply answered his call. His body was too long everywhere it went. Even when he was standing, he was somehow draped across a couch. And that blue jacket, again. Did he not have another?

He kissed me savagely, without hesitation, as if he wanted to taste something deep in my mouth. We could hear the hooting of women above us, leaning from their iron balconies; bringing in their laundry and smoking in the twilight. We gave them a show.

FOR THE NEXT TWO weeks, we were inseparable. It was our happiest time. If I only got to live two weeks, plucked from my whole life, it would be those two. We stayed at Mary Reynolds's place on Rue Hallé, a nest like a giftbox, papered with maps, and a little garden tucked in back. We practically sealed ourselves in that apartment. We didn't leave our borrowed bedroom for days at a time.

Mary was in the hospital, and she'd told me her flat was mine if I wanted it. And I was restless at the Crillon. It was too much part of my past. So I said yes, Mary, I would love that. Looking back, I think of all the things I did not ask her, like *What do you need? What can I do?* But in those years, I always felt that I had already done so much. And what had it ever gotten me? Djuna calling me selfish. Mina saying I'd degraded her work forever.

Sam was different from them from the very start: less focused on what I could give him; more curious about my own pursuits. That first evening on Rue Hallé we stayed in bed for hours, after we fucked; talking about his work and mine. When I told him about the gallery, he grinned. It was the most visible weather I'd ever seen pass across his face. He asked me what I liked about Surrealism, and I told him that I appreciated how brash it was. How it never needed to explain itself. Its arrogant disorder. The art I trusted most, these days, wasn't trying to please you. It didn't need to be what you expected.

He nodded at all this, listening hard. Taking me seriously. After I stopped speaking, it was a long time before he spoke. That was often the case.

Finally he said, It's no small thing, when you find yourself genuinely surprised by anything. I don't think it happens very often.

He was tall, austere, slender. But he had an odd beauty, coiled and alert. He made me think of trestles or branches, objects slender and dangerous. His body was chiseled, which was not surprising once I remembered he had been a boxer in his youth, but it did seem surprising considering he seemed to lie in bed all day and drink all night.

Mary's place on Rue Hallé—number 14, wedged against the train tracks—was deep in Montparnasse, so far from the Paris I'd known as a girl, writing carefully scripted notes about my days at the Louvre, that I would have thought it another country entirely. The flat was a piece of art in its own right. It was Mary's greatest collaboration with Marcel: old maps covering the walls from ceiling to floor, curtains made of strings hung close together, a globe lit from the inside. Her earrings hung from little nails on one wall—beaten silver bangles that caught the sunlight, chunky wooden talismans, every beauty twinned—and for the rest of my life, as I collected my own, some part of me was always comparing my collection to hers; how it caught your eye from all directions. And then her garden, lush and wild as a jungle—throbbing with its vegetal pulse, while everything inside was so carefully constructed. I'd always known her place full of company—not just Marcel and Man Ray but Breton, Djuna, Cocteau, Joyce himself—but when Sam and I stayed there, we didn't have to share it with anyone. It was our own little world.

Not ten minutes' walk away from us—on the other side of the cemetery, near Port Royal—Sam rented a little room at the Hôtel Liberia. But he didn't set foot inside it for those two winter weeks. It made me feel a certain tenderness for him, how he described that room: stains on the walls, damp circles the color of rust; the largest shaped like an ovary. A cot, a desk. Nothing that wasn't brown or white. Only a pair of lovers upstairs, always breaking his quiet.

He was a man who loved silence, that much was already clear. He had arranged his whole life so he would not have the noise of children, of church, of wife. For his quiet, dingy room, he paid twenty francs a week. He made his payments dutifully to the *patronne,* though he could barely afford them on the small amount he got from Joyce and the allowance his mother sent him from Ireland every month. He was thirty-two but seemed, in many ways, like a boy.

Tell me about your days, I asked him.

I keep to myself, he said quickly. And that was it. Nothing else.

So I tried another tack. I said, Tell me about Proust. Then he spoke for hours.

He shared his ideas about the writing—the way attention gets paralyzed by the dull devotions of routine, something about grave sheets as swaddling clothes—but it seemed he was mostly just talking about life. Tragedy isn't about justice, he said. Tragedy is about the sin of having been born.

I sensed this was a man who might understand when I told him, *We were cursed*. But I hadn't told him about all that yet.

All of life was habit, he continued. Habit was just a daily compromise brokered between an individual and his environment. We are locked in certain adaptations until we transition into other adaptations, and these moments of transition are dangerous, vulnerable, fertile; the times when we are most alive. When boredom becomes suffering. Which wasn't a trade everyone would make, he said, but was just fine by him.

Habit is the ballast that chains the dog to his vomit, Sam said. Then his eyes flickered with disgust. He said, I've been trying not to use so many metaphors.

And what about this? I gestured toward our rumpled sheets. Is this a break from your typical routine?

I can assure you, he smiled, I am neither bored nor suffering.

We lay in bed, smoking and drinking champagne straight from the bottle, eating little éclairs that left streaks of cream across the sheets. The sight of those hardened streaks made me giggle, remembering my mother with her Lysol. *I'm too prim to be bohemian,* I'd told her then. Perhaps I'd finally overcome it.

CHAPTER 16

Bird in Space

1938

ON NEW YEAR'S DAY, I WROTE TO EMILY, "I AM IN PARIS working hard for my gallery and fucking." During the fall, all my affairs had been less about needing men and more about enjoying them. I anticipated her skepticism; she always thought I turned too much of myself toward men. So I assured her I wasn't making a fool of myself. "I find men really stimulating but now, thank God I have my own strengths & inner self to fall back on."

Of course, I did not realize then, or had not admitted to myself, that I'd just met a man who would change me forever.

Sam and I were strangely, inexplicably honest with each other from the very start. One day in bed, he told me he found it a bit humiliating, his job with Joyce. Taking dictation was the best of it, really. Odd jobs. Errands. But it was the only way he could stay in Paris. He needed the money. So he translated, and he dutifully recorded the older man's paragraphs. In return, he was given a humiliating sum, a suit, some ties. He had only one suit of his own, so he should have worn these hand-me-downs, but he couldn't, for some reason. Perhaps pride; or they were simply too large. People often looked at him, confused, for his face was so elegant and haughty, so handsome, but his single blue suit was so odd and cheap.

One time with Joyce and the other assistants, he told me, he got so drunk that they left him in Versailles. He woke in the gardens, hallucinating, his head ringing like a gunshot. How did I end up here? he thought, and there were stains from that evening, still on his suit. He could never quite rub them off.

And yet, he told me, the job was worth it. He loved Paris: the golden stone, the quiet Seine. It could change in any moment, he told me. The most hopeful thing I ever heard him say.

He said Paris was like getting out of jail in the spring. He offered this image despite his desire to stop seeing the world as a poet. And yet he couldn't shake his metaphors.

He'd imagined so much, before we met. But never a woman like me, in a silk dress and furs, with the fortune of a queen.

Sometimes, I confessed to him, I didn't always trust what I loved.

Embrace the art of right now, he said. As if it were a living thing.

"Except when it takes me out of bed?"

He nodded solemnly. "Except when it takes you out of bed."

Even though it was January, Paris felt more like a spring-time jailbreak than it ever had before. In his company, the city quivered with sudden moments of communion: the bright red bursts of window pot geraniums, tended with care; or the laundry hanging from clotheslines, strangely tender and intimate, the socks of strangers. We saw a tree growing bushy and wild from the courtyard of an elegant pink building; and I remarked upon the pleasing contrast: the proper house, the wild garden. "This is what a painting does," I told him. "A good one, anyway. Or a love affair. It lets some wild thing grow from a crack in its composure."

He listened closely, getting his faraway look. Then finally he shook his head. "Chaos comes with its own dull routines," he said. But I liked that he wrestled with the things I said, rather than flattering me with agreement or dismissing me with condescension. Our minds had something to say to each other. I hadn't felt this way with anyone since John. Often not even with him.

On one of our afternoon walks, we saw a beautiful woman in a bathrobe, leaning from a third-floor balcony, smoking, her children playing behind her. She paid them no mind. Her minor negligence—a cigarette, a daydream—threw mine into sharper relief: my children were so far away. But her beauty was interesting to me, part of the landscape, rather than threatening, something that turned me back toward myself, ashamed.

All the time I'd spent in Paris, the beauty of Parisian women had always felt like an affront. It felt like such an open wound, badly hidden behind all my wealth, that an earnest surgeon in Cleveland, paid good money mined from the bowels of the earth, could not give me even a crude approximation of the beauty these women came by naturally and carried easily.

With Sam, though, my face didn't feel like the humiliation it always had. "I love your nose," he said. "I wouldn't want to get rid of a single square meter of it."

I felt his affection. But still, there was a sting.

Sometimes I tried to speak with him about my children, but Sam always found ways to take our conversations somewhere else. He had built a life pointed away from such caregiving. Once I mentioned Pegeen's painting—she had just painted something extraordinary the year before, I told him; the first thing where I could really see the emergence of a particular style. "She called it *Girls in the Arches,*" I told him almost shyly, coaxing him to take an interest, proud that she had been so decisive with her title, so sure of it. Six girls with their hands poised stiffly in front of them, standing in front of arches, yes, but also hovering in other doorways: between innocence and sexuality, childhood and fertility. One, but only one, with a dark fleck on her cheek that could be mistaken for a tear.

"You said she's in Switzerland?" he said, but by the time I nodded yes, he'd already turned away from me, squinting, as if he were gazing all the way toward the Alps.

Just when I'd given up on him saying anything, he started to tell me a story. It did not seem to have anything to do with what I'd just said.

On Christmas, he told me, the day before we met, he'd watched *Modern Times* alone in the theater. He laughed at the pratfalls. He adored Chaplin's grace. But without quite realizing why, he continued, he found himself near tears. What is it, why am I crying? he'd wondered. And then he realized: it was Lucia. The girl with the scar on her chin. The way she'd dress up like Chaplin at parties, how he'd watch her move about the room, in her baggy pants and father's suit jacket, tripping and miming, her short dark hair bobbed. That was what brought him to tears, he explained: thinking of her stilled, in a straitjacket, in Geneva, knowing if he'd loved her more, she would still be in Paris, lively and dancing.

It moved me to hear him describe such naked feeling. It wasn't something he often did.

"Sometimes boredom gives way to suffering," I offered. Trying to show him I'd been listening, that I remembered— that I understood something about the price one might pay for moments of great feeling; that they might be worth it, anyway.

"No," he said sharply. "That's not what I'm trying to say at all."

A WEEK INTO OUR seclusion in Mary's apartment, I almost ruined things by answering the telephone. Sam shot me a glare when he saw me pick up the receiver, but it was too late.

"Have you seen Sam?" Helen's voice was on the other end, panicked.

I whispered to Sam, "It's Helen."

He rolled his eyes and put his hat over his head.

Helen raised her voice. "I know you left with him the other night. James is terrified. You know he is often suicidal. Colm had to drag him out of the Seine."

"I think you're overreacting. He doesn't seem to move anywhere. He's terribly lethargic."

"He's supposed to be at work. He does have a job."

"Maybe he'd prefer to fuck me."

"Oh, Peggy, you're too much."

"You're not the only one who likes younger men."

"James is going to be heartbroken if you steal his favorite assistant. Are you going to bring him on your yacht? Perhaps you're going to bring him to Saint-Tropez?"

"It is nice this time of year."

"You're just trying to start a scandal."

"What, get more publicity for my gallery if I start running around with James Joyce's protégé?"

"Well, I think it's a terrible idea. Beckett likes to break hearts. Everyone knows that."

"Oh, does he like to break hearts?" I repeated her words so he could hear them.

Sam threw his hat at me and smirked. I dropped a bouquet of dahlias so that Helen would hear the smash, then told her that I had to clean up a bunch of dripping flowers. I would call her back later.

"Please tell Sam to come back to work. We have thirty pages to dictate. They are wonderful scenes. Joyce prefers Sam to anyone else."

"I'll tell him," I said, but my voice promised nothing.

When I set the phone down, Sam looked truly disappointed. He said, "Thanks for spilling the secret. I wanted to hole up here and disappear with you."

"Is that what you do with all women? It's much easier, I suppose."

"As you saw at the party, I'm not very good in crowds."

"Oh, but I love crowds! Why don't you join me for dinner tonight? Arp is coming in again from Meudon. We're going

to talk about the sculpture show I want to put him in this
year. Though I think most people will find his work too bizarre."

"Oh?" Sam said. But his voice had a sharpness. He didn't
like that I was leaving.

I tried to win him back by telling him a funny thing Arp
had told me. When I'd asked him how he knew he was finished with a piece, he said simply, "I work until enough of
my life has flowed into its body."

Sam and I giggled at that. You couldn't always take artists
too *seriously*. Even they didn't like that. But still, Sam shook
his head. "I'll just stay here and read."

I grinned. I'd been preparing for this moment. "In that
case, I have a book you might like. It's about a man who stays
in bed all day and tries to write, but only reads."

Sam smiled back. He was game for this joke. I found *Oblomov* and handed it to him. It was affectionate, my teasing,
but I knew there was also some part of me that wanted to dig
at him. It was the old frustration I'd had with John: watching
a genius not making use of his talents. I hated that my father
died before he could fully make use of his.

But I said none of this. Not sure I realized it myself. Instead, I said, "You can read this all night. It's a very long book.
And I'll bring you back some dinner."

He looked at me, bewildered and pleased. Not only was I
letting him hide from Joyce, I was making plans for us, as if
we had already agreed to a strange form of relationship. He
arranged his long limbs on our bed. Mary's bed. But already
it felt like ours.

He said, "I'll just be waiting for you right here."

"You are a strange creature," I said.

"You don't seem too put off by it."

"I've known a lot of strange men. I'm used to your kind."

The next thing I knew, he had lifted me up with his strong arms, set the book and hat on the floor, and was lifting his body over mine. "I'll do this all afternoon," he said, grinning.

Eventually, of course, I had to go meet Arp. But by then my hair was tousled, my dress was off, and Beckett's body in that borrowed bed seemed more important than all the un-framed Surrealist work in Paris.

IT WAS FUNNY, JUST when I'd finally found the feeling of communion I'd been craving for so long, I also had a life that was big enough to take me away from it. By the end of those two weeks, I started peeling myself out of bed, headed to Cocteau's opium den on the Rue de Cambon. "I do have work to do," I told him. "I'm terrified the gallery will be a flop."

"It won't be," he said. Almost sternly, as if I'd been silly to worry. And then, more gently, "I hope you know that."

His voice was earnest then, and full of a sense of possibil-ity it almost never carried. It moved me that he felt that. But there was also a bitterness in his voice, whenever I left. "I'd rather you just stayed in bed," he said. Though I would learn, over the months that followed, how much he liked to come and go.

When he said, *I'd rather you just stayed,* I began to wonder if this was about wanting *me* or about the ways my departures reminded him of the work he was not doing.

"Aren't you writing the perfect novel?" I asked him once.

"Not when Joyce has me buying stamps all day."

"Why don't you quit? He's terribly degrading."

"And do what? I'm nothing but a drunk poet."

"You know you're much more than that, and he knows it, too. Has he read any of your work?"

A flicker of humiliation crossed his face. I wondered if I was the first person to point out how Joyce treated him. He already saw it himself. But this was different from having another person recognize it.

To change the subject, I said, "I think you should meet Cocteau."

I tried to conjure the scene for him, cinematically: Cocteau's hotel room full of opium smoke, the sweet smell. The way he stared at his own reflection constantly. He was so beautiful, you could hardly blame him.

Sam shook his head again, more emphatically. "I've met enough opium fiends," he said. "Don't need to meet one more."

"But Sam, just *look.*" I went to my desk and brought out a whimsical sketch of a horse. "Isn't it marvelous the way the horse seems like it's half fabric, half flesh?"

I saw something flicker in his face: a wry, charmed look. His eyes moved over the sketch, absorbing it, but then, after a moment, his gaze moved back to my breasts. He put his hand on my uncovered nipples. I pulled away from him, electrified, and somehow even more electrified at the thought of leaving him—just for a few hours, and then returning to him once I had done my work. Having a life that did not revolve around

a man; that could in fact displace him, even when I wanted
him desperately; this was a novel drug.

"You are incredibly tempting," I told him. "But I need to
work."

A FEW MONTHS EARLIER, two days after I signed the lease for
the gallery, Wyn showed up at my flat in Bloomsbury with a
box of small ivory cards. The words *Guggenheim Jeune* were in
lower case, a pale brown instead of the expected navy blue.
The address and telephone number were printed off center
below. The effect was arresting. The card looked like an elegant mistake. There was something slightly off in the typography, but it was so subtle that you could not identify what
caused it to look irregular. "They're perfect," I said.

This was November. I'd moved in a few months before,
from our rambling Yew Tree Cottage in the countryside. I
had not yet unpacked. I had lain around for weeks, reading
the memoirs of Tolstoy's wife and settling Pegeen at a boarding school near Wimbledon. The boxes were something I did
not want to open, afraid to find John in them. It gave me a
headache to think about setting up another home. But now,
with Wyn beside me, I felt suddenly energetic. The rows of
boxes mortified me. I lit a cigarette and sat on a trunk. "This
one is full of John's books," I told Wyn. "I can't bear to open
it."

"Don't worry about unpacking now," she said. She
opened a window and waved out the smoke. "I think the
cards worked out quite well. They tried to shove some

swanky Art Deco designs on me, as if I don't know quite a
bit about typography. I ended up making this type myself. It
doesn't exist, letters this tilted and modest. I cut up some old
rubber stamps. Took me about ten hours."

"Is it crooked on purpose?" I said, worried for a moment
that the style was merely an error.

"Of course it is," she said. "An eighth of an inch between
some letters, but a ninth between the letters in your name."
She looked very pleased with herself. I wished I could borrow some of her certainty.

"You're really wonderful," I said. "I don't know what I'd
do without you."

She climbed up onto a box and fussed around in the cupboards until she found some tea. We drank tea and talked
about the space and where we would put our desks. The light
on the second floor was very beautiful, and I told her we
should have all the openings early so we could avoid the glare
of bulbs. The walls were dented, and we agreed we should
patch them up, but not paint them yet. Painting was too
costly, and we'd have artwork to cover the more faded patches.

"I really don't want it to be daunting," I said. "I can't stand
when you go to a gallery and it feels like you have to be rever-
ent. I don't mind if it's a bit grimy and comfortable, more like
a studio."

This idea only came to me as I said it aloud, thinking of
Solomon in his stuffy penthouse, with the names Rembrandt
and Renoir whispered like they were sanctified popes of some
sort. I thought, with a sudden thrill, that he would be appalled by what I dreamed of; he would see it as disreputable,
too rough-and-tumble, one step above a bordello.

Wyn had started drawing some sketches of where we could place the artist's statement when I received a phone call. Even now I can't remember who it was that told me the news. A lawyer, a doctor—perhaps Isaac or Henry or one of my cousins. Because of the rainstorm, there was quite a lot of static on the line. I paled and motioned for Wyn to leave the room. *When?* I asked. Whoever it was, he told me that my mother had died earlier in the New York evening. Though she had been ill with these lightning bolts of cancer in her lungs, it was difficult to think of my mother as anything other than an indefatigable sentry. She'd grown kinder in her last years, able to be around me and my children without that scathing scrutiny.

For years, since I left New York at twenty-one, she'd sent me society pages from *The New York Times,* underlining the marriages of my friends and cousins. *Look at this,* she'd write in the margins, as though she could correct my disinterest. She sent me glossy pages from *Harper's Bazaar* with my old best friend Fay Lewisohn dressed in the latest Molyneux gown. Under a headline, THE JEWESS, they discussed her annual ball for the New York Opera. The theme, Fay revealed, would be carnival. *Won't this be fun,* my mother had written on her ivory note card.

But in the last few months of her life, she sent me only photographs of herself in the Both respirator. She looked as if she were encased in a rocket. Her head protruded out of an iron vessel; portals on the sides allowed nurses to reach in and check her heartbeat. Air was pumped into her lungs through a ventilator. Later, she told me it was like lying in a clattering tomb. *Will you visit me?* she asked, her voice suddenly sweet and girlish. *You're really the only daughter I have left.*

I told her I would come during the Christmas holidays, once I'd picked up Pegeen from school and taken her to her father's. Though I'd avoided New York for years and years, I knew I should be with her. I could hear the life leaving her every time we spoke. I could imagine her in her apartment at the Plaza, lying on her high bed, under stiff, uncreased sheets, beside the Lenbach portrait of Benita, Hazel, and me when we were little girls: our ruffled socks and boater hats. "You should take that down," I'd told her. "It must upset you."

"Don't tell me what to do!" she'd snapped back.

The last time she telephoned me, I told her that I'd booked my tickets and would be there very soon, on Christmas Day. Very soon, I said. The nurse must have given her morphine. *I saw the clouds today,* she said, *the clouds above Central Park beckoned me.* I loved her then, when she spoke as if in a dream. And perhaps it was true. Perhaps when you were dying, the ordinary world turned spectral.

She died in November, before my Christmas visit. She didn't suffer at all, the voice said. Who am I speaking to? I wanted to ask then. Have you no idea? *She didn't suffer at all.* But I only said flatly, "I appreciate the information. I imagine there will be reporters swarming about. I'd appreciate if you didn't tell them the whereabouts of Hazel."

She didn't suffer at all.

Reporters were often trying to find Hazel. We gave vague answers, a sanatorium on Park Avenue. But still they pursued her, four years after the scandal. Even on this quiet street in Bloomsbury, I occasionally turned to see a young man in a trench coat, jostling a recorder and a microphone. *Will your sister talk to the police? Why won't your sister meet with detectives?*

The man said something about wills and trusts and the funeral at such-and-such synagogue, but I was no longer listening.

Once I hung up the phone, I began to cry. If Benita were here, I could hold her, I thought. We could talk about the way our mother always drew up lists with the names of who she would invite to her teas. Nothing made her happier. Mrs. Gladys Straus, Mrs. Fanny Loeb, Mrs. Adele Lewisohn. Then she'd take her pencil and erase some of the names she herself had written, writing in the margin: N.G. *No good.*

Wyn came in when she heard me crying. "The call was from New York. About my mother." I could hardly believe it, still. "I was hoping to visit her, but she died before I could get there." When I did go back to New York, to take care of certain arrangements, I arranged to come back early. I was an orphan there; it held nothing but the past.

Wyn looked rather startled when I told her about my mother's death; it must have been awkward to see me, the *patronne,* red-eyed and shaking. I'd drawn a deep line on the table with a butter knife while I was on the telephone, and now I rose, found a sponge in the sink and began the futile effort of trying to wash away an indentation in the wood. I expected Wyn would excuse herself, mutter something sympathetic, and dash away. But she sat down. She took out some of the cards from a box, spread them near my hands like a fan. Guggenheim Jeune, Guggenheim Jeune. She picked one up like a magician choosing a card. "Take this one," she said. "You must bring it along when you visit Brancusi."

———

BUT BRANCUSI WAS AWAY traveling, and so I turned to Cocteau: his dream visions emerging like curling vapors in his
smoky den. Sketches and designs for his play, *Les Chevaliers de
la Table Ronde:* medieval knights and a burnt tree in a stone
tower; illustrated bedsheets that got me in trouble with a
British customs officer. He didn't like the pubic hair.

Of course, I was interested in who was attending the pre-
miere and who was not. Wyn's invitation went all over London, and I was stunned by the number of acceptances I
received. Wyn sent me letters at 14 rue Hallé, almost daily,
updating me about numbers. In my mind I calculated how I
could afford wine and flowers for a crowd of two hundred. I
would buy a nice dress and perhaps a new pair of earrings. I'd
seen a dashing pair in an atelier on the Rive Gauche . . . inter-
locking brass rings, quite dramatic. Almost too much. Almost.

That day the skies were gray, and one letter slipped from
the pile onto the wet concrete pavement; it was soggy when
I picked it up and carried it inside. It was not from Wyn; my
name was written in a different script.

In Mary's bedroom, Sam was snoring. His scent was almost putrid. I'd tried to buy him tailored tweed, but he insisted on wearing that ghastly blue coat he'd bought from an
endearing salesman in Morocco. For some reason, it was his
only notion of propriety. He said the color reminded him of
Marrakech.

When I read the letter, I nearly gasped. It was from Hilla
Rebay, the Baroness, who kept her thumb on my uncle Solomon's museum back in New York and was also, it was common knowledge, his mistress. She was replying to my offer to
sell them a Kandinsky; a favorite of my uncle's and someone

Duchamp had been urging me toward. He would be our second show.

The Baroness wanted to let me know that they did not want to buy the piece, but she also wanted me to know that I was cheapening the family name. "The name of Guggenheim," she wrote, "became known for great art, and it is very poor taste indeed to make use of it, of our work and fame, to cheapen it to a profit."

To make use of their name? As if it were not mine as well.

I rushed into the bedroom, slamming the door behind me in hopes that the noise might wake up Sam. He kept sleeping, still as a stone. I shook him awake.

"Sam," I hissed, "listen to this." And read it to him.

He listened, groggy at first, then intrigued.

"Of course it's nonsense," he said. "She's saying the opposite of what she means."

"How so?"

"She's not afraid that you are cheapening the family name, she's afraid that you are *making* the family name. That you will do their work better than they are doing it."

"My uncle always believed he was better than my father, but he never had any of my father's spark."

He nodded. Thinking. Not speaking.

So I kept talking. "In fact, my father makes me think of you. Or you make me think of him."

"Lucia used to say the same thing."

After a moment, I said, "She must have been madly in love with you." Resenting that he'd returned us to her.

"It was like she wanted someone to break her," he said, wincing at his own words. "I was quite cruel to her."

"How?"

"I was quite abrupt with her one day. I told her, I don't come here for you. I come here for your father. It was a terrible scene. Hilla said I had a black heart, and I often wonder if she's right."

A black heart seemed a bit excessive. Or perhaps it was just a pale excuse. He was trying to tell me what he wasn't willing to give me.

A FEW DAYS LATER, a letter arrived from Pegeen in Switzerland, mournful and full of longing. *Mother, I miss you and your friends, I have such fond memories of Hayford Hall. I miss Djuna and Emily and their wicked jokes. Do you remember when we went to the movies and I asked you how do you know who the bad people are?* When I read this first bit, I felt proud, for I had so few happy memories of my own childhood. I'd always felt a bit guilty at how we'd always kept the children out of the main hall at Hayford—but seeing *fond memories,* it seemed she had felt a part of things after all. Then I kept reading. She wrote: *I sometimes wonder if the bad people are closer to me than I've realized the whole time.* Was her father hurting her? Or else she was sending me a warning, or a signal. Had he somehow turned her against me? Or perhaps I'd done it myself.

After I read the letter, I felt a sense of dread I hadn't felt in years. Her tone was mostly childish, but there was a darkness in her voice that felt new. As if something had woken up inside of her—a new part of her that I did not know, although perhaps I had helped to create it. I sat there in the garden, waiting for Sam to come out. I wanted to read it to him, to ask him, What should I do? Should I invite her here?

I thought of her arriving like a blond wraith, with her accusing eyes, her beautiful golden hair, knock-kneed and ponylike, always saying something heartbreaking like *Could you have another child? I so want a sister.*

He was probably sleeping, as he often was. His habit bothered me then, more than it ever had before. If I ever asked him why he slept so much, he would say something obtuse and funny, like *I am not alive. I am still in the womb.* This was part of his issue with women, he claimed: it was easy for him to feel suffocated, because he had such vivid memories of being trapped inside his mother before birth.

Still, I found myself wanting to part the folds of his privacy. To push the boundaries of our cloistered life, in that borrowed flat. To see how much weight we could bear.

Finally, I went into the bedroom. He was not sleeping. He was scribbling something, but when he heard the door open, he pushed it away.

"Can I read this to you?" I asked but didn't wait for his answer. He seemed surprised by the mention of my daughter, though I had mentioned her many times. Every time he gave me that same look, as if I were ambushing him with some secret.

He couldn't understand why I was so worried by her letter. So she was unhappy in Switzerland. Perhaps she should come back. He didn't seem to care much one way or another. The way his eyes had sharpened into focus when I read the letter about my uncle's museum, this was the opposite. A blunted vacancy settled over his gaze. He'd been interested in that part of my life; this part didn't concern him. I saw him glancing in the direction of the piece of paper he'd been scribbling on. His questions were listless. Why was it so terrible for her to remember that she'd asked me about the bad people?

I tried to explain. Because she'd asked those questions and then everyone had died. Her little cousins falling seven stories to the pavement below. It was unthinkable. And what I could not say: Because perhaps I was one of the bad people, too. Just a mother who had left her over and over again. I was only vaguely aware then that I was putting everything else on hold. As if everyone could stay safe while I focused on arranging the beauty.

AFTER PEGEEN'S LETTER, I started seeing daughters everywhere. Walking to the boulangerie for a fresh baguette, I passed a jungle tucked into a courtyard between old stone buildings, feral with blackberry bushes behind a creaky iron gate, and saw a boy and girl swinging side by side, pushed by their mother.

Heading to the post office with a letter for Wyn, a set of specifications for the caterers, I passed a mother and her daughter sitting at a café table on the sidewalk, both with a certain toughness in their eyes. The mother had a cigarette in her fingers, a bottle of Coca-Cola on the table, a cane leaning against the wall behind her. The girl must have been fourteen or fifteen, not much older than Pegeen. They had an ease, nothing cloying or performed. They were not even talking.

But their bodies fit together easily. They had moved through this world in each other's company.

ON OUR LAST DAY in the borrowed bedroom, Sam and I spent hours wandering the cemetery. We did not know it then, that this would be our last afternoon in the sudden, stolen climate of those days, their lust and fever. The air smelled like moss and soil; the stones were beautifully mottled, lichen covering the stones in spots that reminded me of aging skin. Sam wasn't one for holding hands, but in the cemetery I often felt his cool dry palm in mine.

The more ornate tombs looked like confession booths, little rooms made of marble.

"I'd like one of *those*," I said. "I want people to visit my grave and confess all their worst secrets."

"You're a gossip," he teased. "It's another one of your collections."

I'd learned this was one of the best ways to get him out of bed: the prospect of being close to death. It was one of the few ways of spending time that genuinely compelled him. We both lived close to death, he and I. For him it was a question of temperament. For me it was a question of circumstance. So many people I loved had died.

In those days I was still in the habit of consulting fortune tellers; they gave me a sense of order. Each of their verdicts a kind of cabinet organizing all my loss. And sometimes I wondered if fate had gotten into the habit of sending people my way just after I'd lost someone it seemed impossible to live without. I met John on the anniversary of Benita's death. I met Beckett so soon after losing my mother. It wasn't a question of replacement, but balm. It seemed Emma was right. I kept on surviving.

LOOKING BACK, THAT AFTERNOON in the cemetery was the end of our innocence. We were burying something we did not know we were burying: the perfection of those early days. Our borrowed bedroom, a world apart.

That week he slept with someone else. A married woman he claimed meant nothing to him. "Making love without being *in* love is like taking coffee without brandy," he said. But he seemed to enjoy his coffee just fine. I didn't answer his calls for a week.

It was just as well. I had the opening on the twenty-fourth; I needed to get to London, and before that I went to see the Surrealist Exhibition at the Galerie Beaux-Arts, which was so sublime it almost made me forget my own sore heart. It wasn't like anything I'd ever seen: a decrepit taxicab in the courtyard off the Rue du Faubourg Saint-Honoré, with a stuffed crocodile in the driver's seat and a mannequin in back: leaves at her feet, snails across her body. Somehow rain was falling inside the car. Inside the gallery, the paintings were illuminated with flashlights, and the air smelled like coffee. There was a telephone shaped like a lobster; a feathered soup pot; a chair with human legs. In that room, among those creaturely objects, I had a sudden memory of Benita in her bourgeois parlor, letting out her gentle bark. Imagining that giving birth would connect her to a certain wildness inside. More strongly than ever, I got the sensation that I was walking into someone else's dream—or perhaps one of my own, before I'd even had it.

JUST BEFORE I LEFT for London, for the opening itself, I had a change of heart. I wanted to see Sam. It came to seem silly, holding a grudge. So he'd fucked someone else. So had I, plenty of times. What I felt for him—what happened when we were in a room together, talking, or walking the streets— it mattered more than those stupid lovers' games of coy punishment. He believed in the gallery; perhaps he could come with me to London, to see what I'd created. At least I wanted to say good-bye before I left, to get his blessing.

But then I couldn't reach him. He wasn't answering the phone. I couldn't find him anywhere. When I finally got hold of Nora, I couldn't believe what she told me. He'd been *stabbed*. At first, I was sure I hadn't heard her correctly. But there it was: a pimp had attacked them on the street, demanding francs. His awful, heavy overcoat, which I had always hated, saved his left lung and heart. Which sounded like another one of his metaphors but was only the simple truth.

AT THE HOSPITAL, I found Joyce wandering around, looking for Sam's room in the maze of corridors; half-blind and moving tentatively down the hallways. The smell of Lysol was overpowering. Somehow I knew intuitively where to go, as if Sam's body had a kind of heat, or scent, that I could follow. I held Joyce's elbow and guided him. We sat on either side of Sam, who was shocked and bemused; not so much by what had happened as by what a big deal it had become. Why all this fuss? He looked a bit pale.

At least you're not wearing that horrid blue coat, I said. For once.

He laughed, and it clearly hurt. I wouldn't say anything else that might amuse him. I didn't want him to speak too much.

I started thinking, wildly, that perhaps I would stay; let Wyn handle the opening. Perhaps I could persuade Marcel, who made a point of never attending openings, to attend this one.

But Sam would not hear of it. You have to go, he said. I sat beside him on the bed, holding one of his hands. He smiled that crooked smile. I insist you get out of this bed right away. For a moment, we were both back in our borrowed bedroom, in our old tug-of-war. *Please stay. I've got to go.* Now he was saying, Go.

OUR LOVE AFFAIR LASTED another year, in various seasons of flurry and heartache, swelling and waning like the phases of the moon. But we never had anything so pure as the happiness of those first weeks in Mary's flat. After I left for London, another woman nursed him back to health. Suzanne. He would eventually marry her. I don't think they fucked much, but she took good care of him. "Suzanne makes curtains," he once told Helen. "Peggy makes scenes."

But still, I could not give him up. I rented a room at the Hôtel Liberia so I could be closer to him; but he told me it was too much. So I resettled in an empty apartment that

Hazel still kept on the Île Saint-Louis. Barely furnished, vi-
brating with ghosts, but beautiful Parisian light. On a Sunday
morning I could lie in bed for hours, watching sunlight ripple
across the ceiling from the Seine. I had always wanted to live
beside a river.

Sam invited me to Joyce's fifty-sixth birthday party, and
we walked all over Paris looking for the perfect present—
a walking stick carved from blackthorn, and just the right
wine from Switzerland. What a joy that party was: the miniature model of Dublin in the living room, with a ribbon as
green as a shamrock snaking through. The Liffey! Joyce
danced a jig, and then it was time to leave.

That night Sam walked me back to the Île Saint-Louis, on
the bridge with the best view of Notre-Dame, and I could
feel the heat of his ambivalence coming off him like a fever,
figuring out whether he would come upstairs with me or not.

There we were, in such beauty: the sturdy river he loved
so much, its gentle splashing against the stone; the brass boat
rings on the stone walls, catching the moonlight. But he was
afraid of what he might be promising by crossing the water.
He never wanted to promise me anything. I told myself that
was all right with me. More than I wanted to be promised
anything, I wanted to be taken seriously.

In the end, he walked me to my doorway, but no further.

Meanwhile my gallery was doing well, and I was trying to
acquire a new piece almost every day. Brancusi used to invite
me to lunch in his studio and cook pork chops for me in his
smelting furnace. He always burned them and then apologized; but I knew he did it on purpose. It was how he preferred them. In his own way, he was a prince. I ended up

paying 4,000 French francs for his *Bird in Space*. Of everything I owned, I loved it most. It eliminated every unnecessary detail to make way for the pure sensation of upward flight.

ONCE SAM AND I stopped sleeping together, we started taking long drunken strolls late at night, crossing the Seine, then back again, and then across once more, seeing all of Paris: champagne straight from the bottle, in the plaza at the base of the Panthéon; gazing up at the towering beams of the Eiffel Tower, remembering my father's dreams of ferrying people straight into the sky. As a girl, it had barely bothered me that my father was gone, I just needed to know that he was doing something extraordinary. I felt the same way about Sam; trusted that his genius could excuse the inconstancy of his presence.

After I finally put on a show for his friend Van Velde, we celebrated for the weekend at Yew Tree Cottage. One afternoon on the beach, Sam took off his shirt, pants, belt, socks, shoes, everything, and walked naked into the frigid sea. Swam out, a dark dot on the horizon; then returned to shore, emerging from the waves, used his shirt as a towel, and never spoke a word about what he had just done. He needed to be able to do things like that, without explaining himself. I could never give him his privacy. I wanted too much from him. I had to take so many other lovers, just so I could remain in his life without getting my heart broken six times a month.

I knew he had a great intensity inside of him, and felt I was the one, perhaps the only one, capable of drawing it out. He felt differently. He insisted that a certain part of him was dead inside. His black heart, he called it. Like she had. Nothing but a stone.

We had beautiful times that year: a trip to Dijon, where we saw the tombs of the Burgundy dukes at the Musée des Beaux-Arts, and the small marble figures beneath each tomb: *Pleurants*. The mourners. Each one intricately carved into some expression of grief. Not a city of the dead, a city of those left behind. The place I'd always lived. It was always a pleasure to look at beautiful things with Sam. There was no mind whose company I enjoyed more than his. What I also remember from Dijon: trying to enter his hotel bed, how he pushed me away.

Oh oh oh stone. The tenderness I felt for him was supple, brutal. The weight of my unmet love had come to feel almost pleasurable to me, as if I were sharing a burden with him, by loving him too stubbornly, that normally he shared with no one.

Eventually it was a fortune teller who persuaded me that we were done. This was at Christmastime, nearly a year after we met. She said it was time to get married or at last say goodbye to this man.

So I did.

BUT BEFORE ALL THAT—that year of waxing and waning, leaving and returning—my gallery opened. It was the night of January 24. Bitterly cold, a bright moon. Strange lights glowing eerily across the sky, flickering crimson arches across the horizon; in certain parts of the city, it looked like the streets were on fire. The guards at Windsor Castle even sum-

moned the fire brigade. There was a certain magic. The opening was a triumph. They loved Cocteau; but even more, they
loved the *occasion* of it, the sense of a world being created.
And I had to admit, they loved me. I'd never even considered
this as a possibility. That I might be worth getting excited
about. I'd always thought that if the gallery succeeded, it
would have to succeed *despite* me. I kept the bedsheets out of
the gallery, as I'd promised the customs officer, but I hung
them in my office, pubic hair and all, and invited people back
to see them. It made me smile to imagine my mother, frantically scrubbing them with Lysol.

Everyone who came said I threw a great party. No denying it, they said. One journalist said I had an "attractively
jerky" way of talking. Who could have imagined, after all
these years: my flailing gesticulations, good for something at
last. It was the headline I'd written for myself all those years
ago, before my debutante ball. PEGGY GUGGENHEIM STARTLES
THE CROWD. Finally, I'd made the dead birds fall from the sky.

But nothing made me happier than a telegram wired from
Paris that night. It was a message of congratulations, signed
by *Oblomov.*

Epilogue

1958

PEOPLE SAY THAT VENICE IS BEST WHEN YOU ARE IN LOVE, but I prefer it alone. You end up falling in love with the city anyway; there's barely room for anyone else.

There's so much I have fallen in love with: The green algae growing on the stone steps of the palazzos. The crooked bricks. The gondoliers who sweat and smoke. The sweet filth in everything. The small bridges lit by lanterns at night. The bits of garbage bobbing in the smallest canals. The broken shutters, hanging at odd angles. The way the canals are not one shade of green but twenty, depending on the sun: Cloudy absinthe. Eye of peacock. Burnt lime. I've come to love the tinge of grime and disorder. The sense of something seething beneath all this beauty. The torture rooms behind the treasure at the Doge's Palace. Like my father told me at the museum, all those years ago, how he pointed at the chaos of a painting I adored and said, *This is life*. Then dropped a coin, *and this is death*. This city is both.

They call my home *palazzo non finito*, the unfinished palace, which means I'm free to do as I please. All their stuffy aristocratic regulations can't reach me here, in my home that will never be done, where I fall asleep to the sounds of lapping water and keep Marini's *Angel of the City* poised above my water gate, his erection pointed toward the sky.

Every April, I start sunbathing on the roof. That's how the city knows it's spring.

TWENTY YEARS AGO, as the Germans got closer and closer, all I could think about was collecting as much beauty as I could. *A painting every day,* I said, and once I'd said it, they all came knocking; I could have bought ten a day, twenty. Gala forgot how much she despised me long enough to sell me *Birth of Liquid Desires;* buying Léger's *Men in the City* for a thousand dollars on the day Hitler invaded Norway. Mary called me terrible, indifferent—saying I was doing nothing for the people and only cared about my artwork; that I would have plowed through a line of refugees, just to get my art to safety. In the resistance they called her "Gentle Mary," but she was not always gentle with me.

My collection. The only issue was finding somewhere to put it. There wasn't room in my flat on the Île Saint-Louis; and I gave up my place on the Place Vendôme after two weeks, once I'd torn out all that hideous rococo molding, because there was nowhere to keep the paintings safe underground if an air raid. The Louvre wouldn't store the work, and before long Nellie and I fled the city in my blue Talbot convertible, headed toward my children in the countryside; with the Germans nearby, lighting oil fires that blackened the air; Nellie's white coat dark with soot by the time we stopped for lunch in Fontainebleau. Eventually it was René who helped me get the paintings to America. *Ship them like dinner plates,* he said, and so we packed them up with linens and cookware and lamps, made sure my Jewish name was nowhere on the shipping crates; and sent them on a ship across the water.

The rest of us followed by air: me and the children and Laurence and witchy Kay, with her cruel sense of humor and her lover waiting for her in America, and Max, who was still years from breaking my heart. We all flew on a Clipper over the dark blue sea, drinking whiskey and eating cream of mushroom soup from bone china while the children were sick into their airbags. When we stopped for fuel in the Azores, I bought a sunhat the size of a small island; and everyone called me ridiculous; which I was and still am.

VENICE EMPTIES IN THE winter, the noise and bustle gone, though there's a price: the skies gray, the gloom incessant. At the palazzo, however, there's always someone passing through. My guestbooks are full of sketches. Eugene drew one of my Lhasa apsos perched on a column, like the winged lion above San Marco; Giacometti drew something messy and then wrote beneath it, *There is absolutely no way I can get this drawing right this evening.* Wyn came to visit and wrote, *Unlike Catullus it was to Venice I came to nestle in the pillow of my dreams!* Paul Bowles signed his entry, "To Mrs. Bowles," my title when I posed as his wife to lease a house from anti-Semites in East Hampton. Max brought Dorothea and made our reconciliation official, as if it were a court document, signing, *Peace forever a real friend has come back for ever.* Sindbad's poem I could hardly stand to look at, for its final line, *This town where one does not always find love.*

Just last week I hosted a young American poet for dinner. Gregory Corso, a friend of Ginsberg's, practically *worships* him. Though I find I prefer Corso himself. He is brash and crude and served three years in prison before he was twenty-one. He loves poetry with his bones, in the way you can only really love it when it's saved you from something.

In any case, we have fun. He loves my butterfly spectacles, and the fact that my bedroom is right on the canal. He loves that I wake to the water under my strange and ridiculous headboard: Calder's dangling silver dragonfly. He loves that come spring I am not ashamed to bare my aging body in the Venice light for everyone to see. That I let my big nose bake in the sun. He loves that my floors hold big chunks of mother of pearl. "My foster parents never had shit like this," he said. "I'll tell you that much."

Whenever I see him, I want to give him a haircut. I feel half like his mother, half like his lover. He tells me that Pegeen is Persephone and I am Demeter, jealous of her boyfriend; trying to get her back from the underworld. But Ralph is hardly king of the underworld. Couldn't imagine him king of anything. I suspect Corso just wants to sleep with Pegeen himself. He's also keen to eat squid ink. He's told me three different times, as if he had not mentioned it before.

He's always rambling about minor squabbles across the Atlantic, which I frankly couldn't care less about. He wrote a five-page apology to three other poets he was afraid he'd offended, just because he criticized them in some Dutch newspaper they'll never read. When I told him, "They'll never read it," he snapped. "Oh, Ashbery's already read a translation. He won't ever forgive me. Koch and O'Hara might."

"So they're angry," I shrugged. "So what?"

He gazed at me, dumbfounded as a disciple, so I kept going. "If I lost sleep over every woman whose husband I slept with, much less everyone I'd ever offended . . ."

"You'd never sleep again."

"Exactly," I laughed. "And I sleep like the dead."

THE LAST TIME CORSO was here, he asked me if I had any heroin, and I laughed harder than I can remember laughing in quite some time. He didn't seem too bothered. He's been asking all his friends in America to tuck a bit of hash into their letters, if they can. He consoled himself by signing the guestbook with a poem I couldn't understand but loved anyway. *All the canvases grow sea lonely sure. The butterfly spectacles tremble!*

He told me he's been hassling Ferlinghetti for finished copies of his new book, and hustling to put together an anthology for a German publisher. This anthology is his other great obsession, apart from the three poets who may or may not be angry with him, and I prefer it as a topic of conversation. The work of an anthology is not so different from the work of a gallery, after all, except that you don't get to walk through it, when you're done. You don't get to feel the work all around you, keeping you company.

He read me some lines of a poem he's been composing about Venice, but I didn't like them nearly as much as the weird fragments he jotted down in my guestbook. Too much gauze and fantasy, drunken boys in golden tights on little bridges, crooning violins and the onion-skinned atmosphere. When he started talking about gondolas carrying coffins to San Michele, stinking faintly in the sun, I told him, Why don't you write about *that*?

Just past midnight, he invited himself into my kitchen and made me a perfect sandwich: thick focaccia warmed in the oven, thin slivers of pork shoulder, soft Taleggio, onions cooked to sweetness. "You serve too many cocktails and not enough *food*!" he said. He moved fluently in my unfamiliar kitchen with the practiced ease of a perpetual houseguest, someone who is always staying with others, cooking for them to earn his keep. But it felt so good to be taken care of. Even in that small way. To be fed. He told me that he sees a certain grief in me. "You are what I call 'a liver of life,'" he said. "It pains you to feel it slipping away."

There was a thread of cruelty twined into his compassion. But he wasn't wrong. I took him out to the corner of my garden, to visit the plot where all my dogs are buried. We brought a jug of water, to pour on their grave. He took it seriously. He takes me seriously. The way my father did in the museum. He believed I'd seen something and could share it. Which is what I've tried to do with my life.

In any case, Corso sees how much I've lived and likes to hear about it. When he heard I'd had a love affair with Sam, he certainly wanted to hear about that. So I told him about our beautiful week in Mary's apartment on Rue Hallé, with Marcel's maps on the walls and our dirty sheets, the graveyard just down the boulevard. Looking back, it seemed clear that he'd been one of the only people who ever saw me as more than a spoiled heiress, or the possibility of a monthly allowance; who thought I could do something that mattered. I could still hear the crisp derision in Laurence's voice when I'd been trying to help Mina sell her lampshades, and he said, *You do have the peddler's genes.*

Telling Corso about Sam felt like turning our love affair into a composition, after all these years. All that heartache arranged into meaning: The nights he wouldn't come to my bed. How I begged. Like the way I used to stand back and look at my life, when I was a girl, as if it were a painting and even the ugliest parts could become beautiful.

Sometimes you can see the shape of a thing fully only when you are looking back at it. That's how I feel about the way Sam believed in me; the way I believed in him. Easy to call him a genius now, but I saw it then, when he was just a glorified secretary, buying Joyce's stamps and waking up hungover in the gardens of Versailles.

I told Corso that love is always the very best thing, even when it's painful. Then laughed, thinking of Madge. *It is suicide to be sentimental.* What would she think of me now?

I thought Corso might spend the night, but he didn't. Though he did tell me that he felt like a man with me, and took me in his arms and kissed me. Perhaps this was simply from sympathy, perhaps I have reached that age. Though desire never came at me without a few questions attached, the question of money especially.

Whatever his reasons, it felt good. It felt good to be a woman in the arms of a man, in Venice at night. The flickering shadows of the water rippled against the villa walls, and it made me think of that night with Sam—walking back to Hazel's place on the Île Saint-Louis, the Seine glittering with moonlight as he tried to make up his mind about me, whether to stay or go. He brought me to my doorway, and then he left. And in a sense, he brought me to the doorway of the rest of my life—the gallery, and everything that followed—though I could not see it then.

That night I told Corso something curious, something I've never told anyone: That looking back, I think Sam might have been the great love of my life. That he walked me to that doorway. And in the end, it was enough.

By the time things ended with Sam, I'd come to believe it was my destiny: ending after ending. Everyone else had gone away or died: first my father, then Benita. John. My mother. So much of Hazel left, too, when her boys fell through the sky. Either I was the only one who had escaped the curse, or else I was the one stuck with the brunt of it. Cursed with continuing.

It felt like a series of endings only because I couldn't see what was only just beginning, that I was making something bigger than myself, bigger than all of us: our family, our name, the curse. I could see the start of a new world coming into focus, strange as our dreams and answering to no one. Made of bold lines, molten bronze, paint splattered across canvas. I didn't make that world. But I helped it survive.

As a girl, I used to imagine my father had risen from the bottom of the sea, his pockets full of jewels, and found his way to somewhere better: a painting made of jagged brushstrokes, disorderly beauty, unapologetic light. He would wait for me there, I knew. And now I've arrived.

A Note on
the Text

WHEN SHE DIED FROM CANCER IN OCTOBER 2022, Rebecca Godfrey had been working on *Peggy* for ten years. She had written almost three hundred pages of a working manuscript, assembled across a few different documents, and was determined to finish the novel in the time she had left. When it started to seem likely that that wouldn't happen, Rebecca was clear about her wishes: she wanted the novel to be completed rather than published in unfinished form.

In her final months, spent in a hospital room in lower Manhattan, Rebecca tried to leave behind as many notes as possible for the material she hadn't yet written. Her husband, Herb Wilson, sat beside her bed and transcribed scenes and ideas for Part III, mostly dedicated to Peggy's relationship with Samuel Beckett and the opening of her first gallery, Guggenheim Jeune, which would mark the beginning of her career as one of the most influential art collectors of the twentieth century. Rebecca also spoke to so many good friends about her wishes for the end of the book, including dictating an extensive outline to her best friend, Janet Johnson, imagining a final coda at Peggy's palazzo in Venice. During my own visits with Rebecca in the hospital, we often spoke about her desires for the end of the book, especially the relationship with Beckett—how she wanted to give Peggy, as she put it, "some bliss and triumph."

After Rebecca died, her agent and literary executor, Christy Fletcher, approached me to ask if I would consider helping in the task of finishing the novel. It was an honor to be asked, and a daunting task—for many reasons—to imagine. When I began to work on the book, I inherited a tremendous archive of materials assembled by Herb, Janet, Christy, and Rebecca's mother, Ellen Godfrey: a draft of Part I that was nearly final; extensive drafted material for Part II that comprised much (but not all) of the final version here; a working file for Part III with the scenes and notes that Rebecca had dictated to Herb; the outline for the ending that Rebecca had dictated to Janet; and numerous other early drafted materials assembled from the files Rebecca had left behind; as well as thoughts and guidance from friends who had seen the manuscript through many iterations, including Janet as well as Rebecca's longtime co-conspirator and confidante Stephanie Savage.

The vast bulk of this book is Rebecca's voice and her materials. It is all her vision. Part I and Part II are almost entirely her writing, with some editing that tried to stay faithful to her own editing impulses—as best as I and others could discern and re-create them—and some original composition from me in the final two chapters of Part II, "The Dangerous Month" and "Bird Bones." Part III involves more of my writing, although I also incorporated all the material that Rebecca left behind, including many scenes, especially the ones devoted to Peggy and Wyn starting Guggenheim Jeune; and a few dialogue exchanges between Peggy and Beckett. The Epilogue is my attempt to manifest the vision that Rebecca described to Janet before she died.

The process of working on this book was unlike any creative task I'd previously undertaken: a posthumous collaboration with Rebecca that carried out her vision as best I could, completing the tremendous work she'd already done, adding a few of my own words to carry out a conception that was utterly, powerfully hers. In Peggy, Rebecca found and sculpted a character worthy of her own luminous soul—sharp, funny, and keenly observant, wry and determined, alive to the rich infinitude of experience. Now she has left the rest of us the gift of her vision: startling, singular, unforgettable.

LESLIE JAMISON

BROOKLYN, 2023

Acknowledgments

REBECCA BEGAN COMPOSING HER ACKNOWLEDGMENTS for this book in the weeks before she died, but she was not able to finish them. Here is what she dictated to me:

> This book would not have been possible without the enduring love, beauty, and intelligence of Ada and Herb.
>
> It began after I discovered Peggy's "scandalous" autobiography in my grandmother Mary Swartz's bedroom closet two days after her death. Mary's spirit was a guiding one, as were the charisma, elegance, and bravery of her two daughters, Ellen Godfrey and Diane Williams.
>
> In 2010 we moved to an unexpectedly creative, idyllic town, and the spirit and talent of the mothers and artists I met there were inspiring and singular: Jenny Offill, Hallie Goodman, Samantha Hunt, Dawn Breeze, Jackie Goss, Rebecca Wolff, Maggie Goud-

smit, Melora Kuhn, Amy Huffnagel, and Diann Bauer among them.

At Columbia University I was lifted to the high shelves of learning by Binnie Kirschenbaum, Lucy Brock-Broido, Elissa Schapell, Leanne Shapton, Leslie Jamison, and the many students (too many to name here) who surprised me with their fierce innovation and startling beauty: Devyn Defoe, Madelaine Lucas, Tibo Halsberghe, Amber Medland, Naima Coster, Zoma Galaxia Crum-Tesfa, Nicola Goldberg, Iris Cohen, Natty Berry, Sean Conroe, Bethany Hughes.

This book could not have been written without the groundbreaking analysis and investigation of Mary Dearborn and Deirdre Bair, both women who refused to accept the conventional portrait of Peggy as a sex-starved dilettante and saw an intelligence and tragedy in her, intelligence and tragedy that helped form this portrait. It was greatly helped by the dynamic and pioneering gallerist Beatrice Monti della Corte von Rezzori.

Thanks to Robin Desser for her loyalty and love for this lost character. I couldn't have asked for a more stylish and "peggyish" editor than David Ebershoff, and I always look forward to his sophisticated taste for the fashion and politics of a secret time. From the beginning, Christy Fletcher has made sure in every way that this book could come to be.

To Sarah Reiter for always being faithful and off-beat and a genuinely radical assistant, and to Nik Slackman for his kind and helpful presence.

Thank you to Paul La Farge, Sarah Stern, Gary Shteyngart, Esther Won, and Johnny Won Shteyngart for warmth and love always, and to Janet Johnson, Stephanie Savage, Fi Campbell, and Juliette Consigny for everything.

There are many other people and institutions Rebecca wanted to thank: Mary Gaitskill, Darcey Steinke, Karen Cinorre, Sam Levy, Lisa Farjam, Quinn Shepard, the Mac-Dowell Colony, the Writers' Trust of Canada, Josh Ferris, the Authors' Guild, Paul Williams and Leslie Berger, Elizabeth Sacre, Dr. Abraham Chachoua, Melissa Martinez, Lila Margulies, Andrew Carboy, Lanny Jordan Jackson, Robert Irish, Ariel Dearie, Colm O'Leary, Callie Garnett, Aaron Peck, Doretta Lau, Brigitte and Marian Lacombe, Hannah Appelbaum, Dean Jamieson, Mitchell Watson, Mel Sokolow, Caitlin Harris, Abbie Jones, Josiah Powe, Cecilia Twanmo, and of course Dave Godfrey.

Rebecca passed away before she got the chance to compile a full list of her sources. The works that most informed her understanding of Peggy Guggenheim's life and her writing of this novel include Guggenheim's own memoir *Confessions of an Art Addict;* Mary Dearborn's *Mistress of Modernism: The Life of Peggy Guggenheim;* Laurence Vail's unpublished memoir *Here Goes* (the episodes of Vail's arrest and imprisonment in Paris are especially indebted to this manuscript: at times Rebecca quotes Vail in her dialogue); *Samuel Beckett: A Biography* and *Parisian Lives: Samuel Beckett, Simone de Beauvoir, and Me,* both by Deirdre Bair; *Art Lover: A Biography of Peggy Guggenheim* by Anton Gill; and the selected letters and writings of

Emma Goldman and Samuel Beckett. If a source has been left off this list, this was done inadvertently.

On Rebecca's behalf, I would also like to thank Leslie for seeing so truly what needed to be done, Christy for putting all the pieces together, Stephanie and Ellen for providing some important perspective, and Janet for her singular and unwavering support of Rebecca through all of it. And Rebecca: I wish we could have had more.

HERB WILSON

TIVOLI, N.Y., 2024

I BECAME REBECCA'S LITERARY AGENT IN 2008 DURING A period of great transformation for both of us, not the least of it that we were both pregnant with our daughters who were due a month apart. Although Rebecca could be private about her personal life, she was utterly unguarded about her work, her process, her drive and commitment to her identity as an artist. That candor and directness carried through to when she became ill. That summer she told me she needed to be able to talk about *what if* without self-consciousness. Then eventually it became about *when* . . . it was the only way she could know that I had clarity around what she wanted to happen to her work when she was no longer here to direct it herself.

There are a few people who were directly involved in the publishing of this book I know Rebecca would want to acknowledge: David Ebershoff, Andy Ward, Maddie Woda, and Craig Adams at Random House; my colleagues Sarah Fuentes and Melissa Chinchillo; and Jocasta Hamilton, Kiara Kent, Kristin Cochrane, and Sylvie Rabineau.

Last, my own personal thank-you to Herb Wilson, Ellen Godfrey, Janet Johnson, Stephanie Savage, and Leslie Jamison for finding your way through your grief to support this effort at every turn. Thank you to Robin Desser for being there all those years. This would not be possible without all of you.

CHRISTY FLETCHER
FEBRUARY 13, 2024

REBECCA GODFREY (1967–2022) was an award-winning novelist and journalist. Her books include *The Torn Skirt,* finalist for the Ethel Wilson Fiction Prize, and the award-winning true crime story *Under the Bridge,* adapted into a Hulu limited series starring Lily Gladstone and Riley Keough as Rebecca Godfrey. Godfrey earned her MFA from Sarah Lawrence College and taught writing at Columbia University. She lived with her husband and daughter in the Hudson Valley.

LESLIE JAMISON's books include *The Empathy Exams, The Recovering,* the novel *The Gin Closet,* and the memoir *Splinters.* She teaches at Columbia University and lives in Brooklyn.

This book was set in Bembo, a typeface based on an old-style Roman face that was used for Cardinal Pietro Bembo's tract *De Aetna* in 1495. Bembo was cut by Francesco Griffo (1450–1518) in the early sixteenth century for Italian Renaissance printer and publisher Aldus Manutius (1449–1515). The Lanston Monotype Company of Philadelphia brought the well-proportioned letterforms of Bembo to the United States in the 1930s.